No Ocean Too Wide

Center Point
Large Print

Also by Carrie Turansky and available from
Center Point Large Print:

Shine Like the Dawn
Across the Blue

**This Large Print Book carries the
Seal of Approval of N.A.V.H.**

No Ocean
Too Wide

A Novel

Carrie Turansky

Center Point Large Print
Thorndike, Maine

This Center Point Large Print edition
is published in the year 2019 by arrangement with
Multnomah, an imprint of the Random House,
a division of Penguin Random House LLC, New York.

The text of this Large Print edition is unabridged.
In other aspects, this book may vary
from the original edition.
Printed in the United States of America
on permanent paper.
Set in 16-point Times New Roman type.

ISBN: 978-1-64358-324-2

The Library of Congress has cataloged this record
under Library of Congress Control Number: 2019943468

To Shirley Turansky, my dear mother-in-law, encourager, and friend, who was born in Windsor, Ontario, Canada, and whose ancestors came from England. May this story give you another glimpse of Canadian history.

Defend the weak and the fatherless;
    uphold the cause of the poor and the oppressed.
Rescue the weak and the needy;
    deliver them from the hand of the wicked.

—PSALM 82:3–4, NIV

No Ocean Too Wide

1

London 1909

Katie McAlister's heart pounded out a frantic beat as she gripped the rickety railing and rushed down the back stairs. She shoved open the heavy door at the bottom and jumped into the dark alley behind the dress shop. Cool, gray mist swirled around her, carrying the smell of rotting food and choking coal smoke.

She darted a quick glance to the left and then the right, and tremors raced down her arms. She never went out alone at this time of night. It wasn't safe, not in this part of London. She couldn't let her fears keep her from doing what she must.

If only her older sister, Laura, were here. She would know what to do, but she was miles away.

Katie took off down the alley, dodging wooden crates overflowing with broken bottles and stinking trash. A cat's screech pierced the air. Katie gasped and jumped to the side. The cat dashed past, a black shadow in the faint light of the gas streetlamps.

She pulled in a ragged breath as she rounded the corner, her footsteps slapping on the cold, slick cobblestones. She should have gone for help sooner, but Mum had begged her not to leave.

She ran past the boot shop and bakery, then cut through an alley and dashed up to the Grahams' door. With a shaky hand she knocked three times, then bit her lip and stood back. No one came so she pounded again, harder this time. "Mrs. Graham!"

The door finally swung open, and her mother's friend squinted out at her. She wore a white ruffled cap over her hair and a gray woolen shawl draped around her shoulders. "Goodness, Katie, is that you?"

"Yes ma'am. Can you come? Mum has taken a turn for the worse. She's burnin' with fever, and her breathing is so raspy we don't know what to do."

A fearful look flashed across the woman's face, and she gave a quick nod. "Of course, love. I'll just gather some things."

Katie closed her stinging eyes and blew out a heavy breath. Everything would be all right now. Mrs. Graham knew how to nurse the sick. Katie swallowed hard, praying Mrs. Graham's help would be enough. But the painful memory of her dad's accident eighteen months earlier came rushing back.

He had been injured in a terrible train wreck. Mum had nursed him around the clock for three days. The whole family had prayed he would recover, but he'd slipped away from them and shattered their world.

They'd been forced to leave their modest home and move into the three small rooms over the dress shop where Mum worked long hours doing hand sewing, finishing dresses for Mrs. Palmer. At least Mum had worked for Mrs. Palmer until eight days ago, when she had come down with a fever and taken to her bed.

Mrs. Graham stepped outside, carrying a basket over her arm. "Come along, child."

Katie stiffened. She wasn't a child. She was fourteen, and she worked alongside Mum most days, caring for her younger sister, Grace, and doing some of the cooking and laundry. But this was no time to argue the point. She hurried after Mrs. Graham, sending up a silent prayer as she followed her mum's friend through the neighborhood and then turned into the alley behind the dress shop. She ran ahead and opened the door for Mrs. Graham.

"Blimey, it's as dark as a cave in here." Mrs. Graham grabbed up her skirt and climbed the creaking stairs.

Katie stopped at the bottom step and looked up. Gray light shone through the lone window, spreading ghostly shadows over the steps. Cold dread filled her stomach. If only she could turn and run away from the painful scene that awaited her. But her twin brother, Garth, was upstairs with Mum and seven-year-old Grace. They were counting on her, and she wouldn't leave them to face this frightening night alone.

Pulling in a deep breath, she straightened her shoulders and climbed the stairs. When she reached the top, she followed Mrs. Graham inside. Dank odors from the alley penetrated their small flat even though she and Mum did their best to keep everything clean. A single lantern burned by Mum's bedside, spreading a faint light around the chilly room.

Mrs. Graham bustled toward the bed where Mum lay. Katie's brother and sister sat on the other bed. Grace curled up beside Garth and hid her face in his shoulder. He looked across at Katie, his anxious gaze penetrating hers, reading her thoughts.

It had always been that way, ever since she could remember. Mum said when they were toddlers they had their own language—"twin-speak," she used to call it. And though many years had passed since then, they still had a strong connection and could usually tell what the other was thinking. There were no secrets between them.

Katie moved toward the bed where Grace and Garth waited. She gently ran her hand over her sister's blond curls. Poor dear. It was almost midnight. She should be asleep, dreaming of happier days.

Mrs. Graham spoke softly to Mum as she straightened the sheet and blanket across her chest, but Mum did not answer. Instead, she tossed her head, her cheeks flushed and damp.

Grace looked across at Mrs. Graham. "Is she going to be all right?"

Mrs. Graham hesitated. "Of course, love." But her words were unconvincing. She shifted her gaze from Grace to Katie. "Why don't you go in the kitchen and put on the teakettle? Garth, you and Grace go with her. A cuppa will help us all."

"Yes ma'am." Katie reached for Grace's hand and helped her sister off the bed. Garth stood and followed them into the adjoining room.

Garth added a small scoop of coal to the stove, his expression distant and troubled. Katie filled the kettle and tried to ignore the ache in her chest. Grace climbed into one of the chairs at the round table, watching them both with wide blue eyes.

Katie took four cups from the shelf and set them on the table, then reached for the canister of tea. It was almost empty, and they had no sugar. The bread was gone. All they had left were a few shriveled potatoes and an onion. With a weary sigh, she added tea leaves to the pot and let them steep.

Grace leaned her elbow on the table and placed her chin in her hand. "Can I have hot chocolate?"

Garth sent Katie a quick glance, his meaning clear. *Don't upset Grace.* He turned to their

15

younger sister. "Not tonight, Gracie. Maybe tomorrow."

Grace crossed her arms on the table and lay her head down with a tired sigh.

Garth opened the cupboard and scanned the empty shelves. He gave his head a slight shake, then turned to face Katie. "I'll speak to Mr. Davies. Maybe he'll give me my wages early."

Katie nodded, hoping the butcher would agree. Garth worked for Mr. Davies after school and all day on Saturday as his delivery boy. The man was notoriously stingy and always made Garth wait until the end of the month for his pay. It wasn't much, but Mum hadn't earned any money since she'd been feeling poorly, and they needed Garth's wages as soon as Mr. Davies would pay him.

Mrs. Graham stepped into the kitchen, her hands clasped tightly together. "Garth, I need you to run back to my house and tell Mr. Graham to fetch the wagon. We have to take your mum to the hospital."

Katie's heart lurched. "Mum doesn't want to go to the hospital. Surely there's something we can do for her here."

Mrs. Graham's expression softened as she looked from Katie to Garth. "Your mum needs a doctor and trained nurses looking after her, or I fear she . . ." Her voice drifted off, and she shot a pained look at Grace.

16

Katie laid her hand over the cross necklace beneath her dress and tried to swallow back her fear. She knew Mum's illness was serious. But they couldn't afford to summon a doctor. How would they ever be able to pay a hospital bill?

But what choice did they have? With Dad gone and Laura working so far away, someone had to make this choice for Mum.

Garth grabbed his cap and sweater from the hook on the wall and strode toward the door without a word. He would do as Mrs. Graham asked and fetch her husband.

Katie poured a cup of tea for Mrs. Graham and took it to her. Then she sat with Grace beside Mum's bed. Fearsome questions filled her mind while they waited for Garth to return with Mr. Graham. Mum's face grew even more flushed, and she tossed her head from side to side, murmuring words Katie couldn't understand.

Finally, footsteps sounded on the stairs. Garth strode in, followed by Mr. Graham and the Grahams' son, Jacob. They quickly placed a heavy blanket under Mum to use as a stretcher. Mr. Graham took two corners near Mum's head, and Mrs. Graham and Jacob each took one of the other corners.

Katie reached for her sweater. "We'll come with you."

"No, love. It's late. You'd best stay here." Mrs. Graham sent another pointed glance at Grace, her meaning clear. Grace was too young to see all the suffering at the hospital. "I'll send word when we know more."

Katie looked at Garth, who gave a solemn nod, but cold fear gripped her heart as the Grahams started across the room. Grace burst into tears and clung to Katie's leg, hiding her face in the folds of Katie's skirt.

Katie patted her sister's back. "Hush now. It'll be all right." But her own hot tears overflowed and rolled down her cheeks.

Garth stood next to Katie, his cap in his hand, his cheeks ruddy and his jaw tight. He shed no tears, but his eyes turned glassy as the Grahams carried Mum out the door and down the steps.

"What will we do now?" Katie's throat felt so tight she could barely force out the words.

Garth closed the door and glared at the floor for a few seconds. Finally, he looked up. "We have to send word to Laura."

Katie's thoughts shifted to her older sister. Laura was twenty-one and worked as a lady's maid for a wealthy family on a large estate near St. Albans, about an hour's train ride north of London. "Do you think she'll come?"

"I don't know."

"But what if she does, then loses her position?"

"They wouldn't sack her for coming to help her family, would they?"

Katie rubbed her tired eyes. They counted on

the money Laura sent each month to help pay the rent for their flat. Still, Garth was right. They had to tell their sister what had happened to Mum. She sighed. "It's late. We can write to Laura tomorrow."

Garth nodded. He reached into his sweater pocket, pulled out a small, round paper-wrapped package, and held it out to Grace.

Grace's tears slowed, and she hiccupped. "What is it?"

"Open it and see."

Grace wiped her nose on her sleeve and pulled off the paper, revealing a currant bun inside. Her eyes lit up. "Where did you get it, Garth?"

"Jacob gave it to me while we waited for his dad to bring the wagon 'round." He took another bun from his pocket and held it out to Katie.

Her stomach contracted, but she pushed it back toward him. "You eat it."

"I already had one. This one's for you."

A wave of gratefulness flowed through her. She slipped the bun out of the paper and took a bite, savoring the sweet, buttery treat. "It's really good."

Garth's mouth tipped up. "Jacob is kind, like his mum."

Katie nodded and took another small bite, wanting to make the bun last as long as she could.

Garth frowned toward the small clock on the shelf. "It's late. We should try to get some sleep."

Katie glanced out the window. "I guess you're right."

The sky was dark except for the moon's faint glow through the shifting clouds. She yawned and finished the last bite of her bun. Her eyes felt gritty, and her neck and shoulders ached. She'd lie down with her sister in the bed they shared, but she doubted she'd be able to fall asleep. Too many troublesome thoughts tumbled through her mind tonight.

How long would Mum have to stay in the hospital? What would it cost? How would they get along without her? What if she didn't get well? Would they be left alone to face the future as orphans without a home? She'd seen children begging on the street and others who turned to stealing to survive.

She closed her eyes, trying to block out those painful images. That would never happen to them. Everything would be all right in the morning. Mum would get better, she'd come home, and they'd all be safe and happy together.

Katie stared out the rain-streaked window, searching the street below, but saw no sign of Garth. She glanced at the small clock on the shelf above the sink and bit her lip.

Where could he be? When he'd left that morning, he'd told her he would come home as soon as he finished making deliveries for Mr.

Davies. On Saturday he usually finished by one or two o'clock at the latest, but it was almost three now. Why was he so late? Had he convinced Mr. Davies to give him his pay and then stopped to buy some food on the way home? She blew out a deep breath. Yes, that must be the reason.

She walked over to the table where her little sister sat drawing on the back of an old wrinkled flyer. Grace hummed while she worked on her picture, looking lost in her imaginary world. Katie laid her hand on Grace's shoulder, as much to comfort herself as her sister.

Grace looked up, her blue eyes soft and innocent. "When's Garth coming?"

"I'm sure he'll be here soon." Katie forced a smile. "Tell me about your drawing."

Grace pointed to the stick figures. "This is me and Mum, and this is you and Garth. We're at the park, by the lake, feeding the ducks."

Katie nodded and swallowed. "Very nice." She blinked her stinging eyes. Oh, to be young and feel safe and believe everything was going to be all right.

She'd spent the day trying to keep busy and not worry about Mum. As soon as the dress shop opened, she'd gone downstairs and told Mrs. Palmer that Mum had been taken to the hospital. The stern woman seemed more concerned about who would do the hand sewing than about Mum's illness. Katie offered to take Mum's place, but

Mrs. Palmer wouldn't hear of it. Mum had been teaching Katie how to do the intricate stitching, and she was becoming quite skilled. But Mrs. Palmer didn't believe it.

The dressmaker sent her off with a warning that she would not let them stay in the rooms over the shop unless Mum got well and came back to work soon. Katie slowly climbed the steps with the woman's harsh words ringing in her ears. Back in the flat she'd written a letter to Laura, but she had no stamp or money to buy one. She set it aside and read a story to Grace before tidying up to prepare for Mum's homecoming. Surely she wouldn't have to stay at the hospital too long.

At noon she fried the last of the potatoes and the onion and gave Grace the largest portion. She'd thought about saving some for Garth, but Mrs. Davies usually slipped him a small meat pie or slice of bread and butter before he left to make his deliveries. Grace hoped that was the case today. If not, Garth would be hungry.

Someone knocked, and Katie quickly crossed the room and opened the door.

Mrs. Graham waited in the hallway, her basket over her arm. "Hello, Katie. May I come in?"

"Yes please. Have you been to the hospital? How is Mum?"

Mrs. Graham glanced at Grace and gave her a slight smile. "Hello, love. I've brought you a

22

treat." She took a small orange from her basket and handed it to Grace.

Her sister's face brightened. "Thank you!" She accepted the orange, sat down at the table, and started pulling off the peel.

Mrs. Graham motioned Katie to move away from Grace, then lowered her voice. "I'm just on my way back from the hospital. There's no change in your mum's condition."

Katie gave a slight nod. It wasn't the news she'd hoped for, but Mum was still alive and that gave her hope.

"I spoke to the doctor," Mrs. Graham continued. "He says she has pneumonia. She's weak but stable."

"Can we go see her today?"

"That's a long way, love, and they wouldn't allow Grace to go in. She's too young."

Katie sighed and nodded. She wasn't sure why she'd asked. They couldn't afford to pay for a ride across town, and it would be too far to walk.

"Now, you mustn't worry. Your mum is getting good care, and with time I'm sure she'll get well." Mrs. Graham reached in her basket and took out another orange. Her eyes glowed as she handed it to Katie. "The Lord will take care of her. You just keep a good eye on Grace and say your prayers."

"I will." Katie accepted the cool, smooth orange, and her mouth watered.

Jumbled voices sounded below, and then heavy footsteps pounded up the stairs.

Mrs. Graham glanced toward the door. "Gracious saints above, who is that?"

The door burst open and a policeman hustled in, tugging Garth by the arm.

Katie's heart lurched, and her gaze darted from the policeman to Garth. Her brother's face burned red, and he set his mouth in a grim line. As soon as he met Katie's gaze, he clenched his jaw and looked away.

The officer glared at Mrs. Graham. "Are you Mrs. Edna McAlister?"

"No sir. I'm Mrs. Ruby Graham."

Katie fisted her hands. What had Garth done? He could be headstrong, and he liked to tease, but he'd never been in trouble with the police.

Mrs. Graham's face paled. "What happened, Officer?"

"This lad was caught stealing a loaf of bread from Pinkham's Bakery." The officer jerked Garth's arm. "He said his family was starving and that he only wanted to bring them something to eat, but no one here looks to be starving."

Heat rose in Katie's face. *Oh, Garth, you know Mum would never want you to steal anything, no matter how hungry we are.*

"I shouldn't have taken it." Garth looked up at the officer, a challenge in his eyes. "But I'm not lying. Look around. You'll see I'm telling the truth. We've no food."

The policeman dropped his hold on Garth's arm and strode across the room. He pulled open the cupboards and searched the empty shelves. He huffed, then turned around, glaring at Mrs. Graham. "Is it true their mother is in the hospital?"

"Yes sir. We took her there last night. But I didn't realize the children had nothing to eat. They never said as much to me."

The bobby frowned and scanned the room, his gaze eventually resting on Grace. "How old are you, young lady?"

Grace darted a frightened glance at Katie and shrank down in her chair.

Katie placed her hand on Grace's shoulder. "She's seven."

"And you?"

Katie lifted her chin. "I'm fourteen."

"The same age as your brother?"

"Yes sir. We're twins."

The policeman narrowed his eyes. "You don't look like twins to me."

Katie would've laughed if it hadn't been such a serious situation. "No sir. We're fraternal twins, not identical."

"Well, three children can't be staying alone in a place like this with no food. You'll have to come with me."

Panic shot through Katie, and she tightened her hold on Grace's shoulder. He couldn't really take them away, could he?

Garth crossed the room and stood beside Katie. "Our mum will be coming home from the hospital any day. We can't leave."

The bobby turned to Mrs. Graham. "Is that true?"

The woman hesitated. "Well, we hope she'll be coming home soon, but there's no way to know for sure."

"I can't leave young children on their own with no food and no parents to watch over them." He lowered his voice. "Can you take care of them until their mother returns?"

Mrs. Graham's eyes widened, and she lifted her hand to her chest. "Oh . . . I'd like to, but I don't know what Mr. Graham would say. We have six children of our own and barely enough room for our family."

"All right, then." The officer stepped toward Garth. "I'll take them to the Grangeford Children's Home."

"No! Please, we want to stay here." Garth gripped Katie's hand. "I have a job delivering for Mr. Davies, the butcher on Layton Street, and Katie does piecework for Mrs. Palmer, the dressmaker downstairs. We'll be paid soon. That will give us enough money to buy food until Mum comes back."

"Sorry, lad. You need to come with me." The policeman stepped toward Garth.

"What if we refuse?" Katie wrapped her arm around Grace's shoulders.

The policeman narrowed his eyes and studied her. "Then I'll have to arrest your brother for stealing that bread and take him to jail."

She looked at Garth, trying to read his thoughts, but for once she couldn't. Maybe he felt as confused and panicked as she.

The bobby crossed his burly arms. "You only have two choices. All three of you must come along with me now, or I'll take the lad to jail, then return and take you girls to the children's home."

Garth shot a fearful glance at Katie. Then resignation filled his eyes. He looked back at the policeman. "We want to stay together."

"It will only be until your mum gets well." Mrs. Graham forced a slight smile. "You'll have plenty to eat and a safe place to sleep. Your mum can come and fetch you when she's well."

Katie's stomach roiled, and a dizzy wave swept over her. It all sounded reasonable, but what if Mum didn't get well? What would happen then?

Laura McAlister slid Mrs. Frasier's burgundy silk dress off the ironing board and held it up to make sure she'd pressed out every wrinkle. Sunlight

27

streamed through the laundry room window, making the black beads on the bodice sparkle. She turned the dress slowly, checking the back and sides. Satisfied with her work, she tucked a hanger into the neck of the dress, draped the long skirt over her arm, and headed out to the lower hall.

It was almost noon and time for the servants' midday meal. She'd take the dress upstairs and hang it in her mistress's room, then join the rest of the staff in the servants' hall. Perhaps the morning post had arrived, and she'd find a letter from Mum waiting for her. She usually received letters from home once or twice a week, but for some reason there had been no word for almost two weeks.

Anxious thoughts rose in Laura's mind, and her chest tightened. If she didn't hear something soon, she would ask for a day off so she could travel to London and check on her family.

It was painful and worrisome to be separated from them, but after Dad died, Laura needed to find work to help support her family. Through a friend she heard about Mr. and Mrs. Harrington, a wealthy family in London who were looking to hire a new maid. She'd gone to the interview and been hired that same day.

Everything had gone well at first, but then their nephew, Simon, came to stay. He'd made her life miserable with his suggestive comments, which had quickly progressed to cornering her in the hallways and finally to grabbing her on the back stairs. She'd escaped that last time with a torn dress. But she was so frightened she'd left that afternoon without giving notice.

Laura shuddered, pushed those sickening memories away, and started up the servants' stairs. It was a miracle she'd found a new position working for the Frasier family only one week later. Mr. and Mrs. Frasier lived a quiet life with few visitors. Mrs. Ellis, the housekeeper, and Mr. Sterling, the butler, kept a good eye on everyone, and they didn't allow any carrying on between members of the staff.

She felt safe at Bolton House, and she was grateful for her position.

When she reached the main floor landing, she saw Millie, her friend and a housemaid, standing by the green baize door, peeking into the entrance hall.

"What are you doing?" Laura whispered.

Her friend gasped and spun around. "Laura! You scared me."

"Sorry. What's happening out there?"

Millie grinned, and dimples appeared in her rosy cheeks. "Come and see for yourself."

Laura joined her friend and leaned close to the door. Tipping her head, she looked through the crack, and her breath caught in her throat. A tall, handsome young man stood at the bottom of the staircase, speaking to Mrs. Frasier. He wore a

29

stylish gray suit that was perfectly tailored to fit his slim build. His blue paisley tie stood out against his white starched shirt and tanned face. From this distance she couldn't tell the color of his eyes, but he had light brown hair and a square jaw. Pleasant lines creased the areas around his mouth and eyes as he smiled and greeted Mrs. Frasier.

Laura pulled back and kept her voice low. "Who is he?"

"Andrew Frasier, Mr. and Mrs. Frasier's son."

Laura's stomach dropped. "Has he come to stay?"

"I hope so. Isn't he handsome?" Millie leaned closer. "He'll be the master of Bolton one day."

Laura bit her bottom lip and peeked through the crack once more. Mrs. Frasier had mentioned she had one married daughter and a son. But she said the son lived in London, and she didn't see him as often as she'd like. "What do you know about him?" Laura whispered.

"He's twenty-four, and he's training to be a solicitor."

Laura's shoulders tensed. How long would he stay at Bolton? Was he an honorable man or dangerous like Simon Harrington? She searched Andrew Frasier's face, trying to read past his smile, but it was impossible to discern his true character.

She would have to be very careful and stay far away from him.

Andrew handed his hat and coat to the footman. "It's good to see you, Mother." His voice carried easily through the entrance hall.

Mrs. Frasier looked up at him with shining eyes. "This is such a wonderful surprise. I wasn't expecting you until next week."

"We finished our business early, and when we heard there was a ship departing in two days, we decided to leave straightaway so we could be home in time for Easter."

"I'm so pleased. We've missed you, Andrew."

"And I've missed you as well."

Mrs. Frasier slipped her arm through his. He patted her hand, and they walked toward the drawing room together.

Laura turned to Millie. "It sounds like he's been away on a journey."

Millie nodded. "He's been in Italy for the last two months."

Laura's eyes widened. "Italy? Oh my, I didn't realize."

"Yes. Doesn't it sound wonderful?"

"What was he doing there?"

"He went with another man for their work." She squinted and tapped her chin. "I think his name is Mr. Dowd. He's the one training Mr. Frasier to be a solicitor."

"Why would Andrew Frasier take a position like that when he's the heir to Bolton?"

Millie shrugged. "His father could live another

twenty or thirty years. I suppose he wants to be useful and do something with his life."

"Still, it seems odd for someone in his position to go off to London and work in a law office."

"Not all wealthy men like to lead idle lives."

"I suppose you're right." Laura glanced toward the door through which Mrs. Frasier and her son had disappeared. "I wonder if he's just here for the Easter holiday or if he plans to stay longer."

Millie grinned and got a dreamy look in her eyes. "I hope he'll be staying for a good long while."

A shiver raced up Laura's back. If Andrew Frasier did plan to stay at Bolton past Easter, she might be looking for a new position very soon.

"*What* are you doing?" Mr. Sterling walked down the stairs toward them, a scowl lining his face.

Laura pulled in a quick breath and straightened. "Nothing, sir."

He narrowed his eyes. "The staff at Bolton are concerned about their duties and do not eavesdrop on the family. Is that clear?"

"Yes sir," Millie and Laura said in unison.

"Now, off with you, and don't let me find you lurking on the servants' stairs or peeking through doorways!"

"Yes sir." Laura gripped the hanger and dress and started up the stairs.

Millie caught up and chuckled under her breath. "Mr. Sterling is such an old windbag."

"Don't let him hear you say that." Mr. Sterling was in charge of all the staff along with Mrs. Ellis. He could sack her and send her packing if he wasn't pleased with her work or behavior. It was best to keep her mouth closed, keep her mind on her work, and be respectful of those above her.

"I wonder if Mr. Andrew Frasier has a lady love?"

Laura's stomach tightened. "It's none of our business. I'm sure he would not like to hear two of the maids discussing his private affairs."

"I suppose," Mille said with a saucy grin. "But there's no reason a girl can't do a little dreaming."

"A letter arrived for you this morning." Mrs. Ellis held out the slim ivory envelope toward Laura. She peered at Laura through wire-rimmed spectacles that rode halfway down her long nose. Her silver-streaked hair was parted in the center and pulled back in a small, severe bun.

"Thank you, ma'am." Laura took the letter and slipped it into her apron pocket. She quickly downed the last of her tea, rose from the table, and slipped out of the servants' hall. Tucking her hand in her apron pocket, she wrapped her fingers around the letter and headed down the lower passageway. Hoping to take in a bit of sunshine and read her letter outside in private, she pushed open the door and stepped outside.

The fresh scent of newly mown grass and spring flowers greeted her as she walked out to the back courtyard. She followed the gravel path around the side of the house and entered the holly hedge border garden. Yellow and white daffodils with silvery-green leaves bobbed their heads in the light breeze. Pink, purple, and yellow tulips lined the flower beds, with feathery green ferns unfurling around them. Overhead, the plum tree looked like a pink cloud floating above the pathway.

Laura sat on the stone bench in the shade of the holly hedge and carefully tore open the envelope. She pulled out the single sheet of paper, and a rush of surprise flowed through her. Mum and Katie were the only ones who wrote to her, but this handwriting was unfamiliar. She turned over the letter and found Mrs. Graham's signature at the bottom. Her shoulders tensed.

Dear Laura, I'm sorry to say your mum has had a very difficult time these last few weeks, and she is quite unwell. Katie and Garth did the best they could to take care of her, and I came most days, but she had a high fever and was growing weaker, so my husband and I took her to St. Joseph's Hospital last Friday night.

Laura's heart clenched, and she stared at the letter. How could she have gone about her duties every day and not realized her dear mum was suffering so? Tears filled her eyes, and she had to blink a few times before she could continue reading.

The nurses are giving her good care, and the doctors are hopeful she will recover from her pneumonia, but it is not certain. I wanted to prepare you in case the worst happens. I will visit her as often as I can, and I promise to send word when the situation changes.

The next paragraph was just as upsetting as Mrs. Graham told how her brother had been arrested and her three siblings had been taken to a children's home.

I hope you will come to London if you can. I'm sure it would cheer your mum to see you and know that you are doing what you can to look in on your sisters and brother and let them know they are not forgotten. Please write and tell me if you're coming. I will keep you and your family in my prayers.
Your friend,
Ruby Graham

Laura clutched the letter to her heart, her throat aching. After all they'd already suffered, now they were facing another round of painful hardships. Her brother and sisters had tried to take care of themselves and Mum, but it was too much for them. All the while they'd been hungry and not known where to turn. Her poor brother had felt so desperate he had stolen food. That was not like him, not at all.

She closed her eyes and rubbed her forehead. Katie, Grace, and Garth must be terrified. Which home had they been taken to? Were they together, or had they been separated? Many of the homes accepted only boys or only girls.

She had to go to London. Her family needed her. Would Mrs. Frasier allow it, or would she sack her and hire someone else to take her place? If she lost her position, she would have no money to help her family. She might be able to find a new position in London, but how could she care for her siblings if she was working every day?

A choked sob rose in her throat, and she lifted her hand to cover her mouth. She ought to pray for Mum and her siblings, but she couldn't seem to form her churning thoughts into words. Bowing her head, she waited, wishing for some comfort, but the heavens seemed distant and silent.

A breeze ruffled the plum blossoms overhead,

and a few pink petals fluttered to the ground around her. She raised her hand, covered her eyes, and let her tears fall.

Andrew clasped his hands behind his back and strolled across the emerald-green grass in the old rose garden with his mother by his side. It was too early for the roses to bloom, but he could see the new shoots leafing out with the promise that they would put on a fine show in a few weeks. Now was the time for the borders to shine with rows of colorful tulips, bleeding hearts, grape hyacinths, and forget-me-nots.

It was good to be home and walk through his family's private gardens. He'd spent hours out here when he was a boy, following Mr. Harding, the gruff but softhearted old gardener who'd taught him how to till the fertile beds, transplant perennials, and prune the climbing roses. In between those gardening lessons, Andrew chased rabbits and watched robins build their nests and feed their young.

He had stayed outside and followed Mr. Harding whenever the weather was agreeable— and sometimes even when it wasn't. He had enjoyed those hours with the old man, soaking in the secrets of the garden. It kept him out of the house and away from his father, who had a fiery temper and was rarely pleased with anything Andrew said or did.

He clenched his jaw, pushed that thought away, and turned to his mother. "So, where is Father?"

"He's in Scotland on a fishing trip. He should be back tomorrow or Saturday."

Andrew nodded, thankful he and his mother would have some time together before his father returned.

"So, tell me about Italy." She looked up at him with a warm smile. "I hope you didn't spend all your time taking care of business."

Andrew's gaze drifted off across the garden as he recalled the highlights of the two months he'd spent in Italy with his friend and mentor, Henry Dowd. "Rome was amazing. There is a lot of history there and so many sights to see. But we spent most of our time near Florence. The countryside is beautiful, with several historic hilltop towns that date back to medieval times."

"That sounds lovely."

"Yes, it's a charming area. Those hilltop towns have colorful, narrow streets and sun-drenched town squares they call *piazzas*. The artwork is remarkable, and the people are so friendly. The food is outstanding as well."

"No wonder you enjoyed it so much."

He grinned. "I did, and I hope to return someday."

"And your business? Everything went well?"

"Yes. We settled the estate of one of our

clients and completed the sale of all his Italian holdings."

Their footman approached. "Excuse me, ma'am, but Mrs. Jackson has arrived."

"Oh dear. Please tell her I'll join her soon."

The footman nodded and hurried back toward the house.

"I'm sorry, Andrew. I forgot Althea was coming today. She and I are heading up the Spring Fete Committee for St. Luke's. We have all kinds of details to discuss."

"That's fine, Mother." He bent and kissed her cheek. "Enjoy the time with your friend. I'll see you after."

"Thank you, dear." She patted his arm, then walked toward the house.

Andrew pulled in a deep breath, savoring the scent of moist earth and fragrant flowers. A peaceful stroll around the rest of the garden to see what else was blooming would give him time to consider what he would say to his father when he returned from his fishing trip. The conversation most likely would not be pleasant, but it was long overdue.

He reached the end of the rose garden and set off down the gravel path that went toward the pond, then on to the orchard.

An unusual sound stopped him, and he cocked his head to listen. Was that someone crying on the other side of the holly hedge? After listening a moment more, he took a few steps in that direction.

When he reached the end of the hedge, he stopped and looked around the side. A young woman dressed in a black maid's uniform and white apron sat on the stone bench. Her blond hair was pulled back under her maid's cap, and she clutched a letter to her chest. Her shoulders trembled, and tears glistened on her cheeks.

His chest tightened, and he shifted back out of view. He wasn't sure if he should speak to her or leave her alone to deal with whatever sorrowful news she'd received in that letter. Was it a broken romance or some painful family matter that caused her tears?

Either way, she might be helped by a compassionate word. He stepped around the end of the hedge and walked up the path.

2

Footsteps crunched on the gravel. Laura looked up and pulled in a sharp breath. Andrew Frasier walked toward her. She quickly rose to her feet, swiping the tears from her cheeks. How dreadful to be caught crying in his garden. What would he think of her? Worse yet, what would he say to his mother?

He slowed to a stop a few feet away. "I'm sorry to disturb you." He studied her with a cautious look. "I was just out for a walk, and I thought I heard someone over here." He glanced toward the hedge, then back at her. "Are you all right?"

She sniffed and straightened her shoulders. "Yes sir. I'm fine, thank you." Though she was sure her nose glowed bright red and tears still glistened in her eyes.

He studied her a moment more, his gaze softening. "I'm Andrew Frasier, Mr. and Mrs. Frasier's son. And you are . . . ?"

"Laura McAlister, sir." She gave a brief curtsy. "Mrs. Frasier's lady's maid."

"Ah yes." He glanced at the letter in her hand. "You seem upset. Did you receive some bad news?"

Heat filled her cheeks, and she lifted her chin. "I'll be all right, sir. There's no need for you to be concerned." She might be a servant, but that didn't mean she had to tell him about her personal affairs.

His gaze remained steady. "I only wanted to offer a listening ear and be of help if needed."

She swallowed, surprised by his soft reply. He sounded kind, but he was a wealthy gentleman, the man who would inherit this estate. How could he understand what it was like to work long hours to meet the needs of your family, then be cut off from them and worried about them every single day?

Still, it might ease her sorrow to tell someone what had happened. She slowly looked up and met his gaze. "My mum is very ill. They've taken her to St. Joseph's Hospital in London. I have a brother and two sisters who are too young to stay alone, and the police have taken them to a children's home."

His brows dipped. "I'm sorry. That sounds very serious."

Tears blurred her vision, and she looked away. She wasn't used to receiving sympathy from those she served. Mrs. Frasier was not a cruel mistress, but she focused on her own affairs and had never asked Laura about her family.

She looked down at the letter again, and a sense of urgency flowed through her. "I need to go to London to see my mum and find out what can be done for my brother and sisters. But I'm not sure if Mrs. Frasier will allow it. I don't want to lose my position."

He took a step closer.

Laura stiffened, gripping the letter.

"I'm sure when my mother hears about the situation, she'll let you go take care of family matters in London. That shouldn't put your position at risk."

She studied his face, debating whether she should believe him.

"I could speak to her if you'd like."

Why would he suggest that? The answer rose in her mind, and a shiver traveled down her back. "No, I . . . I don't want to trouble you." And more importantly, she didn't want to be in his debt.

"It's no trouble at all. I'm a solicitor. I'm used to speaking up for others." A smile pulled up one side of his mouth. "I can be quite persuasive, especially where my mother is concerned."

His words sounded sincere, and she was tempted to agree to the idea. But how could she be certain he wasn't like Simon Harrington? What if he had offered his help only to try to win her trust and convince her to lower her defenses?

He studied her a moment more. "Well, what do you say?"

"I'm not sure how long I'll need to be in London. I can't abide the idea of my siblings forced to stay in a children's home."

"My mother is a compassionate person,

especially where the needs of children are concerned. I'm certain she'll understand." He lifted his eyebrows and watched her expectantly.

If the request came from her son, Mrs. Frasier might be more likely to agree to an extended leave. Then Laura could travel to London to help her family without the fear of losing her position. That would also take her far away from Andrew Frasier. There would be no need to worry about feeling indebted to him.

She looked up. "All right. I'd appreciate it if you would speak to her."

"I'll be glad to do it." He thought for a moment, then focused on her again. "I admire your commitment to your family. That says a lot about you." He reached in his pocket and pulled out his card. "This is the address of my office in London. I'll be back in town on Tuesday. If you need any assistance, I hope you'll call on me there."

Laura eyed the card. She had no money to pay a solicitor. What would he expect her to give him in exchange for his services? Her stomach recoiled.

"I have some contacts with those who oversee children's homes," Andrew continued, still holding out the card. "My family supported Dr. Barnardo, and I attended a few of his fund-raising events. Perhaps I could see what's being done for your siblings."

That comment tipped the scale. She slowly

reached out and took his card. It might be a mistake, but she'd do just about anything to help her brother and sisters. She glanced at the address, but she didn't recognize the street. No doubt his office was in an area of town she didn't frequent.

She murmured her thanks and slipped the card into her apron pocket. "I should be going."

He nodded. "My mother is meeting with a friend, but I'll speak to her as soon as she's finished. Then hopefully you can pack your bags and set off for London this afternoon."

"Very good, sir." She dipped a curtsy and strode down the path toward the servants' entrance.

Andrew Frasier seemed to be a respectable man with honorable intentions, but she'd thought the same thing when she'd first met Simon Harrington. It would take more than a few kind words and an offer of assistance to gain her trust.

Katie held tightly to Grace's hand and followed the long line of girls down the stone steps of the Grangeford Home for Poor and Destitute Children. One hundred seventy-three girls, ages five to sixteen, stayed in the three-story stone building. Katie rubbed her arms, trying to banish the chill as the girls' footsteps echoed through the stairwell. Grangeford was a cold, gloomy place, but they were served three meals a day and each girl had her own bed. At least she and Grace had been allowed to have beds next to each other.

She and Grace had been given two plain brown dresses the day they arrived, and they wore an ivory-colored apron over them to keep them clean. Though they were fed and clothed, it was nothing like home. Everything seemed strange and different, and she'd struggled to take it all in. Each day she felt like she was walking through a dreadful dream that would never end. If only she could wake up and return to their rooms over the dress shop and to the love and comfort of Mum's care.

Grace looked up, her face pale and solemn. Gray shadows below her eyes reflected her fitful night's sleep. "Do you think Mum will come today?"

Katie's heart felt like a heavy stone in her chest, but she forced a slight smile for Grace's sake. "I hope so."

This was their fifth day at Grangeford. They'd received no word from their mum or Mrs. Graham since they'd arrived, and with each sunset the hope that Mum would get well and come to claim them grew dimmer.

Was she still alive? That was the question that pounded through Katie's mind every waking hour and stirred her ghostly dreams at night. A tremor passed through her, and she tried to push that frightening question away. Surely if Mum had died, someone would've told her. Since she'd heard nothing, that must mean Mum was still in the hospital and would get better. And when she did, she would come and take them home so they could all be together again.

"Hurry along, girls." Mrs. Hastings, the matron's assistant, held open the door at the bottom of the stairs as Katie, Grace, and a dozen other girls passed through. The older woman wore a simple gray dress and a solemn expression. When the last girl stepped outside, the woman closed the door and turned toward them. "I want you to gather sticks and put them in those wooden crates by the shed." She pointed across the open grassy area to a small whitewashed shed near the tall wooden fence.

An overnight windstorm had littered the lawn with broken branches from the tall trees surrounding the property. It was the second time they had been sent outdoors to clean up the lawn and collect sticks for kindling. Katie didn't mind being assigned this chore. Gathering sticks and branches was a blessed change from sweeping, mopping, and dusting inside the home.

Grace gave a weary sigh, dropped Katie's hand, and trudged across the grass. She scooped up a few small sticks, collecting them in her apron. Katie followed behind, gathering some of the larger branches and dragging them across the lawn toward the shed.

Boys' voices rose from beyond the fence. Katie looked up, and her heartbeat quickened. Could it be Garth? They'd been separated as soon as they'd arrived at the home, and she hadn't seen him since. But she'd been told all the boys were housed in the building beyond the fence. When she'd asked Mrs. Hastings if she could speak to Garth, the woman scowled and said, "Boys and girls are not allowed to speak to each other."

"But he's my twin brother. Surely there wouldn't be any harm in letting us talk to one another."

The woman narrowed her eyes. "Watch what you say, young lady. We'll have none of your cheeky remarks at Grangeford!"

Katie grimaced at the bitter memory and threw the branches she had collected into the crate. The boys' voices rose again, calling out to each other. She glanced over her shoulder. No one looked her way, so she slipped quietly behind the shed and studied the tall wooden fence. If only she could look over, then perhaps she would see Garth on the other side.

Just above her head she spotted a small knothole, and a plan took shape in her mind. She crept back around the side of the shed, grabbed one of the empty crates, and tugged it toward the fence. Positioning it beneath the hole, she turned it over and stepped up on top. Leaning closer, she peeked through the knothole.

Several boys raced around the lawn, looking as though they were enjoying a game of tag, while a few others waited on the side. Katie scanned their faces, and her heart leaped. Garth stood about fifty feet away talking to another boy, his arms folded across his chest as he watched the game. He wore unfamiliar brown knickers and a gray sweater and brown cap.

The urge to call out to him rushed through her, but those who disobeyed the rules were severely punished, and she didn't want Garth to receive a beating for speaking to her. Still, there had to be some way she could let him know she was there.

She bit her lip. *Please, Lord, let him come closer.*

"What are you doing?"

Katie gasped and turned, almost falling off the crate. "Gracie! Don't sneak up on me like that."

Grace looked up at her with wide eyes, clutching her pile of sticks. "Sorry. I didn't mean to scare you."

"It's all right. Come here." Katie held out her hand.

Grace dropped the sticks and climbed up on the crate next to Katie. She wasn't tall enough to look through the hole, so Katie grabbed her by the waist and boosted her up.

Grace peeked through and sucked in a quick breath. "It's Garth!"

"Shhh! We don't want anyone to hear."

"Why not?"

"We're not supposed to talk to the boys. But let's see if he comes closer."

Katie shifted Grace to her hip, and they took turns looking through the knothole, watching their brother.

"Here he comes!" Grace whispered.

"Let me see." Katie moved into place, and when Garth was only about ten feet away, she softly called his name.

He frowned and looked toward the fence.

"Psst," Katie hissed. "Over here."

Garth's eyes flashed. He looked over his shoulder toward the stone building, then slowly walked toward the fence. "Katie, is that you?"

"Yes! Grace and I are here."

A smile broke across his face, but then he sobered and turned away from the fence. "I'll be in deep trouble if anyone finds out I'm talking to you."

"I know. The matron told me the same thing when I asked if I could see you."

"Have you heard from Mum or Mrs. Graham?"

"Not a word. Have you?"

"No." He kept his voice low and his back toward her.

"Do you think Mrs. Graham wrote to Laura for us?"

He huffed. "If she did, why hasn't Laura come?"

Grace looked up at Katie, and her chin wobbled. "Laura's not coming?"

Katie laid her hand on Grace's shoulder. "Don't cry, Gracie. Laura will come if she can." She looked through the knothole again. "Do you think Mum is all right?"

Garth turned toward her, a fierce light burning in his eyes. "I don't know, but I'm going to find out."

Katie froze. "What do you mean?"

"I'm not going to stay here forever, waiting and wondering what's happened to Mum."

"Garth, you can't run away!"

He frowned and stuffed his hands into his pockets. "I've got to get out of here and see Mum. Then I'll find some way to get you and Gracie out."

"But how would we survive on our own?"

His expression hardened. "We'll find a way. We can't let them keep us locked up here, separated from each other."

"I'm sure Mrs. Graham told Mum where we are. She'll come for us as soon as she can. I know she will."

Garth's eyes clouded, and he looked away. The doubt in his expression pierced Katie's heart. If Garth didn't believe Mum was coming, how could she?

"Garth, come on!" A boy ran toward the fence and motioned for him to join their game.

"I have to go."

Katie gulped in a breath. There had to be a way to stay in touch with Garth. An idea popped into her mind, and she poked her finger through the hole. "The next time you come outside, check this hole in the fence. If I hear anything, I'll leave you a note, and you do the same for me."

"All right." He glanced over his shoulder, then reached for her finger and gave it a squeeze. "Take care of yourself and Gracie."

"I will. I promise." She sighed as his fingers slipped away.

Grace peered through the hole once more. "Goodbye, Garth." Her voice wobbled, and she sniffed as she slid down.

Katie leaned in again, watching Garth as he rejoined his friends, then walked back toward the boys' building. With each step he took, she felt like another piece of her heart was being torn off and tossed away. She climbed down from the crate and released a shuddering breath. For fourteen years she and Garth had never been separated, and it was even longer if one considered their time together in Mum's womb.

Being sent to Grangeford and made to stay in separate buildings was hard to bear, but at least she had the comfort of knowing he was on the other side of the fence. If he ran away, how would she find him? She couldn't imagine not knowing where he was and whether he was safe and well.

She glanced down at her sister and pressed her lips tight. She'd promised Garth she would watch out for Grace, and she had to keep that promise. "Come on, Gracie. We need to get back to—"

"Girls! What are you doing?" Mrs. Hastings marched toward them, her face flushed. "Come away from that fence this instant!"

Katie gripped Grace's hand and stared at the woman.

"Well? Why are you just standing there?"

Katie blinked, her heart pounding so hard she felt like it would leap out of her chest. She couldn't tell the truth. What could she say?

Mrs. Hastings pointed a bony finger toward the pile of sticks at their feet. "Pick up those branches and get busy with the job I gave you!" She clucked her tongue. "Idle hands are the devil's workshop, and we'll have none of that at Grangeford."

"Yes ma'am." Katie shot Grace a quick look, and they both bent down and gathered up the prickly pile of broken branches.

As Katie rose, she lifted her eyes to the overcast sky. *Help us, Father. We've no one else to turn to.*

Laura folded her gray wool sweater into the suitcase on her bed, then glanced around the sparse room she shared with Millie on the top floor at Bolton. Her eyes lit on the photograph of her family on the small table by her bed. She couldn't leave that behind. It was the only photograph she had of all the family together. She lifted it off the table and studied the image.

It had been taken three years earlier, before Dad passed away and before she'd gone into service. Life had been so very different then. She could see it reflected in the peace and contentment on each of their faces.

Mum sat in front with shining eyes and a gentle smile. She'd worn her best dress with the high neck and lace collar. Four-year-old Grace sat on her lap, wearing her ruffled white dress with a large white bow holding back her blond curls.

Dad stood behind Mum, tall and handsome in his black suit and tie, with Garth standing on his right. The top of her brother's head barely reached Dad's shoulder. She smiled, remembering how they'd tried to slick down Garth's dark brown curls, but they'd been unable to keep a few from breaking free across his forehead.

She and Katie sat on either side of Mum, wearing matching dresses and leaning in close, completing the family circle. Her throat tightened with those bittersweet memories. None of them had known how much their lives would change in the next few months.

She sighed and carefully tucked the photograph between the folds of her sweater. It wasn't easy working so far from her family, but the ties of love and devotion remained strong even though they lived miles apart.

She added her brush and comb to the case, then lowered the lid and snapped it closed.

The door opened, and Millie looked in. "Are you all packed?"

Laura glanced around the room once more. "Yes. I think I have everything I need."

"Mr. Frasier said to come downstairs as soon as you're ready to go."

"Mr. Frasier? I thought he was away on a fishing trip."

Millie grinned. "I mean the younger, Mr. Andrew Frasier."

A warning flashed through Laura. "What does he want?"

"I don't know, but you'd best hurry and not keep him waiting."

Laura slipped on her coat, then reached for Millie and gave her a hug. "I'll miss you, Millie."

"And I you. Take care. Let us know how you're getting on and when you'll be coming back."

"I will." Laura lifted her handbag and suitcase off the bed and carried them into the upper hallway. She started toward the servants' stairs, but then changed her mind and turned around. If

Andrew Frasier was waiting for her, she would take the main stairs. She didn't want to risk a chance meeting with him in the secluded back stairwell.

She pulled in a steadying breath and set off. When she reached the lower landing, she spotted Andrew Frasier standing at the bottom of the steps with Mr. Sterling. The stout butler sent her a concerned look. He'd always been kind to her, and for that she was grateful.

Andrew Frasier looked up and smiled. "Ah, Miss McAlister, there you are." He took his watch from his vest pocket and glanced at the time. "I believe you can catch the three-thirty train to London if you hurry."

She looked at the tall clock by the fireplace in the great hall as she descended the last few stairs. It was already close to three. There was no way she could walk to the station by three thirty. It took at least forty minutes to reach the village, even if she could keep up a brisk pace carrying her bags.

"Layton is bringing the car around," Andrew continued. "He'll drive you to the station."

Laura stopped at the bottom step. "Oh, no sir. That's not necessary. I can walk."

"But if you miss the afternoon departure, there's not another train until a quarter after seven. I don't want you to wait at the station that long." He glanced toward the window. "And it looks as though rain is on the way. Please, let me offer you a ride into the village."

He seemed sincere, and she'd much rather take a quick ride in the motorcar than a long, damp walk down the road. "All right. Thank you, sir."

Elsie, the young kitchen maid, came through the doorway at the end of the great hall and hurried toward them carrying a small basket. "Here you are, sir."

"Very good." He took the basket. "Please thank Mrs. Lindquist."

"Yes sir." Elsie dipped her head and scurried back toward the servants' stairs that led down to the kitchen.

Outside, tires crunched on the gravel drive, and Laura glanced that way.

"I believe that's the motorcar now." Andrew motioned toward the front door.

Mr. Sterling strode ahead of them, across the black-and-white-tiled entry hall, and pulled open the heavy wooden door. Andrew Frasier walked out first and Laura followed. As she passed the butler, he nodded. She gave a slight smile, thanking him with her eyes.

Stepping outside, she looked out across the circular drive to the lawn and gardens beyond. The scent of rain and freshly mown grass floated toward her. She pulled in a deep breath, and her throat suddenly felt tight. It was silly to feel sentimental about leaving Bolton. This wasn't her home. She was returning to London, where she'd been born and raised. But her family was broken and scattered, and there would be no warm welcome awaiting her when she arrived in town. Her closest friends were here, among the staff.

The chauffeur hustled around the motorcar and approached Mr. Frasier.

"Please take Miss McAlister to the train station."

"Yes sir." Layton took Laura's suitcase and walked around back to strap it on.

Mr. Frasier opened the rear passenger door and turned toward her.

Laura sent him an uncomfortable glance. "I usually sit up front whenever I ride in the motorcar with Mrs. Frasier."

"She's not going along today, so it's all right." He motioned toward the back seat. "We don't want you to be late and miss that train."

Laura slid into the back seat and tucked her skirt around her, though she couldn't help but feel it wasn't proper for her to ride in the back like a member of the family.

"Here you go." He handed her the basket.

She blinked and looked up at him, then accepted the small wicker hamper.

"I'm not sure what Mrs. Lindquist packed, but whatever it is, I'm sure it's better than what you'll be offered on the train."

"Thank you." She was so surprised that was all she could think to say.

"Mrs. Lindquist is the one to thank, and you can do that when you return." He took an envelope from his suit jacket pocket and held it out to her.

She stared at the crisp white envelope with her name written on the front. "What . . . what is this?"

His brown eyes warmed, and his mouth tugged up at one corner. "It's for you."

She bit her lip, uncertain if she should take it.

"It's just a small sum to help you on your journey."

Still, she hesitated. Why would he give her anything?

"Please, Mrs. Frasier and I want you to have it."

If his mother was also behind the gift, she could accept it. "Thank you. And please thank Mrs. Frasier for me."

"I will. Have a safe journey." He closed her door.

The chauffeur cranked the motorcar, then climbed in up front. The first few drops of rain splashed on the soft roof of the motorcar.

Mr. Frasier lifted his hand, and Laura nodded to him as the motorcar pulled away.

Easing back in the black leather seat, she looked down at the basket and envelope. Why had he gone to all this trouble and been so kind to her? He didn't seem to expect her to repay him, but she couldn't be sure. She carefully tore open the envelope and pulled out a sheet of creamy white stationery. When she unfolded it, two crisp five-pound notes fell into her lap.

She gasped and stared at them. Her wages were only four pounds a month since she also received her room and meals. It was an amazing gift that would be a great help to her when she reached London. She looked down at the letter and read it silently.

Miss McAlister, I hope you will accept this small gift to help you and your family during this difficult time.

It might be small to him, but it would make a big difference to her.

I pray your mother's health improves soon, and you'll find your siblings happy and well cared for at the children's home. Please call on me for any assistance you may need while you are in London. I expect to return to town on 13 April. You may contact me at the office of Mr. Henry Dowd.

Sincerely,

Mr. Andrew Frasier

She refolded the letter and slipped it and the five-pound notes deep into her coat pocket for safekeeping. With this money in hand, she wouldn't have to worry about how she would get to the hospital to see Mum or how she would travel across town to visit her siblings. Her spirits lifted, but a moment later they deflated as confusing questions and doubts rose in her mind. She must put a stop to these anxious thoughts!

They had faced many hardships before and come through them all. They would find a way through these as well.

She closed her eyes, struggling to form a prayer. She wanted to believe God cared about her and her family, yet she'd prayed for her dad after the accident and the Lord had taken him away. Still, she had to try.

Lord, please heal Mum and watch over my brother and sisters. Help me trust You even though I don't understand why You allowed this to happen and have no idea what the future holds.

She opened her eyes and stared out the window as raindrops splattered on the glass. She waited to feel a calming assurance or to hear a quiet voice telling her the answer was on the way. But all she heard was the rumbling of the motorcar as it splashed through the puddles and made its way toward the village.

Would He answer and make a way for them all to be together again? That was her heart's cry . . . but her fears loomed larger than her faith and quenched the little spark of hope she carried in her heart.

3

I t's out of the question! I won't allow it!" George Frasier banged his fist on the library desk and glared at Andrew. "How can you even think of doing such a thing? You are a gentleman, not a money-grasping, middle-class solicitor!"

Andrew's heart pounded, but he set his jaw and kept his gaze steady. He would not give in this time, no matter how volatile his father's threats. "Henry Dowd made the offer, and I accepted the position. It can't be changed."

"It most certainly can. You have a responsibility to your family and to Bolton. That must come first, above any ill-thought-out agreement you made with Dowd."

"I don't see how accepting the position with Henry Dowd means I would be neglecting my responsibilities." Andrew pulled in a breath, trying to calm his temper. "You oversee Bolton with the help of a very capable estate agent and staff. I'm not needed here, and I won't be needed for years to come."

"You have no idea when those responsibilities will fall on your shoulders. It could come sooner than you think. And you'll have a very difficult time if you have to take over without having any experience."

What was that supposed to mean? Did his father have an issue with his health?

Father's mouth drew down at the corners. "I would think you would be grateful that you'll inherit your family's estate one day."

Those words pricked his conscience and sent a wave of doubt through him. Was his father facing a health challenge and truly hurt by his decision, or was he simply trying to manipulate the situation?

"I am grateful, Father." Andrew softened his tone. "And when the time comes, I will look after the family and Bolton, but until then I want to put my education and legal training to good use and do something to help my fellow man."

His father's mouth puckered as though he'd tasted something bitter. "How can slaving away in a solicitor's office, working for a man who is not your equal, help your fellow man?"

Irritation burned in Andrew's throat. "Henry Dowd is my mentor and friend. He has impeccable character and is well respected by everyone I know."

"I thought letting you train under that man for a few months would make you see what's required and you'd come to your senses."

"I have seen what's required, and I find it challenging and fulfilling."

"Oh, Andrew, you're not making sense!"

Andrew rose from his chair and stalked to the window. Why couldn't his father understand times were changing? He did not want to spend his life in the country, wasting his days hunting, riding, and fishing—not when important issues stirred him and called for strong legal support.

"Be sensible, Andrew, and give up this foolish daydream!"

Andrew swung around. "Working as a solicitor, or one day a barrister, is not a foolish daydream! I've spent the last six years preparing for this, and I intend to follow through on my commitment."

His father stood and lifted a quivering finger. "If you continue with this headstrong behavior, you're going to permanently tarnish our family's reputation."

"That's ridiculous!"

"No, it is not! Who will respect you if you give up your role at Bolton and take up an occupation in town?"

"Anyone who has common sense and is not living in the last century!"

His mother walked into the library, her eyes wide and her face lined with concern. "For goodness' sake, George, why are you shouting?"

"I'm not shouting!" His father cleared his throat and tugged down the front of his vest. His voice was softer as he continued. "I'm simply trying to convince your son to change his mind about a very foolish decision."

Understanding lit her expression, and she took a few steps closer. "Well, I suggest you lower your voices so the staff can go about their business." She raised her eyebrows and nodded toward the doorway leading to the great hall.

Andrew glanced that way, and his face warmed. Sterling and a few other staff members had probably been listening to the entire argument. Well, it couldn't be helped.

His father pointed his way. "Andrew wants to live in London and spend his days working with that Dowd fellow rather than taking up his responsibilities here at Bolton."

Andrew rolled his eyes. Was his father going to repeat the entire conversation for his mother's sake?

She clasped her hands. "I'm aware of his decision."

His father's eyes flashed. "You knew about this?"

"Yes. I've known for quite some time."

"And you agree with him?"

Her expression remained calm. "I believe Andrew is old enough to make up his own mind about his future, and if he feels called to practice law in London, then I think we should support his decision."

"Ha! You would. You're American."

"Oh, really, George! I've lived in England for over thirty years, and I'm well aware of the differences between English and American culture and family expectations."

"Then you ought to know it's not acceptable for Andrew to take up an occupation and live in London when his family estate is in Hertfordshire. He is a gentleman, the son of a gentleman, and the future heir of Bolton. That ought to be enough for him, but evidently it's not!"

His mother looked his way, an appeal in her eyes. She wanted him to try to ease the situation and restore some calm and order to the day.

Andrew pulled in a deep breath, determined to make one more attempt. "Father, I understand you would like me to follow in your footsteps and remain at Bolton rather than practice law in London, but I wish you would try to see things from my perspective. I respect you and Mother, and I'm proud of our home and heritage, but I'm not content living the life of a country gentleman.

"I'd rather spend my days in a law office or in the courtroom and focus my energies on defending those who have been falsely accused and seeing that justice is upheld. Those are worthy pursuits and the best way for me to use my gifts and training."

"That's not the kind of life I want for my son!"

So much for his efforts to help his father understand his perspective. Well, he was done trying to persuade him. Andrew drew himself up.

"I am going to practice law as a solicitor, Father, and one day I hope to be a partner with Henry Dowd."

"So, that's it?" His father lifted his hands in the air. "You're going to run off to London, live a fast life, and never darken the door of Bolton again?"

"That's not what I said nor what I meant." He took a moment to calm his voice. "I will work and live in London the majority of the time, but I'll come home to see you and Mother as often as I can. And when the time comes that I'm needed here at Bolton, I will do my duty."

His father crossed his arms and glared at Andrew. The rigid set of his shoulders made it clear he was not going to back down from his position.

Andrew glanced at his mother, urging her to speak up on his behalf.

She gave a slight nod, then shifted her gaze to his father. "George, I think it's time we accept his decision and move forward." She walked across the room and stood before her husband, a look of patient understanding on her face. "I know this is difficult, but if we want to maintain peace and goodwill in our family, then we must support Andrew's decision."

The tick of the clock sounded loud in the strained silence between father, mother, and son. Andrew stood tall and silent, his gaze focused on his father.

Finally, his father huffed out a deep breath. "I warn you, if your work brings you into association with a scandal and our family name is tarnished, then you must come home immediately. Do you understand?"

"I hear what you're saying, but I doubt that will ever be the case."

"Promise me you'll do everything possible to protect the honor of your family."

"Of course I'll do my best to guard our family's reputation. That goes without saying." Andrew waited, hoping his father would offer his support, even if grudgingly.

His mother lifted her eyebrows. "George?"

"Very well, you may go, but don't expect me to celebrate your decision. I cannot, and I believe you'll come to regret it, but it will be too late to repair the damage that's been done." He turned and strode out of the library.

His mother watched him go before turning to Andrew, her eyes soft. "I'm sorry, son. Your father is set in his ways and steeped in tradition. I hope you'll forgive him."

Andrew forced his words past his tight throat. "I wish he would try to understand I want a different kind of life and see the value in it."

"I know, and I wish the same. But at least it's out in the open and not a secret anymore."

"That was never my intention."

She nodded. "I appreciate you waiting this

long. I only wish your conversation could've been after Easter." She'd asked him to put it off so they could enjoy the holiday, but it had been impossible.

"I'm sorry, Mother. When he asked me directly about my plans, there was no way around telling the truth."

"It's all right." She reached out and patted his arm. "We'll get through it. I just hope he calms down before your Aunt Eloise and Uncle Bertram arrive."

Andrew nodded. The thought of his father's sister and her husband adding their stuffy ways to the already turbulent atmosphere made him want to groan. "That should be interesting."

His mother sent him an understanding smile. "Please, let's just try to keep the peace and not discuss your London plans while they're here."

Andrew nodded. "I'll do my best."

She sent him a tender smile. "Thank you, Andrew. And regardless of what your father says, I am proud of you. I know you'll be a fine solicitor."

His father might not approve, but at least he had his mother's support. They had always had a special connection. She listened, she understood, and he was grateful.

The old man seated behind the hospital reception desk looked up and studied Laura through cloudy spectacles. "I'm sorry, miss. I understand you want to see your mother, but hospital visiting hours ended at four o'clock. You'll have to come back tomorrow."

Laura clutched the handle of her suitcase and tried to suppress the panicked feeling rising in her chest. "I only learned about my mother's illness today, and I've come all the way from St. Albans on the train." She placed her hand on the reception desk and leaned forward. "Please, sir, I have to see her."

The old man's expression softened. He cleared his throat, adjusted his spectacles, and lowered his gaze to the papers on his desk.

Laura held her breath and waited. Was he going to tell her how to find her mum or insist she leave? She darted a glance around the reception area, wishing there was someone else she might appeal to, but no one sat in the three dilapidated wooden chairs behind her, and the two hallways leading away from the reception area were empty.

She pulled in a breath, and the smell of stale coffee and strong antiseptic stung her nose. How could anyone get well in such a foul-smelling place?

Finally, the man looked up. He glanced down the hallway to the left and then the right and pushed a few pieces of paper across his desk toward her. Lifting his eyebrows, he pointed to the title at the top of the page: *Patient List.*

Laura's gaze darted up to meet his, her hopes flickering to life.

"I'm sorry I can't help you, miss," he said in a rather loud voice. "I have to step away from my desk for a few minutes." His mouth quirked up on one side, and he whispered, "Take the stairs at the end of that hallway. All the women's wards are on the second floor."

She nodded and mouthed a silent *Thank you.*

He returned a slight nod. Then he stepped around the desk and walked down the hall to the left, disappearing through a doorway.

Laura quickly scanned the list and spotted her mum's name near the bottom of the first page. She ran her finger across and read, *Ward D, Bed Six.* Her pulse leaped.

She slid the list back across the desk, then walked quietly down the long hall to the right. At the end she opened the heavy door and looked into the dimly lit stairwell. Faint light shone through the window on the landing, spreading shifting shadows and making her stomach tighten.

What would she find when she reached ward D? Would her mum recognize her and speak to her?

She climbed the stairs, hauling the heavy case up with her. She must not give in to fear and anxious thoughts. She would hold on to hope and think of good things—Millie's hug and promise to pray, Mr. Andrew Frasier's gifts and kindness, and the way she'd made her journey to London and across town without any trouble.

When she reached the second floor, she opened the door and peeked down the hall. A nurse wearing a gray uniform and a white apron and headscarf strode away from her and stepped through a doorway into one of the wards. No one else was in sight.

Laura slipped quietly down the hall, checking the signs over the doors until she came to the one that read *Ward D*. She walked in and scanned the row of patients, then started down the center aisle between the beds. When she reached the sixth bed, she stopped and her eyes widened. Was that pale, gaunt woman really her mum?

Wisps of silver threaded her dark blond hair, and gray shadows hung beneath her closed eyes. She lay still and silent beneath an ivory blanket that looked too similar to the color of her skin.

Laura walked closer and laid her hand on her mum's shoulder. "Mum, are you asleep?"

Mum's eyelids fluttered, and then her eyes widened. "Laura, is that you?" Her voice was weak and hoarse, and her blue-gray eyes looked dazed.

Laura's heart swelled and she leaned down. "Yes, Mum, I'm here."

"I asked Mrs. Graham to write, but I didn't know if you'd come."

"I just received her letter today."

"Just today?" Mum's brow creased. "What . . . what day is it? How long have I been here?"

"It's Thursday, the eighth of April."

Confusion clouded Mum's eyes. "I'm glad you've come. But what about your work at Bolton?"

"It's all right. The Frasiers are very kind. They let me come."

Mum slipped her hand out from under the blanket, but she didn't seem to have the strength to lift it any higher.

Laura clasped Mum's cool fingers, and her throat tightened. "Everything is going to be all right."

"Yes." Mum closed her eyes and pulled in a slow, shallow breath.

"Have you spoken to the doctor today?"

"He says I'm improving." Mum gave a weak smile, but it was unconvincing.

"I'm glad to hear it." Laura wanted to ask when she might be able to leave the hospital, but it didn't look like it would be anytime soon. She decided not to upset her mum by asking.

"Have you seen the children?" Mum tightened her grip on Laura's hand. "I'm so worried about them. Mrs. Graham told me they've been taken to a children's home."

"Yes, that's what she said in her letter." Had Mrs. Graham also told Mum that Garth had been caught stealing food? Laura didn't want to add to Mum's burden, so she didn't mention it. "Do you know the name of the home?"

Mum's gaze drifted toward the window. "I believe it's the Grangeford Children's Home. I don't know the number or street."

"That's all right. I'll find out and go there tomorrow."

Mum nodded and closed her eyes. "Thank you. Tell them I'll come for the children as soon as I can. I sent word through Mrs. Graham, but I haven't seen her for a few days. I don't know if she delivered the message or not."

"Don't worry. I'll make sure they know."

Mum closed her eyes again with a tired sigh. "Please tell the children I'm doing better. I'm sure they're upset and confused by all this."

"They'll be fine." She forced confidence into her voice, but some of the stories she'd heard about children's homes made disquieting questions rise in her mind.

Footsteps sounded behind her, and Laura looked over her shoulder.

A nurse strode down the aisle toward them, her eyebrows slanting in disapproval. "I'm sorry. Visiting hours are over. You'll have to leave." But she didn't really look the least bit sorry.

"This is my daughter Laura. She's come all the way from St. Albans to see me. Surely you can make an exception for family members."

"Family or not, the rule still stands." She shifted her sharp look to Laura. "Your mother needs her rest. You may see her tomorrow between one and four, not before or after."

Laura leaned down and kissed Mum's forehead. "Rest well, Mum. I'll visit Garth, Katie, and Grace tomorrow, then come here directly after."

"Thank you, dear." Mum's eyes drifted closed.

Laura's heart lifted. Their visit might have been short, but her promise to visit the children had renewed Mum's hope. That would have to be enough for now.

An hour later Laura trudged down Larchmont Street, her arm aching from toting her suitcase all afternoon. Daylight had faded, and gas lamps glowed in the house and shop windows she passed. She shifted the case to her other hand and turned down the alley behind the dress shop. Piles of broken and abandoned furniture and heaps of trash littered the alley. She lifted her hand and covered the lower half of her face, trying to block the sour stench of rotting food.

What a dreadful place! She must find a way to move her family to more suitable lodgings. But how could they afford it, especially now that her mum had lost so many days of work because of her illness?

She reached the entrance to her family's flat, set down her bag, and tried the door, but it was locked. She glanced around, looking for someplace Mum might have hidden a key. She ran her hand over the top of the doorframe and checked under the trash bin, but she found nothing. What would she do now?

Lifting her hand, she rubbed her stinging eyes, trying to fight off the wave of hopelessness rising in her heart. She wanted to sit down right there on the back steps and have a good cry, but that was not an option. Her family needed her to be strong and think clearly.

She pulled in a deep breath, trying to sort through her jumbled thoughts. Mrs. Palmer, the widow who owned the dress shop, would have a key to the flat. Perhaps she was still at the shop.

Laura set off down the alley and rounded the corner. Many of the shops were dark and shuttered, but light still glowed from Palmer's Dress Shop. She peered through the front window, past the two mannequins on display. Mrs. Palmer stood on a step stool behind the counter, placing a box on a high shelf.

Laura summoned her courage and pushed open the front door. The bell rang overhead. Mrs. Palmer turned, and her expression hardened.

"Good evening, ma'am." Laura forced cheerfulness into her voice, hoping it would warm the woman's chilly reception.

Mrs. Palmer stepped down from the stool, her

expression unchanged. "What are you doing here?"

"I came to town to see my mother."

"And have you seen her?"

"Yes ma'am. I've just been to the hospital."

"How is she?" The woman's tone carried no hint of compassion.

"She's improving. Though she still needs some time to regain her strength." Laura glanced around the shop, wishing Anna and Liza, Mrs. Palmer's daughters, were there. Perhaps if Mrs. Palmer remembered Laura's friendship with them, it might make her more willing to help. "I tried to go up to our flat, but the door in the alley is locked, and I don't have a key."

Mrs. Palmer's gaze turned icy, and her lips firmed.

"I'll be in town for a few days, and I need a place to stay."

"Well, you can't stay upstairs, not unless you plan to pay the past-due rent."

Laura's stomach twisted. "The rent hasn't been paid?"

"Not since the beginning of April. And if your mother doesn't pay what's owed and return to work soon, I'll have the flat packed up and her things put out on the street."

"Oh no! Please don't do that. I can pay." Laura reached in her pocket and pulled out a five-pound note, three one-pound notes, and a few coins and held them out to the woman. It was almost all she had left from the money Andrew Frasier had given her earlier that day.

Mrs. Palmer sniffed and lifted her chin. "The rent is twelve pounds."

Laura's chin dropped. "Twelve pounds!"

"That's right. I only charged your mother six, but I can't give her that rate unless she comes back and takes up her duties."

"I'm sure she will as soon as she can."

"And when will that be?"

"I . . . I don't know."

"Well, I can't hold her position open forever. We're working our fingers to the bone, doing all the hand sewing ourselves." She narrowed her eyes and looked at Laura. "If your mother doesn't return to work by the end of the month, I'll have to hire someone else to take her place."

The tight band around Laura's chest constricted, making it hard for her to pull in a breath. There had to be some way to reason with the woman and make her give them more time. "My mother is an excellent seamstress. You'll be hard-pressed to find anyone so skilled."

"Maybe, but I have enough troubles of my own. I can't carry your mother's load as well."

Heat rushed into Laura's face, and she clenched her jaw. How could Mrs. Palmer be so uncaring?

"It won't do you any good to stand there giving me the evil eye. I won't change my mind. I have a business to run, and I have to do what's best for me and my girls."

"I'm sure your daughters would understand and want to help."

Mrs. Palmer huffed. "You can't expect me to take food from their mouths to feed you and your family!"

"That's not what I'm asking. My mother is ill, and most likely it's due to the long hours and unhealthy conditions in this shop."

The woman's expression turned stormy. "Don't blame me for your mother's poor health. She always caught every illness that passed by."

"My mother is a loyal, hardworking widow who is doing the best she can to care for her children. I thought you of all people would understand her situation and have a little more compassion. Evidently that's not the case."

"You're a rude, ungrateful girl! And I won't listen to any more of your foolish talk." Mrs. Palmer grabbed her hat and coat from the hook on the wall behind her. "Go on! You won't be staying upstairs tonight!"

"Please, Mrs. Palmer. I have nowhere else to go!"

"That's not my problem." She waved her hand. "Now take yourself right out that door before I change my mind about giving you until the end of the month to come up with the rent money."

Laura spun away, strode out the door, and gave

it a hard shove. The door banged closed behind her. That woman had no right to scold her like that. She silently rehearsed all she would've liked to say to put Mrs. Palmer in her place. But by the time she'd marched twenty paces, her anger had drained away. A stubborn lump lodged in her throat, and tears welled up in her eyes.

Where should she go now? Since her dad died and they'd moved to this part of town, they'd lost touch with most of their old friends. She'd lived here only a few months before she'd left to go into service. Who would help her?

Her thoughts flashed to Andrew Frasier, but he was at Bolton and would not return to London until early next week. If she was going to come up with a solution, she needed to slow her racing thoughts and be sensible. Surely there was someone who might take pity on her and give her a place to stay while she helped her mum and siblings.

Mrs. Graham's letter came to mind. Perhaps her mum's friend would have more compassion than Mrs. Palmer. Laura set off in the direction of the Grahams' home, fighting each step of the way not to give in to despair.

Five minutes later, she knocked on the Grahams' door and held her breath. If the Grahams turned her away, she'd be sleeping on the front steps of the church or on a park bench.

A shudder traveled through her, and she rubbed her hands down her coat sleeves.

The door opened, and Jacob Graham looked out at her. His brown eyes widened, and a smile broke across his face. "Laura! What a surprise. Come in." He stood back and pulled the door open wider. "Here, let me take your case."

"Thank you." She released it to him, and he set it on the floor just inside the door. "Is your mum home?"

"Yes, she's in the kitchen, making dinner." He studied her face with an admiring gaze. "It's good to see you again, Laura."

"Thank you. It's good to see you as well." She considered Jacob a friend, but before she'd gone into service, she'd sensed he hoped for more. She pushed that thought away. This was no time to worry about Jacob's feelings or intentions. "I received your mum's letter and came as soon as I could get away. I've just come from the hospital."

"How is your mum?"

"She looks so pale and thin I hardly recognized her. But she wasn't coughing, and she says she's improving."

"That's what my mum said after her last visit. I'm so sorry your mum is ill. We've all been praying for her."

"Thank you. I appreciate it. May I speak to your mum?"

"Sure. Come with me." He motioned toward

the hallway behind him. "She's right this way." He led Laura into the warm, steamy kitchen where his mum stood by the stove, stirring a large pot.

Mrs. Graham turned as she entered. "Laura, I'm so glad you've come!" She wiped her hands on her apron, then stepped forward and embraced Laura. The comforting scents of apples and cinnamon clung to her clothes.

The tender hug and warm welcome made Laura's throat grow tight.

Mrs. Graham stepped back. "Have you been to the hospital?"

"Yes, I slipped in even though visiting hours were over." Laura recounted her visit with her mum, and then she explained what had happened when she'd gone to the dress shop and spoken to Mrs. Palmer.

Jacob's face reddened as he listened. "How could she treat you like that?"

Mrs. Graham released a soft sigh. "Ethel Palmer still hasn't recovered from the loss of her husband and young son. She's angry about the past and fearful of the future. And I'm afraid that makes her say and do things that are thoughtless and hurtful at times."

Jacob made a noise in his throat. "That's no excuse for locking Laura out of her family's flat."

"No, it's not, but we don't have to let that ruin our reunion." Mrs. Graham turned to Laura.

"You're welcome to stay with us if you don't mind sharing a bed with Sarah."

Relief poured through Laura. "I don't mind at all. Thank you so much."

"Well, it's the least I can do for the daughter of such a fine friend." Mrs. Graham glanced over her shoulder. "Did you know she sewed those curtains for me? Aren't they lovely? And she wouldn't even let me pay for the fabric."

Laura studied the butter-yellow curtains with the ruffled valance hanging across the kitchen window. That was just like her mum, so kind and generous, always thinking of how she could use her skills to bless others even when she had so little. She deserved so much more out of life than what she had been given. Laura determined to find a way to make life easier for her mum and siblings from now on.

Jacob took a step closer to Laura, his gaze intense. "You don't have to worry. We'll watch out for you, Laura."

Her cheeks warmed, and she sent him a slight smile. She needed the Grahams' help, but she didn't want to mislead Jacob. He was a fine young man, but she couldn't imagine ever feeling more than friendship for him.

4

Andrew slipped his watch from his vest pocket, lowered it beneath the dining room table, and discreetly checked the time. He stifled a groan and tried to focus on the dinner conversation. With effort he'd managed to contribute a few polite comments during the last hour, but his patience was wearing thin.

If they would just clear away the final course, he could excuse himself and return to the library. He'd much rather spend what was left of the evening reading the latest issue of the *Law Journal Reports* than listen to Aunt Eloise complain about her arthritic knees or her milliner's lack of creativity.

If only his sister, Olivia, were here with her husband and two children. She always kept the dinner conversation going. But with the recent birth of a new baby boy, they had decided to stay home this Easter rather than visit the family at Bolton.

"I do hope you'll be coming to town for the season." Eloise dabbed at her mouth with her napkin and looked around the table. "The Royal Academy Summer Exhibition opens soon."

His father scowled across the table at his sister.

"I am not a fan of art exhibitions, and I have no plans to attend."

"But, George, it's expected. You should make an appearance."

"I detest all the noise and mad rush in town." He turned his cool gaze toward Andrew. "You know I prefer country life, away from the stifling crowds and dirty streets of London."

Andrew clenched his jaw. He would not argue with his father about the virtues of life in town versus life in the country.

"I quite agree with you." Uncle Bertram nodded to Father. "Country life is much more peaceful. Fresh air, fine walks down country lanes—who could complain about that?"

"I enjoy time in the country as much as the next person," Aunt Eloise continued, "but if you want to maintain your connections, you must take part in the London season."

His father huffed. "I've no desire to maintain connections with people who waste the best months of the year parading from one event to the next, trying to impress the other fools who have nothing better to do."

Andrew's mother shifted her gaze to Andrew, an urgent plea in her eyes. She obviously wanted him to join the conversation and try to ease the situation.

He cleared his throat. "I'm looking forward to attending the Henley Royal Regatta and the

Royal Ascot. Father, you've enjoyed those in the past. Perhaps you'll consider attending this year." He wanted to add they could go together, but that was too much to hope for. His father never invited him along when he went to town or anywhere else. He hunted alone, he fished alone, and he traveled alone. He was an austere, solitary man, as uncompromising as anyone Andrew had ever known.

"I may go to the Royal Ascot, but only the first day," his father said. "I see no need to stay for the other four."

"Will you open your London house for only that one night?" Aunt Eloise asked.

"No, I'll stay at the club and return the next morning."

Andrew glanced at his mother. Was she hurt by his father's comments? Her expression revealed little, but Andrew couldn't help feeling offended for her. Didn't his father even consider she might like to attend the Ascot or some of the other events in London this spring and summer? Andrew shook his head. He was tired of his father's thoughtless ways.

"Well, I'm glad you're going to come in for the Royal Ascot," Eloise added. "At least making an appearance there will squelch the rumors you've become a complete recluse."

Mother cringed and lowered her gaze to her plate.

Father's face reddened. "Honestly, Eloise, you spend too much time worrying about what other people think!"

Uncle Bertram darted a glance at his wife, then at Andrew's father. "I understand your dislike for spending time in town, especially during the season. Between the crowds and the noise, it can be intolerable and sometimes even dangerous."

Eloise leaned forward. "I'm afraid Bertram is right. Tell them what happened last week."

"A young ruffian stole my wallet right out of my pocket!"

Eloise placed her hand over her ample bosom. "We were coming out of Victoria Station, and the boy bumped into Bertram, nearly knocking him down. He apologized and ran off, and we didn't even realize he'd stolen Bertram's wallet until we tried to pay the cab driver and had nothing!" Her gaze darted around the table. "It is dreadful the way decent people cannot even walk through certain areas of town without being accosted by vagrants and street Arabs!"

"They ought to sweep the whole lot of them into jail!" Bertram waved his hand, nearly knocking over his water glass.

Father scowled. "There aren't enough jails to contain all of London's gutter rats."

Andrew's mother frowned. "George, how can you call them that? They're only children."

"I don't care how old they are. They're a

nuisance, and we ought to clear them from the streets."

Aunt Eloise gave a vigorous nod. "I quite agree. Something has to be done!"

"Those young thieves are no better than their parents," his father continued. "We can't take pity on them simply because of their age. Once a thief, always a thief. That's what I say."

Andrew clenched his hands under the table. "Children who resort to stealing do so only because the adults who should be responsible for them have neglected their duty. You can't blame them for their hunger or poverty. Where are their mothers and fathers?"

"I agree," Mother added. "Most of them have no home or family to care for them. What do you suggest they do?"

Father's chin jutted forward. "Homeless or not, thievery is not the answer."

His mother's cheeks flushed pink. "And neither is jail!"

"Then what's to be done?" Aunt Eloise looked around the table. "When they turn to crime, the authorities have no choice but to arrest them and lock them up."

"There is another solution," his mother said. "And it's one I believe we should support."

"And what is that?" his father asked.

"There are homes for those children, like those begun by Dr. Barnardo. They take boys and girls out of the workhouses and off the street and give them training so they can prepare for useful, productive lives."

Aunt Eloise wrinkled her nose. "I don't believe Dr. Barnardo was a respectable gentleman. I've heard there were all kinds of accusations against that man and his work. He was constantly in court for one problem or another. How could you support someone like that?"

"He was a controversial figure, but I heard him speak," Mother continued. "And I was quite impressed. He was a man of deep faith with a powerful commitment to helping children. He believed no child should ever be turned away."

Father lowered his dark eyebrows. "You attended one of Barnardo's presentations?"

"Yes, we heard him at Cliffside. And after his speech, some of the children in his care gave a very heartwarming presentation. They sang and had such lovely voices. I was nearly in tears by the end. I wish you all could've been there."

His father scowled. "When was this?"

"A few years ago, while you were away on a hunting trip."

"That is not the kind of event you should attend. They only want to play on your sympathies and get you to empty your pockets."

Andrew straightened in his chair. "Well, something has to be done for those children. And rather than sitting around a dining room table discussing the issue, Dr. Barnardo stepped forward and took thousands of poor and destitute children off the streets. Surely, Father, you have to admit that is a worthy cause we ought to support."

Irritation lined his father's face. "What I see is a self-righteous man who tried to build up his own reputation by parading those children in front of an audience. All he really wanted to do was raise enough money to keep his name in the public eye." He shifted his glare to his wife. "The man was a charlatan, and I don't want you to have anything more to do with his charity."

"George, you didn't even know the man. How can you judge him so harshly?"

"I know enough about him and his type. And I forbid you to attend any more of those meetings!"

His mother opened her mouth to reply, but his father lifted his hand. "The topic is closed. I'll hear no more of it!"

Andrew clenched his jaw, his anger seething. He was done listening to his father on this topic or any other. The sooner he left Bolton and stepped out from under his father's control, the better. His only regret was leaving his mother behind to deal with his father on her own.

How had she coped with his selfishness and angry outbursts for so many years? She had her friends, her church, and the local charities she supported. Those gave her a focus for her energies, and her faith would give her strength. But would that be enough to sustain her? He'd have to return as often as he could to lift her spirits and make sure she knew how much he valued her.

Laura adjusted her umbrella against the wind and rain as she hurried down Rushley Lane. She looked up, scanning the buildings, searching for Number 326. Would there be a sign for the Grangeford Home for Poor and Destitute Children? Just thinking about that name made her chest ache. Her family might not be wealthy, but they were rich in love and devoted to one another.

Raindrops splashed around her feet, dampening her skirt hem and coat. The gusty wind made the umbrella almost useless. She swiped water from her cheek, and a few cold drops made their way down the back of her neck. She shivered and pressed on. No matter how chilled and damp she felt, nothing would stop her from finding her brother and sisters and making sure they knew they were loved and not forgotten.

After she visited them, she would travel across town and see her mother at the hospital. Bringing word from Garth, Katie, and Grace would surely brighten her mother's outlook and encourage her healing.

Up ahead she spotted a faded sign for the

children's home on the side of a three-story stone building. Her hopes rose but then fell just as quickly. An imposing iron fence with a sturdy gate enclosed the property. Shifting her umbrella to the other hand, she pulled the gate handle, but it wouldn't open. A short rope attached to a bell hung to the right of the gate. She gave it a tug. No one came, so she pulled the rope again, all the while shivering beneath her dripping umbrella.

Finally, an old man in a navy rain slicker came striding toward her, splashing through the puddles on the gravel drive. "Can I help you, miss?"

"Yes, thank you. I've come to see my brother and sisters."

His eyebrows rose. Then he frowned slightly and glanced over his shoulder at the building behind him. "This is a girls' home. Your sisters may be here, but your brother would be down the street in the boys' building. It's just past the fence, beyond those trees." He nodded to the left, and as he did, rain drizzled off his cap and ran down his whiskered face.

The ache in Laura's chest cut deeper. They had separated Garth from the girls. That must have been painful, especially for Katie, though Grace also dearly loved her brother.

She looked up and met the old man's gaze. "I'd like to come in and see my sisters."

He gave a brief nod, reached in his pocket, and

pulled out a large metal key ring. With rainwater dripping off his hand, he sorted through the keys. "Here we are." He unlocked the gate, and the hinges squealed as he pulled it open. "Come with me."

She followed him up the drive, dodging the puddles, then mounted the stone steps leading to the tall wooden door.

"Knock there, and someone will come and let you in." He started down the steps but then stopped and looked back. "I hope you have a nice visit. Good day to you, miss." He turned and set off down the drive.

She faced the door and knocked three times. A few seconds later, the door opened and a serious young woman looked out. She appeared older than Katie but younger than Laura, perhaps sixteen or seventeen. Her light brown hair was braided and pinned around the crown of her head. She wore a plain brown dress covered by a long ivory apron. Her scuffed brown shoes were visible beneath her skirt.

"Good morning. My name is Laura McAlister. I've come to see my sisters, Katie and Grace."

The girl's brow creased. "You'll have to speak to the matron. I'm not sure if that's allowed."

Laura nodded. "All right. If you'll show me the way, I'll be glad to speak to her."

The girl pulled open the door. Laura collapsed her umbrella and shook it off before stepping inside. Still, she left a trail of rainwater on the gray tile floor as she followed the girl down the dim hallway. They stopped in front of the last door on the right, and the girl knocked.

"Come in," a woman called.

The girl stepped aside, sent Laura a brief glance devoid of emotion, then walked away.

Laura straightened her shoulders and entered the matron's office.

The older woman sat behind a large wooden desk. Bookshelves filled the wall behind her. The heavy navy blue curtains around the only window blocked most of the sunlight that would've brightened the office even on a rainy day like this one. Instead, an oil lamp on the corner of the desk shed a stark yellow light.

The woman looked up. Her severe, unwelcoming expression seemed a perfect match with her dark gray dress and sallow complexion. She wore her salt-and-pepper hair parted in the middle and pulled back in a bun, and small wire-framed spectacles perched halfway down her nose. A sign on her desk read *Mrs. Stafford, Matron.* She didn't rise but scanned Laura from head to toe.

"Good morning, ma'am. My name is Laura McAlister. I understand my sisters Katie and Grace McAlister are staying here at Grangeford, and I've come to visit them."

"I don't recall admitting them." Her tone was

cool, her words were clipped, and she didn't waste a smile. "I'll see if they're in residence." She pulled open her desk drawer and searched through several files. Her hand stilled and she looked up. "We have a Katherine McAlister, age fourteen, and a Grace McAlister, age seven."

Relief rushed through Laura. "Yes, those are my sisters."

"You may take a seat." The woman nodded to a chair in front of her desk.

Laura stepped forward and sat on the hard wooden chair.

The matron laid the two files on her desk. She opened the top file and began reading. Her frown deepened as she continued to scan down the page.

Laura clasped her hands in her lap and tried not to fidget. Why was the woman's expression so disapproving? What had her sisters done? Katie did have a strong will and was not afraid to speak her mind, but Laura couldn't imagine her causing any real trouble, especially not in a fearsome place like this.

The matron looked up. "I'm afraid it won't be possible for you to see your sisters."

Laura blinked. "What? Why not?"

"Katherine and Grace have only been at Grangeford a short time. It's too soon for a family visit. It would be upsetting for them."

"But I've come all the way from St. Albans on

the train. Our mother is in the hospital, and I need to give them news about her condition."

The matron skimmed the file once more, then lifted her gaze. "Your sisters have had a difficult time adjusting to the daily routine. I'm afraid a visit with a family member would unsettle them and set back what little progress they've made."

Laura leaned forward. "I'm very close to my sisters. I'm sure my visit would be an encouragement, not upsetting."

Mrs. Stafford's expression firmed. "I'm sorry. I cannot allow it."

Laura clenched her hands beneath the folds of her skirt. How could the woman refuse to let her see her sisters? It wasn't fair, and it probably wasn't even legal. She straightened in her chair. "If you won't allow me to see them, then I want to remove my sisters from your care and take them with me today."

The matron's eyebrows arched. "That is not possible."

Laura lifted her chin. "Why not? I am of age and they are my siblings."

"They were brought here by the police and entrusted into our care. I can't just hand them over to you."

"Surely if a family member comes and claims them, you have to release them."

"No, I do not! And they won't be released to you or anyone else unless you can prove you are their legal guardian and the circumstances that brought them here have been corrected." She looked at Laura over the top of her spectacles. "Then there is the matter of paying the fees associated with their care."

"What fees?"

"There is a daily charge for the shelter, food, and clothing we provide the children. You will have to settle their accounts before they're allowed to leave Grangeford."

"How much is owed?"

The matron glanced at the open file and wrote the calculation on a piece of paper. She turned the paper and slid it across the desk toward Laura. "This is the amount."

Laura stifled a gasp. "That's outrageous!"

"That is the fee for one girl. You will need to double that figure if you intend to take both your sisters."

A dizzy, heartsick feeling washed over Laura. How could they expect her to pay such a large sum? She had no savings and no idea where she might borrow that much money. And what about Garth? She would have to triple the fee in order to release him as well.

"And I will remind you the fee continues to increase each day the children remain in our care."

Laura's chest squeezed tight. This was so unfair! Why would a charitable institution charge families for the care it gave the children? There had to be some way around that rule.

Laura forced her voice to remain calm. "I'm sure when you hear our situation, you'll want to make an exception. You see, our father passed away two years ago from injuries he received in a railway accident. Our mother has worked as a seamstress since then. My brother works after school as a delivery boy for a butcher, and I've gone into service as a lady's maid. We all contribute toward the support of our family. And we've taken good care of each other until just the last few weeks when our mother had to go into the hospital and wasn't able to continue working."

"Miss McAlister, every child in this institution has a story of hardship and loss. That is what brings them to Grangeford. Your situation is not unique. We have rules and regulations in place for the safety of the children, and those rules must be followed for every child and every family."

"Yes, I understand. But I'm willing to take responsibility for my siblings. There's no need for them to take up valuable space at Grangeford. I'll watch over them and provide for them." She had no idea how she would actually accomplish that, but she had to try to convince the woman it was true.

The matron pursed her lips. "As I've already said, I can't release them to you unless you can show evidence of guardianship and the ability to support them, as well as settle their accounts. Are you prepared to do that today?"

Laura shifted in her seat. "No, I'm not, but there has to be some other way—"

"There is no other way, Miss McAlister!" The matron swiped the files closed and rose from her chair. "You may write to your siblings, but that is the only contact allowed. Now, you will have to excuse me. I have pressing duties I need to attend to."

Laura stood, her heart hammering. "Please, Mrs. Stafford, I just want to see them!"

"Good day, Miss McAlister." The matron strode past Laura and out the office door without looking back.

Heat radiated in Laura's face, and her hands shook. Why were rules and regulations more important than keeping a family from being torn apart?

Laura snatched up her umbrella and marched out the door and into the hall. Mrs. Stafford might think she had the last word, but Laura was not giving up! She would find a way to see Katie and Grace in spite of the matron's hardhearted decision and Grangeford's unbendable rules. And she would make sure they did not have to stay in this cold, impersonal institution one day longer than necessary.

She pushed open the front door and stepped

outside. A misty fog hung over the grounds, and rain still drizzled from the gloomy sky. She opened her umbrella and started down the drive.

How did someone prove guardianship? She would probably need some kind of official document. Could she draw that up on her own, or would she need the help of a solicitor?

Andrew Frasier's offer of assistance flashed in her mind. She reached in her coat pocket and wrapped her fingers around his card. Biting her lip, she considered contacting him.

Would he take on their case? Was it even fair to ask for his help when she had no income and no home to offer her siblings? She shook her head. He was a solicitor, not a miracle worker. He couldn't just snap his fingers and solve these problems. She'd have to find someone else who could help her without expecting a financial payment or anything else from her.

There had to be some way to free her brother and sisters. And she would not stop trying until they were safely in her care.

Katie slipped quietly out Grangeford's side door and hurried down the stone steps. Moonlight cast stark shadows across the grass. A cold wind whistled under the eaves, making a keening sound and sending shivers down her back. If anyone found her outside at this hour, she would be in serious trouble. Keeping to the shadows, she crept around the side of the building with careful, light steps.

This hour before lights out was the only free time she had each day. Most of the girls were resting on their beds, reading, or talking with friends. After telling them she needed to visit the water closet, she'd tiptoed down the steps and out the side door.

She took a quick glance over her shoulder, then ran across the grass toward the shed, hoping she would find a note from Garth. On the way she grabbed an empty crate at the side of the shed and dragged it around back. With a silent plea toward heaven, she climbed up and reached into the knothole. Her fingers wrapped around a folded piece of paper. She pulled it out and held it up to the bright moonlight.

Dear Katie, I hope this message reaches you in time. They put me on the list to go to Canada. I'm taking the place of another boy who was chosen but then couldn't pass the medical exam.

Katie blinked and stared at the words. Garth was going to Canada? It couldn't be true! How could he even think of leaving her and Grace behind? She had heard some of the girls talking about friends at the home who had been sent to

Canada, but it hadn't made sense to her. Why were they sent away? What had they done?

I told them Mum was coming for me, and I didn't think I should be put on the list. But Mr. Gumblich, the overseer of all the boys, shook his head and said she won't be coming for me. I don't want to believe Mum is truly gone, but what else could he mean?

Katie's heart plunged, and a dizzy wave nearly knocked her off the crate. She grabbed the fence and held on. Mum wasn't coming? She was gone? How could that be? Wouldn't they tell her if Mum had died? Wouldn't she somehow sense it? She lowered her gaze and read the rest, trying to make sense of Garth's words.

Have you heard from Mum? It's been almost two weeks since the Grahams took her to the hospital. Why won't someone tell us what happened? I thought Laura would come by now or at least Mrs. Graham would send word about Mum, but I've heard nothing. Please tell me what you know.

They say I'll be leaving on Tuesday. First I'll be sent to a children's home in Liverpool to prepare for the trip. I'm not sure how long that will take. After that, I'll board a ship with a group of boys going to Canada. I asked Mr. Gumblich if they take girls, and he said they do. So, I think you should try to get on the list with Grace, so we can all go.

Katie lifted her hand to cover her mouth and stifle a cry. He wanted her to ask to go to Canada? That was crazy! She didn't want to sail across the sea! Even if Mum couldn't come for them, then surely Laura would come. Her sister wouldn't leave them here forever. Katie shook her head and continued reading.

They say Canada is a grand place with miles and miles of open country. There are families there who take in boys and girls to help on their farms and in their homes. Mr. Gumblich says it's a good opportunity, and I should be glad to take that boy's place. He says some people call it crossing the golden bridge, and we can build a new life there.

But I can't stop thinking about Mum and our life here in London. Things have been hard since Dad died, but at least we were together and we always took care of each other. I'm sorry I tried to steal that bread. I didn't know it would set off this terrible chain of events. If only I could go back and make a different choice, but I can't.

I wish I could talk to you and be sure you'll be coming to Canada with me. Somehow we must find a way to stay together, no matter what happens.

Please leave me a note. I only have four more days here at Grangeford. I need to hear from you before I go!

With love from your brother,
Garth

Hot tears blurred her vision, making it nearly impossible to reread that last part of the letter. Garth was leaving and going to Canada to make a new life. Mum was gone and would never come for them. Her shoulders sank, and a sob rose in her throat.

Oh, Father, what should I do? I can't imagine leaving England and going so far away.

A small light flashed off to her left, then bobbed toward her.

Katie froze and stared at the lantern, for surely that was what it was.

"I say there, young lady, what are you doing out here in the dark by yourself?"

Katie's heart thumped hard. "Who . . . who are you?"

"Charlie Peterson." He lifted the lantern higher so the light shone on his craggy face. "I'm the groundskeeper and night watchman. And who are you?"

"Katie . . . Katie McAlister."

"Well, Miss Katie, you best step down from that crate and come with me." When she didn't move, he looked her up and down. "Did you hear me, lass?"

She snapped out of her daze and stepped down, still clutching the message from Garth. No doubt she would be punished for sneaking outside without permission.

His gaze dropped to the note in her hand, and a frown creased his forehead. "Are you passing messages to the boys?"

"No! I mean yes, but only with my brother, Garth. We're twins. And they wouldn't let us see each other."

"Well now, that is a problem." He motioned toward the building. "I think you best come with me."

She gave a resigned sigh and followed him, all the while trying to think of what she would say when he turned her over to the matron. But he passed the main entrance, walked around to the back of the building, and led her down a set of steps. When he reached the bottom, he pushed open the door and motioned her through.

She stepped inside, and they walked down the hall and into a small room where a fire burned brightly in the grate. Another lantern sat on a small table with two chairs nearby. The only other furniture in the room was a desk in one corner, piled high with books and papers.

"Now then, take a seat and you can tell me your story." He pulled out one of the chairs for her.

"My story?"

"Yes, why you're here and more about that brother of yours. You said his name is Garth?"

"Yes sir." Katie lowered herself into the old wooden chair facing the fireplace. Mr. Peterson gave her a cup of tea, and she told him what had happened to bring them to Grangeford.

The old man sat opposite her, nodding now and then and asking her a few questions, but mostly he just listened, watching her with a soft light in his gray eyes. Finally, he said, "I'm sorry to hear about your mum. I lost my mum when I was about your age, so I can imagine how hard that must be for you."

Katie swallowed and tried not to cry. She'd barely had time to think it through, but the old man's kind words helped ease that dreadful ache in her chest a bit. It had been a long time since anyone cared enough to ask about her family and truly listen to what she had to say.

Mr. Peterson poured himself a second cup of tea and stirred in a spoonful of sugar. "So, Miss Katie, it sounds like you have a decision to make and not much time to make it. Will you ask to be put on the list for Canada?"

"I don't want to go so far away from home." But did she really have a home now that Mum was gone and her brother was being sent away?

"Do you have any other family who might take you in?"

Katie stared into the fire. "I have an older sister, but she works as a lady's maid at an estate north of London."

"Does she know you're here?"

"Our neighbor said she would write to her for us, but we've not heard from her or our neighbor since we arrived."

"Then I say, write again." He rose from the table, crossed the room, and opened the top desk drawer. After pushing things around for a few seconds, he pulled out a few sheets of paper and a pen and walked back to the table. "Here you go. And while you're at it, pen a letter to your brother and I'll see that it's delivered to him." He lifted his finger. "But you must promise, no more creeping 'round in the dark or sending notes through the fence."

Katie accepted the pen and paper and met his gaze.

"Will you give me your word, lass?"

"Yes sir." She lifted the pen, considering who she ought to write to first, but then she looked up. "I don't have any money to buy stamps."

His smile returned and created crinkled lines at the corners of his eyes. "Not to worry. I'll deliver your brother's letter and buy a stamp for the other. You just write your letter, and you best be quick about it. It'll be time for bed soon, and you don't want the matron to make her rounds and find your bed empty. If you're not there, she'll think you've run away and send for the police." His eyes twinkled at the prospect.

On some other night she might have smiled or even laughed as she imagined the matron's overreaction when she found Katie's bed empty and set off on a frantic search. But the heartbreaking news she had received about Mum stole any possibility of a lighthearted response.

She bit her lip and stared at the blank piece of stationery. Now that she had paper and a pen and even the promise of a stamp and delivery, she had no idea what to say.

Should she promise Garth she would try to find a way to sail to Canada with him? Was there time to alert Laura and convince her sister to come and rescue them before she and Grace had no choice but to follow Garth across the sea?

5

Andrew tossed the tennis ball in the air and swung his racket hard. The ball flew across the net and bounced just inside the service area. It felt good to be back in London and back in the company of his friend and mentor.

Henry Dowd stepped up and lobbed the ball back. Andrew dashed forward and volleyed the ball, skimming it just over the top of the net.

Henry hesitated a moment too long before he shifted to the left and swung. He missed the ball by at least two inches. Groaning, he shook his head. "Good shot, Andrew. That's the game." He jogged across the court, scooped up the ball, and walked toward the net to meet Andrew.

"Good game." Andrew reached across and shook hands with Henry.

His friend grimaced. "Not my best, that's for certain."

"You don't usually let me beat you by that much." Andrew's grin faded. "You seem a bit off. Is everything all right?"

Henry lifted his racket and rested it on his shoulder. "Let's blame it on being distracted."

"What's on your mind?" Andrew scooped up two more balls and walked toward the side of the court. He followed Henry out through the gate and into the shade of the tall cedar tree.

Henry nodded toward the bench beneath the tree. "Let's sit down."

Andrew studied Henry as they walked toward the bench. Traveling to Italy together had helped them forge a strong bond. Now they shared a friendship as well as their business connection. And though Henry was ten years Andrew's senior, their common background and shared interests had solidified their friendship.

Henry lowered himself to the wooden bench. "I received a letter from Reginald Hayworth just after we returned from Italy."

Andrew sat beside him. "Isn't he the chief legal assistant to the home secretary?"

"Yes, and he has a close connection to the royal family, which gives him a great deal of influence."

"What was the letter about?"

"Apparently, Richard Jansen had a stroke and he can't continue his investigation into child emigration. Hayworth wants me to take his place. He sent a huge packet of documents and information Jansen collected."

Andrew gave a thoughtful nod. "I'm familiar with child emigration. Our family has been a supporter of Dr. Barnardo's work for a few years." At least he and his mother had supported the cause. "What's prompting the investigation?"

"There is a longstanding disagreement between those who are in favor of it and those who are opposed."

"I'm surprised anyone would be opposed. I've always heard child emigration benefited both Canada and Britain. We clear the workhouses and streets of poor orphans, giving those children the opportunity for a better life. And Canada benefits by adding to their population."

"That's been my opinion as well, but some unfortunate incidents in Canada have made some people, including Her Majesty Queen Alexandra, question the practice."

Andrew frowned. "What kind of unfortunate incidents?"

"Children disappearing, others who have been neglected or injured by those who have taken them in." Henry's brow creased. "I'm afraid there may be a darker side to child emigration that has been hidden by those who stand to benefit from it."

"What do you mean?"

"Our government pays the sending organization two dollars Canadian for every child we send, and Canada matches those funds. The receiving homes also charge an application fee to those who want to take in a child. When you multiply those funds times the number of children emigrating, we're talking about a significant amount of money."

Andrew gave a solemn nod. "Wasn't there some kind of government investigation in the past? I seem to remember reading about it in my law studies."

Henry nodded. "About thirty years ago, a man named Andrew Doyle was commissioned to look into it and report his findings. He traveled to Canada and visited several receiving homes and some of the children who had been placed with families. When his report was published, it caused quite a stir."

"What were his conclusions?"

"He was critical of those who were sending the children and of the process itself. He believed the program failed the children and was doing more harm than good. In fact, he recommended the government put a stop to it or at the least make several changes."

"What were his chief concerns?"

"He said there needed to be more screening of those who took the children and a better system to check up on them after they were placed."

"Were those changes made?"

Henry shook his head. "Initially, a few organizations took steps to improve things, but from what I've read, not many followed through. The number of children sent to Canada has steadily increased since then. And I'm afraid most of the troublesome policies have not been corrected, and that's why Hayworth has been asked to launch an official government investigation."

Andrew fingered the handle of his racket, pondering Henry's comments. "I heard Dr. Barnardo speak and saw a presentation given by some of the children in his care. It was quite impressive, especially knowing most of those same children were living on the streets before they were taken in."

"Dr. Barnardo was the undisputed leader in child emigration before his passing, but he was not the only one emigrating children to Canada. It seems more than fifty thousand have already been sent."

Andrew turned to his friend. "I didn't realize there have been so many."

"Yes, it's quite a surprising number, but it has been going on for many years. I believe Dr. Barnardo began sending children in the early 1880s, following in the footsteps of Annie MacPherson, Maria Rye, and a few others."

"It sounds like there is quite a history."

Henry nodded. "I've been reading up on it. I believe those who started it had good intentions, and probably most still do. But it's grown so large, and with the number of children emigrating, it's easy to see how some would slip through the cracks and come to a bad end."

Andrew sobered. Were those isolated cases, or were hundreds or even thousands of children suffering because of lack of proper guidelines and oversight? He glanced at Henry. "So, will you take up the investigation?"

"It's an important issue. Someone needs to look into it and give a fair and unbiased report. That person must be free to travel and able to spend some time in Canada this spring and summer." Henry rested his racket across his knees. "I'm ready to accept the commission, but I'd rather not handle it alone."

Andrew studied his friend's face. "You want me to go with you?"

"Yes. I think if we tackle this project together, we can be much more efficient. We'll need to visit some of the children's homes here in London and Liverpool before we travel to Canada to gather information and evaluate the situation there. When we return, we'll need to write a report summarizing our findings, then give our recommendations. Hopefully we can finish by the end of summer."

Andrew chuckled. "That's all?"

"It will take a good deal of intense work. I'm thinking we could take care of matters here and be ready to leave for Canada in two or three weeks."

"Can we make our travel arrangements that quickly?"

"I'll have Phillips start working on it today." Henry sent him an expectant look. "So, what do you say?"

Andrew considered it a moment more. "It sounds challenging. You know I like to travel, and I've always wanted to see Canada."

Henry cocked his eyebrow. "I thought you were going to say you've always had a heart for helping children and caring for the poor."

Andrew's face warmed. "I am concerned about justice for the poor, especially the children."

Henry slapped him on the shoulder. "I know you are. I was just trying to see if I could ruffle your feathers a bit." His grin faded. "But in all seriousness I consider this a very important commission. We'll be responsible to the government, but more importantly to the Lord. And we must be firmly resolved to give it our best effort and cover our work with prayer."

"Yes, of course."

"Why don't we start now?" Without waiting for a reply, Henry bowed his head.

Andrew quickly ducked his head as well. He was still a bit uncomfortable with his friend's habit of praying aloud at the most unusual times. But he appreciated his sincere faith and his practical example of seeking God's guidance in everyday situations.

"Father, we come to You with our hearts and minds focused on this new commission we've been given to investigate child emigration. We know You are infinitely aware of all the issues and people who are involved. We know You care about the poor and have a special place in Your heart for orphans and abandoned children. Help us have that same genuine concern for them. Guide us and lead us to the truth. Help us see the situation clearly and know what to include in our report and what to recommend. We ask for traveling mercies once again, and we place ourselves in Your hands. We pray all these things in the name of Jesus Christ, our Lord. Amen."

"Amen," Andrew added and lifted his head.

Henry placed his hand on Andrew's shoulder. "Well, my friend, this is a significant responsibility, but it also sounds like it could be a great adventure."

Andrew returned the smile. "It does indeed, and I'll be ready."

Katie gulped in a deep breath and forced out her words. "I want to go to Canada."

Mrs. Stafford's eyebrows rose, and she looked at Katie over the top of her spectacles. "We only send our best girls to Canada, those who are obedient and hardworking. Would you describe yourself that way?"

Heat rushed into Katie's cheeks. "Yes ma'am. I try to be." Thank goodness Mr. Peterson had never told the matron she'd been sneaking outside after dark to exchange messages with Garth. She looked across the desk and met the matron's gaze.

Mrs. Stafford pursed her lips and looked at the open file in front of her. "Tell me about your family."

A lump rose in Katie's throat, and she had to swallow hard before she could speak. She still couldn't believe her mum was gone. It hurt too much to even think about it. "My parents were good people, very kind and loving. Dad worked as a carpenter, building houses and repairing buildings. Mum cared for our home and family until Dad died. Then we had to move, and Mum started working in a dress shop. But she's gone now, and we're on our own."

Mrs. Stafford frowned and looked down at the file. "Both your parents are dead?"

Katie swallowed hard and nodded.

"And your siblings?"

"My twin brother, Garth, is at the boys' home next door, and my little sister, Grace, is here with me. We have an older sister, Laura, who works as a lady's maid on an estate near St. Albans." Painful disappointment rose and nearly stole her voice. "But she can't care for us."

"I see." The matron dipped her pen in ink and wrote in the file for a few seconds. She looked up. "Tell me why you want to go to Canada."

"Garth said he'll be going soon, and that's why Grace and I want to go too, so we can stay together."

Mrs. Stafford closed the file and studied Katie.

"You appear to be healthy, and you're not a bad-looking girl, though you are short for your age." The matron scanned her once more. "It's a shame your eyes aren't blue."

Katie clasped her hands behind her back and tried not to let the matron's comments sting, but they did. She would never be as pretty as her sisters. They both had lovely blue eyes and wavy blond hair. Her eyes were hazel like her dad's, and her hair was more red than brown. That wouldn't keep her from going to Canada, would it?

Katie met the matron's gaze. "A person can't help the color of their eyes."

"Oh, don't fret, child. There still might be a family that would take you."

Katie smoothed out her expression. She didn't want to anger the woman or make her think she was moody and fractious.

"The Dominion of Canada is one of the most prosperous areas of the British Empire—a land of opportunity for those who are willing to work hard and be responsible and obedient." She narrowed her eyes. "Are you willing, Katherine?"

"Yes ma'am. I always helped my mother with cooking and cleaning and taking care of my younger sister. I know how to darn and knit, and I've been learning to do the hand sewing to finish dresses and shirts. I'm sure I'll be a fine seamstress one day."

Mrs. Stafford's mouth pulled down at the corners. "It's not becoming to boast about your skills. Wait until someone asks you about them before you reel off your list."

Heat surged into Katie's face once again, and she pressed her lips together.

"Remember, Katherine, humility will take you much further than pride."

"Yes ma'am."

"Heaven knows we are overcrowded here." The matron looked through the papers in the file once more and heaved a sigh. "We have four girls leaving for Liverpool on Wednesday. I'll put your name on the list to go with them."

Katie leaned forward and gripped the edge of the matron's desk. "Please, ma'am, my sister Grace must go too. We have to stay together."

The matron pulled another file from her desk drawer. She frowned as she scanned the first page. "Grace is only seven. She's too young to be of much help to a family."

"But I'll take care of her. She won't be any trouble."

The matron tapped her fingers on the desk as she looked through the rest of the papers in Grace's file. Finally, she looked up. "All right. There might be a family willing to take you both."

Relief rushed through Katie. "Thank you, ma'am. I promise we'll do what we're told and be respectful. As long as we can stay together, that's all that matters to us."

The matron's eyes softened for a second, but then a shadow crossed her expression. "I'm sure you'll be fine. Mrs. Hastings will see that you have what you need for the trip to Liverpool. The staff at the home there will help you prepare and pack your trunk for sailing. You should be off for Canada very soon to start your new life." She closed the file. "You may go."

"Thank you, ma'am." Katie turned and left the matron's office, her emotions rising and falling like she was already aboard a ship. They had to follow Garth. That was their only choice now that Mum and Dad were gone. Laura hadn't answered her letter, and Mrs. Graham seemed to have forgotten about them too.

Her eyes stung, but she blinked back her tears as she climbed the stairs in search of her sister. When she reached the top-floor dormitory, she spotted Grace standing by her bed, brushing her hair.

Katie hurried across the room. "I talked to the matron."

Grace spun around. "Has she heard from Mum?"

Pain pierced Katie's heart. She hadn't told her sister the sad news in Garth's last note. She couldn't seem to find the courage to say those painful words aloud. Grace loved Mum so much.

How could she tell her they would never hear her gentle voice or see her caring smile again? She'd have to tell her sometime, but not today.

She shook her head and reached for Grace's hand. "The matron said we can go to Canada."

Grace's blue eyes rounded. "But what about Mum? Won't she be worried if we go so far away?"

Katie ran her thumb over the top of Grace's hand, searching for the right words to reassure her sister. "I think Mum wants the three of us to stay together. And since Garth is going, we should go too."

"But then Laura won't know where to find us."

Those words hit Katie like a fresh blow to the chest. She pulled in a deep breath, sat on the bed, and patted the blanket beside her. "Sit down, Grace."

Her little sister sank down next to her.

"Laura hasn't answered my letter or come to see us. She probably can't get away to come to London. And even if she could, I don't think she'd be able to take care of us."

Grace's chin wobbled. "But Laura loves us."

Katie nodded, though she wasn't sure of it anymore, and then pulled Grace into a hug.

Why hadn't Laura answered her letter? Katie had told her sister what happened to Mum and where they'd been taken. It didn't make sense. Laura usually wrote every week and visited the family as often as she could. They had always been close . . . at least she'd thought they were.

Katie patted her sister's back. She had to be the one to comfort Grace now that Mum was gone and Laura had left them on their own. And she would always take care of Grace no matter what happened. "It will be all right," she said softly. "The matron says Canada is a wonderful place, and we'll be able to stay together with a family."

"Garth too?"

Katie hoped that was true, but doubts rose in her mind. What if they were sent somewhere far away from Garth? What if this decision to go to Canada was a terrible mistake? She'd lost Dad and Mum. How would she survive without Garth?

She closed her eyes, a silent plea rising from her heart. *Please, Father, watch over us, keep us safe, and help us find a way to stay together.*

Laura pushed Mum's wheelchair outside, into the small garden behind St. Joseph's Hospital. What a relief to leave the dingy, antiseptic-smelling ward even for a few minutes.

Mum was still weak and could walk only a few steps, but Laura had pleaded with the nurse for permission to take her outside for some fresh air. The nurse had reluctantly agreed as long as Mum bundled up, and Laura promised not to keep her out too long.

Early afternoon sunlight filtered through the tall trees around the edge of the garden, sending lacy shadows across the brick path.

Mum lifted her face and closed her eyes. "It's wonderful to feel the warmth of the sun again. And just listen to the birds."

"Yes, it's lovely out here." Laura glanced around the garden, taking in the winding path and the wisteria vines climbing the walls with purple blossoms just coming into bloom. She parked the wheelchair next to a wooden bench at the side of the path and tucked the soft blanket tighter across Mum's lap. "Are you warm enough?"

"Yes, dear, I'm fine." Mum smiled up at Laura and reached for her hand. "Thank you. It's such a comfort to have you here."

Laura squeezed Mum's fingers. "I'm glad I can be here."

Mum shifted in her wheelchair. "Were you able to see Reverend Bush?"

"Yes, we talked for almost an hour this morning." Laura sat on the end of the bench closest to Mum. "I was glad to speak to someone who actually wanted to listen to our story."

"What advice did he have for us?"

Laura glanced away and chose her words carefully. "He was sympathetic, and he said to tell you he is praying for you. But guardianship is a legal matter, not one that he can solve for us."

Mum's hopeful expression faded. "I'm sorry

124

to hear that. I thought a letter from him might convince that matron at Grangeford to let you take the children."

Laura was disappointed as well, but Reverend Bush had helped her realize she wasn't ready to accept full responsibility for her siblings. She had no income until she returned to Bolton or found a new position, and she couldn't expect the Grahams to house and feed them all indefinitely.

She pushed her discouragement away and focused on Mum again. "He said he would try to help me find a new position. Then I can save my earnings toward renting a flat and paying the fees at Grangeford."

Mum gave a tired sigh. "I don't understand why they charge us for the children's care. It doesn't seem charitable, especially when they know no loving parent wants to put their child in a home."

"I agree, but Reverend Bush assured me they would be well cared for until we're able to bring them home with us."

Hopeful light flickered in Mum's blue-gray eyes. "So, you're going to stay in London?"

Laura nodded. "I think it's best."

"Oh, thank you, dear. I'm so grateful. Will you stay with the Grahams for now?"

"Yes. They've been very kind. And Reverend Bush said I may call on him again in three days, and he'll let me know if he has heard about any open positions. He suggested I check the newspapers and contact an employment agency."

Mum took Laura's hand. "That sounds like a fine plan. I'll pray for the right position with a good family."

Laura's stomach tensed. She'd thought the Harringtons were a good family until their nephew arrived and made her life miserable. How could she be sure she wasn't putting herself in a dangerous situation again?

"Your experience as a lady's maid for the Frasiers should be helpful."

"I hope so." But she couldn't count on it. The competition would be stiff here in London. She might have to start at the bottom again, as a chambermaid or perhaps even a kitchen maid, but that didn't matter. She would take whatever position she could find to stay in London and be near her family.

She needed to write to Mrs. Frasier and explain why she couldn't return to Bolton. She was a kind woman, and Laura hoped she would understand. But leaving without giving proper notice put her mistress in an awkward position. She might not give Laura a letter of recommendation.

What would Andrew Frasier think about her decision? Would he believe she had taken advantage of the situation, accepted the money, and never intended to return? Her heart sank at that thought.

"Laura?" Mum tipped her head. "Did you hear what I said?"

"No, I'm sorry."

Mum smiled. "You looked like you were miles away."

"I was just thinking that I have to write to the Frasiers and tell them I won't be coming back to Bolton."

"Yes, you should. I'm sure when you explain why your family needs you here, they'll understand." Mum gazed across the garden for a few seconds, then looked back at Laura. "Perhaps I should write a letter to the matron at Grangeford."

"I don't think she'll let the children go until we pay the fees."

"She might not release them to you, but at least I could appeal for a visit. I'd feel so much more at ease if you could see them and assure them I'm going to get well, and they'll be able to come home soon."

Laura wasn't sure a letter would sway the matron, but it would make Mum feel better to try.

"And I'll write to each of the children as well," Mum added with a smile. "That should cheer them and give them something to hold on to."

"I'm sure they'd love to receive a letter from you."

"All right, then. Let's go inside and see if we can find some paper and a pen."

Laura pushed Mum back across the garden, and her thoughts shifted to Katie and Grace. The matron had said the girls were having a difficult time adjusting to the routine at Grangeford. What did she mean by that? How could anyone be happy in such a stark, gloomy place?

A new surge of determination filled her. She would go to Grangeford again and take Mum's letter to the matron. That might open the door for a visit. If not, she could at least make sure her siblings received a comforting message from Mum so they would not think they were forgotten.

6

Katie held tight to Grace's hand and followed Mrs. Hastings and the other four girls through the crowded train station. Her heart pounded in her ears, and her face felt hot. She'd never ridden on a train before. Her father had died after his train careened off the tracks and tumbled down a hillside, killing or injuring everyone on board.

Were she and Grace headed for the same fate?

She lifted her hand to her mouth and swallowed hard, trying not to lose her breakfast.

Back at Grangeford, when she learned they would travel to Liverpool by train, she'd almost refused to go. But she had promised Garth they would follow him to Canada, and she could not break a promise to her brother, no matter how much the thought of riding a train frightened her.

Somehow she would have to find the courage to board that train for the first leg of their journey.

Grace sent an anxious glance around the bustling station. "I'm scared, Katie."

"Just hold tight to my hand, and you'll be all right." But Katie couldn't hide the tremor in her own voice.

"Will Garth be on the train?"

He had probably already left for Liverpool.

Still, she didn't want to dampen Grace's hopes. "I don't know. We'll have to wait and see."

Mrs. Hastings stopped under a sign that read *To the Trains* and turned toward the six girls. "I'll speak to the gate agent, and I want you all to pass through and wait for me on the other side."

Katie and Grace fell in line behind Jenny, Alice, Martha, and Ethel. Mrs. Hastings showed their tickets to the man at the gate, and he motioned the girls through the turnstile.

Katie stepped out onto the train platform and glanced around. A high arched roof sheltered the tracks and platforms. A few pigeons flew back and forth, cooing and fluttering their wings. A large round clock displayed the time, and several signs hung overhead: *Booking Office, Cloak Room, Enquiry Office, Way Out.*

"Come along, girls." Mrs. Hastings led them down Platform Number Two, and they lined up under a sign that read *Wait Here for Third Class.*

Katie brushed a piece of lint from Grace's shoulder and folded down her sister's coat collar in the back. They both wore ivory straw hats with a navy blue ribbon around the crown and navy blue hip-length coats over light blue dresses. Each girl carried a small satchel containing a nightgown and undergarments. Mrs. Hastings had told them they would receive a trunk of new clothing for their trip to Canada when they reached Liverpool.

A train whistle blew in the distance. Katie turned and looked down the tracks. A huge locomotive rolled into the station, looking like a fearful, fiery dragon billowing black smoke from a chimney up top. The brakes screeched and steam hissed out, creating a misty cloud around them as the train slowed to a stop by their platform.

Katie clasped Grace's hand and stepped back while the other girls surged forward.

Mrs. Hastings held out her arm. "Not yet, girls. We must wait until the arriving passengers disembark."

Katie watched as several people stepped down from the train. Most were well-dressed men in business suits, along with a few women wearing large hats and colorful coats and dresses. One woman carried a baby in her arms, and another held tight to the hand of a young boy wearing a sailor suit.

"All right, girls, follow me." Mrs. Hastings grabbed up her skirt and mounted the steps to the train car. Katie, Grace, and the other girls hurried after her.

They found their seats in the middle of the car and stowed their satchels in the rack overhead. Katie and Grace sat together across from Jenny and Martha. Mrs. Hastings sat on the other side of the aisle, facing Alice and Ethel. The air in the car was stuffy and smelled of cigar smoke.

Katie wished she could open the window, but she wasn't sure how the latches worked. The seats were slightly padded on the bottom, but the back was hard wood. She shifted on the bench seat and tried to get comfortable. How long would it take to reach Liverpool? No one had told her, and she hadn't thought to ask.

"What's wrong? Seat too hard for you?" Jenny's voice carried a taunt.

"No, it's fine." Katie turned and looked away, hoping to squelch the conversation. Jenny had continually mocked and teased her at the home, and it seemed she planned to continue doing the same on their journey.

"Why are you moping? We're the lucky ones." Jenny sent her a smug smile. "We got away from Grangeford."

"I'm not moping."

"Well, you don't look very happy."

Katie clenched her jaw, determined not to answer.

"You ought to be glad they picked you. Not everyone gets chosen to go to Canada."

Martha leaned toward Jenny. "Of course she's not happy. She thinks she's better than everyone else."

Fire flashed through Katie. "I do not!"

Mrs. Hastings looked their way, a warning in her stern expression.

"You're no better than us." Jenny lowered her

voice, but it held the same hurtful tone. "You're an orphan off the street just like we are."

"We're not orphans!" Grace jutted out her chin, and pink splotches colored her cheeks. "And we didn't live on the street! We have a mum who loves us!"

Pain throbbed in Katie's chest. Grace didn't know the truth, and she couldn't tell her now, not in front of these girls. If she did, they'd only torment them and bring Grace to tears.

Jenny narrowed her eyes. "If you're not orphans, then why were you sent to Grangeford?"

Grace darted a frustrated glance at Katie, urging her to speak up for them.

Katie lifted her chin. "Our mum was ill and had to go to the hospital. That's why we were sent to the home."

Jenny shook her head. "I don't believe it. You're lying!"

Grace leaned forward. "We are not!"

"Yes, you are! You just don't want to admit you've got no family left!"

Mrs. Hastings rose from her seat. "Girls, lower your voices at once! That is no way to behave, especially not in public." She pursed her lips, glaring at Katie and Grace, then shifting her sharp gaze to Jenny and Martha. "Now, you will act like well-mannered young ladies and remain silent for the rest of the trip."

"But, Mrs. Hastings, it was Katie who—"

133

"I expect you to obey! Not one more word or you will stand at the back of the train car until we reach Liverpool. Do you understand?"

"Yes ma'am," they all replied.

But as soon as Mrs. Hastings returned to her seat, Jenny smirked and rolled her eyes toward the ceiling. "She's such an old goat," she whispered.

Martha lifted her hand and covered her mouth, choking back her laughter.

Katie stared at them. They didn't care what Mrs. Hastings said. It was all a joke to them. They were used to being scolded every day for breaking one rule or another.

But Katie had been raised to respect her elders and treat everyone with kindness. She wasn't used to being taunted and teased by other children, and she certainly wasn't used to being considered a troublemaker by the adults in her life.

She sighed and slipped her hand into Grace's. Her sister looked up at her with a flushed face and glassy eyes. Katie silently mouthed, *Don't worry. It will be all right.*

Grace leaned in closer, resting her head against Katie's arm. Thank goodness they were making this journey together. She couldn't imagine traveling without her sister or sending her off alone.

The whistle blew. The train jerked and rolled

forward. Katie gripped the edge of the seat with one hand while she held tight to Grace with the other. The car rocked and swayed as the train left the station and picked up speed. Soon they were rolling down the track, racing past buildings and crossing the river on a bridge that looked too narrow to keep them from falling into the water.

The other girls' faces glowed with excitement as they watched the city pass by, but all Katie could think about was everything they were leaving behind.

Where was Garth? How would she find him? And what about Laura? What would she think when she received the letter telling her the three of them had left for Canada? Would she ever see her brother and sister again?

Laura clutched Mum's letters in her hand and walked down the main hall at Grangeford. Would the heartfelt message convince the matron to change her mind and allow a visit? If only she could have a few minutes with Katie and Grace, she could let them know Mum would soon be leaving the hospital, and Laura was looking for a new position in London. Surely knowing they wouldn't have to stay at Grangeford too much longer would ease their minds and give them hope.

As she passed the main staircase, girls' voices floated down from the floor above, reciting mathematic facts. Laura approached the matron's door and knocked twice. She waited a few seconds, but no one answered.

Footsteps sounded down the hall, and Laura turned. Two girls walked toward her, each carrying a mop and a bucket of gray water. As they came closer, they watched Laura with suspicious looks.

"Excuse me." Laura smiled, hoping to put them at ease. "I'm looking for Mrs. Stafford. She doesn't seem to be in her office. Do you know where I might find her?"

The taller girl exchanged a glance with the other, then turned back to Laura. "Sorry, miss, we don't know."

"Is there someone else I could speak to, perhaps an assistant?"

The shorter girl shifted her bucket to the other hand, and some of the water sloshed over the side and dripped to the floor. "Mrs. Hastings is her assistant, but she's not here. Maybe you could speak to Miss Richter. She's one of the teachers."

"Could you tell me where to find her?"

The taller girl glanced down the hallway. "Her classroom is the second door on the right."

"Thank you." Perhaps these girls could tell her more or even deliver the letters to her sisters. "I've come to visit Grace and Katie McAlister. Do you know them?"

They exchanged wary glances again, and the taller girl adjusted her hold on the mop. "They're not here anymore."

Laura's eyes widened, and she stared at her. "What?"

"They left with the other girls who are going to Canada."

Laura tensed. "No, you must be mistaken. They couldn't send them to Canada without our mother's permission. She would never agree to that."

The girl shrugged. "All I know is, they left with Mrs. Hastings and four other girls."

Laura slowly shook her head. This couldn't be true. Katie and Grace couldn't have been sent so far away.

A middle-aged woman with dark brown hair stepped out a doorway just down the hall. Her gaze darted from Laura to the girls. "Is everything all right, Elsa?"

"Yes ma'am."

Laura turned and faced the woman. "I'm Laura McAlister. I'm looking for my sisters, Katie and Grace McAlister."

The woman nodded. "I know Katie and Grace."

"Oh, thank goodness! I was so worried. They said my sisters had left Grangeford."

The woman shifted her gaze toward the girls. "You may be excused from mopping the hall. Go back to your other duties."

"Yes ma'am." They turned away, whispering to each other as they set off.

The woman stepped into the hallway and shut the door behind her. "I'm Miss Richter. And I'm afraid what the girls told you is true. Katie and Grace left with an emigration party last week."

Laura gasped. "Why would you send them away?"

Miss Richter straightened. "I'm sorry. I don't know the particulars of their situation. You'll have to speak to Mrs. Stafford, the matron, for those details."

"She's not in her office. I knocked on her door, but she didn't answer."

"Oh yes, that's right. She is out for the day, but she'll be back tomorrow."

"This can't wait until tomorrow! My sisters should never have left Grangeford! We had no warning, no opportunity to pay their fees and bring them home."

The teacher stepped back, obviously wanting to put distance between herself and Laura. "Miss McAlister, I know this is upsetting news. I'm sure that when you come back and speak to Mrs. Stafford, she will explain everything."

"Oh, I'll come back, you can be sure of it! You had no right to send them anywhere, especially not to Canada!"

"Please, Miss McAlister, calm yourself!"

"How can I be calm when my sisters have been stolen away and sent to a foreign land!"

A man carrying a toolbox stepped through the doorway at the end of the hall and walked toward them. He was the one who had greeted her at the gate on her first visit to Grangeford.

The teacher turned toward him. "Mr. Peterson, this is Miss McAlister. We've finished our discussion. Will you please show her out?" The woman's firm tone matched her rigid posture.

The man's gaze darted from Miss Richter to Laura. "Yes ma'am." He touched the brim of his cap, then motioned down the hall. "This way, miss."

Laura's throat burned. "This is wrong, terribly wrong, and you know it!"

Miss Richter's face flushed, but she didn't answer. Instead, she stepped into her classroom and closed the door.

"Come along, miss." Mr. Peterson tilted his head toward the main door, compassion in his eyes. "Miss Richter can't help you. She's not the one who makes decisions 'round here."

Mr. Peterson started down the hall, and Laura reluctantly fell in step beside him. "They sent my sisters to Canada without our permission! How could they do that when they have family members who want to care for them? It's a terrible mistake!"

"I believe Katie asked to go."

Laura's steps faltered. "You spoke to my sister about this?"

He nodded, his expression somber.

"But why? Why would she want to go?"

"She wasn't too keen on the idea at first, but then she heard her brother was going, so she thought she should go too."

Laura's heart sank. "Garth is gone as well?"

"I believe so, but you'll have to check with the staff at the boys' home to be sure."

Her mind spun as they continued down the hall. Why would Garth want to go to Canada? Didn't he realize she was doing everything she could to bring them all home?

When they reached the main door, Mr. Peterson pushed it open for her. "I'm real sorry, Miss McAlister. I thought you knew they were going. Katie wrote to you."

Laura shook her head. "I never received her letter." She stopped in the doorway as the truth became clear. Katie had sent the letter to Bolton, and the staff had held it there, expecting Laura to return.

Poor Katie! She'd been torn and needing her sister's advice, but she'd never received a reply. No wonder she'd asked to go to Canada with Garth. She probably thought he was the only one left who cared about her. Hot tears filled Laura's eyes, and she lifted her hand to cover her mouth.

"Oh no, miss. Don't cry." He pulled a folded handkerchief from his pocket and pressed it into her hand. "Here, take this."

"Thank you." She sniffed and blotted her cheeks. "When will the ship set sail?"

"I don't know. All the girls go through the Hughes Home in Liverpool first."

"How long do they stay there?"

"Some stay a few months for training. Others board a ship within a few weeks or days. It all depends on the sailing schedule and the number of children and escorts in each emigration party."

Laura's thoughts raced ahead. "So there might still be time to speak to someone at the Hughes Home and bring them back to London."

He sent her a worried glance. "I don't know about that, miss."

"I have to try. I can't just give up and let them be sent across the ocean."

"Don't go alone, miss. I doubt they'd listen to you unless you take an older male relative or you have some sort of legal papers to prove you can claim them."

She had no male family members living in London and no guardianship papers.

Andrew Frasier's offer of help came to mind once again. She didn't like the idea of being indebted to him, but what other option did she have? She needed his advice and assistance if she was going to rescue her siblings and bring them back to London before they boarded a ship for Canada.

She reached out and touched the old man's jacket sleeve. "Thank you, Mr. Peterson. I appreciate your kindness."

His shook his head as he slipped his hands in his jacket pockets. "You've no cause to thank me. I've done nothing."

"But you have. You helped me when no one else would." She leaned forward and kissed his cheek. "God bless you, sir."

His ears turned pink, and a smile creased his whiskered face. "I hope you find them and that the folks at Hughes will listen."

Laura nodded, her throat so tight she could barely speak. "So do I." Then she reached in her pocket, took out Andrew Frasier's card, and started down the drive.

Andrew scanned the next page of notes Henry had given him to review. The articles and interviews gave a great deal of helpful information about child emigration. Some said it was a wonderful opportunity for Britain's poor children to have a fresh start and hope for a better future. Others thought it was a national disgrace, and they insisted most of the children were treated no better than slaves. Both opinions couldn't be right. There obviously needed to be an independent investigation that would establish the truth and make sound recommendations for the future. He was glad he and Henry were taking this on.

He sat back, perplexed by the wide range of opinions. When he and his mother had heard Dr. Barnardo speak and listened to the children's voices raised in song, they'd both been deeply touched. Tears had shimmered in his mother's eyes, and he'd reached for his wallet, eager to give toward Dr. Barnardo's work. He had to admit he believed the positive reports about the man, and he admired his dedication to helping London's poor and orphaned children.

There would always be those who exaggerated the negative side of every issue and made a huge fuss about small matters. Still, he needed to have an open mind and let the facts speak for themselves.

He and Henry planned to visit two children's homes that afternoon. He looked down and checked the names—Grangeford and Barkingside. Their visits were purposely unscheduled, with the hope that a surprise visit would allow them to see a true picture of how the homes were run and how the children were treated.

Andrew ran his finger down the list of homes Henry wanted to visit before they left for Canada. There were five more in London and three in Liverpool. Would they have enough time to see them all before their ship sailed?

Jonathan Phillips, Henry's assistant, was still working on their travel arrangements. It seemed odd he hadn't been able to confirm the date for their departure. How difficult could it be to purchase tickets?

A knock sounded at his door.

"Come in," Andrew called.

Phillips leaned around the door. "Mr. Dowd would like to see you in his office."

"Thank you." Andrew rose from his desk and followed Phillips into the reception area. The young man took a seat and shifted some files to cover a newspaper on his desk.

Andrew frowned as he passed Phillips. Why was he reading the newspaper when he ought to be working on their travel arrangements? Andrew blew out a breath, trying to let go of his irritation. The timing of their trip was in the Lord's hands, and no irresponsible assistant would keep them from setting sail on the appointed day.

He proceeded into Henry's office. "You wanted to see me?"

Henry looked up and set aside his pen. "Yes. I received a letter from Reginald Hayworth."

"The legal assistant to the home secretary?"

"Yes. He's eager to hear more about our assessment of Jansen's preliminary work. He'd like to meet with us before we leave for Canada. I thought I'd suggest Monday afternoon. That would give us time to visit one or two of the children's homes in the morning."

Andrew nodded. "That sounds like a good plan."

"All right. I'll have Phillips send a reply to Hayworth." Henry rose and reached for his suit jacket. "Are you ready to go?"

"Yes, I just need to collect my hat from my office." Andrew followed Henry out the door. As they rounded the corner to the reception area, he spotted Phillips sitting with his feet propped up on the desk, reading the newspaper. As soon as Phillips saw them coming, he lowered his feet and stuffed the newspaper under the desk.

Frowning, Henry stopped by his assistant's desk. "Mr. Phillips, we're going out, and we don't plan to return until four o'clock. By that time I expect you to have confirmed our travel arrangements. If that means leaving the office to pick up our tickets, then please do so."

A muscle twitched in Phillips's cheek, betraying his irritation. "I'll take care of it, sir."

"I'd also like you to send a message to Mr. Reginald Hayworth. Tell him Mr. Frasier and I are available to meet with him on Monday afternoon at one o'clock if that's a convenient time for him. Ask the messenger to wait for a reply."

"Yes sir."

Henry studied Phillips for a moment, looking

as though he wanted to say more, but he turned to Andrew. "Why don't you collect your things and meet me downstairs?"

Andrew agreed and returned to his office, giving Henry a moment to speak to Phillips in private. This wasn't the first time Henry's assistant had been reprimanded for laziness or coming in late and looking as though he'd had too much to drink the night before. Andrew shook his head. That young man needed to change his ways, or his days of working for Henry were numbered. The fact that he was Henry's distant cousin was the only reason he'd been allowed so many chances to mend his ways and hold on to his position.

He took his notebook and pen from his desk, then collected his hat from the hook by the door.

As he walked out of his office, he glanced at Phillips. The young man sat at his desk, looking down at something in his lap. Andrew quietly walked closer and spotted the *Tatler* newspaper resting on his knees. Of all the nerve!

Phillips looked up, but he didn't bother to hide the newspaper or appear ashamed at being caught reading it again. "Did you want something, Mr. Frasier?"

"Yes, I want to see you doing your work rather than reading that gossip rag."

Phillips leaned back in his chair. "I don't answer to you. Mr. Dowd is my employer."

"That may be true, but if you want to keep your position, I suggest you toss out that newspaper and finish your assignment. This trip to Canada is important. We need those arrangements settled as soon as possible."

Phillips's face reddened, but his expression remained defiant. "You always act so righteous, so high and mighty, but you're no better than I am."

Andrew leveled his gaze at Phillips. "You'd get a lot further in life if you'd treat others with respect and do an honest day's work."

"What are you—a Sunday school teacher?" Phillips huffed, and his voice turned taunting. "You better hurry along now. You don't want to keep Mr. Dowd waiting."

Andrew sent him a final scathing look and strode out of the office, his opinion of Phillips dipping to a new low. Laziness was one thing, but rude and disrespectful behavior was entirely another.

Laura glanced at Andrew Frasier's card and checked the address once more. She continued down the street a few more minutes and finally spotted the sign for the law office of Mr. Henry Dowd posted by the door of a large limestone building.

She rested her hand over her fluttering stomach and pulled in a deep breath. She could do this.

Her family needed legal help, and she knew only one solicitor . . . Andrew Frasier.

She returned the card to her coat pocket, mounted the steps, and entered the building. The sign in the lobby listed his office on the second floor. She smoothed her hand down the front of her coat, adjusted her hat, and climbed the stairs.

Only four offices were on the second floor. She approached his door, knocked, and waited. Someone called, "It's open," and she stepped inside.

A young man seated in the reception area looked up. His sullen expression faded as she approached. "Well, hello there, miss."

His quick smile and informal greeting surprised her, but she tried to look confident as she met his gaze. "Good afternoon. My name is Laura McAlister. I'd like to see Mr. Andrew Frasier."

"Do you have an appointment?"

"No sir, but I believe he'll want to see me."

He cocked one eyebrow and grinned. "I'm sure he would."

A warning flashed through her, and her stomach tensed.

He tipped his head and scanned her from head to toe. "Now, why would a pretty young woman like you want to see a lawyer?"

Laura stiffened. "That is something I want to discuss with Mr. Frasier."

The man rose from his chair and walked around

the desk. "Mr. Frasier is not in. But I'm sure I can help you."

She stepped back. "No, thank you. When do you expect Mr. Frasier to return?"

He sent her a slow, suggestive smile. "He's going to be out of the office for several hours."

A tremor traveled through Laura, but she did her best to mask her discomfort. "Then I'd like to make an appointment to see him as soon as possible."

"He's a very busy man, but I work closely with Mr. Frasier. Why don't you step into our inner office, and we can discuss your . . . situation?"

No way was she was going anywhere with this man. "No, thank you. I want to make the appointment with Mr. Frasier."

He stepped closer. "He can't help you. I'm the one you want."

Alarm flashed through her, and she spun away.

He grabbed her arm. "Come on. You don't have to be afraid of me."

She jerked away and lunged toward the door.

But he dashed around and blocked her path. "You're a feisty one, but I like a challenge."

Panic throbbed in her chest. Her gaze darted around the room, looking for another way out, but she saw none.

Grinning, he reached for her again. But she grabbed up her skirt and kicked him hard. Her foot landed a powerful blow just below his belt.

He yelped, groaned, and bent forward, muttering a curse.

She ran around him, yanked open the door, and dashed into the hall. With her heart hammering, she charged down the steps.

Footsteps pounded on the floor above. "Wait! Come back!"

She nearly flew around the landing and ran down the next flight of stairs. Once she reached the main floor, she shoved open the front door and ran down the street. People stared as she passed, but no one stopped her or asked if she needed help.

Jumbled thoughts tumbled through her mind, and her throat clogged. How could this happen again? What was wrong with her? Did she wear a sign around her neck that said, *I'm young and defenseless. Do whatever you'd like to me?*

She must never, ever put herself in that kind of situation again!

7

Katie knelt on the floor by the large wooden trunk at the foot of her bed. She brushed her hand across the top, then traced her finger over her name painted there in white letters.

Tonight they would pick up her trunk, and tomorrow morning she and Grace would board a ship called the *Corinthian* and sail across the ocean to Canada. She had no idea how long the trip would take or how difficult the journey might be. She'd never been on a ship before or even ridden in a rowboat.

Closing her eyes, she sat back on her heels, trying to fight off the sick, lonely feeling knotting her stomach. She should be excited to finally be on her way, but she had not seen Garth since she arrived at the Hughes Home in Liverpool. Only girls stayed here. She didn't know where the boys were sent, and though she'd asked, no one had been willing to tell her. She shifted her gaze to the window and dark sky outside.

Was Garth nearby in Liverpool, or had he already left for Canada? Would he be aboard the *Corinthian*? Was there still a chance they would find each other and make the trip together?

She pulled in a deep breath, trying to calm her

fears. The journey and the future held so many unknowns, but the staff at Hughes had not been harsh or unkind. She'd been given three meals a day and some time outdoors after lessons and chores. The weather had warmed, and she was not cold at night. And most important of all, she and Grace had been able to stay together.

Please, Father, help me be grateful and not weighed down with worries and cares.

She rose up on her knees and lifted the lid of her trunk. Reaching inside, she adjusted the stacks of new clothing. Everything was neatly pressed and folded, ready for the journey. She gazed at the paper attached to the inside of the lid and read it once more.

Girls Outfit List: One nicely trimmed dress and straw hat for Sabbath wear; Two print dresses for summer; Two warm dresses for winter; One dark felt hat for winter; Two white aprons; Two print aprons; Three nightgowns; Two chemises; Two pairs of drawers; Two cotton petticoats; Two flannel petticoats; Two pairs of boots; Five pairs of stockings; One warm overcoat for aboard ship; One jacket with hood; One scarf; One pair of gloves; One hairbrush and comb; One sewing kit with needles, pins, thread, and worsted for darning; Writing materials;

One Bible; One hymn and prayer book;
One copy of *Pilgrim's Progress.*

They said she had everything she needed for
her new life in Canada . . . everything except
Garth and Laura.

She reached up and touched the cross necklace
Mum had given her on her twelfth birthday, only
a few weeks before her father died. Life had
been so different then. Oh, how she wished she
could go back in time and make her father stay
home that day. If only he'd not taken that train. If
only . . .

"What are you doing down there on your
knees? You're not praying, are you?" Jenny's
haughty tone scraped across Katie's nerves.

She quickly glanced away. "No, I'm just
looking through my trunk."

Jenny glared at Katie. "I don't know why
they're letting you go to Canada before the rest
of us. It's not fair."

Katie knew why. She was ahead of other girls
her age in schooling, and she could cook, clean,
sew, and care for children. Her parents had taught
her to be respectful to adults and considerate of
others, and the staff at Hughes had taken notice.
Most of the other girls would spend weeks or
months catching up on basic skills and manners
before they would be ready to go.

Katie had been surprised when they told her

she'd be leaving with the next group, then panicked, fearing Grace would not be allowed to go with her. She'd pleaded and assured them she would take good care of her sister. Finally, the matron agreed Grace could join Katie's group. She'd been so relieved she'd almost cried.

"Did you hear what I said?" Jenny moved closer and stood over her.

Katie rose and faced Jenny. "Yes, I heard you."

"Well then, I want to know how you got them to put your name on the list ahead of everyone else."

Katie couldn't very well tell Jenny it was her ignorance and rude behavior that were keeping her at Hughes. That would cause a fight for sure. She met Jenny's gaze. "It wasn't my decision. If you want to know more, you can speak to the matron."

Jenny huffed. "She'd never listen to me."

"You won't know unless you try."

Jenny's face reddened. "She doesn't care about us. To her we're all nothing but dirty street rats, and she can do whatever she wants with us." Her chin trembled, and she quickly folded her arms over her stomach.

Katie's heart softened as she watched Jenny. The girl had been mean and spiteful since the first day they met, but she looked so miserable Katie couldn't help but feel sorry for her. Jenny had lived on the streets of London before she came to Grangeford. And as far as Katie knew, she had no family, no one who cared what happened to her. And now she faced an unknown future that would take her far away from England.

"Why are you looking at me like that? Don't you believe me?" Jenny's voice rose. "I heard the matron talking to one of the teachers, and that's exactly what she called us—dirty street rats!" She spun away and paced across the room. "That old witch! I bet she only took this job for the money. She doesn't care what happens to us! I've a mind to go down to her office right now and tell her what I think of her."

"That might not be the best idea."

"Why not?" Jenny demanded.

"You don't want to make her angry. She's the one who decides when you can go to Canada."

Jenny's face crumpled, and she sank down on the nearest bed. "I'll be stuck here in Liverpool longer than anyone else. You'll all go on and start new lives and forget all about me."

Katie sat down beside her. "I won't forget you, Jenny."

The girl swiped a tear from her flushed cheek.

Katie wanted to help Jenny, but she wasn't sure what she could do. Then an idea struck and she turned toward her. "I think I know how you can move up the list."

Jenny sniffed and looked up. "What do you mean?"

"If you want to go with the next group, then you have to show the matron you're ready."

"How am I supposed to do that?"

Thoughts rushed through Katie's mind. How could she condense all her parents had taught her since she was a little girl? Their kindness, love, and training had given her a great advantage over Jenny and many of the other girls. Even though her parents were gone, their example and instruction were still with her.

How could someone like Jenny understand what she had never experienced? She had nothing to draw on but what she had learned from other children who had grown up in the same sad circumstances. Still, that didn't mean she couldn't learn and change. Perhaps a bit of practical advice would help—if she was willing to listen.

Katie faced Jenny. "The staff is watching how you treat them and the other girls. You can show them you're ready by following the Golden Rule."

Jenny frowned. "What's that?"

Surprise rippled through Katie. How could Jenny not know the Golden Rule? But Jenny had probably never attended church or Sunday school until she arrived at Grangeford.

She focused on Jenny again. "The Golden Rule is part of Jesus's teaching. He said you should do unto others as you would have them do unto you."

Jenny gave a slight shrug. "That doesn't sound too hard."

"It might sound simple, but it can be a challenge, especially when others don't treat you the way you would like."

Jenny pondered that for a moment. "So, you think if I start treating others the way I want to be treated, the matron will let me go to Canada with the next group?"

Katie nodded. "You have to show her you know how to get along with others, and following the Golden Rule will help you with that."

"I'm not sure how to start."

"You want to be respected, right?"

Jenny nodded.

"Then you need to show respect to others. You wish people would speak kindly to you. Then you need to speak to others with kindness. It means putting others first and doing what's best for them even when they're not doing the same for you."

Jenny's brow wrinkled. "I suppose I could try to do that."

"It will help you now and when you stay with your new family in Canada."

Jenny clasped her hands in her lap. "Do you really think there'll be a family who'll want me?"

Katie leaned her shoulder against Jenny's. "Of course. You're strong and determined, and I've seen how hard you can work when you want to. You'll be a great help to a family."

"They said we'll most likely go to families who have farms. But I don't know anything about living in the country or doing farm chores. I can't imagine how you milk a cow or collect eggs from chickens."

Katie grinned. "I don't know how to do those things either, but I'm sure they'll teach us."

Jenny sighed, lines still creasing her forehead. "I suppose so. I just wish I was going on the same ship as you."

Katie pondered Jenny's comment for a moment, then realized she also wished that were true. She crossed to her open trunk and reached down to the bottom. Pushing aside her nightgowns, she found her new Bible and lifted it out. She walked back to the bed and held it out to Jenny. "Here. I want you to have this."

Jenny took the Bible and looked up at Katie. "Won't you want to take it with you?"

"I'll ask for another. I'm sure they'll give it to me."

"I'm not much of a reader."

"That's all right. Just start with the book of John. That tells about Jesus. That's the best part."

"All right." Jenny's fingers grazed the smooth black cover. Then she looked up. "Thank you, Katie."

Katie smiled. She had won a friend. And she had a feeling Jenny was well on her way to building more friendships and winning a spot in the next group going to Canada.

She glanced at the Bible in Jenny's hand, her

heart warming. If she found Jesus in the pages of that Bible, she would have a friend who would never leave her side . . . and that was what she needed most for the journey ahead.

Laura wrapped her arm around Mum's waist, supporting her as they slowly made their way toward the Grahams' front door. Mum hardly ever coughed anymore, but her strength was still lacking. It had been a long, exhausting day of travel across the city, and Laura was eager to help Mum settle in with the Grahams.

The door opened, and Ruby Graham stepped out, followed by Mr. Graham, Jacob, and their five young daughters.

"Oh, Edna, it's so good to see you. Please come inside." A caring smile wreathed Mrs. Graham's face as she ushered Mum into the house and helped her take off her coat.

"Thank you, Ruby. It's kind of you to let me come." Mum's voice faltered.

"Of course. We're glad to have you." She motioned toward the hallway. "Let's all go into the kitchen and have a cup of tea."

"That sounds wonderful."

Jacob glanced at Laura, a warm welcome in his eyes as he helped her slip off her coat. "I'm glad your mum is doing better." He hung her coat on a peg by the door, and they started down the hall toward the kitchen.

"She's not fully recovered." Laura kept her voice low. "But I'm glad she is well enough to leave the hospital. I think she'll improve more quickly now that she's here."

He nodded. "My mum will take good care of her. I can promise you that." Jacob ushered her into the kitchen.

Laura's gaze followed her mum as she slowly lowered herself into a chair at the kitchen table. How long would it take for her to regain her full strength? Thank goodness the Grahams had said she could stay with them as long as needed.

Mrs. Graham set the teacups on the table. "So, what news do you have about the children?" She looked across at Laura. "Were you able to see them today?"

Laura hesitated and took a seat. She hadn't told Mum about her visit to Grangeford that morning. But now that her mum had the support of her friends, it was time she told her the truth.

Mum watched her carefully. "Laura, what is it?"

She steeled herself and met Mum's gaze. "The children have been moved to Liverpool."

Mum's eyes widened. "Why would they send them there?"

Laura glanced around the table. "Apparently, there was some kind of misunderstanding and they assigned them to a child emigration group going to Canada."

Mum's hand flew up to cover her mouth. "Oh no!"

Jacob's face grew ruddy. "How could they do such a thing?"

Mr. Graham banged his fist on the table. "Blasted busybodies! Why can't they leave well enough alone?"

"Albert, please!" Mrs. Graham turned to Laura's mum. "Don't worry, Edna. We'll send word. I'm sure they'll return the children as soon as they learn about the mistake."

"What if it's too late?" Tears filled Mum's eyes. "What if they've already sent them across the ocean?"

Ruby rose and placed her arm around Mum's shoulders. "Now, Edna, calm yourself." She took a handkerchief from her apron pocket and handed it to her. Then she nodded to Laura. "Tell us what they said at the home."

Laura relayed her conversations with Miss Richter and Mr. Peterson, but she didn't tell them about her visit to Andrew Frasier's office. It hadn't helped matters, and hearing those details would only make Mum more distressed.

Jacob leaned forward. "I think you should go to the police."

"But they're the ones who took the children away!" Mum sniffed and blotted her cheeks with the handkerchief. "I doubt they'd want to help us."

"I'm afraid Edna is right," Mr. Graham said. "Especially now that the children have left London and gone to Liverpool."

"What should we do?" Mum's voice trembled. "I can't just let them take my children away to Canada!"

"No, of course not." Mrs. Graham's gaze darted toward her husband, but he gave a slight shrug and looked away.

The pain in Mum's face was too much for Laura to bear. "I'll go to Liverpool and bring them back."

Mum gasped. "You can't go all the way to Liverpool by yourself!"

"I'll be all right. I'm used to taking the train between St. Albans and London. It can't be much farther than that." Laura willed confidence into her voice, though she didn't like the idea of traveling to Liverpool on her own.

Mr. Graham folded his arms across his chest. "It's at least three hours by train. You'd be hard-pressed to make it there and back in a day."

Jacob turned toward her. "I'll go with you."

"No, son. I'm afraid you can't do that." Mr. Graham's voice was firm. "You risk losing your job if you miss a day's work, and we can't afford to let that happen."

"But Laura shouldn't have to go by herself. This is important."

"Laura will be all right," Mrs. Graham said.

"She's a clever young woman, and she knows how to take care of herself." She focused on Laura. "My cousin Dorothy lives in Liverpool. I can give you her name and address and a note from me. If you need help, just go see Dorothy. And if you have to stay over, I'm sure she'll give you a meal and a bed for the night."

Mum's worried gaze shifted from Laura to Mrs. Graham. "Even if Laura is willing to go, how can we afford the train ticket?"

"I have some money." Laura reached in her pocket and pulled out a five-pound note. This was the last of the money Andrew Frasier had given her. "Do you think that will be enough?"

Mr. Graham rubbed his chin. "It might buy you a one-way ticket, but if they let you take the children, you'll have to buy four return tickets for the journey back."

Laura's hopes deflated. Five pounds definitely wouldn't be enough for them all to take the train back to London.

Jacob reached in his pocket. "Here's two pounds." He laid the notes on the table.

"No, Jacob." Laura shook her head. "I can't take your money."

He pushed it to the center of the table. "I want you to take it and bring your brother and sisters home."

Laura gave a reluctant nod. "All right. Thank you."

"You'll need more than that." Ruby rose from her chair and took a metal tin off the shelf above the sink. She popped off the lid and poured several coins on the table. "I've been setting this aside for a rainy day, and this looks like a storm for sure."

Before Laura could thank her, Mr. Graham took three notes from his shirt pocket and added them to the pile. "You might as well take these too, in case you need them."

Mum looked up with a teary-eyed smile. "Thank you all so much. I'll repay you as soon as I'm able to go back to work."

"Please don't worry about that." Mrs. Graham laid her hand over Mum's. "The most important thing is keeping your family together."

Mum pushed the money across the table toward Laura. "You take this and put it in a safe place. I'll write a letter and explain the circumstances. Surely they can't send my children to Canada without my permission. We can give them Reverend Bush's name and address as a reference. Then they'll have to release the children into your care."

Laura nodded, but doubts tugged at her heart. No one from Grangeford had contacted her mum about assigning the children to an emigration party. They had refused Laura's request to visit her siblings and acted as though they were well within their rights to do so. It seemed they wanted to sever all ties between the children and their family.

Would the staff in Liverpool be more sympathetic? Laura hoped so, for Mum's sake. If Laura failed to bring them back, it would be a terrible blow, and her mum might never fully recover. Somehow Laura had to convince the staff at Hughes a mistake had been made and they needed to release the children and allow her to bring them back to London.

She met Mum's gaze. "I'll go tomorrow and do everything I can to bring them home."

Once again, tears glistened in Mum's eyes, and she pulled Laura in for a tight hug. "Thank you, Laura. I'll keep you in prayer and ask God to guide you each step of the way. He loves you all even more than I do. He'll take care of you."

Laura's throat felt so tight she couldn't speak. So she kissed Mum's cheek, holding back her own tears. Was that true? Did God really love them? If so, then why was He putting them through these painful trials? It didn't make sense, and she wasn't sure it ever would.

Katie stood on tiptoe and leaned to the left, trying to see around the girls in line ahead of her. Three women and more than fifty girls waited with their group to board the huge steamship tied up at the dock beside them. They had been paired up with partners, and she held tight to Grace's hand.

It wasn't noon yet, but it seemed like they'd been standing on this pier for hours.

Finally, the first girl passed the inspector and walked up the gangplank with one of the escorts. Katie sighed, shuffled forward a few steps, then stopped again. To her right, workmen loaded huge stacks of trunks and boxes onto wooden pallets. They attached ropes, then raised the heavy pallets to the deck of the ship. The workmen's shouts mixed with the cries of gulls circling overhead.

Water splashed against the black hull of the ship, sending up a fine spray. She studied the ship's name, the *Corinthian*, painted in large black letters on a wide white strip near the top railing.

Her throat felt dry and scratchy, and her stomach contracted and growled. She'd been too nervous to eat more than a few bites of toast at breakfast, and she regretted it now. Who knew when they would have their next meal or what kind of food they would be served on the ship?

Pressing down her anxious thoughts, she adjusted the shoulder strap of her travel bag and glanced down at Grace. Her sister looked up, her blue eyes wide and her forehead creased above her pale eyebrows. "How much longer till we get on the boat?"

Katie looked toward the head of the line where two men questioned each girl and checked her boarding card before they let her pass. "It will be a little while."

Grace gazed toward the ship. "It sure is big."

"Yes, it is." Katie placed her hand on Grace's shoulder and forced a smile while she tried to think of something reassuring to say. "There should be plenty of room for everyone."

Grace looked up at her again. "I wish Laura was going with us."

Pain pierced Katie's heart, and her smile faltered. If only that were true. Would they ever see their sister again? If Laura wrote to her now, what would happen to her letter? How would she know where to send it when they didn't know who would take them in? She swallowed hard and closed her eyes.

She had so many questions and no answers.

When they were settled with a family in Canada, she would write to Laura again and ask her to come and join them. Maybe her sister could find work nearby so they could at least see each other. But would she give up her position and travel across the ocean without knowing where she would work or live?

"Look, here come the boys!" A tall, redheaded girl pointed behind them.

Katie turned to follow her gaze. A large group of boys strode down the pier toward the ship, marching four abreast. They were all dressed alike in brown coats, black pants, and red caps.

Each one carried a travel bag over his shoulder that looked exactly like the ones Katie and Grace carried. Two men in black suits and bowler hats marched in front of the group, leading the way. Two more men marched at the back with the tallest boys.

Grace pulled on Katie's sleeve. "Do you see Garth?"

Katie searched the lines, her heart pounding. It looked as though the younger boys marched in front and the older boys came behind. Garth would fall somewhere in the middle, but the boys weren't close enough yet to see their faces clearly.

Grace tugged on Katie again. "Is he there? Can you see him?"

"Wait, Grace." Katie scanned the boys' faces as the group came closer. But those in front blocked her view of the boys behind, and there were at least one hundred of them.

"Turn around, girls." One of the escorts, a plump blond woman in a brown traveling suit and small brown hat, walked toward Katie and Grace. "Keep your eyes ahead, and don't hold up the line."

Katie and Grace stepped forward, filling in the gap. But as soon as the escort moved away, Katie looked over her shoulder and watched the parade of boys move into place behind her group.

She held her breath and searched through the crowd, checking each face. Two boys shifted apart, and her heart leaped. Garth stood behind them in the fourth row, his gaze fixed on the ship.

She gripped Grace's shoulder. "There he is! There's Garth!"

"Where?" Grace spun around, hopping from one foot to the other, trying to catch a glimpse of their brother.

Katie rose up on her toes and lifted her hand. "Garth, Garth!"

Oh please, Father, let him hear me!

But the voices of the children around them and the noise of the workmen loading the ship drowned out her call. She waved her arms back and forth and yelled his name again.

Garth jerked his head to the right, his gaze intense as he scanned the group of girls.

"Garth! We're over here!" Katie jumped up and down, ignoring the startled glances of the girls around them.

He spotted them, and a smile burst across his face.

Then, just as quickly, some boys stepped in front of him, blocking her view. "Garth!" she yelled again.

"Stop that shouting at once!" The plump escort strode toward Katie, grabbed her arm, and jerked her around. "Lower your voice! This is not a cricket match!"

"But that's my brother!" Katie pointed toward the boys.

The woman slapped her hand down. "I told you to keep your eyes forward! Now behave yourself and act like a proper young lady."

"But I haven't seen him for so long. I didn't know he was going to be on our ship. I prayed he would be, but I didn't believe it would really happen."

"That's enough! Settle down and be quiet. You are making a spectacle of yourself!"

Katie clamped her jaw and glared at the woman. She had every right to call out to her brother. How else could she get his attention in a crowd like this? If that woman thought she could keep her from talking to Garth, then she was mistaken.

One of the other escorts approached. "Miss Hotchkiss, we need your assistance at the head of the line."

Miss Hotchkiss leaned toward Katie and squeezed her arm. "Do as I say, or you will be punished after we board the ship." She dropped her hold and strode up the line.

Katie waited a few seconds, then took her sister's hand. "Come on, Grace."

"Where are we going?"

"To see Garth."

Grace's eyes widened, and she shot an anxious glance over her shoulder.

"I'm not missing a chance to talk to him."

Grace nodded, and they stepped out of line and let the other girls pass until they were at the very end of the girls' group. Katie tried to be calm and not draw attention as she glanced back at the boys. Where was Garth? Why couldn't she see him now?

An official-looking man in a navy blue uniform approached the two men leading the boys' group. The three of them stepped aside to look at the official's clipboard. He pointed to the stack of trunks waiting to be loaded onto the ship and then at his clipboard again. There seemed to be a problem about the number of trunks.

The younger boys in the front of their group filled in the space left by their two leaders, bringing them right up behind Katie and Grace. They jostled each other, and their eager chatter rose around them.

The line inched forward. Katie glanced toward the ship. Only about a dozen girls waited in line in front of them now.

Please, Father, help me find Garth! I just want to speak to him.

"Hey, you can't push ahead of us!" a young boy shouted behind Katie.

She turned to look as Garth elbowed his way through the crowd toward the front. "Katie!"

Her heart soared. "Garth!"

He rushed forward and grabbed her, and she flung her arms around his neck. Grace ran to them and joined in the hug.

Katie closed her eyes, soaking in the comfort of her brother's arms, joy pulsing through her.

"Oh, Garth. I've missed you so much!" Behind her several girls giggled and pointed their way. Katie didn't care. Let them laugh and make fun of her. She'd found her brother.

Hoots and whistles rose from the boys, but Garth ignored them. "I'm so glad we're going on the same ship."

She smiled, blinking her damp eyes. "Yes, God answered our prayers."

Garth grinned. "That He did." He stepped back a little but kept his arm around her shoulder.

"Let go of that girl!" One of the men with a bowler hat rushed toward them and jerked Garth away from Katie. "We'll have none of that!"

"We didn't do anything wrong. That's my sister!"

The man scoffed and jabbed his finger toward Katie. "Get back with your group!"

She clenched her hands tightly and stood her ground.

He huffed. "We try to teach you street Arabs to be civilized, but you're born into sin and prone to continue in it."

Heat filled her face. They were not street Arabs!

Garth stepped forward. "Don't talk to my sister like that!"

The man shoved Garth's shoulder. "Get back in line, young man, before I box your ears! And stay away from the girls!"

Garth looked at Katie, and she read his thoughts. They had no choice right now, but that man did not have the final word. Once they boarded the ship, they would find each other, and nothing would ever separate them again.

8

Laura rose before dawn, gathered a few items of clothing in case she needed to stay overnight in Liverpool, and kissed her mother goodbye. Jacob insisted on going with her to Victoria Station, and though she'd been reluctant to agree, in the end she was glad he'd come along. She caught the first train to Liverpool and spent most of the three-hour trip rehearsing what she would say when she arrived at the Hughes Home. She tried to stay calm and remain hopeful, but she couldn't seem to stop fearful thoughts from rushing through her mind.

What if she was too late and the children had already been sent to Canada? What would she do then? She reached in her coat pocket and ran her fingers across her mother's letter. So much depended on what happened today. She wasn't sure if God was listening, but she decided to offer a prayer.

Please, Lord, Mum has suffered so much, and her health is fragile. For her sake help me find the children and bring them home.

She waited, hoping the prayer would calm her and give her some reassurance, but uneasy feelings kept her unsettled for the rest of the trip.

Just after ten o'clock she stepped through the

front door of the Hughes Children's Home and started down the long, empty hallway. The building looked at least twice the size of Grangeford, and though it was newer, the stale smell and dim lighting made it feel just as oppressive.

She spotted the sign for the matron's office over an open doorway and looked in. A young woman about Laura's age sat behind a small wooden desk, sorting through a stack of papers. Her red hair was caught up in a neat style, and she had an abundance of freckles sprinkled across her nose and round cheeks. She looked too young to be the matron, and Laura assumed she was an assistant or receptionist.

Across the room a middle-aged woman sat in a straight-backed chair against the wall. She wore a gray dress and a modest hat of the same color. Was she a mother waiting to visit her children staying at Hughes? Laura searched the woman's face, but she didn't seem anxious. In fact, she appeared calm and perhaps even a little bored.

The young redhead looked up and noticed Laura in the doorway. "May I help you?"

Laura stepped into the room, but before she could speak, the door to the inner office opened and a tall, thin woman in a black dress strode out.

"Miss Langdon, why did you admit that woman?" Her voice rang with authority as she glared at the redhead.

The young woman's eyes widened. "I'm sorry,

Miss Williams. She . . . she had such a compelling story I didn't feel right turning her away. I thought it would be best to let you decide."

Miss Williams's dark eyes snapped. "I thought I made it clear we only allow family visitation on the last Saturday of each month."

"Yes ma'am, you did, but I—"

Miss Williams raised her hand to stop her. "If you want to continue in this position, you need to obey my instructions."

"Yes ma'am." Miss Langdon bobbed her chin twice.

"The only people I want to see today are those applying for the open positions. Is that clear?" Miss Williams shot a glance at Laura, then at the woman waiting in the chair.

Laura's stomach dropped. What was she going to do now?

Miss Williams turned and strode back into her office, leaving the door open but disappearing from view. "Mrs. Hudson, as I've already said, this is not visitation day. I am sorry, but you'll have to leave."

"Please, I just want to see my children." The other woman's voice was soft and pleading.

Laura couldn't see Mrs. Hudson, but she knew exactly how the poor woman felt.

"The children have a set schedule, and they cannot be disturbed. The next visitation day is May twenty-ninth."

"But that's almost a month away! I can't wait that long."

"You signed the papers and agreed to the terms when the children were admitted."

"Yes, but I didn't know I wouldn't be allowed to see them!"

The matron appeared in her office doorway, her mouth set in a firm line.

Mrs. Hudson stepped into sight. She wore a bedraggled green dress with a stained and torn hem and clutched a black shawl around her shoulders. Her mousy gray hair hung in neglected strands, and her face was pale and thin. She reached for Miss Williams's arm. "Please, promise me you won't send my children to Canada. I can take care of them now. I'm living with my sister, and I—"

Miss Williams brushed the woman's arm away. "It's time for you to leave."

Mrs. Hudson's chin trembled. She lifted her hand, covered her mouth, and bolted past Laura. Her sobs rose in the air as she hurried out the door and down the hall.

Miss Williams turned toward her assistant. "Who's next?"

Miss Langdon nodded to the middle-aged woman seated in the chair. "Miss Cunningham."

Miss Williams arched her eyebrows. "Are you here to apply for a position?"

"Yes ma'am. I am."

"You may come in."

Miss Cunningham rose from her chair and followed the matron into her office.

When the door closed, Miss Langdon looked up at Laura. "I'm sorry about that," she said in a hushed voice. "I hope you're here for an interview and not a visit."

Laura's mind spun as she stepped up to the desk. It seemed she would have to take a different tack if she was going to learn anything about her siblings. "Yes, I'd like to interview for . . . one of the positions."

Miss Langdon offered a slight smile. "That's a relief."

Laura forced a smile in return. "Could you tell me a little about the positions?"

"Of course. We have two openings. One is for the head laundress, and the other is for an escort to accompany the girls emigrating to Canada."

Laura's nerves tingled. "And what exactly are the responsibilities of an escort?"

"They work with the girls here at the home and help them prepare for the trip. Then they escort them on the sea voyage. When they arrive in Canada, they travel by train to the receiving home, where the girls are transferred into the care of our workers there. Some stay on for a time until the girls are all settled, and others return right away to help the next group preparing at Hughes."

"Only girls?"

"Yes, we don't have boys here. They're all housed at Mifflin Hall."

Laura nodded, tucking that information away for later. "How many girls travel together?"

"Most of our groups have about sixty girls. Three or four groups go out in the spring and three or four more in the early fall. The next group is leaving on May 13."

Laura tensed. Were her sisters assigned to that group? If she was hired as an escort, she could find out, then see what could be done to remedy the situation. This might be just the answer she needed. Laura glanced toward the matron's closed door.

Miss Langdon leaned forward and motioned Laura closer. "Miss Williams is strict. But you'll do all right if you mind your manners and speak only when you're spoken to."

Laura nodded. "Thank you."

Miss Langdon pointed toward the chairs. "You can go ahead and sit down. It won't be too long."

Laura crossed the room and took a seat.

"Oh, I'm sorry. I forgot to ask your name."

Laura stilled. If she used her real name, they might become suspicious when she started asking questions about her sisters. "My name is . . . Mary Hopkins." The lie slipped out before she even had time to think it through. Mary was her middle name, and Hopkins was her mother's maiden name, so it wasn't really too far from the truth.

Miss Langdon jotted it down.

Laura tried to stifle her guilty feelings, but it wasn't easy. Her parents had taught her to always tell the truth. But what would they say in this situation? What had happened to her family was unfair, and those in charge had refused to listen. She had to protect her siblings, and if using a false name was the only way to save them from going to Canada, then she would lie to the king himself. She had no other choice.

The door to the inner office opened, and the woman who had finished her interview walked out. She wore a slight smile and nodded to Miss Langdon as she passed. It looked as though her meeting with the matron had gone well. Which position had she been offered?

The matron appeared in her office doorway and glanced at her assistant.

Miss Langdon looked up. "This is Miss Mary Hopkins. She's here to interview for a position."

Miss Williams scanned Laura from head to toe, looking none too pleased. "You may come in."

Laura rose and walked into the office, her knees feeling a bit shaky.

Miss Williams motioned to a chair facing her desk, and Laura sat down.

"You look too young to be applying for a position here. How old are you?"

"I'm twenty-one, ma'am." Remembering what Miss Langdon had said, she waited for the next question rather than adding more to her answer.

"Do you have any experience?"

"I've been in service for the last two years, first as a house maid in London and the last few months as a lady's maid for the Frasier family of the Bolton Estate near St. Albans."

Miss Williams's forehead creased. "Hughes is a children's home for waifs and strays. We receive children from all over England and prepare them for emigration to Canada. Do you have any experience working with children?"

"Yes ma'am. I am the oldest of six. I helped my mother care for all of them." She didn't add that two of them had died shortly after birth. That was a private matter.

"May I see your references?"

Laura froze, her throat going dry. How would she explain she had none? "I can give you the name and address of our clergyman in London, Reverend Samuel Bush. I'm sure he would be happy to give me a recommendation. But I didn't bring any letters of reference."

Miss Williams sniffed. "How do you expect me to make a decision about your character and work habits without any letters of reference?"

Laura pulled in a deep breath. "I'm sorry. My mother has been ill, and I left my position in St.

Albans a few weeks ago to go to London and care for her."

Miss Williams arched her eyebrows. "But now you've come to Liverpool?"

"Yes ma'am. My mother is improving, and I'm staying with a friend here." At least she hoped Mrs. Graham's cousin would allow her to stay. Oh, how had she gotten in such deep water so quickly? One lie just seemed to lead to the next.

Miss Williams stared toward the window for a moment, then looked back at Laura. "We usually send at least two escorts to oversee each group of girls going to Canada. One of our experienced escorts fell and broke her ankle earlier this week. She's unable to walk, and we have fifty-some girls traveling to Quebec City and then on to Kingston and Belleville, Ontario, on the thirteenth. I need to find another escort."

Laura shifted on her chair, her stomach churning. Should she just tell the truth and risk being thrown out, or should she continue her ruse to help her sisters escape from Hughes before they were sent across the sea?

She could see no other way to protect her sisters. "I would like the opportunity to care for the children."

"You've no qualms about sailing with the group?"

"I'm willing to do whatever is needed." That wasn't a direct answer, but it was true.

182

Miss Williams studied her, still looking unconvinced. "I'm very selective about hiring staff. Under normal circumstances I would never consider taking on someone without references, but perhaps this one time I could make an exception." She clasped her hands on her desk. "Are you willing to obey those over you and do as you're told?"

"You can trust me to do what's right."

The matron reached down and pulled a sheet of paper from her drawer. "Very well. Fill out this form. You can start tomorrow morning at seven."

Relief rushed through Laura. "Thank you."

Miss Williams held up her index finger. "But you will have a one-week trial. That's all I can offer you at this time. I think we both need time to discern if this is the right decision."

"That will be fine." She accepted the pen and paper. One week would be more than enough time to discover if her sisters were still at Hughes and, if they were, to find a way to free them and return to London.

Andrew adjusted his hat as he stepped down from the cab. Henry paid the driver and climbed out after him. They turned and faced the large, impressive building set back among the trees and surrounded by a high stone wall. The sign above the iron gate read *The Hughes Children's Home.*

Andrew scanned what he could see of the

grounds and building. "It looks to be in better condition than some of the other homes we've visited."

"Yes, it does." Henry started toward the gate. "I hope their concern for the building reflects their care of the children."

Andrew fell in step beside his friend, recalling the children's homes they'd visited in London. It had been a busy and enlightening experience. The realities of institutional care had been unsettling, to say the least, and his positive view of child emigration had been challenged at every turn.

Only two other homes in Liverpool remained on the list. Their ocean passage was secured. Within two weeks, they would board the *Parisian* and set sail for Canada to continue their investigation.

They passed through the open gate and started up the gravel drive. "How many children are housed here?"

Henry cocked his eyebrow. "I'm not sure I appreciate your use of the term *housed*. It sounds as though you're speaking of prison inmates rather than children."

"Sorry. That was not my intention."

A slight smile lifted Henry's mouth. "I didn't think so." He pulled a folded paper from his jacket pocket. "Up to two hundred fifty children are in care here. It's the main girls' sending home in Liverpool, so the number fluctuates as the emigration parties leave for Canada."

Andrew nodded as they mounted the stone steps, then knocked on the front door.

How would this home compare to the others once they moved past the well-kept exterior? Would the children be happy and healthy, or would they have emotionless, pale faces like so many of the children he'd seen at the other homes?

An elderly woman in a simple gray dress answered the door.

"Good morning. My name is Mr. Henry Dowd, and this is my associate, Mr. Andrew Frasier. We would like to speak to . . ." He glanced down at his paper. "Miss Agatha Williams, the matron."

"Yes sir. Her office is this way. If you'll follow me." The woman turned and shuffled down a long hall at a slow pace.

Andrew glanced around. The floors looked clean, and the walls appeared to have been painted recently. But an odd smell permeated the air. He sniffed, trying to decide if the musty scent came from mold or if it was a foul cooking odor.

Down the hall a door opened, and a woman stepped out. She was slim and dressed in a blue suit with black piping. A few strands of blond hair were visible beneath her straw hat. She glanced his way, and her blue eyes widened.

His breath snagged. Was that Miss McAlister?

Before he could decide, she spun away

and hurried off down the hall in the opposite direction.

He slowed and gave his head a slight shake. It couldn't be his mother's lady's maid. She had gone to London, not Liverpool.

Henry looked his way. "Everything all right?"

"Yes. Sorry. I thought I recognized that woman, but I must be mistaken."

Henry glanced at her receding figure, then turned to the woman leading them down the hall. "Do you know who that was?"

"No sir, I've never seen her before." She motioned to the next door on the right, the same door the young woman had walked out of moments before. "This is the matron's office."

"Thank you." Henry opened the door and turned to Andrew. "Coming?"

"Yes." Andrew cast one last glance down the hall before he followed his friend into the matron's office. He'd seen the woman's face for only a split second, but she looked so much like Laura McAlister. Did his mother's lady's maid have a cousin or sister in Liverpool? Or was he just imagining the similarities for some odd reason?

What had happened to Laura McAlister and her family? He'd offered a few prayers for her mother's recovery and for the safety of her brother and two sisters who had been sent to a children's home after their mother's illness.

A children's home . . . that was odd. Perhaps that was Laura McAlister after all. But even if that were the case, he could do nothing about it now. She had disappeared out the rear door without looking back.

Laura shoved the door closed and quickly stepped to the side, her heartbeat pounding in her throat. Was that really Andrew Frasier? The surprised look on his face when he'd seen her banished the last of her doubts. He knew exactly who she was.

What was he doing here? Surely he wasn't looking for her, was he?

She leaned back against the stone wall and tried to slow her breathing. She needed to calm down and think clearly. She had not revealed her real name to the matron or her assistant. Even if he asked about her, what could they say?

Everyone here thought she was Mary Hopkins.

But Andrew Frasier knew the truth.

Her thoughts darted back to her frightening encounter in his London office with his assistant. She had given him her name, but he wouldn't dare tell Mr. Frasier about her visit and risk her reporting how he had treated her. She hadn't revealed the reason she wanted to speak to him. That man had nothing to pass on. There would be no reason for Andrew Frasier to follow her to Liverpool.

This just had to be a very strange coincidence.

Still . . . she had better be certain. Summoning her courage, she cracked the door open an inch and peeked through. The hall was empty now, but she could hear voices in the distance. She slipped inside and tiptoed back toward the matron's office, stopping just outside her door.

"How may I help you gentlemen?" That was the young redhead's voice.

"We'd like to speak to Miss Agatha Williams."

Laura frowned. That wasn't Andrew Frasier's voice.

"May I give her your name?"

"Of course. I'm Mr. Henry Dowd, and this is my associate, Mr. Andrew Frasier."

"Thank you. I'll let Miss Williams know you're here."

It was quiet for a moment, and Laura held her breath, waiting.

"Do you think she'll give us a tour or send us packing?" That was Andrew, and she could hear a touch of humor in his voice.

"Once she sees the letter from the home secretary, she'll have no choice but to cooperate."

Laura cocked her head. The home secretary? What was that about?

A door opened. "Gentlemen, what can I do for you?" The matron's tone made it clear she was not expecting their visit.

"We'd like to speak to you about an important matter."

A second ticked by before the matron replied. "Very well. Come into my office."

Footsteps shuffled, and a door closed.

Laura waited in the silence for a few more seconds, then hurried down the hall and out the front door. Questions swirled through her mind as she walked down the drive. Why had Andrew Frasier come to Hughes? It didn't seem to have anything to do with her. That was a relief, but it still seemed very odd to see him here.

She passed through the gate and looked down the street, searching for someone who could give her directions to Mifflin Hall. Would the staff there be more willing to listen and help her? It seemed an unlikely hope after the way she had been treated at Grangeford and Hughes, but she had to try. She could not leave Garth languishing there with no word from his family.

Turning, she looked down the street to the left. Two policemen stood in front of a bookshop, and she set off in that direction. As she walked, she reached into her pocket and fingered Mrs. Graham's note with the directions to her cousin's house. She would ask the policemen how to find the boys' home, then how to get to the address on Lime Street. Hopefully Mrs. Graham's cousin Dorothy would give her a place to stay for at least one night and maybe more.

The weight of her choices, her lies, and her concern for her siblings pressed down on her, making her steps heavy. The impression that she ought to pray rose in her mind again, but she clenched her jaw and pushed it away.

She had set her course and accepted a position at Hughes under the name Mary Hopkins. Right or wrong, she would do what she must to free her sisters and brother and reunite her family.

Andrew and Henry sat across from Miss Williams in her office. The tall, austere matron wore a plain black dress with a high collar. Silver strands laced her dark brown hair, and her expression looked as though it had been chiseled from stone. She was obviously not pleased with their unannounced visit.

"Please be seated." Miss Williams motioned to the two chairs opposite her desk, and Henry and Andrew took their seats.

"What brings you to Hughes?" She watched them with a wary expression.

Henry began. "Mr. Frasier and I have been commissioned to write a report about child emigration and give recommendations to the Office of the Home Secretary." Henry took their official letter of introduction from his coat pocket and handed it to the matron.

Her dark eyebrows arched. "The home secretary?"

"Yes ma'am. We've been asked to do a thorough investigation into all aspects of the children's care here in England and then in Canada. The information verifying our investigation is in the letter."

The matron unfolded the sheet of stationery and scanned the page. Her mouth firmed, and she looked up and met Henry's gaze. "I can assure you we follow all the appropriate rules and regulations. The girls at Hughes receive excellent care and preparation for their new lives in Canada." She folded the letter and slid it back across the desk.

"That's good to know." Henry picked up the letter and placed it in his pocket again. "We would like to tour the home and see the children's quarters, classrooms, and dining hall. We'd also like to know how the children are selected and prepared for their journey to Canada."

Miss Williams's eyebrows rose. "I'm not sure that will be possible today. I have a full schedule. I would prefer you make an appointment later this week or next. Then I can give you my full attention."

"I'm sorry. That won't be possible. We're leaving for Canada soon to inspect the receiving homes there and visit some of the children who have been placed with families. It's important that we tour Hughes today and learn all we can before we depart."

Her gaze darted from one man to the other. "Very well. It's inconvenient, but we will do our best to accommodate you."

"Thank you." Henry took a small notebook and pencil from his pocket. "Let's start with a few questions. Can you tell us how long you've been the matron of Hughes?"

"Twelve years, and before that I was the head teacher for five years."

Henry jotted that information in his notebook. "Excellent. I'm sure your years of experience have given you important insight into the needs of children and the issues surrounding child emigration."

"Yes, I have learned a great deal during my time at Hughes."

"That should make your comments very helpful to us. We'll certainly appreciate hearing your opinion on these important matters."

She lifted her chin, looking pleased. "Of course. I've dealt with all types of children, and I have always done my best to see that they are well trained for useful and productive lives in Canada."

Andrew stifled a smile. Henry was so clever. He knew exactly what to say to gain the matron's cooperation.

Henry held his pencil poised over his notebook. "What are the ages of the children in your care?"

"The girls are five to sixteen."

"And what would you say is the best age for a child to emigrate to Canada?"

"I've always believed the younger they are,

the better. That allows them to make a fresh start and forget the poverty and deprivation of their early lives." Her lips puckered as though she'd tasted something unpleasant. "Most of these girls come directly off the streets or from the workhouses."

Andrew had been content to listen up to this point, but he couldn't resist questioning that statement. "Surely not all the children come from such difficult backgrounds. Aren't some placed in your care because of a parent's loss of employment or the illness or death of one or both parents?"

"Some, yes, but most of these girls were pulled from the slums and saved from a life of degradation that would most likely lead them to . . . terrible circumstances in the future." She sent them a meaningful look.

"Yes, we understand." Henry glanced down at his notebook. "So, back to the question about the best age for emigration. You said the younger, the better."

"That's right. The younger ones have the best chance of being adopted into a family, but it can be difficult to transport them."

Andrew leaned forward. "Aren't all the children available for adoption?"

"Yes, but that's not possible for every child. Most girls will be taken in as domestic servants with a commitment to work for a family until they are twenty-one. The majority of the boys work on farms until they're eighteen."

Andrew's chest tightened as he considered what that meant for the children.

"What is the age of the youngest child you've sent to Canada?"

"Last fall we sent a three-year-old, but that was an unusual case. She had two older sisters in our care, and we wanted to send them all together. As I stated, most of the girls who emigrate are between the ages of five and sixteen."

Henry looked up. "Even the girls who are five are expected to work as servants?"

Miss Williams stiffened. "We teach them all how to do simple household chores, and the family who takes them in finishes any needed training."

Henry's forehead creased as he made note of the matron's comment.

She frowned at Henry. "Do you have children, Mr. Dowd?"

"No, I am not married."

"Then perhaps you're not aware that it is completely normal for children of all ages to assist their family with household chores. That's how they learn the skills they will need to manage their own homes one day. The families who take them in are doing them a great service, giving them food and shelter, as well as the opportunity to prepare for life as adults."

"Yes, but expecting a five-year-old to take up household duties raises questions in my mind."

Miss Williams pursed her lips. "Of course a five-year-old would not do the same amount of work as an older girl. The family would know that when they took her in."

"I see." Henry made a few more notes, then closed his book. "I believe that gives us the background information we need for now. Shall we start the tour?" He rose without waiting for her reply, and Andrew followed his lead.

Miss Williams stood and showed them out of her office. She gave a brief explanation to her receptionist, then took them up the stairs to the top floor.

The matron opened the first door on the right and stood back. "This is one of the girls' dormitories."

Andrew followed Henry into the long open room while the matron waited in the doorway. Four rows of narrow beds filled the space beneath the eaves. Each bed was neatly made with white sheets, gray wool blankets, and one rather flat pillow. A wooden trunk sat at the end of most of the beds, and Andrew supposed that was where they kept their clothing and personal items. The walls were bare of decorations, and the windows had no curtains. It all seemed adequate but sterile and decidedly gloomy.

Andrew turned to Miss Williams. "How many girls sleep in this room?"

"Sixty when all the beds are filled."

"You have other dormitories?"

"Yes. Two on the floor below." The matron gave an impatient glance at her watch. "The classrooms are on the first floor." She motioned toward the hallway.

They took the stairs down and looked in on two classrooms. The girls were learning hand sewing in the first room and some basic cooking skills in the next.

Andrew turned to Miss Williams as they stepped into the hall again. "Are the girls taught the regular school subjects, such as mathematics and reading, while they're here?"

The matron sent him a sharp look. "Most of these girls will be working for farm families. Their greatest need is for the practical skills that will make them valuable workers."

"I understand, but they shouldn't be denied an education simply because they are emigrating to Canada."

"They are not denied." Her tone was firm and decisive. "They receive the training that will be most useful for them in their new lives."

Andrew couldn't let that statement stand without a challenge. "The information we were given said we send our most intelligent and promising children. Surely children like that need a basic education as well as practical skills."

She stopped at the end of the hall. "The type

of girls wanted in Canada are those who are obedient, respectful, and trained to work hard."

Andrew was about to give a sharp reply, but Henry shot him a stern glance. Henry had warned him he needed to keep his opinions to himself during these tours. A critical comment could prompt the matron to send them away before they'd seen the rest of the facility and learned all they could.

He pushed down his irritation and followed Henry and the matron down the hall. One thing was clear: he and Miss Williams had a very different perspective about the proper training and education these girls needed and deserved. He might not be able to speak up now, but when it came time to write their report, he would recommend changes were made in their schooling and training.

They walked into the empty dining hall, then toured the kitchen, where the midday meal was being prepared. Several young girls, wearing aprons and caps, assisted the adult cooks in preparing the food. Some of the girls stood on crates to chop vegetables with knives that looked too large for their small hands. Others stirred bubbling pots or rolled out dough. Henry observed it all with keen interest, and Andrew could tell his friend did not approve of the girls using those knives or working so close to the hot stove.

They looked into the nurse's office, the laundry, and the storage room, which was stacked with the same wooden trunks they'd seen upstairs in the dormitory.

Miss Williams pulled the storage room door closed. "Well, I think you've seen everything."

"Thank you, Miss Williams." Henry nodded to her. "I believe we have the information we need."

She started toward the stairs. "Our goal is to prepare the girls for a successful transition to life in Canada." A hint of uneasiness lined her face as she looked their way. "I hope you'll pass on a good report regarding our work here."

"We appreciate you taking the time to meet with us and give us a tour. It's been very interesting." Henry's tone remained as noncommittal as his words.

Her expression hardened. "You'll have to excuse me. I need to meet with our cook. You'll find the exit at the top of these stairs." Without waiting for their reply, she turned and strode down the hall.

Henry shook his head. "Well, that was certainly an enlightening visit."

"That's not the word I would choose to describe it." Andrew huffed out a breath. "That woman's approach is not only outdated—it's harmful. The preparation she gives those girls guarantees they'll be locked into a servant's position the rest of their lives."

Henry cocked one eyebrow and smiled. "Now that's the kind of response I've been waiting to hear." He turned toward the stairs. "Come on, we have another home to visit before we call it a day."

9

Katie rose from her swaying bunk and grabbed hold of the pole at the end. The ship dipped, and her stomach dropped with it. She closed her eyes and prayed she would not lose her supper.

Grace turned over and looked up at her through glassy eyes. "I'm thirsty, Katie." Her sister's pale face and miserable expression tugged at Katie's heart. The poor dear! She had barely been able to leave her bunk since their first afternoon at sea. And though Katie brought her tea and toast after every meal, Grace had managed to keep down only a few bites since they'd come aboard ship four days ago.

Katie laid a gentle hand on her sister's shoulder. "Rest easy, Grace. I'll get you some water."

"Thank you," she whispered. Closing her eyes, her sister turned her face away.

Most of the girls in the emigration party had been laid low with seasickness. Even the escorts had taken to their bunks by midmorning the second day of the voyage.

Katie made her way across the large, open steerage room toward the pantry where meals were prepared for those who were able to eat. She asked for a glass of water, then started back toward her sister's bunk.

If she had known they would be this sick on the voyage, she might not have come. She paused and shook her head. That wasn't true. She would endure almost anything if it meant she and her brother and sister would not be separated. Garth and Grace were all she had left now that Mum was gone and Laura was too wrapped up in her own affairs to care about them.

How could Laura turn her back on them when they needed her so much? Why hadn't she come to claim them before it was too late and they had to set off on their own to a strange new land?

Laura's silence and rejection hurt almost as much as Mum's death. But Mum hadn't chosen to leave them. She'd been taken. Katie pulled in a slow, deep breath and blinked back hot tears. The same was true of Dad. She had begged God for healing after the accident, and they had all grieved when hope was gone. But that was not true for Laura. She had chosen to ignore their pleas when they had needed her most.

Katie wiped her eyes and pushed those painful thoughts away. She ought to forgive her sister and let go of the hurt, but she had no idea how to do that when the wound was still so fresh. Maybe it wouldn't be so hard if she wasn't also still reeling from Mum's passing.

She returned to Grace's bunk and helped her sit up so she wouldn't spill her water.

Grace took a sip and then licked her dry lips. "How long till we reach Canada?"

"Miss Allen said about four more days." Katie glanced at the youngest escort resting in the bunk across the way. She had been kind to them that first night, comforting them and bringing a bucket and towel when they were overcome with seasickness. Now the young woman's face was pale, and she was as ill as Grace.

Her sister drank the last of the water and handed the cup back to Katie. "I wish my stomach would stop hurting."

Katie patted her sister's back. "I know. I'm sorry, Grace. Some of the girls are doing better today. I think you'll be up and around soon."

Grace sighed and lay back on her pillow. "I hope so." She closed her eyes and snuggled down in her blanket, looking a bit more at peace.

"Try to sleep for a while. That will help." Katie rose and returned the empty cup to the pantry. The ship creaked and swayed, and she reached for the wall to steady herself. The smell of greasy onions, burnt coffee, and sickness assaulted her nose. If she could just get some fresh air, it would be such a relief.

She glanced at the stairs leading up to the deck, then glanced back at Miss Allen and the other escorts. They all rested on their bunks with their eyes closed.

She bit her lip, considering her choice a

moment longer. They had been told to stay in the steerage compartment, but if she was careful, she might be able to slip away for a few minutes.

Clutching her sweater close, she quietly climbed the first set of stairs and then three more. At the top she glanced around and spotted a set of double doors leading outside. The passageway was empty, so she hurried across and pushed open the door.

A fresh, cool breeze rushed across her face and ruffled her skirt as she stepped out on the deck. Pulling in a deep breath, she filled her lungs and let the wind blow away the last of the stale scents from steerage that clung to her hair and clothes.

She crossed to the railing and held on tight while the ship rose and fell. The deep blue water stretched for miles and miles. To the west the sky glowed orange and gold, with sunbeams setting the clouds on fire just above the horizon. Rippling lights bounced off the water like a thousand diamonds sparkling in a golden path across the sea.

The wind whistled past her ears, mixing with the sounds of the chugging steam engine and the whooshing waves as the ship cut through the water.

"Katie!"

Her heart leaped and she turned.

Garth and another boy strode across the deck

toward her. Her brother's smile spread wide as he drew closer. "I was hoping I'd see you." He gave her a quick hug, then stood back. "How are you? How's Grace?"

"I'm all right now, but Grace isn't doing so well."

Garth's eyebrows dipped. "Is she seasick?"

"Yes, and she's pretty miserable. But she's sleeping now." Katie glanced toward the door. She shouldn't stay on deck too long, but now that Garth was here, she didn't want to leave.

"Most of the boys were sick for the first two days." Garth stepped up to the railing beside her. "But we got used to it. Grace will too."

Katie glanced past Garth to his companion. He looked a little older than her brother and was a few inches taller, with dark blond hair and eyes as blue as the sky.

"This is my friend, Rob Lewis. We met at Grangeford, then came to Mifflin together." Garth nodded to Katie. "This is my twin sister, Katherine, but we call her Katie."

Rob touched his red cap. "I'm glad to meet you, Katie. Garth has told me a lot about you and your family." He tipped his head slightly and studied her face.

Her cheeks warmed, and she returned a smile. "Thank you. It's good to know Garth has a friend."

Garth grinned and bumped his shoulder into

Rob's. "That's for sure. Some of the boys can be pretty rough. But Rob and I stick together."

"That we do. Remember that time Paul Grimes stole my shoes?"

Garth chuckled. "We sure taught him a lesson."

"He won't be doing that again to me or anyone else." Rob gave Garth a good-natured slap on the back. "Thanks for standing up for me."

"That's what friends do." Garth leaned both arms on the railing. "I would've been in a lot of trouble if you hadn't helped me finish up that last trunk."

Katie sent Garth a questioning look.

"The boys at Mifflin make all the trunks for those going to Canada. We were behind, and Mr. Parker singled me out and said I was not working fast enough. He threatened to keep me in the workshop until the last trunk was finished, and that meant I would've missed supper. But Rob gave me a hand. We finished it up in no time."

Rob grinned, his eyes glowing. "I know you'd do the same for me."

The boys bumped shoulders again, obviously enjoying the memories of their shared experiences at Mifflin.

Katie's gaze darted from Rob to Garth, and she tried to make sense of her uneasy feelings. It was good Garth had a friend and wasn't alone. She had Grace, and that was a comfort. But she and Garth had always shared a strong bond, not just as brother and sister but also as best friends. Now that Garth had Rob, maybe she'd been replaced.

Her heart sank. She clutched the railing and stared out to sea.

Garth looked her way. "Have you heard any more about what happens once we arrive in Canada?"

She shook her head. "Our escorts haven't been well. I don't know what happens next."

A gust of wind blew past, and Rob tugged his cap lower. "I heard Mr. Stratford say once the ship docks we'll take a train to Kingston. There's a boys' home there."

Katie turned to Rob. "What about the girls?"

Rob gave a slight shrug. "I don't know. He didn't say where the girls will go. I suppose they have a separate home for them."

Katie's chest tightened, and she looked up at Garth. "What are we going to do? How are we going to stay together?"

He reached out and touched her arm. "Don't worry. I'll speak to Mr. Stratford and tell him I want to go to the same family with you and Grace. That should take care of it."

That was just like Garth, always believing the best about people and situations. But no one had promised them they could all stay together. In fact, they would've lost touch with each other if they hadn't passed messages back and forth at Grangeford. Unwelcome tears filled her eyes, and she blinked them away. She was not going to cry, not in front of this boy she hardly knew.

"It will be all right, Katie." Garth stepped closer, his arm brushing against hers. "You'll see. This will be a new beginning for us."

But she couldn't hold back her anxious thoughts. "What if we have to go to different families or different towns? How will we find each other? What if I lose track of you and we never see each other again?"

Garth slipped his arm around her shoulder. "Come on now, Katie. Remember what Dad used to say: don't go borrowing trouble from tomorrow. We've come this far together. I'm sure it will all work out for the best."

She leaned against Garth and tried to believe what he said was true, but nagging fears gripped her heart and would not let go.

Laura followed Miss Williams up the stairs toward the top floor of the Hughes Children's Home. Her hands tingled as she grasped her skirt and passed the next landing. Would she find her sisters this morning? And if she did, what would she do then?

The need to pray pressed down on her heart, but the words wouldn't come. How could she ask God for help when she was using a name that was not her own? She would just have to do what she must and hope for the best.

Yesterday afternoon, after accepting the position at Hughes, she'd gone to Mifflin Hall, hoping to find her brother. She'd used her real name there. The man in charge, Mr. Randolph, had invited her into his office and listened to her story with surprising sympathy. After searching through his records, he told her he was sorry but Garth had already left for Canada.

Laura was so stunned she could hardly process what he was saying. She knew Garth might not be at Mifflin, but she had held on to hope until that last moment.

Mr. Randolph told her there was no way to contact Garth until after he was settled in Canada and the staff there sent his new address back to England. Mr. Randolph offered to forward Garth's address as soon as he received word.

Fighting back a wave of despair, Laura thanked him and gave him the Grahams' address in London.

"Miss Hopkins?" Miss Williams looked over her shoulder as they reached the top floor.

Laura blinked and focused on the matron. "Yes ma'am?"

"You will be in charge of Dormitory Number Three along with Miss Rose Carson. She has been carrying the full responsibility of looking after the girls and helping them prepare for their journey since Miss Worthington fell and broke her ankle. She will inform you of your duties."

Laura thought she would begin searching for her sisters as soon as Miss Williams assigned her a task and left her on her own. Working with Miss Carson might make it more difficult, but it would not stop her.

"There are sixty girls assigned to this dormitory," the matron continued. "Fifty-two will be traveling to Canada in the next party. Eight will be staying behind to prepare themselves to join a future group." The matron stopped in front of the first door on the left. "Do you have any questions, Miss Hopkins?"

Laura had a thousand questions, but she didn't dare ask even one of them. "No ma'am. I'll do my best to help Miss Carson."

"I hope you do. Remember, you are here on trial. You have only one week to demonstrate your ability to handle your responsibilities." Miss Williams pushed open the door without waiting for her reply. "Miss Carson."

A petite woman with dark brown hair stood across the room, talking to one of the girls. She turned and looked their way. All the girls straightened and stilled as the matron strode in.

Miss Williams glanced at Laura before letting her gaze travel around the room. "This is Miss Hopkins. She will be assisting Miss Carson. I expect you girls to obey her and treat her with respect. Do you understand?"

"Yes, Miss Williams," the girls chorused.

"I have made my decision and selected the girls who will be going to Canada in the next party."

A few whispers rose from the girls, and several glanced at one another with hopeful expressions. It looked as though they were all eager to be chosen for the journey.

Laura scanned the faces of the girls she could see clearly. There were four rows, and some girls stood behind others, making it difficult to see all their faces. If Katie and Grace were here, she prayed they would not call out.

Miss Williams opened her notebook. "The following eight girls will be staying behind to improve their character and bring their manners and skills up to our standards." She read the eight names, prompting a few gasps and red faces. When the last name was called, a short, blond girl burst out crying and threw herself down on one of the beds.

Miss Williams glared at the girl and snapped her notebook closed. "We can all see why Alice Palmroy is not ready for a new life in Canada. Hughes girls know how to behave themselves. They don't have emotional outbursts or wilt like a flower when the wind changes direction."

Alice's crying softened, but she didn't raise her head from the pillow.

"The rest of you will finish your packing and prepare yourselves to leave on Thursday,

May 13." Miss Williams's stern gaze traveled around the room once more.

A shiver traveled down Laura's back. She could well understand one reason the girls might be eager to leave Hughes. Miss Williams was one of the most austere, unlikable women she'd ever met.

"Miss Carson and Miss Hopkins will check your trunks and see that you have what you need." The matron turned to Laura and Rose. "Ladies." Without any further explanation, she strode out of the dormitory.

Rose crossed the room and met Laura by the door. Her smile was warm and genuine, and her pretty blue-green eyes sparkled as she offered her hand. "Welcome to Hughes, Miss Hopkins. I'm very glad you've joined us."

"Thank you. I'm happy to be here." Laura glanced past Rose to the girls farther down the first row, hoping to spot Katie and Grace, but she didn't see them.

"We have twenty minutes before classes begin. That doesn't give us enough time to check every trunk, but we can get started and then finish up after lessons this afternoon."

Rose picked up a large basket filled with books. "I finished distributing clothing and most of the personal items yesterday. Today we'll give each girl a Bible, a hymn and prayer book, and a copy of *Pilgrim's Progress*." She held out a basket to

Laura, then picked up a second basket. "Why don't you come with me while I see to the first girl? Then you can check on the other girls in this row."

Laura nodded and followed Rose as she approached the nearest girl, who looked about ten years old. She had large brown eyes and an abundance of curly, dark brown hair pulled back in a thick braid. She wore a plain brown dress covered by an ivory pinafore and thick-soled brown shoes.

"Ellen, would you please open your trunk?"

"Yes ma'am." The girl knelt and lifted the lid on the large wooden trunk.

Rose smiled. "Everything looks very neat." She shifted the stacks of clothing and looked deeper into the trunk. "Did you add the sewing kit and the extra stockings we discussed yesterday?"

"Yes ma'am. I went down to see Mrs. Robbins. She didn't believe me at first, even though I told her you said I needed them. She thought I was making up a story and said I should leave. But I just crossed my arms and told her I was going to stay right there until she gave them to me. She fussed and fussed, and I had to wait almost an hour, but she finally handed them over." The girl scowled. "I don't know why Mrs. Robbins had to be such a mean old—"

Rose held up her hand and cut her off. "Ellen, I'm sure you don't want to say anything unkind about Mrs. Robbins. Remember what we talked about."

Ellen closed her eyes and released a deep breath. "Yes ma'am. I remember."

Rose took a Bible from the basket and handed it to the girl. "Keep this Bible close and read it often. Take the truths to heart, and they will help you build a good life in Canada."

The girl's expression softened as she accepted the Bible. "Thank you, ma'am."

"This will help you as well." Rose handed her the hymnbook. "I often like to sing while I'm working. It lifts my spirits. I hope you'll do the same."

Ellen nodded and accepted the hymnbook.

"I've read this book many times." Rose handed her *Pilgrim's Progress.* "It's been a great encouragement to me."

"Thank you. I'll be sure to read it." Ellen held the Bible and books to her chest.

Rose laid her hand on Ellen's shoulder. "You're a good girl, Ellen. I'm sure you'll be a great help to your new family, and you'll make us all proud."

"I'm glad you're going with us, Miss Carson. I wouldn't want to go alone."

Rose touched her cheek. "You're never alone, Ellen. Remember that."

The girl nodded and smiled at Rose.

Rose turned to Laura. "Why don't you go ahead and check the next girl's trunk?"

Laura leaned closer and lowered her voice. "I'm not exactly sure what I'm looking for."

"Don't worry. I've already gone over the packing list with each girl and seen they have the clothing they need. You're just checking to make sure it's neatly folded, then you can give them the Bible and books." Rose sent her an encouraging smile. "And take a few minutes to meet each girl and encourage her."

"All right." Laura took the second basket of books and greeted the next girl, twelve-year-old Lucy. She looked through her trunk and asked her a few questions, then gave her the Bible, hymnbook, and *Pilgrim's Progress*. Their conversation wasn't as meaningful as the one shared by Rose and Ellen, but Laura did the best she could.

As she moved down the row, she continued to look around the room for Katie and Grace, but she didn't see them anywhere. Were they in another dormitory? Perhaps when it was time for their next meal, she would have a chance to see the rest of the girls and find her sisters.

When she came to the last girl in the row, she set down the basket by her open trunk. "I'm Miss Hopkins. What's your name?"

"Jenny Crawford, ma'am." The girl was thin and pale and had short, light brown hair. Her features were plain, and her eyes slanted down on the ends, making her look sad even when she smiled.

"How old are you, Jenny?"

"Fourteen, but I'm turning fifteen in June."

Laura bit the inside of her mouth. Katie's birthday was June 3. She would turn fifteen that day. She focused on Jenny again. "Where are you from?"

"I was born in Whitechapel, London, ma'am."

Laura's heart clenched at the mention of that poor area. What circumstances had brought the girl here? This wasn't the time to ask. She nodded and looked down at Jenny's trunk. "Everything is nicely packed. It looks as though you're taking good care of your clothing."

"Thank you, ma'am. I try to do what I'm told."

Laura took a Bible from the basket and held it out to Jenny. "We'd like you to have this Bible."

"No, thank you, ma'am. I already have one." The girl reached under her pillow and pulled out a Bible that looked just like those in the basket. "My friend gave me her copy before she left for Canada. She didn't want me to have to wait for mine."

"That was kind of her."

The girl smiled. "Yes ma'am. Katie's very kind."

Laura stilled. "Katie?"

"Yes ma'am. Katie McAlister. She's the one who gave me this Bible."

Laura stared at her. "You said she left?"

"Yes, she and her sister sailed with the last group."

Laura stifled the cry rising in her throat. She was too late! Her sisters were not at Hughes. They were already headed across the Atlantic Ocean and on their way to Canada!

Jenny's brow creased as she studied Laura's face. "Don't worry. Katie got another Bible before she left." She ran her fingers over the cover, and her expression eased. "She told me to read it every day and follow the Golden Rule and they'd choose me for the next group. And she was right."

Laura had to force out her next words. "You'll need these as well." She passed Jenny the other two books.

"Thank you, ma'am." The girl carefully tucked them into the corner of the trunk.

Laura straightened and glanced around the room. Her head throbbed, and she had a hard time focusing her thoughts.

Rose looked her way, and concern flashed in her eyes.

Laura quickly shifted her gaze away, but she was too late.

Rose crossed the room toward her. "Miss Hopkins, are you all right? You look quite pale."

Laura lifted her hand to her forehead, shading her eyes from view. "I'm sorry. I'm not feeling well."

"Come with me." Rose placed her arm around Laura's back and guided her across the dormitory and through a doorway into a small adjoining room. It was furnished with two beds, a desk, and a comfortable chair by the fireplace. "This is my room. You can rest here, and I'll go and get you a drink of water." She motioned to the chair. "Please sit down, or you can lie down if you'd like."

"No, the chair is fine."

Rose watched her a moment more. "Rest easy. I'll get the water and be right back."

"Thank you." Laura sank into the chair and lowered her head. How could this happen? She had come as quickly as she could, but she was too late! What would she tell Mum? After Dad's passing and Mum's suffering through her recent illness, losing her three youngest children would be a heartbreaking blow.

Pain throbbed at her temple. What should she do now?

Slowly she lifted her head and glanced around the room. Her gaze landed on the large wooden trunk at the end of the bed. Rose Carson would be traveling to Canada as an escort with the next group of girls.

Laura straightened in her chair. If she could hold on to this position, she would have free passage to Canada. Then, once she arrived, she could continue her search for Katie, Grace, and

Garth. Her salary would probably be enough to cover her expenses.

But Canada was such a vast land, much larger than England, and the children could be sent anywhere. How would she find them? The memory of her conversation with Mr. Randolph at Mifflin came to mind, giving her the answer. The Canadian receiving home would keep a record of where the children had been placed. All she had to do was find that information, then . . .

Tremors traveled down her arms. She had no idea what she would do after that, but she had to go and try. Katie, Grace, and Garth couldn't spend the rest of their lives in Canada separated from their family, never knowing they were loved and cherished by those back in England.

Someone had to speak up for them, right this terrible wrong, and bring them home. Mum couldn't go, and no one else cared enough to travel across the sea to find them. It was up to her. She had to sail to Canada and continue the search.

The ocean breeze ruffled Andrew's hair as he leaned on the railing of the *Parisian* and scanned the sky. The temperature was cool for mid-May, but the sun broke through the clouds, warming the shoulders of Andrew's black topcoat.

Down on the dock, a long line of passengers waited to show their travel documents to the agents and come aboard. Some of the ladies wore colorful dresses in the latest fashion and elaborate hats covered with feathers and flowers. The men with them were dressed in finely tailored suits, and several were accompanied by servants in uniform. Other passengers dressed in plain clothing waited in a separate line. They were probably headed for the second- or third-class accommodations, but they wore the same expectant look as they gazed up at the huge steamship.

On the upper promenade deck, where he and Henry stood at the railing, well-dressed men and women paraded past, taking in the view of the ship and the other passengers while they exchanged polite conversation with their companions.

Henry smiled. "It's quite a show, isn't it?"

Andrew glanced at those standing along the railing. "Yes, it is."

He had sailed across the Channel several times on similar ships, but this would be his first voyage across the Atlantic. Eight days of relaxation aboard ship would be a welcome change from the intense work of the past few weeks and the travel they expected to undertake for their investigation once they reached Canada.

Seagulls swooped overhead, calling out to each other as they circled the ship. The crew on the dock attached ropes to a shiny new motorcar.

It rose up in the air on an elaborate crane-and-pulley system and hovered over the deck for several seconds before it was lowered aboard.

Henry nodded toward the motorcar. "Someone must have paid a hefty sum to bring that along."

"I wonder if he knows he could buy a new one when he arrives in Canada?"

"I suppose he is attached to that particular model and has the funds to do as he pleases." Henry shook his head, then turned his attention to the dock once more. "Look, here comes a group of children."

Andrew followed his friend's gaze. "Do you think those are the girls from Hughes?"

Henry studied them for a few seconds and nodded. "I suppose they'll stay down in steerage with their chaperones."

Andrew's brow creased as he thought of their spacious, first-class cabin with its large windows and comfortable beds. No doubt he and Henry would have the best of everything, including dinner with the captain one night. He was quite certain the girls' accommodations wouldn't be nearly as comfortable.

"I was bothered that Phillips took so long to secure our passage, but it seems Providence was behind the delay. Sailing with the girls from Hughes will give us an opportunity to see how they fare on the voyage. Those observations should be helpful in our report."

Andrew watched the girls as they lined up at the second- and third-class gangplank. They were all dressed alike in navy blue jackets with lighter blue dresses beneath. Each girl wore a cream-colored straw hat with a wide, navy blue ribbon around the crown and carried a satchel with a long strap over her shoulder.

The two chaperones were dressed in traveling suits and simple hats. From this vantage point he couldn't see their faces. Both were young and slim and moved among the girls at a quick pace, answering questions and offering reassurance. He quickly counted heads. "It looks like there are about fifty girls with two chaperones."

Henry studied the group. "I'm not sure that is an adequate number of adults to supervise that many girls."

"I suppose the older girls will help the younger ones."

"True, but a sea voyage can be quite rough if the weather turns stormy." Henry glanced at him. "I recall you had a bit of trouble with seasickness on our last voyage to Italy."

Andrew chuckled. "Don't remind me. I'm hoping I'll gain my sea legs more quickly this time."

Henry clapped his hand on Andrew's shoulder. "I'm sure you will. And if the weather stays mild like this, we shouldn't have any trouble."

The girls reached the bottom of the gangplank

with the shorter chaperone in the lead. All around, people stopped to watch their group. Even the men working on the dock turned to take a look as the long line of young girls waited to board the ship.

Andrew smiled. It was an unusual sight with them all dressed alike and such a large number with only two adults to accompany them. How would they fare on the voyage? Recalling his bout with seasickness, he hoped they wouldn't suffer as he had. He wouldn't wish that on anyone.

Laura ushered the girls forward to join the long line of passengers waiting to board the *Parisian*. She scanned the length of the mammoth steamship, and her stomach did a nervous flip. There would be no turning back once she walked up that gangplank. The next time she set foot on land, she would be in Canada, on her own to search for her brother and sisters.

The last few days had been so full of learning all she needed to know in her new position, she'd barely had a minute to herself. The first day Miss Williams had informed her she would be required to stay at the home, so she'd moved in and shared a room with Rose Carson.

She had put off writing to Mum until she passed the one-week trial period. When Miss Williams confirmed she would be going to Canada with the next group, she'd written to tell Mum her plans. But she'd posted that letter only two days ago, so there hadn't been time to receive a reply. Perhaps that was best. Mum might not approve of her making this trip, especially if she knew Laura was using a false name.

She had left that detail out of her letter, and she refused to question her decision now. It was too late to change her mind. She didn't have time to wait for Mum's reply. If she was going to catch up with her siblings at the receiving home before they were placed with families, she had to leave now. And still, she might be too late.

She glanced at Rose, and another sliver of guilt pricked her heart. Her new friend had been so kind, lending her clothes and helping her prepare for the journey. She wished she could confide in Rose and tell her the whole story. But Laura wasn't sure Rose would keep her secret or even want to be her friend if she knew the truth.

Six-year-old Anna May, the youngest girl in their group, tugged on Laura's sleeve and looked up at her with wide brown eyes. "Miss Hopkins, how long will we be on that big ship?"

Laura smiled, hoping to ease the girl's fears. "About a week."

"That's a long time."

Laura placed her hand on the little girl's shoulder. "It'll be an adventure. And when the week is past, we'll arrive in Canada."

Rose joined them. "There's no need to worry, Anna May. I've sailed to Canada three times on ships like this. We'll be just fine."

"But what if we get lost or there's a big storm?"

"I'm sure we have a very experienced captain and crew, and even more important, Jesus promises to be with us wherever we go. He tells us to have faith and not be afraid. He can calm any storm."

Anna May sighed. "I'll try, but it won't be easy."

Rose's eyes twinkled. "You're a good girl, Anna May. And you can depend on Miss Hopkins and me to watch over you as well. You might even enjoy your week at sea. Then, before you know it, we'll arrive in Quebec City, and you'll be on your way to your new home and family."

Doubt still shimmered in Anna May's eyes, but she gave a tentative nod, then turned to look up at the ship again.

The boarding agent at the bottom of the gangplank waved Rose forward. He spoke to her for a few moments and handed her a packet of travel documents. She tucked them into her bag and motioned Laura forward to join her. "We have to wait. There's some question about our accommodations."

Laura frowned. "What kind of question?"

Rose sighed. "Not enough rooms for the

number of girls in our group. But we don't need to worry. I'm sure they'll straighten it out."

Laura certainly hoped so. She couldn't imagine having to turn around and take all these girls back to Hughes.

Rose lifted her gaze and studied the ship. "The *Parisian* looks much newer than the ship we traveled on last time. Our quarters were so cramped that time, it was nearly impossible to . . ." Her voice trailed off as she stared up at the deck.

"What is it, Rose?"

"Don't look up now, but I believe the inspector is on the top deck."

"The inspector?"

"Yes, the man who paid a surprise visit to Hughes."

Laura peeked out from beneath her hat brim. A large crowd of men and women stood at the railing on the upper deck. "I don't know who you mean."

"Oh, that's right. You weren't working at Hughes when he came." Rose took another discreet glance up at the ship. "He just showed up, unannounced, with his associate, asking for a tour and a great deal of information. You should've heard Miss Williams after he left. I've never seen her so angry. She made it very clear she did not appreciate surprise visits from nosy government inspectors."

Laura could easily imagine the matron's response. Though she'd been at Hughes only a short time, she'd seen the matron display her temper on several occasions. "I'm surprised she didn't turn him away."

"She couldn't. He's conducting an official investigation for the government."

Unease prickled along Laura's arms. "A government investigation?"

"Yes, and not just Hughes. They visited several other children's homes as well. They're looking into the issues surrounding child emigration." Panic rose in Laura's chest, snatching away her breath. She peeked up at the top deck again. "Which one is he?"

"Do you see the woman in the lavender dress with the large white hat with the ostrich feathers? Mr. Dowd is on her right."

She spotted him, and her gaze jumped to the man standing on his right. Andrew Frasier leaned on the railing, looking down at her group. She quickly lowered her head, praying her hat would block his view of her face.

"I'm sure that's Mr. Henry Dowd," Rose continued. "Miss Williams introduced him when they toured my classroom. I don't remember his associate's name, but he's up there as well."

Laura closed her eyes, wishing she could shrink out of sight. If Andrew Frasier discovered she was aboard the *Parisian* escorting a group of girls to Canada and using a false name, her whole story would crumble. Rose would find out she'd lied to gain her position and secure her passage to Canada. They'd probably have her arrested or locked in her cabin. "Oh, this is terrible," Laura muttered under her breath.

"What?" Rose turned to her.

Laura's face flushed. "I just . . . don't think it will be helpful to have inspectors watching us during the voyage."

"I suppose they may pay us a visit in steerage, but we have nothing to hide."

"Yes, of course."

A slow smile formed on Rose's lips. "In fact, this may be an unexpected opportunity."

"What do you mean?" Laura couldn't imagine anything positive coming from the situation.

"If Mr. Dowd observes us caring for the girls and sees how well behaved and prepared they are for their new lives, that will give him a positive impression of our work at Hughes and child emigration in general."

"I suppose." The line began moving forward again, and Laura leaned to the left, trying to see what was happening up ahead. If they could just hurry and board the ship, then he might not see her.

"I think we should make sure we cross paths with them."

Alarm zinged along Laura's nerves. "Oh, I don't think we need to do that."

227

Rose smiled, undeterred from her idea. "I'm sure they're traveling in first class, so we won't see them at meals. They'll have a separate dining room, but we might see them strolling on the deck when the weather is fine."

Laura moaned softly and lifted her hand to her forehead. Running into Andrew Frasier was the last thing she wanted to do. She hadn't even boarded the ship and already her lie was putting her in a difficult position. What did she expect? This was what happened when you made a hasty decision, compromised your convictions, and tried to manipulate the situation. One lie led to the next and took you deeper into trouble.

Rose placed her hand on Laura's arm. "Are you feeling all right, Mary?"

"I'm sure I'll be fine once we're aboard." She looked away, unwilling to meet Rose's eyes. She liked Rose, and she wished their friendship would grow and deepen, but that wouldn't happen unless she was willing to tell her the truth . . . and that was impossible.

Finally, the boarding agent returned and gave their group permission to board. Rose led the group, and each girl stepped forward in turn and gave the agent her name. He checked them off and motioned them up the gangplank. Laura followed the last girl. She stepped onto the ship and glanced over her shoulder.

She was leaving the security of her homeland

and heading off into the unknown. What would be the outcome of her journey? How much time would pass until she returned home to England? She had no answers for those questions, but she was certain of one thing—she would not return without her siblings.

10

Katie looked up at the tall clock tower rising above the Belleville Town Hall and tightened her hold on Grace's hand. The imposing brick building was much larger than the surrounding buildings and looked a little out of place, especially in a small town like Belleville. Maybe the people here expected the town to grow and prosper in the future. Surely that was a good sign, wasn't it?

The scene reminded her of London, and that brought bittersweet thoughts of Mum and Dad to mind. Oh, how she missed them! How long would it be before she could think of them without this terrible ache in her chest or tears stinging her eyes?

She blinked away the moisture and pulled in a shallow breath, trying to ease the ache. She had to focus on what was happening today and take care of Grace. That was most important now. Only time and God's grace would heal her grieving heart.

She glanced down at her sister as they followed the line of girls under the arched entryway and into the town hall. It was their fourth day in Canada, and she still felt as if she was walking through a confusing, unsettling dream.

They'd left the ship in Quebec City and taken a train overnight to Montreal, then traveled on to Kingston, where half the girls left the train with one of the escorts. The rest of the girls, including Katie and Grace and the other two escorts, traveled on to Belleville, arriving at the receiving home around noon. Their chaperones served them a simple lunch of bread and soup, then took them upstairs to the big dormitory to rest. Yesterday they'd all taken baths and washed their hair and spent time sorting out the clothing in their trunks. Today they'd left for the town hall directly after breakfast.

She hadn't seen Garth since the last day on the *Corinthian*. Some of the boys in his group had boarded the same train as Katie and Grace, but Garth was not with them, and the fear of losing track of him had nearly sent her into a panic. She'd been so tired and upset during the train ride that she'd spent half the time in tears, and that made Grace cry as well. One of the escorts finally sat with them and encouraged them to dry their tears. She said they could ask about their brother when they reached Belleville. But so far, no one had been able to tell her anything more about Garth.

"Come along, girls." Miss Delaney, the tall Irish escort, motioned them through the dim hallway and down the steps into a large open room on the lower level of the town hall. She turned and scanned the group with a no-nonsense expression. Freckles were sprinkled across her plain face, and a small brown hat covered most of her curly red hair. "Line up by the wall and wait quietly."

Katie crossed the room and took her place next to Grace along the side wall. Twenty-four girls, half of the original group from Hughes, waited with them to meet the people who would take them to their new homes.

Grace looked up at her with a frightened expression. "What if the people aren't nice?"

"Don't worry. It'll be all right." Katie forced confidence into her voice. "Anyone who would take in children who are not their own must have a kind heart." She prayed it was true and the family that chose them would treat them well.

She placed her hand over her aching stomach and released a soft sigh. The lukewarm porridge she'd eaten at breakfast felt like it had congealed into a solid lump. So many questions swirled through her mind, but there was no way to answer them or know what would happen to her and Grace.

Two men and an older woman sat at a long table near the front of the room. The blue curtain on the stage behind them was closed. A Canadian flag stood on one side of the stage, and some other flag she didn't recognize stood on the other. Miss Delaney approached the table and introduced herself.

The man seated in the middle nodded to her. "I'm Reverend Fuller, and this is Mr. Rook and Mrs. Abernathy. We're here to oversee the placement of the girls."

"I'm pleased to meet you." She took a folder from her bag and passed it to Reverend Fuller. "This is the list with the girls' names and ages. If anyone wants to know about a girl's background, I have their files with me, but it's usually best not to offer that information unless someone asks."

Reverend Fuller nodded and searched across the group. Frowning, he lowered his gaze and scanned the list. "We were told you were bringing at least fifty girls." He lifted serious eyes to meet Miss Delaney's.

"We brought fifty-two girls from England, but half of our group was dropped off in Kingston."

"You should have informed me you were only bringing twenty-six girls." He tapped the stack of papers on the table. "I have fifty-five applicants waiting outside, each one planning to take in a girl as a domestic. They all paid their three-dollar fee, and they expect to take a child home today. What do you suggest I tell the other twenty-nine?"

Her cheeks flushed pink beneath her freckles. "That is up to you, sir. I am simply following the directions Miss Williams, the matron of Hughes, gave me when we left England."

Reverend Fuller leaned to the left and spoke

to Mr. Rook in a hushed voice. Then he turned and consulted Mrs. Abernathy. Finally, he straightened and looked up at Miss Delaney. "We're prepared to go ahead. We'll bring in one couple at a time to see the girls and make their choice. When the girls are all distributed, I'll step outside to speak to the others and explain the situation."

"Very well. We're ready to begin when you are." Miss Delaney turned and strode back across the room toward Katie and the others. Her face was still flushed as she approached and looked them over. "All right, girls. I want you to stand up straight. Look smart and be quiet and respectful to the people who come in to see you."

Katie straightened her back and glanced at Grace. She'd taken extra time combing and braiding Grace's hair this morning, and she'd made sure her sister's face and hands were clean. She wore the green print dress with an ivory pinafore, blue jacket, and straw hat, just like Katie and all the other girls. With her big blue eyes and sweet face, she was bound to be one of the first chosen.

Mr. Rook crossed the room and stepped out through a side door. A few seconds later, the first couple walked in.

The man was tall with dark hair and eyes, and he had a full mustache covering his upper lip. He was dressed in a fine black suit with white shirt and a dark green tie. He removed his black bowler hat and guided the woman across the room toward the line of girls. His expression grew serious and searching as he came closer.

The woman looked younger than Mum, with light brown hair, blue eyes, and rosy cheeks. Her copper-colored suit was trimmed with a scroll design and a double row of covered buttons. It was much nicer than any of the outfits she and Mum had worked on in Mrs. Palmer's dress shop. The woman's large hat was covered with flowers and feathers and gathered netting that matched her suit.

They walked down the row of girls, looking at each one carefully. The woman slowed as they approached Grace and Katie. A smile lifted her lips as she studied Grace.

Katie's heartbeat sped up, and she stepped closer to her sister. The woman looked her way. Katie lifted her chin and met the woman's gaze. The woman smiled at her, then looked at her husband.

His brow creased as he scanned Grace and Katie. Then he took his wife's arm and guided her down the row to look at the other girls.

Katie released a deep breath, and tingles raced down her arms. They had not been chosen. She stared after the couple, unsure if she was relieved or disappointed.

"They didn't like us?" Grace's voice quavered as she looked up at Katie.

"Don't worry." Katie slipped her arm around Grace. "I'm sure there are more families coming in soon."

The couple walked up to the table and spoke to Reverend Fuller in low tones. The reverend looked around the couple at the girls. He lowered his gaze to the list and pointed to something written there. The woman smiled at the man and nodded. They turned back to Reverend Fuller. He spoke to them again, then passed a paper to the woman seated next to him. She looked it over and wrote something across the bottom. She rose from her chair and walked over to speak to Miss Delaney. The escort nodded a few times as she listened, then walked toward Katie and Grace.

Katie's heartbeat sped up again. The couple wanted them after all.

Miss Delaney approached. "I'd like you to come with me, Grace."

Katie gripped Grace's hand. "Why? Where are you taking her?"

"That couple would like to talk to her."

Grace looked up at Katie, her eyes filled with questions.

Why were they asking to speak to Grace and not to both of them? Maybe they were allowed to talk to only one girl at a time, and they had decided to start with the youngest. Yes, that was probably the reason. Everything was all right.

"Go ahead, Grace." Katie released her sister's

hand. "Just be sure to tell them I'm your sister and we have to stay together."

Grace nodded. "I will."

Miss Delaney sent Katie an impatient glance, then guided Grace across the room to where the couple waited.

Katie bit her lip, praying they'd like Grace, then call for her to come over as well. Surely once Grace told them she had a sister, the couple would take them both.

The well-dressed woman sat in a chair and smiled at Grace. She took her hand, leaned closer, and spoke to her in a voice so low and soft Katie couldn't hear what she said.

Grace lowered her head and looked reluctant to answer. Katie's stomach tensed. This was not good. Grace needed to look up and speak to the woman or they might think she was shy and difficult. The man stood nearby, turning his hat in his hands and looking as though he wished the conversation would hurry along.

Mr. Rook crossed to the door again and let in the next couple. The man who entered was short and wiry with a grizzled face. He walked with a limp, and his plain clothes and straw hat made him look like he was a farmer who lived in the country. The woman with him was plump with straggly brown hair. Her gray dress was stained around the ragged hem, and she carried an empty basket over her arm. They started down the row, slowing to look at the older girls, but neither smiled nor made any comments.

Katie looked down at the floor as they came closer. She did not want them to think they could choose her. She was going with the first couple as soon as they called for her.

"Look at me, girl." The woman's voice sounded dry and raspy, as though she yelled too often.

Katie slowly lifted her head.

The woman squinted at her. "This one looks old enough."

"She looks a mite thin to me." The farmer scanned her from head to toe. "Not sure she could do much work."

Katie's face heated, and she lowered her head again. How could they be so rude and talk about her like that?

A cry rang out across the room. Katie's head jerked up.

The man in the bowler hat tugged Grace toward the far door. Grace writhed and tried to pull away from him, but it was no use.

"Wait!" Katie started across the room. "Where are you taking her?"

Miss Delaney caught up with Katie and grabbed her arm. "Where do you think you're going?"

"Stop them! They're taking my sister!"

"Of course they are. That's the reason we're here." Miss Delaney gave her arm a rough shake. "Now stop this foolishness and get back in line."

Katie tried to pull away, but Miss Delaney held on with a viselike grip.

"But Mrs. Stafford said we could stay together!"

Miss Delaney marched Katie back toward the wall. "You misunderstood. She would never say that."

"You're wrong! She did!" A sob caught in Katie's throat. "She promised!"

"That's enough! Settle down and mind your manners."

"Please, let me go with Grace! I'll do whatever kind of work they want."

"They don't want house help. They're here to adopt a young girl, and Grace caught their eye." Miss Delaney leaned closer to Katie's face. "You should be happy for your sister. They look like a fine family. I'm sure they'll treat her well."

Katie squeezed her eyes shut, but tears leaked out at the corners.

"Now, unless you want to be the very last girl chosen, I suggest you hold your tongue and wipe those tears off your face."

Searing heat pulsed through Katie. She clenched her jaw and turned her face away. This wasn't right! They should not separate her from her sister!

The other girls all looked on with somber gazes. One or two watched with sympathetic

239

expressions, but no one spoke to her or offered any words of comfort.

Katie lowered her head and closed her eyes as another painful round of tears clogged her throat. First they had taken Garth away, and now Grace. She was all alone—no one to care for and no one who cared for her.

The next hour passed in a daze as one by one girls were chosen and taken away. Katie's tears dried, and she felt numb all over as she watched each girl walk out the door with a new family. Finally, only Katie and two other girls were left.

A tall, thin man in a rumpled suit walked in and approached the girls. He had a long, hawk-like nose and small dark eyes. A black beard covered the lower half of his face, but it couldn't hide his sour expression.

He slowed for only a moment to look at the other two younger girls, then stopped in front of Katie. "How old are you?"

She swallowed. "Fourteen."

He studied her with a frown as though he didn't believe her. "Do you know how to cook and clean?"

"Yes sir."

"Open your mouth."

Katie blinked. "What?"

"I said, open your mouth."

She parted her lips an inch while the other girls stared at them.

"Tip your head back and say 'ah.' " He stepped closer. "Open wider."

She did as he asked but felt mortified. What was he looking for?

"Hmm, good teeth."

She snapped her mouth closed. How dreadful! Did he think she was a horse?

"Have you had the measles and mumps?"

"I don't know . . . I think so."

He glared at her. "Did you have them or not?"

"I'm not sure."

He snorted. "I can't take a chance on spreading disease to my wife and children."

Miss Delaney approached. "Is there a problem, sir?"

"I'm a doctor, and I want to know if she's healthy. I'd like to see her medical records before I decide if I'll take her."

Miss Delaney glanced at Katie. "I have her file. It will give you some information, but I can guarantee she is in good health. Each girl has a medical exam before they leave England and again when they arrive in Canada."

Katie recalled seeing the doctor in England, but when she arrived in Quebec City, a medical officer had asked her only a few questions after she left the ship. She wouldn't really call that a medical exam, but it didn't matter. She didn't have any diseases.

"Come with me, sir, and I'll check her file."

Miss Delaney led the man to the table at the front of the room. She opened a folder on the table, shuffled through a few papers, and pointed out something to him.

The man lifted the paper from the file and scanned it closely. Finally, he nodded. "I'll take her. Where do I sign?"

Katie's heart plummeted. How could she go with that man? He might be a doctor, but he didn't seem to have a compassionate bone in his body. He hadn't even asked her name.

"Come along, Katherine." Miss Delaney motioned her to join them at the table.

Her feet felt like weighted bricks as she slowly crossed the room. She glanced around, looking for any way she might escape, but she had nowhere to go and too many people who would stop her if she tried.

"Katherine, this is Dr. Thomas Richardson. You'll be going home with him."

Katie stared at Dr. Richardson as he signed a document and passed it back to Reverend Fuller. "I'll give the girl a trial. But if I'm not happy with her work, I'll send her back."

Reverend Fuller nodded. "You have that option if things don't go well, but I expect she'll work hard and be helpful to you and your wife."

"She'd better be, or I'll ask for my money back." He started toward the door.

Katie stood there, too numb to move.

The doctor turned and looked over his shoulder. "Come along, girl. I have patients to see and no time to waste."

Katie blew out a breath and forced herself to take the first step. She had no choice. She had to follow him.

Mrs. Abernathy's eyes clouded as Katie walked past.

Miss Delaney waited by the end of the table. She lifted her chin, her expression firm. "Do your best, Katie, and everything will be fine."

She couldn't answer. Words wouldn't come. She felt hollowed out, empty of thoughts and feelings. Grace and Garth were gone. Her hope was lost. Not one of these people really cared what happened to her.

Andrew clasped his hands behind his back and strolled down the promenade deck of the *Parisian*. He lifted his gaze to the clear blue sky overhead and pulled in a deep breath. "What a beautiful day. I can't believe the weather has been so clear and calm."

Henry smiled. "It certainly makes for smooth sailing."

"I'm grateful for that." It was their second day at sea, and Andrew had felt only a slight wave of seasickness that morning. Fortunately, it faded quickly and he had been able to enjoy his breakfast in the luxurious first-class dining room.

They walked past a row of people resting in deck chairs, reading books, and soaking up the midday sunshine.

As they strolled on past several lifeboats, Henry shifted his gaze toward the water. "I'm always inspired when I see the ocean. Who could observe such a wonder and not believe in the Creator?"

Andrew gave a thoughtful nod. The ocean certainly was a wonder with its vast size, and they could see only the surface. Another world thrived beneath the shimmering water.

"The ocean is an amazing reflection of His awesome wisdom and creative power," Henry added. They exchanged a smile and continued around the deck.

They'd spent the morning poring over their notes and discussing how they ought to outline the first section of their report on child emigration. After the introduction, they decided to tell how children came into the care of the homes, then how they were selected and prepared for emigration to Canada. After that, they would describe the accommodations at the homes, discuss the qualifications of the staff, then comment on the health and fitness of the children they'd observed. They also wanted to include information about the children's schooling, training programs, meals, and medical care.

The breeze picked up, and Henry lifted his

hand to his hat. "I'm pleased with the progress we made this morning."

Andrew nodded. "It's a good start." His thoughts shifted to the group of girls he'd seen come aboard the ship yesterday morning. "It would be helpful to see how the children are cared for on the voyage."

"Yes, we'll want to include that in our report." Henry's expression sobered. "I've heard the steerage area of the ship can be rather dank and unhealthy."

"That doesn't sound like good accommodations for children."

"No, it doesn't. But this is a newer ship. Perhaps it's not as bad as I've been told."

"Why don't we go down and pay them a visit? Then we can see how the children are faring."

"We may not need to. It appears they're coming to us." Henry nodded down the deck, and Andrew followed his gaze.

Six young girls, all dressed alike in green print dresses, walked toward them. He studied them as they drew closer and guessed they were between the ages of six and twelve. They looked to be in good spirits and none the worse for their time in steerage.

He lifted his gaze to the two women caretakers walking behind them, and his steps faltered. The woman on the right looked like Laura McAlister or her identical twin sister.

Henry glanced his way with a lifted brow. "Something wrong, Andrew?"

He shook his head as the truth became clear. That was his mother's lady's maid. There was no mistake about it. What in the world was she doing on the *Parisian* overseeing a group of girls on their way to Canada?

Laura looked his way, and her eyes flashed. She lowered her head and turned her face away.

The other woman smiled at them as they approached. "Good morning, Mr. Dowd."

"Miss Carson." Henry tipped his hat and smiled. "It's a pleasure to see you again."

His friend certainly had an excellent memory. Andrew remembered meeting the petite brunette teacher, but he didn't remember her name.

Miss Carson's eyes sparkled as she looked up at Henry. "We're happy to see you as well. I hope you're enjoying the voyage."

"Yes, we were just saying what a lovely day it is and how grateful we are for the smooth seas." Henry glanced at Laura.

"Oh, I'm sorry." Miss Carson turned to Laura. "Let me introduce my friend. This is Miss Mary Hopkins. She is also one of the escorts for the girls from Hughes."

Andrew stared at Laura. *Mary Hopkins?*

Her startled gaze darted from Rose to Henry. Her face had gone pale, and she seemed unable to gather her words. Finally, she looked at Andrew, her eyes begging him not to question her about her name.

He hesitated a moment, then lifted his hat. "I'm pleased to meet you, *Miss Hopkins*. My name is Andrew Frasier. I'm Mr. Dowd's associate." He would play along for the time being, but he would get to the bottom of this questionable behavior.

Relief filled her face. "It's a pleasure to meet you, Mr. Frasier."

Henry grinned at the girls. "Now I'd like to meet these young ladies."

Miss Carson introduced the six girls, and they offered shy smiles and polite responses to Henry's questions. The youngest, six-year-old Anna May, had big brown eyes and a sweet set of dimples that would surely melt some man's heart when she was older.

"As you know," Henry said, "Mr. Frasier and I are gathering information for a report about child emigration, and we were wondering if you might show us the girls' accommodations."

Miss Carson smiled. "We would be happy to show you our cabins."

"It would also be helpful to see where they take their meals. And we'd like to hear your thoughts about the journey and any suggestions you might have for groups coming on future voyages."

She glanced at Laura, then smiled at Henry again. "We'd be very pleased to answer your questions."

Henry nodded. "Thank you. That would be most helpful."

"Our cabins are this way." Miss Carson motioned down the deck, and Henry stepped up to walk beside her. The girls fell in step behind them.

Andrew walked beside Laura. She stared straight ahead, pretending to ignore him, but her stiff posture and the twitching muscle in her cheek gave away her embarrassment.

"There are fifty-two girls in our party," Miss Carson continued. "We have ten cabins for our group, with six beds each. Miss Hopkins and I each have five of the youngest girls with us in our cabins. An older girl is assigned to oversee the girls in the other eight cabins."

Henry held the door open, and their group entered the passageway. They started down the stairs with Miss Carson leading the way and Henry behind her. The six girls clattered down the metal steps after them, and Laura and Andrew followed.

When the group of girls rounded the corner and started down the next flight of stairs, Andrew slowed and stepped closer to Laura. "So, it's *Miss Mary Hopkins* now, is it?" He kept his voice low enough so no one but Laura could hear.

Her cheeks flushed bright pink. She lifted her chin and walked on without answering.

"What kind of game are you playing, Miss McAlister?"

"It's not a game!" Urgency filled her hushed voice.

"Then why are you pretending to be someone you're not?"

"I can't explain right now, but I assure you I have a very good reason for what I'm doing."

"Ha! That's what every criminal says when they're caught in the act."

Her eyes flashed. "I am not a criminal!"

"Then you had better tell me your *very good reason,* or I'll have to put an end to your charade."

"Please, I can't tell you right now. Not here!"

He studied her as she hurried after the girls. She was obviously trying to put some distance between herself and him, but he easily caught up again. "If you won't tell me now, then meet me on the promenade deck at nine tonight. And you had better be prepared to give me an honest explanation, or I will speak to Miss Carson and tell her what I know about you."

She stopped and turned to him, her blue-eyed gaze betraying her fear. "I don't know if I can get away at that time."

"You had better find a way." He was giving her a chance to do what was right, and he would not listen to any excuses.

Her shoulders sagged. "All right. I'll do my best to meet you at nine."

Disappointment tightened his chest as he

watched Laura descend the steps. When he'd met Laura McAlister at Bolton, he'd thought she was an honest, caring young woman in need of his help. Did she even have a mother who was ill in London? And what about her claim that she had three siblings who had been taken away to a children's home? Was any of that true, or was it all a lie?

He abhorred dishonesty. And he wasn't about to let her take advantage of his family, those in charge of the Hughes Home, or even more importantly, these girls.

If she did have some explanation—though he couldn't imagine one that would justify her actions—he would listen. But if he wasn't persuaded, he would expose her lies to those in charge of her party tomorrow morning.

11

Laura leaned over Anna May and listened closely. The girl's slow, steady breathing assured her she was fast asleep. She glanced around at the other four girls who rested quietly in their bunks, then tiptoed to the cabin door. She waited there, listening to be sure they didn't stir. When all remained quiet, she cracked open the door and looked out. With no one in sight, she slipped out and closed the door softly behind her.

She hurried down the long passageway but slowed as she passed Rose's cabin. Would her friend be upset with her for leaving the girls alone, or would she understand? Laura's girls had all slept peacefully the night before. She prayed the same would be true tonight and Rose would never know she'd left the cabin to go up on deck.

Her thoughts raced ahead to her meeting with Andrew Frasier. She stopped at the bottom of the stairs and pressed her hand over her heart.

Lord, I need Your help. I know I am not worthy to ask for it when I'm deceiving Rose and the others, but still, I'm asking for Your mercy. Please help Andrew Frasier understand this was my only choice.

Her prayer faltered, and the weight of those thoughts pressed down on her.

Was that true? Could she have found some other way to travel to Canada and right the wrongs that had been done to her family?

Oh, Lord, please help me out of this mess!

She waited on the bottom step with her eyes closed and her stomach churning. Sorrow and shame battled in her heart. Of course God wouldn't answer her prayer. Why would He listen to someone who knew the right thing to do yet didn't do it?

Her only option was to climb those stairs, face Andrew Frasier, and hope she could convince him not to tell anyone the truth about her.

She gripped the railing and started up the steps. When she reached the level of the promenade deck, she crossed to the door and looked out. Andrew stood at the railing, a dark figure against the backdrop of the silver sea. Her heart sank to her toes. She had hoped he might not come and she wouldn't have to face him tonight. But there he stood, waiting for her.

She summoned her courage and pushed open the door. The cool evening breeze ruffled her skirt and blew a few strands of her hair into her face. She brushed them away, approached the railing, and claimed a spot a few feet down from him.

He turned toward her. Moonlight shone on the smooth planes of his face, outlining his strong jaw. He was a handsome man, but that only made her more certain she shouldn't trust him.

She glanced around the empty promenade deck, and a shiver traveled down her back. There was so much she didn't know about Mr. Frasier. She would have to be on her guard.

He cocked one eyebrow. "I wondered if you'd come."

"You didn't leave me much choice."

He acknowledged her statement with a slight tip of his head. "You can imagine my surprise when we were introduced today. I was under the impression your name was Laura McAlister and you were employed as my mother's lady's maid. But now I find you bound for Canada, overseeing a group of young emigrants, and going by the name Mary Hopkins. I think that requires an explanation."

She couldn't look at him any longer, so she turned away.

"So, which is it really—Laura McAlister or Mary Hopkins?"

She straightened. "Laura McAlister, but I have a good reason for using the name Mary Hopkins."

"All right." He faced her and crossed his arms. "What's your story?" Was it his training as a solicitor that made him respond in such a cool, logical manner?

She called her practiced explanation to mind and began. "When I left Bolton, I fully intended to return and resume my duties. But my mum's condition was very serious, and I knew I would need to stay in London longer than I expected. My mum was very concerned about my brother and sisters, and she urged me to visit them at the Grangeford Children's Home."

"They're at Grangeford?"

"They were for a time, but when I tried to see them, the matron refused to allow it. She said a visit would be too upsetting, and it would keep them from settling into the routine at the home." Laura gripped the railing, the memory of the woman's dismissive attitude stirring her anger. "I told the matron I was ready to accept responsibility for the children and take them with me, but she refused that as well. She said she wouldn't release them unless I could prove guardianship and pay their fees."

"What fees?"

"If a family wants to reclaim their children, they have to pay for all the food, clothing, and care they received while they were at the home. Of course those fees are outrageous, and that makes it nearly impossible for anyone to recover their children." Bitterness tinged her voice, but she wasn't sorry. It was a dreadful, unjust rule.

"Are you sure about that?" His tone revealed his doubt.

"Yes, the matron made it quite clear."

He pondered that for a moment, then met her gaze. "What did you do after that?"

"I spoke to our clergyman, Reverend Bush. He

offered to help me find work in London, but he said guardianship was a legal matter. He wrote a letter for me, and my mum did as well, but by the time I took them to Grangeford, Katie, Grace, and Garth had been put on the list for Canada and sent to Liverpool—all without my mother's knowledge or consent."

Andrew frowned. "I find that hard to believe. There must have been some kind of mistake. Surely, if they're not orphans, the home must have permission from at least one parent to emigrate the children."

"They never contacted my mother. We have no idea why they were put on the list, and we definitely didn't want them sent to Canada."

He was listening now, and his serious, concerned expression gave her hope.

"As soon as I learned their fate, I took the train to Liverpool. But when I arrived at Hughes, I learned they only allow family visits once a month and I had just missed visitation day. I had to find out if they were still there, so when I heard the matron was conducting interviews to fill some staff positions, I applied."

He gave a slight nod. "I thought I saw you there the day we toured Hughes."

She remembered seeing him and Mr. Dowd and gave a slight nod.

"And you were hired as an escort?"

"Yes, but I was too late." Her throat tightened,

and she had to swallow before she could continue. "My first day working at Hughes I learned my sisters had already left for Canada, and my brother had been sent as well."

"Your mother never received an emigration notice from the home?"

"I don't believe so. I wrote and told her I was following them to Canada with the next group, but I left Liverpool before I received her reply."

He looked out across the ocean, a frown still creasing his forehead.

"I wrote to your mother as well and explained why I couldn't return to Bolton. I told her I'd pay back the money you gave me as soon as I'm able, and I intend to keep my word."

He looked her way, and his expression softened. "There's no need."

"But I know you gave it to me thinking I was coming back."

"I did, but my main intention was to help you and your family."

"It helped a great deal, and I'll always be thankful for your kindness."

His mouth pulled up on one side into a slight smile. "I'm glad to hear it."

The tension in her neck and shoulders eased a bit. She seemed to have gained his understanding and perhaps even his sympathy.

"You still haven't told me why you're using the name Mary Hopkins."

That was the sticking point. Somehow she had to convince him her reasons were justified. She looked up and met his gaze. "The matron at Hughes made it very clear she would not see any family members asking for a visit. I watched her send one poor mother away in tears. And I was afraid if she realized I was looking for Katie and Grace, she'd send me away as well. So I used my middle name and my mother's maiden name to come up with Mary Hopkins."

"Why didn't you just tell the matron the truth? Surely if you explained there'd been a mistake and your mother didn't want them sent to Canada, she would've listened. You had the letters from your clergyman and your mother to substantiate your claims."

"I don't believe she would've listened."

He sent her a doubtful glance. "You didn't try."

"You don't understand." Her voice became more insistent. "The people overseeing those homes don't value family connections. In fact, they seem to do everything in their power to break all ties between children and their parents."

His frown returned, and he leaned on the railing. "It's not fair to paint every organization helping poor and orphaned children with such a broad stroke and especially to imply they all intend to separate families. Most of the children's homes were started by sincere Christians who saw children living on the streets, begging and stealing to survive. In the last fifty years they've rescued thousands of children from desperate situations and given them an opportunity to build new lives."

"But do they have to send them across the ocean to do it? Why can't the children stay in England so they at least have a chance to be reunited if their family's situation improves?"

He tipped his head. "I see your point, but the homes face a number of significant challenges. With the changes in society and so many people moving into the cities, the number of poor and abandoned children continues to increase. Caring for all of them is very costly, and most of the homes don't have sufficient funds. If the children remain in England, their opportunities for the future are limited. Many believe emigration to Canada is the best solution."

"But is it what's best for the children?"

"That's what Henry and I hope to learn through our investigation."

She'd listened patiently to his explanation, but she was not convinced. "Here's an important point you may want to include in your report." She took a step closer. "No one should have the right to take children away from parents who love them and are able to care for them."

He watched her with a steady gaze.

"My family is suffering greatly because some people believe their solution is best, and they couldn't be bothered to listen to the truth of our situation. I'll tell you this: my family may not be rich, but we love each other. And no one should have the power to separate us."

Silvery light shone in his eyes. "I understand what you're saying, and I see why you've gone to such great lengths to follow your brother and sisters to Canada."

His open expression spurred her on. "So . . . will you help me?"

"What are you asking?"

"I'm asking you not to tell Rose who I am or that I'm searching for my siblings."

He frowned and glanced away. "I don't believe hiding your identity or intentions is the best way to go about this."

"I'm not hurting anyone by using the name Mary Hopkins. I'm carrying out my duties as an escort and looking after the children just as I promised I would."

"But what happens when you arrive in Canada? Will you desert them to take up your search?"

"No, I won't desert them! I'll stay and care for them as long as I'm needed."

"And what then? How do you propose to find your siblings?"

She lifted her hands. "I suppose I'll start at the home and learn where they've been sent. Then I'll go there and find a way to take them back to England."

"Just like that?" He sent her an unbelieving look, making it clear he thought she was foolish and naive.

Her face heated. "I don't know exactly how I'll accomplish it, but I'm not giving up. I have to find them. My mother is depending on me, and I won't let her down."

He blew out a long breath. "Even though I believe a mistake was made in sending your siblings, it could be a complicated process to find them and secure their release. You can't do it alone. You'll need legal help."

She looked up at him, hope and expectation making her rise up on her toes. "I'm sure you're right."

He looked away, obviously pondering all that was involved in her request. Finally, he turned back to her. "I can only take this on if you're willing to drop the charade and use your real name."

She gasped. "I can't do that!"

"You'll have to if you want my help. I can't mislead Henry or jeopardize our investigation."

She opened her mouth to reply, but a loud, clanging bell cut her off. She lifted her hands and covered her ears. "What is that?"

Andrew stiffened, and his gaze darted around. "It's an alarm. Come with me!" He set off down the deck.

"Where are we going?"

"We have to find out what's happening." He pushed open the door and strode inside.

"But what about my girls? I should go down to them."

"Let's see what the problem is first. Then we'll decide what to do."

The bell continued to clang as they hurried down the upper passageway. People stepped out of their cabins and looked around with questioning expressions. Some called out, asking about the bells.

"It's a fire alarm!" one man shouted.

Dread raced through Laura, chilling her to the bone. They were trapped on this ship. Could the crew fight the fire and get it under control, or was their ship doomed and all the passengers with it?

Andrew pushed open a cabin door, and Laura followed him inside.

Henry Dowd stood in the center of the large cabin, buttoning his shirt. His eyes widened. "I wondered where you were."

"Someone said that's a fire alarm."

Henry nodded. "I believe they're right. Remember the drill. Grab your important documents and life jacket. Then we'll head up to our emergency station."

"I have to go down to my girls." Laura turned toward the door.

"Wait! I'm coming with you." Andrew grabbed his papers and life jacket from the closet.

Henry shoved his arms into his suit jacket sleeves. "I'll come as well. You'll need help managing them all." He grabbed his life jacket from the bed and slung it over his shoulder.

Andrew jerked open the cabin door, and they set off down the passageway with the alarm bell still ringing and people milling around them.

Laura scanned the air and sniffed. There was no sign of smoke on this deck, but what about down in steerage? She picked up her pace.

As they rounded the corner and started down the stairs, she felt as though she was swimming upstream against the swarm of passengers trying to reach the promenade deck where they'd all been told to report in case of an emergency.

"Make way!" Andrew shouted, forging ahead and moving people aside so they could continue down. Laura stayed close behind him, and Henry came behind her.

Finally, they reached steerage level, and Laura's heart clenched. Several of the girls stood in the passageway, clutching their life jackets. Some were in tears, and others clung to their friends with pale faces and fear-filled eyes.

Rose stepped out of one of the cabins and rushed down the passageway toward them. "Thank heavens you've come!" Laura was about to explain and apologize, but Rose went directly to Henry.

He placed his hand on her arm. "How can we help?"

"We have to make sure every girl has a life jacket before we start upstairs."

"Let's divide the group." Andrew motioned toward the girls. "You have ten cabins, correct?"

"Yes." Rose watched him eagerly.

"You and Miss Hopkins take five cabins," Andrew continued. "Henry and I will oversee the other five. Have the girls line up against the wall so we can be sure everyone is accounted for."

Rose gave them the cabin numbers, and Laura hurried down the passageway to collect her girls. A few were ready and waiting inside the cabin, but she had to help the youngest find their life jackets under the bunks and put those on.

"Line up out in the hall and wait for me there." Laura rushed into the next cabin. Only two girls sat together on one of the bunks. "Where are the others?"

Tears streamed down nine-year-old Lilly's face. "They ran out, looking for you."

Pain pierced Laura's chest. Her girls needed her, but she'd left them on their own to face this frightening night. How could she have been so selfish and irresponsible? She forced those condemning thoughts away. She was here now, and she would do all she could to make sure they were safe.

She pulled in a breath to steady her nerves.

"Let's be calm and do as we practiced in the drill." She bent down and pulled their life jackets from under the bunk. With trembling hands, she helped the girls don their life jackets. She took their hands and led them out to the passageway and told them to stand with the others.

With a quick glance down the row, she found the rest of her girls among the others and moved them all into one group. She checked to be sure each wore a life jacket and it was secure.

Andrew walked down the passageway, looking in each cabin. He slowed and glanced at Laura. "Do you have all your girls?"

She glanced over the group. "Yes. We're ready to go up."

He sent her a reassuring nod, then moved down the row, checking with Rose and helping a few of the girls secure their life jackets.

"Miss Hopkins, look!" Twelve-year-old Sophie pointed toward the ceiling.

Laura glanced up and froze. Thin wisps of smoke curled along the ceiling. She sniffed, and the scent of burning oil filled her nose. There was no time to waste. She charged down the hall toward Andrew. "There's smoke! We have to get the girls up to the promenade deck now!"

He followed her gaze. His eyes widened, and he started toward the stairs. "Tell the girls to stay in line and follow me."

Laura hurried back down the row, giving

instructions and encouraging them to stay calm and follow Andrew. She stepped into line, rejoining the girls from her cabin. A few were still in tears, but most seemed focused and ready to do as they were told.

Laura looked over her shoulder as they reached the top of the first flight of stairs. The line of girls filled the stairwell. Henry stayed at the bottom and finally took his place at the end of the line after the last girl in Rose's group.

A prayer rose from Laura's heart as they started up the next flight of stairs. *Have mercy on us, Lord. Not for my sake but for these dear girls.*

When they finally reached the promenade deck, Andrew held the door open while the girls passed through. Laura rushed to the head of the line and led them down the deck toward their assigned stations. It was difficult to squeeze past all the other passengers who huddled in groups along the deck, but the girls stayed together.

"What is your station number?" Andrew called.

"S-72 and 73," Laura answered.

"We're almost there!" He hurried forward and joined her.

They passed the entrance to the first-class lounge and reached their assigned stations. Laura gathered the girls to stand together. The cool wind off the water blew across Laura's face and sent a shiver down her back. Her girls were all barefoot and dressed in their nightclothes. Why hadn't she made them collect their shoes, socks, and sweaters?

The answer sent another wave of guilt through her heart. She'd left them alone to meet Andrew on deck, then lost several minutes going back to his cabin before going down to help them.

Rose walked among the girls and encouraged them to sit down and huddle close to try to stay warm. All the while the alarm continued to sound and send tremors through Laura.

Andrew approached Laura. Frustration lined his face as he searched the deck past the other groups of passengers. "I don't understand why they haven't sent someone up to give us instructions."

"I'm sure they'll let us know something soon."

"I'm going to look for a crew member and find out what's happening."

Laura tensed. His presence had helped her stay calm. What if they were told to board lifeboats and set out to sea? Could she manage all the girls without his help?

She laid her hand on his arm. "Please don't go yet."

Before he could answer, one of her girls shouted, "Miss Hopkins! Where is Anna May?"

Laura spun around, searching for her youngest charge, but she didn't see her sitting with the others. She strode forward, scanning the faces of the girls in her group and then the others, but Anna May was not there.

How could she have left Anna May behind? She'd counted all the girls—but somehow she must have counted wrong. She scanned the girls once more. "Did anyone see Anna May in the cabin or in the passageway downstairs?"

The girls all looked at one another and shook their heads.

She turned and started down the deck. "I'm going back for Anna May."

Andrew grabbed her arm. "You can't go back to steerage!"

"I have to!" She pulled her arm away. "I can't leave her down there by herself!"

"Then I'll go. You stay here."

"She doesn't know you. She'll be frightened." She stepped around him.

He growled something under his breath and set off after her. "It won't help the other girls if you become trapped in steerage."

She strode on. "I have to find her!"

He stepped past Laura and pushed open the door. "Then we'll do it together."

They exchanged a split-second glance, and a silent agreement passed between them. She grabbed up her skirt and quickly followed him down the three flights of stairs. When they reached steerage, the veil of smoke swirled in the air near the ceiling. Laura lifted her hand to cover her mouth and nose and started down the passageway.

"Anna May!" Andrew flung open the first cabin door on the right and looked inside. He called again, but there was no answer.

Laura coughed and ran to the opposite door. "Anna May, are you in here?" She scanned the empty bunks, searching past the twisted sheets and blankets, but no one was there.

Smoke stung her eyes, and the alarm bell continued to ring, making her feel as if her head would explode with the dreadful noise. She bent low, trying to stay beneath the stinging haze and hurried down the passageway, checking each cabin.

She yanked open the door to the last cabin, tore the blankets from the beds, and bent down to look underneath. All she found was a stray stocking and a rumpled handkerchief.

Tears flooded her eyes. *Where is she, Lord? Please help us find her!*

Andrew dashed back into the passageway and met Laura in the doorway to the last cabin.

She looked up at him, her throat burning. "She's not here!"

Deep lines creased his forehead as he looked past her into the empty room. "We have to go back up on deck. Maybe she's with one of the other groups and we just didn't see her."

Laura spun around and searched the empty passageway once more. Her chest ached so much she could barely pull in a breath. She couldn't go up on deck and give up her search!

The lights flickered, and the alarm bell suddenly stopped.

Laura stilled, staring at Andrew. "What does that mean?"

Andrew looked up at the lights. "Maybe the fire burnt through the alarm system."

"Or it could mean they have the fire under control, and they—"

Andrew held up his hand. "Wait! Listen!"

Laura turned, straining to catch the sound Andrew had heard. A soft whimper reached her ears, and she gasped. "Anna May!"

Andrew took off toward the opposite end of the passageway, and Laura hurried after him. The soft cries led them to the stairway.

"She must be under here." Andrew pushed aside a rolling cart filled with towels and cleaning supplies and looked beneath the steps.

Laura hovered close behind him. She spotted Anna May and bit her lip. The frightened little girl was curled up on the floor, clutching her knees to her chest and hiding her face in the folds of her nightgown.

Andrew leaned closer and laid his hand on her shoulder. "It's all right, Anna May."

Laura knelt beside him. "We're here now. You don't have to be afraid."

Anna May looked up through red-rimmed eyes. Tears flowed down her cheeks.

"What happened, sweetheart? Why didn't you

come up with us?" Laura kept her tone soft, not wanting to upset her any further.

"I had to go to the WC, and when I came back, everyone was gone." Her chin trembled, and her tears overflowed again.

Laura pulled Anna May into her arms and patted her back. "There now, everything will be all right."

Anna May leaned back to look up at Laura. "That bell was so loud."

Laura nodded, then glanced at Andrew. The alarm might have stopped, but they still needed to rejoin their group and find out what was happening.

He turned to Anna May. "We have to go up on deck. How about I give you a lift?"

The little girl sniffed and nodded. Andrew scooped her up and carried her toward the steps as though she weighed nothing.

Laura's heart warmed as she watched him climb the stairs with Anna May in his arms. She couldn't help but admire the tender way he held the little girl and spoke softly to her. Had she finally met a man who was truly kind and caring, one who might even come to have a special place in her heart?

She stifled a groan and looked away. What a foolish thought! Andrew Frasier was a wealthy gentleman, a solicitor, and the future heir of Bolton. She was a working-class woman with little money and no social standing. She had no hope of a future with him, and she had better put that idea out of her mind before she embarrassed herself and him. She needed to focus her thoughts on her girls and protecting them from the dangers ahead.

Would the fire rage out of control and force them to climb aboard lifeboats and set out to sea? A shiver traveled down her back, and she slowed as she climbed the last flight of stairs.

Andrew glanced over his shoulder at her. "Are you all right?"

What could she say? Her life had turned upside down, and she had no idea what would happen tonight or in the future. But Andrew had cared enough to help her search for Anna May . . . and maybe he would do the same to help her find her siblings once they reached Canada.

She met his gaze. "Yes. I'm fine." Lifting her skirt, she climbed the last few steps to the promenade deck, then pushed open the door for Andrew. He passed through, and she walked beside him as he carried Anna May back to their emergency station.

12

Katie dunked the heavy pot into the lukewarm dishwater and scrubbed at the sticky ring of sauce stuck to the inside. A strand of her hair fell forward into her eyes. She sighed and used her shoulder to push it off her sweaty face.

She'd been up since six that morning doing an endless list of chores given to her by Mrs. O'Leary, Dr. and Mrs. Richardson's cook and housekeeper. The old woman followed her around all day, looking over her shoulder and scolding her for not working fast enough or doing things the way she wanted them done, though she rarely bothered to explain the tasks ahead of time.

She'd been at the Richardsons' home for five days, but it felt much longer than that. She still wasn't used to the work, and her back and legs ached. And it was no wonder after she'd spent hours sweeping, mopping, dusting, changing bed linens, and washing clothes and hanging them out to dry. And every day the list of chores seemed to grow longer. No matter how quickly she worked, there was no hope of finishing everything they asked her to do.

She glanced at the clock on the wall and blew out a deep breath. It was almost eight thirty. The family was just finishing dinner. She had at least another hour of work before she'd be done in the kitchen and allowed to eat something. Then she could finally set up her cot in the pantry where she slept.

Mrs. O'Leary walked in from the dining room carrying a tray of dirty plates and silverware and set it on the counter next to the sink. "Hurry up with those dishes. I don't want to stay in this kitchen all night."

"Yes ma'am." Katie slowed her scrubbing and glanced over her shoulder at the nearly empty serving platters on the worktable. Her stomach contracted, and her mouth watered. The lamb roast was all gone, but a few potatoes and green beans were still left. If only she could take a break from the dishes and have something to eat.

"Stop staring at that food! You'll get nothing to eat until those dishes are done and the kitchen is clean." The old woman's mouth puckered as she glared at Katie. "Do you hear me, girl?"

"Yes ma'am." Katie focused on the pot again and continued scrubbing. Her fingers stung from the harsh soap and steel wool scrubber.

Mrs. O'Leary huffed and sank down on the stool at the end of the worktable. The wooden stool squeaked from her bulky weight. "I don't know why the doctor didn't bring home an older girl or at least one who was stronger and could do a decent day's work."

Katie clenched her jaw and rinsed the heavy

273

pot. She was doing the best she could. It wasn't her fault she was only fourteen and not used to working from dawn until late at night.

Mrs. Richardson walked into the kitchen, and Mrs. O'Leary jumped up from the stool. "The doctor would like his coffee in the library." She shifted her snooty gaze from the cook to Katie. "Goodness, girl, haven't you finished those dishes yet?"

"No ma'am. I mean . . . I'll be done soon."

"I hope so." She lifted her hand to her forehead. "I have a headache. I need you to go upstairs and put the children to bed."

Katie gasped and dropped the heavy pot on the counter. It banged hard and rolled off onto the floor. She scrambled to pick it up, but she was not quick enough.

"You clumsy girl!" Mrs. O'Leary slapped Katie across the arm.

Katie cried out and jumped back.

"Pick it up! And if that pot is dented, I'll give you a whipping you won't forget!"

Mrs. Richardson rubbed her forehead and sighed. "Goodness, Mrs. O'Leary. Is she always this clumsy? How do you put up with her?"

"It's a trial, that's for sure and certain. I've never met such a lazy girl."

Katie thumped the pot onto the counter, her face flaming. "I am not lazy! I've done everything you've asked the best I can."

Mrs. Richardson strode forward and grabbed Katie's arm. "That is enough! I will not listen to disrespectful talk!" She leaned close, her hot breath smelling like the garlic they'd used on the lamb roast. "All of you home children are alike— willful, disobedient, and ungrateful! Now dry your hands and go upstairs with the children."

"But I haven't had my dinner yet."

Mrs. Richardson's eyes flashed. "And you will not have any dinner if you continue to argue with me! Now do as I say!" She squeezed Katie's arm hard, then dropped her hold and marched out of the kitchen.

Katie stared after her, the woman's stinging words ringing in her ears.

"Well, don't just stand there." Mrs. O'Leary waved toward the door. "Go upstairs!"

"Please." Katie pressed her hand to her empty stomach. "Couldn't I just have something to eat first?"

Mrs. O'Leary lowered her gray, bushy eyebrows. "No, you may not! And no more talk about eating until you do as Mrs. Richardson says and put those children to bed! Go on, off with you!"

Katie trudged out of the kitchen and climbed the back stairs, her empty stomach clawing at her backbone. When would this terrible day end?

The children's voices rang out from the rooms up above. She walked down the hall and looked through the doorway of the boys' bedroom. Ned, John, Fred, and little Timmy were jumping on their beds, laughing and swinging pillows at each other.

A tremor raced down Katie's back. If Mrs. Richardson came upstairs and saw what the boys were doing, Katie would be the one blamed for their wild antics. "Boys, your mother said it's time to get ready for bed." She used her strongest voice, but they didn't even look her way. Instead, the pillow fight grew wilder and louder.

"Please, you have to settle down!"

"We can't hear you." Thirteen-year-old Ned sent her a wicked grin. "You'll have to yell louder than that." He was heavier and taller than Katie, and he never listened to a word she said. With a wild shout, he jumped from one bed to the next and tumbled into his youngest brother, knocking four-year-old Timmy onto the floor. The little boy hit his head and let out a loud cry.

Fred and John dropped their pillows, jumped down, and circled around Timmy. "Are you all right, Tim?" Fred leaned closer and laid his hand on his younger brother's back.

Timmy lay on the floor, facedown, his legs sprawled, howling like he was dying. He rolled over and looked up at them with tears streaming down his red face.

Katie knelt beside him. "Where are you hurt, Timmy?" She brushed his sweaty brown hair away from his forehead and felt the lump. A goose egg was starting to swell there.

"Ow!" The little boy shoved her hand away. "Don't touch me!"

Katie pulled her hand back, and Fred and John glared at her.

"Get away from my brother!" Ned jumped down and shoved Katie's shoulder. She toppled over and landed on her backside.

Five-year-old Lucy and seven-year-old Alice looked in from the doorway.

Ned glared at them. "Go away! You girls aren't allowed in here!"

"What happened?" Alice walked into the room. "Why is Timmy crying?"

"That's none of your business! Go on! Get out of here!"

Alice's cheeks flushed pink. She grabbed Lucy's hand and stalked across the room. "You hurt Timmy! I'm going to tell Mother on you!"

Ned grabbed Alice by the shoulders. "You better not or you'll be sorry!"

"Let go of me, or I'm going to tell on you!" Alice tried to wiggle free, but Ned's grip was too strong. Timmy continued to wail from his spot on the floor.

Katie jumped up. She had to put a stop to all this before Dr. or Mrs. Richardson came upstairs. "Let go of Alice!"

The older boy grabbed Alice around the waist

and lifted her up off her feet. "I don't have to listen to you. She's my sister. I can do what I want with her."

Alice cried and squirmed, kicking her dangling feet. "Put me down!"

Katie grabbed hold of Alice's legs and tried to wrestle her out of Ned's grip. The little girl's cries rose to a piercing wail.

Dr. Richardson stomped through the doorway, his eyes ablaze. "What is going on?"

Ned let go of Alice, and his little sister fell to the floor, taking Katie with her. Ned pointed an accusing finger at Katie. "She was hurting Alice, and she pushed Timmy off the bed!"

Katie's mouth fell open. "I did not! You're the one who grabbed Alice. And you knocked Timmy off, not me!"

"Get up off the floor!" Dr. Richardson pointed his shaking finger at Katie. "I knew the minute we turned our backs you would lash out at my children. You can never trust a home child!"

Katie rose, her legs trembling. "I didn't hurt Alice. I promise, I was just—"

Dr. Richardson sliced his hand through the air, cutting off her words. "I never should've taken you in! You're more trouble than you're worth!"

Katie blinked and stared at him. How could he say such awful things?

"We're done with you!" He grabbed her by the arm and dragged her toward the door. "First thing tomorrow morning, you're going back to the home."

"But it's not my fault! The boys wouldn't listen. Ned was the one who knocked Timmy off the bed, and he's the one who grabbed Alice."

The doctor's face grew mottled. "Liar!" He lifted his hand and slapped Katie across the face.

She gasped and fell back, her cheek stinging.

"That will teach you to speak evil of my children! You're nothing but a street rat! And I will not have you polluting our home with your wicked ways!" He shoved her in the direction of the back stairs. "Go pack your trunk! And don't let me hear one more word from you tonight."

She stumbled down the hall, a sob rising in her throat. How could he be so cruel? She had tried so hard to please him and his wife, but it was impossible. Now she would have to go back to the home and carry their bad report with her. She'd probably be reprimanded there as well.

Swallowing back her tears, she started down the stairs. *Oh, Father, this is too much to bear. I'm so tired and worn out. I've tried to do what's right, but it doesn't matter. They don't want me.*

A terrible wave of homesickness rolled over Katie, and tears coursed down her cheeks. What Dr. Richardson said wasn't true, and he never should've struck her. No one should be treated so unkindly even if they were an orphan and a home child. That didn't make them evil. What a terrible thing to say!

She didn't bother going back to the kitchen. Mrs. O'Leary wouldn't give her anything to eat, not after she heard what happened upstairs. She entered the pantry and unfolded her cot in the corner. The old pillow they'd given her was nothing more than a flour sack stuffed with rags. She took it down from the shelf, then shook out the old stained blanket and laid it and the pillow on the cot.

She lifted her hand to her hot, throbbing cheek and gently ran her fingers across the tender spot. She could fetch a cool cloth from the kitchen, but then she would have to face Mrs. O'Leary, and she didn't want to risk being told she had to finish the dishes and clean the kitchen. That could wait until morning.

She stilled and replayed Dr. Richardson's words. Tomorrow morning he was taking her back to the home. She would leave this house, and she wouldn't have to answer to Dr. and Mrs. Richardson or Mrs. O'Leary anymore. Maybe it was a good thing they were sending her back. The next family might be kinder, and they might even have a girl close to her age who could be her friend. She bit her lip, and another round of tears filled her eyes.

Oh, to have a friend would be so heavenly. It

wouldn't be the same as being with Garth, Grace, and Laura, but a friend would help ease her loneliness and partially fill her longing for her family.

Thoughts of Garth and Grace made her heart ache even more. What had happened to them? Were they happy in their new homes, or were they suffering the same kind of harsh treatment Katie had received at the Richardsons'?

Dear Father, please watch over them and keep them safe. Help me find out where they've been sent. If I could only have a letter and know they're well cared for, I'd be so relieved.

Her prayer rose and faded away like mist rising off the river. She sighed, slipped out of her clothes, and pulled her nightgown over her head as quickly as she could. It was cold in the pantry, so she left her stockings on and climbed onto the cot.

Pulling the blanket up to her chin, she closed her eyes and thought of her family and home in London. She could picture Garth and Grace, but when she tried to recall Mum, Dad, and Laura, their images were a little fuzzy. A surge of stinging sadness filled her.

She must never forget her family and who she truly was. No matter where she was sent or how long they were apart, one day she would find her brother and sister and they would make their way home.

• • •

Andrew strode down the promenade deck past the first-class lounge with Laura beside him and a little treasure in his arms. Even in the dim lantern light, several girls from Hughes saw him coming and jumped up. When he came closer and they realized he carried Anna May, a cheer rose from the group. Rose Carson sent him a grateful smile and hurried toward them.

He carefully lowered Anna May to the deck as her friends called out to her and gathered around. Some patted her on the back, and others bent to ask how she had become separated from them. Rose knelt and gave Anna May a tender hug.

Laura watched Rose and the girls with a soft smile on her lips. Earlier that evening, when she'd confessed why she was using a false name, he'd wondered if she had accepted her position only to gain free passage to Canada, but her true character had shone through tonight. She cared deeply about every one of these girls, and he regretted questioning her commitment to them.

She glanced up at him. The soft glow of the lantern light reflected in her eyes. "Thank you," she said softly. "I'm grateful for your help."

He stilled, caught by her gaze. Was that gratitude reflected there or something more? Pleasing warmth rose in his chest. "I'm glad Anna May is safely back where she belongs."

Her steady gaze remained on him as though

she was searching past his words to understand his thoughts. He wished they had time to talk privately and he could learn more about her and her family and the events that had separated them. Her actions tonight had made him more certain he wanted to help her search for her siblings. But first he had to convince her to trust him and drop the charade.

Henry walked toward them from the other end of the deck, holding up a lantern to light his way. Rose met him, and they spoke quietly for a moment. Then they both walked over to join Laura and Andrew.

Henry lowered his voice, his gaze intent. "I've spoken to a crewman. He told me the fire is in the boiler room."

Laura shot a questioning glance at Andrew.

Andrew turned to his friend. "Can they get it under control?"

"So far they've managed to keep it from spreading, but one of the boilers has been destroyed. There are three others, and there's still a chance they can put out the fire and save those."

Rose lifted her hand to her heart. "So, we won't need to abandon ship?"

"It doesn't look like it, but we won't know for sure until the fire is completely under control and they can assess the damage."

Rose nodded, and her worried glance shifted to

the huddled children sitting around them. "I'm concerned about the girls. The temperature is dropping, and with this wind it feels even colder."

Henry nodded. "I've asked one of the stewards to bring us some blankets. He assured me he'd do what he could."

Rose peered up at Henry. "Thank you. That was very kind."

"I want to do whatever I can for you . . . and for the girls. I'd like to speak to them if I may."

"About the fire?"

"I'll mention that, but mainly I want to encourage them and pray for them, with your permission of course."

A warm smile lit Rose's face. "That would be most appreciated." She turned toward the girls and lifted her hand. "Girls, look up here, please."

The girls quieted and turned toward Rose.

"I want to introduce Mr. Henry Dowd. He has asked to speak to you, and I'd like you to give him your full attention."

Henry stepped up next to Rose. "Thank you, Miss Carson." He turned his gaze on the girls.

Andrew's jaw tightened as he looked at their young, upturned faces. Most had already faced great losses that put them in a position to emigrate to Canada, and now they were spending a cold night on the deck of a ship with the threat of the fire on their minds. If he believed in luck, he would say they had little. But through

Henry's friendship and example, Andrew's faith had grown stronger. Now he believed God had not forgotten any of them, and He was unfolding His plan for each of their lives even through this tragic series of events.

And with that belief, a strong conviction filled his mind. He must do everything in his power to see these girls were safely conducted to Canada, where they could begin new lives and enjoy all God had planned for them.

Henry waited until every eye was on him. "I want to commend each of you for your quick action and bravery tonight. It's no small matter to hear an alarm, don a life jacket, follow directions without question, then spend time up on deck on a cold night like this."

Some of the girls smiled, and others exchanged glances with their friends.

"I know some of you may feel frightened by what has happened tonight. That is natural, and there is no need to be ashamed of those feelings. We all go through times when we feel afraid. And when we do, we can ask the Lord for faith to trust Him and help us overcome those fears.

"He loves each one of you, and He has promised to send His angels to watch over you. His Spirit is also with us to comfort us and remind us of the wonderful promises in God's Word."

Rose clasped her hands beneath her chin as she listened to Henry. It seemed his friend had won the respect and admiration of the kind escort.

"I want to share one of those promises with you now. It comes from the book of Isaiah. I memorized it when I was young, and it's been a great help to me." Henry paused a moment, then scanned the girls' faces once more. " 'Fear thou not; for I am with thee: be not dismayed; for I am thy God: I will strengthen thee; yea, I will help thee; yea, I will uphold thee with the right hand of my righteousness.' " He lowered his head for a moment, letting those words settle in, then began again. "When I remember God is with me and has promised to give me strength, I know I can face anything that will come my way."

Laura watched Henry with careful attention, emotion shifting across her features. Andrew wished he knew what she was thinking. Did his friend's words give her courage and comfort, or was there more Andrew ought to say to her?

Henry looked around the group once more. "I'd like to lead you all in a prayer. Please bow your heads and close your eyes."

Andrew lowered his head, his throat tightening. They were facing a dangerous night, but the Lord was near.

"Dear heavenly Father," Henry began, "we come to You tonight and ask You to watch over us and keep us safe. Please help those fighting the fire to put it out quickly. Thank You that You are always with us and that You have promised to give us Your help and strength. Thank You that we don't have to be afraid but can entrust ourselves into Your care and know You will do what is best for us. Help each of us to put our full faith and trust in You tonight and in the days ahead. We are grateful You hear our prayers, and we can depend on You to comfort and strengthen us. I pray these things in the name of Jesus Christ, our Lord. Amen."

A sense of peace seemed to settle over the group. And as they lifted their heads, Andrew could see it reflected in the girls' faces.

A steward rolled a cart piled high with gray wool blankets out the door of the first-class lounge. Henry called the adults together. They passed out blankets to the girls and encouraged them to wrap up and sit close together. As they finished distributing the blankets, Henry gave the last one to Rose, his hand resting on hers for a moment. She looked up and thanked him. Henry kept his eyes on her as she settled on the deck close to some of the girls and then took his seat not far from her.

Andrew couldn't help smiling as he observed their interaction. It seemed the events of this night had helped their acquaintance grow into a friendship. Would the same be true for him and Laura? He turned and searched for her.

She moved through the group of girls, tucking

blankets tighter around some and kissing others on the head as she reassured them. Several of the girls huddled together and leaned on each other. A few of the younger girls had already fallen asleep. Laura checked on each one and made sure all of them were well covered.

Andrew's appreciation deepened as he watched her. Finally, when they were all settled, she took her own blanket and found a spot by the wall of the ship at the edge of her group.

He picked up his blanket and walked over to her. "May I join you?" His request sounded a bit formal for their current situation, but he didn't just want to plop down beside her without saying something.

She smiled and nodded. "Of course."

He wrapped the blanket around his shoulders and settled in on the hard deck next to her.

She tugged her blanket up a bit higher and shifted slightly away. Her movements made it clear she wanted to keep a respectful distance between them. He'd meant only to block the wind and provide some added warmth, but he supposed she wanted to guard her reputation even on a night like this.

He leaned back and looked out across the railing to the dark sea beyond. The cool, salty breeze ruffled his hair, and he wished he'd taken time to grab his hat. The ship dipped and then rose, still moving ahead at a slow pace. *Please,*

Lord, keep us all safe tonight. He pulled in a slow deep breath and reminded himself of the promise and prayer Henry had spoken over them. The sense of calm returned, and he lifted his eyes to the sky.

Laura looked up as well. "I can't believe how many stars you can see out here at night."

"It's quite different than the usual view of the night sky in London."

"Hmm, yes, it is and very beautiful." Her voice sounded soft and wistful.

He glanced her way, watching as she scanned the glittering expanse.

"Is that the Milky Way?" She gazed up at the broad stripe of stars cloaked in misty clouds, arcing across the sky.

"Yes, I believe it is."

"I've read about it but never seen it so clearly before."

The lantern light cast shadows over her face, but it highlighted her slender straight nose and her softly rounded cheeks. Her wavy blond hair had come loose and now tumbled over her shoulders in an appealing manner. She was a lovely young woman, even lovelier than the starry night sky.

He blinked and shifted his gaze away. Where had that thought come from? He had better keep his mind on track and not let himself get carried away by thoughts that were most likely inspired by the dramatic events of the evening. Still, he couldn't help but appreciate her attractive appearance and her devotion to her family and the girls in her care. The fact that she was a former member of the Bolton staff should've been enough to squelch thoughts of how appealing she was, but somehow it didn't.

"I'd like to hear more about your family and what caused your siblings to be separated from you and your mother."

She glanced his way. "Why would you want to know that?"

"I need to understand the situation if I'm going to help you in your search."

She sat up straighter. "You're going to help me?"

He considered his words carefully. "I'd like to, but first I want to know the background and understand what happened."

"All right." She sounded eager now. "Where shall I start?"

"Wherever you'd like."

She thought for a moment. "I suppose our troubles began about two years ago when my father died from injuries sustained in a rail accident. That's when everything changed for our family."

"I'm sorry for your loss."

"Thank you. My father was a good man— hardworking and kind. But he didn't expect to leave us so soon, and there wasn't much money set aside. That put us in a difficult situation, and we all had to find work. My mum is an excellent seamstress, so she took a position at a dressmaker's shop. My brother, Garth, worked as a delivery boy for a butcher after school, and my sister Katie and I helped Mum with the sewing. But even with all our efforts, that didn't bring in enough money to cover our expenses.

"So it was decided I should go into service. I found a maid's position, working for a family in London, but . . ." She stopped and looked down. "I had to leave there a few months later, and that's when I came to Bolton and began working for your family."

Her hesitation and serious tone stirred his curiosity. "Why did you leave your position in London?"

Her expression fell, and she looked away. "I'd rather not say."

Had she done something dishonest or improper and been dismissed? He hoped not, but he had to ask. "If I'm going to represent you, I need to know your character is not in question."

She shot him a hot look. "It was not my character that caused the problem—the opposite in fact."

"What do you mean?"

She pressed her lips together for a few seconds, then said, "A young man came to stay at the house where I was working. He was their nephew, and he . . ." Her voice faltered, and even in the lantern light he could see the pain in her eyes. "He was not a gentleman. I had to leave for my own safety."

His anger surged, and he had to swallow before he could speak. "I'm sorry."

"It's not your fault."

"No, but I resent any man who would use his power or position to threaten a woman or treat her with disrespect. Women ought to be protected, no matter what their class or station, not misused or made to feel afraid for their safety."

She turned her piercing gaze on him. "If you truly believe that, then you ought to hire a different assistant."

He frowned. "What?"

"I went to your office in London. You weren't there, but I met your assistant."

"You mean Jonathan Phillips?"

"I don't remember his name, but I know his type. He's not an honorable man."

Confusing thoughts clashed in his mind. "You went to our office in London and our assistant was . . . inappropriate?"

"Exactly. And if I hadn't run away, I'm afraid he would've done much worse."

Her reply hit him like a blow to his chest. "I'm so sorry. I do apologize." He shook his head. "I knew Phillips was lazy and deceptive, but I had no idea he would threaten our female clients."

Andrew set his jaw. "I'll speak to Henry and see that Phillips is dismissed as soon as we return to London."

Laura pulled in a sharp breath. "I don't want him to lose his job. Can't you just speak to him and make him understand what he did was wrong?"

Andrew shook his head. "It won't be his first reprimand. Even with the threat of losing his position, I doubt he'll change his ways." He thought for a moment. "When was this?"

"After I learned my brother and sisters had been put on the list for Canada, I knew I needed legal help. You had given me your card, so I went to your office hoping to see you, but . . ."

"I was out, and you had to deal with our wretched assistant."

She nodded, then stared out at the ocean.

"But we're here together now. Please continue." He settled back and listened while she relayed what had happened after she arrived in London to help her mother, then how she had followed her siblings from London to Liverpool.

He grew more concerned as she told him how all her efforts to visit her siblings had been blocked. Her pleas to straighten out the mistake had been ignored as well.

"So, that's why I'm bound for Canada. I have to find my brother and sisters and bring them home."

He gave a thoughtful nod. "All right. Let me speak to Henry—"

"No!" She leaned toward Andrew. "You mustn't tell him."

"But we're partners in the investigation. I can't keep something like this from Henry."

"Helping me and my family won't interfere with your investigation. It's a separate matter. Please promise me you'll keep what I've told you in confidence, at least until we reach Canada and I find out where my brother and sisters have been placed."

He didn't like the idea of withholding the matter from his friend, but she'd set an end point to keeping the secret. He could live with that. "All right. I won't say anything to him now, but I hope you'll come to trust us both to do what's best for you and your family."

13

Katie set her jaw and stared straight ahead as Dr. Richardson pulled the open carriage to a stop in front of the Belleville receiving home. She'd stayed there only one night, and she barely remembered the place.

The doctor climbed down without a word and started toward the front gate. When Katie didn't follow, he stopped and looked over his shoulder. "Well, don't just sit there like a stone statue. Climb down."

She thought of refusing, but if she did, he'd just come and grab her and he wouldn't be gentle about it. She hopped to the ground and trudged up the walk, toward the huge white house with black shutters and a wraparound porch.

What would they say when the doctor announced he was returning her to the home? What would happen to her then? Her stomach swirled, and she put her hand over her mouth and swallowed hard. *Please, Lord, don't let me lose my breakfast.*

When they reached the front door, he turned and gripped her shoulder. "Keep your mouth closed, and don't even think about telling any more of your lies. Do you hear me?"

Katie lifted her chin and looked away, the

memory of his stinging slap silencing her. There was no point in arguing with him now.

He opened the door without knocking, stepped inside, and strode down the front hall. Katie followed him, glancing around and trying to remember what she could of her first and only night there.

A middle-aged woman in a black skirt and white blouse stepped into the hall from one of the rooms on the right. Her eyebrows rose as she saw them approach. "Good day, sir."

"Are you the one in charge here?"

She nodded. "I am Mrs. Woodward. How can I help you?"

"I'm bringing this girl back." He jerked his thumb toward Katie. "We don't want her in our home any longer." He turned away.

Mrs. Woodward's eyes widened. "Wait, sir! What is your name?"

He stopped and looked back. "Dr. Thomas Richardson."

"And the girl's name?"

He shook his head. "I can't recall. You'll have to ask her."

Mrs. Woodward shifted her concerned gaze to Katie. "Young lady, what is your name?"

"Katherine McAlister, ma'am."

The woman nodded. "Dr. Richardson, please come into my office so we can discuss this matter."

He lifted his hand. "I don't have time for a

discussion. I have patients to tend to this morning."

"I'm only asking for a few minutes of your time. Certainly you can—"

"My mind is made up! The girl is obstinate, and she can't do a decent day's work. She was disrespectful to my wife, and she can't care for the children. She's no use to us."

"Some children just need a little time to settle in and—"

His expression hardened into a scowl. "I never should've taken in a home child. They're all tainted and set on sin. It's in their blood."

Mrs. Woodward pulled back. "Dr. Richardson, surely as a medical man you know a home child is no different than any other. They simply need instruction and discipline so they can become productive members of society. That's part of the responsibility you take on when you accept one of our children into your home."

"I don't have time to reform her, and I'm not inclined to believe it's possible." He turned and strode off down the hall.

"Dr. Richardson, there are papers to sign!"

He walked out the front door and slammed it behind him.

Mrs. Woodward closed her eyes and lifted her hand to her forehead. "My goodness. What a way to start the day." She sighed and looked at Katie again. "Well, young lady, it seems you've been released from a hard situation."

Katie blinked, surprised the woman didn't scold her.

"I'm afraid some people have their minds set against home children, and there's nothing you can say or do to change them." She laid her hand on Katie's shoulder. "What he said about you being tainted is not true. I hope you won't take it to heart." She gave Katie's shoulder a gentle pat. "Come with me into my office and we'll see what's to be done for you."

Katie followed Mrs. Woodward and took the chair she indicated in front of her desk.

The woman stopped at a filing cabinet and pulled open the top drawer. "You said your name is McAlister?"

"Yes ma'am, Katherine McAlister, but I'm called Katie."

Mrs. Woodward thumbed through the files. "Here we are." She pulled out a plain brown folder and took a seat at her desk. With one more glance at Katie, she opened the file and adjusted her spectacles.

Katie sat on the edge of her chair, watching Mrs. Woodward as she leafed through several papers. So far, the woman had been kind, but she had no idea what would happen next.

Mrs. Woodward looked up with a slight smile. "The staff at Hughes and Grangeford say you have good character and are skilled in household chores and sewing. They believed you would do well here."

"I tried to do what Dr. and Mrs. Richardson asked, but I'm not used to working from early morning until late at night and managing six unruly children besides."

Mrs. Woodward's eyebrows rose. "That's what they asked you to do?"

"Yes ma'am. They have a cook who is also their housekeeper, but she would rather give me orders than do any of the work herself."

Mrs. Woodward lowered her chin and looked at Katie over the top of her spectacles. "Were you obstinate and disrespectful to Dr. and Mrs. Richardson or their housekeeper?"

Katie glanced away and bit her lip. "I did ask questions when I didn't know how to do something, and I cried and said some things I shouldn't have when they wouldn't give me anything to eat for lunch or dinner."

Mrs. Woodward's brow creased. "They withheld meals from you?"

"Yes ma'am, several times."

"That is not an acceptable means of discipline." The woman pursed her lips and flipped through a few more papers. Finally, she closed the file and looked at Katie. "You've had a difficult beginning, but I'm sure we can find a more suitable placement for you." The kindness in her voice made Katie's throat tighten.

Mrs. Woodward wasn't going to reprimand or punish her. She was going to find her a new home with people who would treat her kindly. "Thank you, ma'am." A thought struck, and she straightened. "Could I stay with my sister Grace? We came over from England together, but she was sent off with another family."

Mrs. Woodward sent her a sympathetic look. "Let me see." She returned to the filing cabinet, pulled out another file, and scanned the papers within.

With a sigh and a sad shake of her head, she placed the file back in the drawer. "I'm sorry, Katie." Mrs. Woodward returned to the desk. "The family who took your sister only wanted one child. They plan to adopt her. They're not looking for a domestic."

Katie sagged back in the chair, painful disappointment washing over her again. When would she see her sister?

"Now, don't be discouraged. I'm sure we can find a place for you." She sorted through a stack of papers on the corner of her desk and pulled out one near the bottom. "Here we are. This may be just the answer we're looking for."

Katie lifted her gaze to meet Mrs. Woodward's, but she had a hard time feeling hopeful.

"Reverend Paxton from Roslin wrote to us about a family in need of a domestic." Mrs. Woodward held the letter out a bit farther and squinted. "Mr. Howard Hoffman and his wife, Ella, live on a farm north of town. Mrs. Hoffman has a new baby and two other young children to care for." She smiled and looked up. "I'm sure you would be a great help to a young mother. And with only two children to look after, that would be a lighter workload than you were carrying at the Richardsons'."

Katie clasped her hands together as Mrs. Woodward read the description of the new family. She'd never lived on a farm. She hadn't even visited one. But she had helped her mum care for Grace since she was born, and watching two children sounded easier than trying to manage six while doing all the household chores.

"I think the Hoffmans would be a good situation for you. Don't you agree?"

Katie shifted on her chair. What choice did she have? She had to go somewhere, and this family sounded like they needed help. She looked up. "Yes ma'am."

"All right. I'll contact the reverend and make the arrangements."

"Thank you, ma'am."

"Now, Katie, you must promise to be respectful and obedient and make every effort to be a good help to this new family."

"I'll do my best."

"Very good." She rose from her chair. "Come

301

with me and we'll get you settled here for the time being."

Katie stood and followed Mrs. Woodward out of her office.

As soon as the woman stepped into the hall, she turned. "What about your trunk?"

"Dr. Richardson brought it with us."

"I hope he left it for you. If not, I'll send someone to his house to collect it."

Mrs. Woodward walked down the hall and out the front door. Katie hurried after her and spotted her trunk at the bottom of the porch steps. Closing her eyes, she sent off a prayer of thanks. That trunk held all she had left in the world . . . except for the cross necklace Mum had given her and her fading memories of her family and home.

Laura snuggled down deeper in her blanket, but she couldn't ignore the gentle rise and fall of the ship or the cool, salty breeze tickling her nose. The sound of water whooshing against the side of the ship finally stirred her from sleep. She opened one eye and peeked out at the early morning sky. Soft pink clouds floated on the horizon over the gray-green sea.

All around her, the girls slept sprawled out on the deck. She sat with her back to the wall of the ship, leaning against something soft but solid. She glanced to the right and stilled. She was leaning against Andrew Frasier's arm and shoulder.

Her face warmed, and the events of last evening came back to her mind, bringing her fully awake. The ship was still moving westward. That must mean the crew had brought the fire under control. If that was true, why hadn't they sounded the all clear and let them return to their cabins?

The last thing she remembered was listening to Andrew talk about his travels in Italy as they watched the full moon rise over the silvery sea. She must have fallen asleep after that and sagged against him, and he'd been kind enough to let her stay.

If she moved now, she might wake him, so she sat still and studied his face. His deep-set eyes were closed, and his lips were slightly parted. His slow, steady breathing assured her he was sound asleep. Brown stubble shaded his strong chin and upper lip, giving him a roguish look, quite different than his usual clean-shaven appearance.

A smile lifted the corners of her mouth. There was no denying he was handsome, and last night he'd proven he was also a man of courage and conviction. In spite of the danger, he had not given up searching for Anna May until he found her and carried her to safety. Then he'd listened to more of Laura's family's story and agreed to keep her secret for now. He'd even promised to help her search for her siblings. All those actions stirred her heart and drew her to him.

But a warning traveled through her, and she gave

her head a slight shake. Andrew Frasier might be a caring man who sincerely wanted to help her, but he would never be interested in her in a romantic way. They came from two different worlds, and she must remember that and guard her heart.

Andrew shifted, and his eyes slowly opened.

She pulled in a quick breath and leaned away.

He blinked against the morning light, then focused on her. "Good morning."

"Good morning, Mr. Frasier." She brushed a hand down her wrinkled dress and stifled a groan. She was a rumpled mess.

He chuckled. "I believe in our present circumstances it would be all right for you to call me Andrew."

Her hand stilled, and she looked at him. "I'm not sure that would be proper."

"I don't see why not." He glanced at the blankets pooled around them on the deck. "I hope you'll consider me your friend, especially after the events of last night."

"I do. I just don't want to make any assumptions about our . . . connection."

His mouth tugged up on one side. "No need to worry about that. Please call me Andrew, and with your permission I'll call you Laura unless, of course, we're with others. Then I'll address you as Miss Hopkins, as you've asked."

Her heart warmed. "Thank you. I appreciate your kindness."

He returned her smile. "Of course. That's what any gentleman would do in a situation like this."

"But not every man is a gentleman."

His smile eased. "I'm afraid that's true, but Henry and I will look out for you and do what we can for you and your family."

Before she could reply, footsteps sounded behind her. She turned as a crewman strode up the deck toward them.

"It looks like he has news." Andrew rose and straightened his suit jacket. He extended his hand to her.

Laura hesitated for a split second, then reached out and took hold. He helped her to her feet. Her face flushed, and she averted her gaze. She tugged her skirt into place. Her hair had come undone, and a few strands fell across her face.

"I must look a fright." She lifted her hand and tried to smooth back her hair.

"Not at all. You look lovely." As soon as the words left his mouth, his face turned ruddy, and he shifted his gaze to the approaching crewman.

Henry, Rose, Andrew, and Laura crossed the deck to meet him.

The man's tired face was smudged with soot. "The fire has been put out. You're free to return to your cabins. Breakfast will be delayed until nine o'clock." He started to step away.

But Henry reached for his arm. "Was anyone killed or injured in the fire?"

"No sir. I'm thankful to report we all made it through with just a few minor burns and raw throats."

"Very good. We're glad to hear it. What about damages to the ship?"

Lines creased the weary crewman's forehead. "We lost two of the four boilers. That will slow us down and add three or four days to the trip."

Rose leaned closer. "But the ship is not in danger?"

"No ma'am. The steel plates in the boiler room helped contain the fire to that area. The captain inspected the damage this morning, and he believes we can safely continue the journey."

Rose nodded, looking relieved. "Thank you, and please thank the captain and all those who fought the fire. We're very grateful."

The crewman nodded and continued up the deck to speak to the next group.

Henry glanced at Rose. "This is a wonderful answer to prayer."

"Yes. I'm so relieved." Rose's gaze traveled over the girls. Some were stirring now, and a few sat up and looked their way.

Rose sent them a warm smile. "Good morning, girls. We have very good news. The Lord has answered our prayers, and the fire has been put out. We are released to return to our cabins."

Some of the girls squinted up at her and rubbed their eyes while others woke their friends nearby.

They spent the next few minutes waking the rest of the girls, folding blankets, and gathering the girls into a line.

Andrew stepped up next to Laura. "Shall we help you take the girls down to their cabins?"

"Thank you, but I'm sure we can manage."

Andrew lifted his hand to his bristly jaw. "All right. We'll head back to our cabin and clean up before breakfast." But rather than turning to go, he waited there, watching as she helped the last few girls fold their blankets and move into line.

"Miss Hopkins?"

She turned his way. "Yes?"

"If I'm going to assist you with the . . . *project* we discussed, then it would be helpful to meet with you again to gather some more information."

Pleasant warmth filled her. "All right. That would be fine."

"When would you be free to meet with me?"

She thought for a moment. "I could be free after lunch for an hour or so."

"Shall we meet here on the promenade deck at one thirty?"

She nodded and sent him a smile. "I'll see you then." Her heart lifted as she ushered the last little girl into line, then walked with them inside and started down the stairs. Andrew Frasier had proven his commitment again.

The old conductor walked up the aisle of the train car and nodded to Katie. "Roslin. This stop is Roslin," he called in a singsong voice.

She glanced out the window, looking for a town, but saw only a few scattered buildings. The train's brakes squealed as it slowed to a stop. She rose and collected her travel bag, then made her way to the back of the car.

The conductor opened the door and stepped down. She followed him and looked out across the sagging wooden platform toward the small station building beyond. It was painted gray and had a lone window but looked deserted.

Past the station, she saw a general store, a livery, and a white church with a steeple rising above the buildings around it. Beyond the church were a few other homes and businesses, but not many. Only fourteen miles north of Belleville, Ontario, Roslin was a tired-looking town, much smaller than Belleville and definitely nothing like London. The streets were muddy and rutted, and weeds flourished around the station. Thick trees filled the land on both sides of the tracks leading away from town.

A man dressed in a navy blue uniform and cap walked out of the station. He carried a gray canvas bag and crossed to meet the conductor. "Morning, Hector."

"Morning, James. I have a trunk for the

girl." The conductor nodded toward Katie, then pulled open the door to the baggage car. The two men grunted as they tugged the heavy wooden trunk toward the opening. They lifted it down to the platform, where it landed with a loud thump.

The stationmaster picked up the gray canvas bag he'd set aside and handed it to the conductor. "Here's the outgoing mail."

"We'll take care of it." The conductor tossed it into the baggage car and slid the door closed with a bang. He glanced back at the stationmaster and touched his hat brim. "We'll see you tomorrow."

The stationmaster lifted his hand. "See you then."

The conductor turned and waved toward the engineer as he climbed aboard the last train car. The whistle blew a loud blast. Clouds of steam puffed out as the train slowly pulled away from the station.

Katie watched it go, and an uncomfortable lump lodged in her throat. Every step of this journey took her farther away from home and farther from those she loved. She tried to pull in a deep breath, but her chest felt so tight it was nearly impossible.

The stationmaster turned to Katie. "Morning, young lady. What's your name?"

"Katie McAlister, sir."

"Well, Miss Katie, who is coming for you?"

"Mr. and Mrs. Howard Hoffman." She had memorized their names, hoping that would make her feel as though she were going to stay with friends rather than strangers.

The stationmaster tipped his head and studied her with a slight frown. "You don't sound like you're from 'round here."

"No sir. I'm from London, England."

His eyebrows dipped. "All the way from England?"

"Yes sir."

He lowered his chin and looked at her over the top of his spectacles. "You're not one of those home children, are you?"

Katie paused, considering how to answer. From the look he gave her, it seemed he didn't approve of home children any more than Dr. Richardson did.

Why were people so set against orphans? It wasn't right to look down on someone just because her parents were no longer living.

She straightened her shoulders. "My parents were fine folks, but they passed away. So I've come to Canada to make a new life." That wasn't the whole story, but it was all she was going to tell him.

"So you *are* a home child." He narrowed his eyes. "You say you're going to the Hoffmans'?"

"Yes sir." She had spent the entire train ride trying to imagine what life would be like with this new family and what she might do to please them and make them want to keep her.

He shook his head. "Now that's a shame . . . a real shame."

Katie's face flamed. Was he saying that because she was a home child, or was something wrong with the Hoffmans?

He motioned toward a wooden bench by the door to the station. "You can sit over there and wait for them if you like." After looking her over once more with a slight frown, he walked back toward the station with a shuffling gait.

She sighed, lifted her traveling bag, and followed him across the platform.

Clouds scuttled across the sky, blocking the sun. She pulled her sweater tighter around herself. It wasn't too cool, but she shivered just the same. She took a seat on the hard wooden bench, then lowered her bag to the platform beside her.

She glanced around the deserted station and bit her lip. Why wasn't anyone here to meet her? Had the Hoffmans forgotten she was coming today? What would she do if they never came? She had no money to take the train back to Belleville, and the stationmaster didn't seem to be very sympathetic. She doubted he would help her, but he wouldn't leave her here alone all night, would he?

Closing her eyes, she reached up and laid her hand over her cross necklace beneath the fabric of her dress. Running her fingers over the shape reminded her of Mum's love and strong faith. Mum always told her if she was feeling low, she should count her blessings and it would lift her spirits. This was certainly a good time to remember those words of encouragement.

She opened her eyes, settled back, and listened. Birds called to one another from the trees beyond the tracks. She couldn't see them, but she could enjoy their songs. The sky held some clouds, but it wasn't raining. That was a blessing. Roslin had a lot of nice tall trees and plenty of fresh air. She might even find some wildflowers when she was free to look around.

Best of all—the Lord was with her. She was not alone. That thought brought the most comfort. Surely if He'd brought her here, then He would help her through whatever was coming next.

The sound of horses' hoofbeats, squeaking wagon wheels, and jingling tack sounded off to the right. She turned that way as a horse-drawn wagon rolled around the side of the station.

A stout man with curly blond hair sat up front, and a small blond boy who looked about six or seven sat next to him. The wagon rolled to a stop at the end of the platform, and the man looked her way. He was dressed in a stained blue shirt, brown work trousers, and heavy leather boots. The little boy's face was smudged with dirt, and she could barely tell what color his clothing was because it was so ragged and soiled.

The man studied her, and his eyebrows dipped. "You the girl from Belleville?"

"Yes sir. I'm Katie McAlister." Her voice came out with a slight tremor.

"How old are you?"

"Fourteen."

He grimaced and jerked his thumb toward the wagon. "Climb in back."

She stared at him. He wasn't even going to step down to meet her? How could he expect her to just climb into the back of his wagon and ride away with a man she didn't know? A sense of panic rose in her chest.

He cocked his head. "Well, what are you waiting for?"

"That's . . . that's my trunk." She nodded toward it.

Scowling, he grumbled something she couldn't understand and jumped down from the wagon. He strode across the platform, grabbed the handle on one end, and scowled at her. "Get up and take the other end!"

Katie grabbed her bag, hurried forward, and reached for the opposite handle. The man lifted his side, and Katie strained to raise hers.

"You'll have to do better than that."

She gritted her teeth and tugged harder, raising the trunk a few more inches. He cursed under his breath and set off toward the wagon. His steps were so quick she could hardly keep up. The strap of her traveling bag slipped down her arm and the bag banged against her knees, nearly tripping her.

They reached the wagon, and the man hoisted up his end. Katie tried to lift her side higher, but it was no use. He grunted and shifted his hands toward her side, finally shoving the trunk onto the wagon.

He huffed and wiped his hands on his trouser legs. "What do you have in there, rocks?"

"No sir, just my clothes and a few books."

He shook his head and walked toward the front of the wagon without another word.

Katie gulped. The bed of the wagon was higher than her waist, and she wasn't sure how she could climb up without his help.

He stepped up and took a seat on the front bench, then lifted the reins. The young boy beside him stared at Katie, his blue eyes wide and his mouth hanging open, but he didn't say a word. Dried tracks from his tears ran down his dirty cheeks, making it look like he hadn't washed his face in a week.

Mr. Hoffman looked over his shoulder. "I don't have all day, girl. Get in the wagon."

She bit her lip, tossed her traveling bag in the back, then scanned the side of the wagon, looking for a foothold.

Mr. Hoffman jerked around on the bench. "Land sakes, girl, are you daft? Just step up on the hub of the wheel."

"Yes sir." She gripped the board on the side, stepped up, and climbed into the back of the wagon. There was no bench, so she crawled over to sit against the opposite side. Before she was settled, Mr. Hoffman clicked to the horses, and the wagon jerked and rolled down the road.

Katie lifted her hand to her hat and tugged it down so it wouldn't fly off in the breeze. The wagon rattled over the rough road, shaking her so hard she thought her teeth would surely fall out. She held on tightly to the side, looking ahead and trying to take in her surroundings.

They passed through Roslin in less than two minutes, then traveled down a country road between open fields and patches of shady forest. Her stomach ached from hunger and worry, and she longed for a drink of water. She had no idea how long the trip would take, and she didn't dare ask Mr. Hoffman. He was a fierce-looking man, and she'd already angered him with her heavy trunk and slow response to his order to get in the wagon.

About ten minutes later, the wagon turned off onto a side road. They passed a large barn with faded red paint. Broken-down farming equipment sat in front with tall weeds growing around it. The wagon rolled to a stop beside a run-down two-story house. It looked like it used to be nice, but now the white paint was peeling off the wooden siding and two of the upstairs windows were cracked. Some of the dark green shutters were broken, and a few others hung loose, swinging in the wind. Part of the picket fence in front had fallen down and was overgrown with weeds. Four chickens strutted around in front of the house, clucking and pecking at the dirt.

A dog ran out from behind the house, barking as Mr. Hoffman jumped down from the wagon. The chickens squawked and ran to hide under the porch.

Katie tensed as she watched the black-and-white border collie. But his barking sounded more like a happy greeting than a dangerous threat, and he wagged his tail as he circled around the wagon.

Mr. Hoffman lifted the boy to the ground and gave him a little swat on his backside. "Go on up to the house."

The boy glanced up at Katie with a solemn expression. The dog sniffed his hand, but the boy ignored him and walked toward the house and up the porch steps.

A woman pushed open the screen door and walked out to the front porch. A little girl with blond curly hair held on to her skirt with one hand and sucked her thumb with the other. She looked about three years old. Katie guessed the woman was Mrs. Hoffman, and the little girl must be her daughter.

The woman's light brown hair was tied back, but several straggly pieces hung around her pale, lined face. She carried a baby wrapped in a blanket, but not in the careful, tender way most mothers held their babies. She didn't call out a greeting or smile as her husband approached.

Her sagging shoulders and vacant expression sent a tremor through Katie. What was wrong with Mrs. Hoffman? Why didn't she hold her baby close or say hello?

Mr. Hoffman stopped on the porch and looked back at Katie. "The girl is from the home in Belleville. She'll help you with the children and housework."

The woman stared at Katie with gray, solemn eyes, but she didn't say a word.

Frowning, Mr. Hoffman motioned to Katie. "Come on down out of the wagon."

Her stomach twisted as she climbed over the side. She glanced at her trunk and traveling bag and decided she should leave them there for now. Summoning her courage, she hopped down, walked across the hard-packed dirt, and climbed up the porch steps.

All the while Mrs. Hoffman just stood there watching her with the sleeping baby sagging in her arms.

Katie's mouth felt so dry she could hardly form her words. "Mrs. Hoffman, I'm Katie McAlister."

"Take her, will ya? I got no strength left." She shoved the baby into Katie's arms.

Katie sucked in a quick breath and grabbed hold. She adjusted the baby to a better position and smoothed the blanket away from her face. "What's her name?"

Mrs. Hoffman shook her head. "She's got no name yet."

Katie blinked. "How old is she?"

"Goin' on six weeks. No . . . must be seven or eight weeks by now." Her voice sounded almost as hollow as her vacant eyes. Katie watched her with growing unease. All mothers were tired after bringing a new baby into the family, but this woman's tiredness seemed to run much deeper.

Katie looked down at the baby and ran her hand over her soft head and pale blond hair. She was a beautiful baby, with rosebud lips and long, light brown eyelashes, and her skin was so pale Katie could see the blue veins beneath. Her nose was a little crusty, and so were the corners of her eyes. She needed her face washed almost as much as her brother.

The little girl with the blond curly hair looked out from around her mother's skirt and pulled her thumb out of her mouth. "I'm hungry." She sniffed and rubbed her dirty hand under her runny nose.

Mrs. Hoffman sighed. "Take Daisy inside and give her something to eat."

Katie stared at the woman. "What . . . what shall I fix for her?"

"There's some leftover mush on the stove." The woman pulled her daughter's hand away from her skirt. "Go on now. She'll feed you."

The little girl whimpered and popped her thumb back in her mouth, but when Katie held out her hand, Daisy reached out and took hold.

Mrs. Hoffman sank down onto an old wooden chair on the porch, and her gaze drifted off toward the fields.

Katie's hands were full, and she struggled to open the screen door, but she finally managed. The house was dim, and a bad smell hung in the air. Was that stench rotten potatoes or something worse?

"Daisy, can you show me the way to the kitchen?" Katie tried not to breathe too deeply as the little girl led her toward the back of the house. The awful smell increased with each step she took. When they walked into the kitchen, Katie's stomach dropped and her mouth fell open.

The counter and sink were piled high with dirty dishes. Crusts of bread and greasy bits of meat littered the plates on the table. Boiled-over food had dried on the side of a pot on the stove. Other pots and pans were half-full of burnt food she couldn't even recognize. Big flies buzzed around the room and crawled over the stinking mess.

Lord, help me. I don't even know where to start.

Daisy tugged on her hand. "I'm hungry."

"All right. I'll fix you something in just a minute." Katie looked around for a safe place to lay the sleeping baby. She walked into the pantry and found some towels and an empty crate.

Daisy followed Katie, sucking on her thumb and watching everything she did with wide blue eyes.

"This should make a nice soft bed." Katie arranged the towels in the crate and carefully placed the baby inside. She couldn't leave the baby in the pantry, so she carried the crate back into the kitchen and cleared off the bench by the back door. She set the crate down and watched the baby for a few seconds. Somehow the little one had slept through all the jostling and seemed content.

Katie walked over to the table and scanned the disgusting scene once more. She would have to start there if she was going to feed Daisy. Holding her breath, she scraped and stacked the dirty dishes, then found a clean cloth and wiped off the table.

How could anyone stand to live in such a mess?

Flies crawled in the pot of burnt mush, so she threw it away and washed out the pot the best she could. She found a basket of eggs on top of the pie safe and lowered it for Daisy to see. "Do you like scrambled eggs?"

Daisy nodded, and Katie breathed a sigh of relief. The kitchen still smelled like a rubbish bin, but at least she'd found something the little girl could eat.

She cleared off the stove and stacked the pots and pans on the floor by the sink since there was no more room on the counter. Holding her hand over the stove, she felt the heat and breathed a prayer of thanks. She scrambled two eggs for Daisy and set her up at the table. With the little girl settled, Katie dug through the dishes in the sink, looking for a spoon. But Daisy couldn't wait. She scooped up the eggs with her hands and shoved the food into her mouth.

"Daisy, I'll bring you a spoon as soon as I wash one."

The little girl ignored her and continued eating with her hands, smearing the food around her mouth as she gobbled up the eggs. Hadn't anyone taught her how to use a fork and spoon?

The sound of the wagon caught her attention, and she looked out the open window over the sink. Mr. Hoffman drove past the house, heading toward the barn. Katie watched as his son ran ahead and pulled open the barn door. Had he forgotten about her trunk and traveling bag?

She glanced at Daisy. The little girl had

finished eating and was already climbing down off her chair.

"Come here, Daisy." She wiped the girl's hands and checked on the baby. The little one still slept peacefully in her crate. She took Daisy by the hand and walked out the back door.

The sun had come out and beat down on her shoulders as she followed the dirt path past the outhouse and on toward the barn. When she stepped inside the shady barn, the scent of hay and animals greeted her. The wagon was parked in the open area in the middle, and Mr. Hoffman was unhitching the horses.

He waved her over. "Come on, girl. Let's lift that trunk down."

Katie hesitated. "Shouldn't we take it up to the house?"

"You'll be staying in here, up in the loft."

Katie lifted her gaze and stared up at the loft. It was nothing more than an open second story filled with piles of hay. "You want me to sleep up there?"

"That's right." He looked her way. "You have a problem with that?" His tone carried a subtle threat.

She stiffened. "No sir." What else could she say?

"There's no room for you in the house. We only got two bedrooms, one for me and the missus, and the other for Daisy and Daniel." He tugged the trunk toward the tailgate of the wagon. "Be glad you're sleepin' out here. You won't have to listen to the baby cryin' all night."

She doubted that was the real reason she'd be sleeping in the barn loft, but she wasn't going to argue with him. "How are we going to get the trunk up there?"

"No need. It can stay down here." He nodded toward the opposite end of the trunk. "Grab hold."

She reached for the handle. They hoisted the trunk out of the wagon, carried it across the barn, and set it down against the far wall.

"Now I got work to do. You go back in the house and take care of things there." He turned and strode back to the horses.

"Mr. Hoffman, how do I get up to the loft . . . I mean, when it's time for bed tonight?"

He pointed to the far wall. "You climb up that ladder."

Katie gulped. She'd never liked heights, and climbing a tall ladder like that one was going to take every ounce of courage she possessed. She closed her eyes, feeling the need to pray. But her new surroundings were so strange and shocking that all she could think of was . . . *Father, help me.*

14

Andrew shifted in his chair and glanced up from the notes he was reviewing on children's receiving homes in Ontario, Canada. Henry sat across from him at a writing table in the ship's beautifully furnished library. A few other passengers relaxed in overstuffed chairs and on comfortable couches around the room, reading books and magazines or newspapers that had been brought aboard before they left Liverpool. Glass-enclosed bookshelves filled two walls, and windows looking out on the promenade deck filled another.

Andrew tried to focus on the notes again, but the memory of his conversations with Laura rose and filled his mind. He was committed to helping her, but he wasn't sure how best to go about it. His promise to keep Laura's true identity a secret and not reveal her real reason for traveling to Canada put him in an awkward position with Henry.

He glanced across the table at his friend. Perhaps there was still a way he might gain some helpful information, but he would have to be very careful. "What do you think a mother could do if she believed her children had been emigrated to Canada by mistake?"

Henry looked up. "What do you mean?"

"Have you heard of any instances where children were emigrated and their parents learned about it after and objected?"

"I suppose it might happen, but it seems rather unlikely."

"But if it did happen, would the parent be able to regain custody and have the children returned to England?"

Henry studied him for an uncomfortable moment. "I'm not sure. I know Dr. Barnardo was taken to court a few times by parents who wanted to reclaim their children. They were not usually successful. He had a lot of influence and quite a strong legal team. Most of those parents could not afford an extended legal battle."

Andrew leaned forward. "But what does the law say? Isn't the sending organization required to have the parents' consent before they emigrate the children?"

"Not necessarily. If the organization believes the child's health or safety is in danger, or the situation is not morally suitable, they have the right to remove the child from the parents' care."

"But what about emigrating them? Can they send them off to Canada or Australia or wherever without the parents' permission?"

"Yes, from what I've read, I believe they can. When a child is removed from the parents' home or the streets, the guardianship transfers from the parents to the organization. All that's required is notification of the parents, and that can be sent after they sail. By that time it's almost too late for the parents to do anything about it."

Andrew frowned at his notes. "It doesn't seem right."

"Is it right for children to live in poverty and suffer neglect because of their parents' poor choices?"

He looked up and met Henry's gaze. "That's not the only reason children go into the care of the homes."

"True." Henry rubbed his chin. "For some it's a series of unfortunate events, such as loss of income, desertion by a spouse, or the illness or death of one or both of the child's parents. If there are no remaining family members who are willing or able to care for them, the children are relinquished to a home."

Andrew nodded. "Those are the cases I'm thinking of—a parent who places the children in care for what he or she believes is a temporary problem, then finds out the children are sent away without warning."

"If the family's issues are temporary, they have the opportunity to reclaim the children before they emigrate."

"But as we've seen," Andrew continued, "children process through the homes at different rates. Some stay for years, others only for a few weeks before they're assigned to an emigration party. It's possible some children could be added to the list before their family has had sufficient time to sort out their issues and reclaim their children."

"I suppose that could happen, but it would be a rare case."

"If it happens to even one child, it's not right. Preserving families ought to be a high priority."

"I agree. However, that must be balanced with doing what's best for the children."

"Still, families who are willing and able to care for their children ought not have that right taken away without due process."

Henry cocked his head and studied Andrew. "You certainly sound passionate about a situation that rarely occurs."

He clenched his jaw and glanced away. He did feel strongly about it, and that made him even more certain he wanted to help Laura and her family . . . and gaining Henry's assistance was key. But if he told Henry more about the situation, he would be breaking his promise to Laura.

He tapped his finger on the table between them. Somehow he had to persuade Laura to trust Henry and confide in him. He had the wisdom and experience to handle the legal aspects of the case, and he would have much more influence than Andrew did at this point in his career.

. . .

The vibrating notes of a Scottish bagpipe rose from the far end of the deck. Laura looked up from the girls' game of double jump rope and scanned the crowd.

"Someone is playing a bagpipe!" An eager expression lit Jenny Crawford's face as she turned and searched for the musician. "There he is!" She looked up at Rose and Laura. "Can we go closer to hear him play?"

Laura exchanged a smile with Rose, then nodded. "Yes, let's all go."

The girls collected their jump ropes, and Rose and Laura led them through the other passengers who had gathered in the open area of the poop deck to talk, play games, and escape the confines of their third-class cabins. They were not locked into the lower decks of the ship, but they had been told they were not allowed in the first-class lounges, salons, dining room, exercise rooms, or library. They could stroll on the promenade deck, but that was the only area they shared with the first- and second-class passengers.

Several people had gathered in a semicircle around the piper and a young boy playing a small drum. The girls maneuvered through and soon reached the front row. The middle-aged piper's loud notes charged the air with excitement. His cheeks puffed out, and his face turned ruddy as he blew into the mouthpiece and the bag filled with air.

Jenny leaned toward Emma and whispered something in her ear. Emma smiled and nodded. Then Jenny grabbed Emma's hand and pulled her into the area in front of the musicians. Both girls faced the crowd, placed their hands on their waists, and bowed.

Murmurs and smiles traveled through those who had gathered around.

Rose touched Laura's arm. "What are they doing?"

"I don't know." But the next moment the girls began hopping from foot to foot in time to the music.

"They're dancing the Highland Fling!" Cecelia clapped to the music, and the other girls joined in. Soon everyone was clapping. Jenny and Emma kicked their feet, lifted one hand, and twirled around in unison, all the while tapping their toes and heels and keeping time to the piper's tune. The girls' skirts swished against their legs, and their hair swung around as they hopped and spun.

Laura smiled and clapped along with the girls, her heart lifting as she watched Jenny and Emma dance with joy and abandon. Where had they learned the Highland Fling? Were their families originally from Scotland?

The girls danced on, and when the final notes of the song faded, they grinned and bowed. The crowd applauded, and Jenny and Emma hurried back to join the other girls. Their friends circled around, laughing and praising their bravery and dancing skills.

"That was a nice surprise." The male voice came from behind Laura.

She turned and lifted her hand to her heart. Andrew Frasier stood just a foot away, smiling down at her with shining brown eyes.

"Yes, it was. I had no idea they could dance like that."

"I'm glad I came down when I did. It's been quite a while since I've been to the Highlands or seen dancing like that."

"I've only seen it a few times myself at festivals in London."

He glanced around, then looked back at her. "Can you slip away for a few minutes and take a stroll on the promenade deck?"

Laura's breath caught, and a pleasant tingling traveled through her. She quickly stifled the feeling and scolded herself. Andrew Frasier didn't have romantic intentions toward her. He wanted only to continue their discussion about searching for her siblings.

She glanced at Rose. "I'm not sure. Let me speak to Miss Carson."

He nodded, then stepped back. "I'll wait for you by the steps."

Laura approached Rose as the piper tuned up

for his next song. "Would you mind watching my girls for a little while?"

Rose searched her face. "Is everything all right?"

"Yes, I'd just like to go up on deck for a few minutes."

Rose glanced past Laura's shoulder. Her eyes widened for a split second before she looked at Laura again. "Are you going with Mr. Frasier?"

She might not be able to tell Rose the full story, but at least she could be honest about this request. "Yes, he asked if I wanted to take a stroll on the promenade deck, and I'd like to accept."

A slight crease appeared on Rose's forehead. "Be careful, Laura. He seems like a respectable gentleman, but you need to guard your heart and your reputation."

"Of course. I'm sure there's nothing romantic about his invitation. We simply have a . . . common interest we want to discuss."

"What kind of common interest?"

Laura clasped her hands together. She hated keeping a secret from Rose. She'd almost confessed everything the morning after the fire, but for some reason she couldn't find the courage. "I can't explain right now, but I promise I'll tell you more later."

"All right. I'll wait for you here or back at the cabins. Let me know when you return, and be sure it's before tea time so I won't worry about you."

Laura nodded. "Thank you." She sent Rose a grateful smile, then crossed to meet Andrew.

He watched her approach. "Are you free to go up?"

"Yes." She smoothed her hand down her skirt, and he motioned for her to precede him up the stairs. Laura took the first two steps, then glanced over her shoulder. "What brought you down to our deck?"

"I heard the bagpipe, and I was curious to see who might be playing." He smiled. "And it was a good excuse to come looking for you."

Her cheeks warmed, but she couldn't help returning his smile. Did he like teasing her, or was he suggesting he wanted to be her friend as well as offer her legal advice? She hoped he had friendship in mind because she needed a friend almost as much as she needed a solicitor.

When they reached the promenade deck, he opened the door for her, and they stepped outside. The afternoon sky was a brilliant blue with mounds of white clouds on the western horizon. A light breeze off the ocean cooled her face and filled her lungs with fresh, salty air.

They walked over to the railing, and she glanced up at him. "You seemed to enjoy hearing that bagpiper. Did your family spend holidays in Scotland?"

"My father's brother and his family live near Aberdeen. We used to visit them often when I was a boy. But my father had a falling out with Uncle Richard. We haven't been back to Scotland since I was fourteen."

"I see." She looked out at the water, trying to think of a different topic of conversation. "Did you hear from your family before we set sail?"

"I received a letter from my mother. She's doing well and keeping busy with her charities and visiting friends."

"And your father?"

"He doesn't write. He could, but he simply chooses not to." Andrew's brow creased as he leaned on the railing. "I'm afraid my father and I are not on good terms at the moment."

"I'm sorry. I shouldn't have asked about your family."

"No, it's all right. I don't mind talking about them. In fact it's probably good to get it off my chest." He looked her way, squinting against the sunlight reflected off the water. "My father doesn't approve of my decision to live in London and practice law. In fact we had quite a heated discussion the last time I was at Bolton."

"Why doesn't he approve? You'd think he would be proud to see his son take up an honorable profession."

"It's not the right choice in his mind. He would rather I stay at Bolton and learn to manage the estate. He says that's where I belong, and I'm shirking my responsibility by running off to London and chasing after a fast life."

Laura pulled back, surprised her former employer would make such an unkind statement to his son. "But that's not true. You provide important legal assistance to people and make sure their rights are protected."

His eyes lit up, and he searched her face with a slight smile. "I'm glad to hear you approve of my choice. I only wish my father held the same opinion."

"Maybe he will one day after he sees all you accomplish."

"Whether he changes his opinion or not, I won't let that stop me from doing what I believe is right."

She smiled, her admiration for him increasing. "I'm glad to hear it. Not everyone is willing to follow the path they believe is right in spite of opposition."

"I respect my father and care about my family. One day, when they truly need me, I'll return to Bolton. But for now I plan to continue my training with Henry." He gazed out at the ocean again. "In some ways he has stepped into the role my father never wanted to take."

She pondered that for a moment. "It's good you have someone like Mr. Dowd in your life."

Andrew nodded. "We've worked side by side

for almost a year, traveled together, and tackled all kinds of legal work."

She smiled, encouraging him to continue.

"Henry has been a great example and inspiration. He lives out his faith in practical ways every day." Andrew smiled, then chuckled. "Do you know Henry will stop in the middle of a meeting or even out on the street to pray aloud and ask the Lord for wisdom and direction?"

Laura tipped her head. "That seems unusual to you?"

"Yes. I've never met anyone who is so bold and honest about spiritual matters."

Laura's throat tightened. "My father was like that."

He looked her way. "Really?"

She nodded. "It used to embarrass me sometimes when I was younger, but now that he's gone, I realize what an amazing man he was and how much his faith meant to him."

Andrew was silent for a moment, then said, "We've both been blessed with good examples to follow."

"Yes, we have."

He turned toward her, his gaze growing more intense. "With the memory of your father in mind, as well as what I've told you about Henry, I hope you'll reconsider keeping your identity a secret."

A chill traveled through her. "Why do you say that?"

"When I asked Henry about your situation—"

She gasped and pulled back. "You told him about me?"

"No!" He reached out his hand, but she took another step away. "I didn't say anything specific. I just stated a hypothetical situation similar to yours and asked his opinion."

She clenched her jaw and turned away. How could he go behind her back and speak to Henry? She should've known she couldn't trust him.

"Laura, please, I didn't give away your secret. I was simply trying to see if I could learn anything that would help us."

"But you promised." She crossed her arms protectively over her stomach.

"Yes . . . I did." He stepped around in front of her. "And I didn't tell him anything that betrayed my promise."

She studied his sincere expression, still trying to sort out what he meant. He'd asked Henry for information, but he'd kept her secret. Curiosity pushed away her fear. "Did Henry say anything that would be helpful?"

"I'm afraid the situation is more complicated than I first realized."

She tensed. "What do you mean?"

"Those who oversee the children's homes in England have the right to remove children for just about any reason. They can also emigrate them without the parents' permission. All that's required is that they inform the parents their children are being sent. And even that can be done after the children leave the country."

Laura stared at him. "So . . . you're saying what happened to my brother and sisters was perfectly legal?"

His expression grew even more solemn. "I'm afraid so."

"Then what can I do? How can I regain custody? There has to be some way around that."

"I'm sure there is. And that's why we need to be honest with Henry and tell him what happened to your family. He'll help us. I know he will."

She shook her head, concern engulfing her. "How can you say that? What if he decides I'm the one who broke the law by using a false name to take this position and gain my passage to Canada? He could have me arrested!"

"I'm sure he wouldn't do that."

"You have no way of knowing what he'll do!"

"I told you, Henry is a God-fearing, trustworthy man. I promise he'll listen to all you have to say and do whatever he can for you and your family, but you must tell him the truth."

She shook her head. "You don't understand. Everyone in authority I've appealed to has treated me with contempt and turned me away in the cruelest manner. How can you ask me to trust

Henry Dowd? I can't even trust you!" She swung away from him and strode off, her thoughts whirling and her aching heart pounding in her chest.

Katie lifted the heavy basket of wet sheets and carried it across the yard toward the Hoffmans' clotheslines. Looking up, she squinted against the bright sunlight. A few wispy clouds feathered across the blue sky. It was only late May, but the heat of the sun burned down on her head and shoulders that afternoon. She set the basket on the ground and wiped her damp face with her sleeve.

She'd spent all morning heating water in a heavy pot over an open fire, and washing and rinsing three loads of laundry. The backbreaking job had to be done outdoors, which made it doubly hard when it was so hot.

When she'd started that morning, the pile of dirty clothes, sheets, and towels had been so high she didn't think she would be able to finish it all in one day. But it was just after two o'clock, and the family's clean clothes were now all pinned on the lines, swaying in the slight breeze. She just needed to hang this last load of sheets, and she'd be done. Sweat dripped down the side of her face, and her empty stomach screamed for something to eat.

She glanced over at Mrs. Hoffman, sitting on

the porch in the shade, staring out across the fields with her empty gaze. Every once in a while, she would pick up her fussy baby girl and nurse her for a few minutes. Other than that, she hadn't moved from her chair.

Katie sighed and shook her head slightly. She'd heard some mothers felt sad and worn out after a baby was born, and that certainly seemed true of Mrs. Hoffman. The poor woman barely spoke to anyone, and some days she didn't even get out of bed until noon. Katie was on her own to prepare breakfast for the rest of the family and start on the day's chores. Mrs. Hoffman kept the baby with her most mornings, but Katie had to watch Daisy and Daniel while she fed the chickens, collected the eggs, washed the dishes, and cleaned the house.

Some afternoons Katie watched the baby for an hour or two when Mrs. Hoffman passed her off. Katie didn't mind. She was a sweet little thing. When Katie had asked again about her name, Mrs. Hoffman told her they had decided to call her Darla, after Mr. Hoffman's mother. The name fit, and Katie was thankful they'd finally given their baby that gift.

Katie picked up the top sheet from the basket. She had to stand on tiptoe to reach up and lift it over the clothesline. Her other foot kicked the basket, and she pulled in a sharp breath. If she wasn't careful, those clean, damp sheets would fall out in the dirt, and then she would have to start all over again.

Daniel stood a few feet away, swinging a stick back and forth, teasing their collie, Charger. The dog watched eagerly, leaping and barking at the stick, but then Daniel jerked it up high, out of reach, and laughed. It wasn't a happy, playful laugh but mean and taunting.

Katie pulled a clothespin from her apron pocket and reached up to pin the sheet in place. "Daniel, why don't you throw that stick? I'm sure Charger will fetch it for you."

"I don't want to." He gave Katie a surly scowl. "He's just a dumb old dog."

Katie sighed and draped the next sheet over the line. What was wrong with that boy? Charger was a beautiful dog, lively and obedient, eager to please—nothing like Daniel.

His little sister Daisy sat at the bottom of the porch steps, playing in the dirt. She had collected a few stones and was stacking them up and pouring dirt over them. Her hands, face, and dress were smeared with dusty brown streaks.

Katie groaned under her breath—more laundry for her to wash. But at least Daisy was content and not hanging on Katie's leg.

Mrs. Hoffman glanced at her daughter. "Daisy, get out of the dirt." Her slow, monotone words hung in the hot air, but the woman didn't move from her chair.

Daisy kept right on playing, ignoring her mother. She seemed to know her mother wouldn't get up and make her obey.

The dog let out a painful yip, and Katie spun around.

Daniel swung the stick again and brought it down across the dog's back.

Katie gasped. "Daniel, stop! Don't hit him!" She dropped the wet sheet and lunged for the boy, but she was too late. He whacked the dog again. Charger yelped and dashed off toward the barn.

"What is wrong with you?" Katie grabbed hold of his arm and tried to pull the stick away, but he held on tight.

"Let go of me!" The boy squirmed and twisted.

"Not until you give me that stick!"

Daniel growled and tried to wrestle free, but Katie wouldn't let him go.

"Take your hands off my boy!" Mr. Hoffman's voice boomed behind her. He grabbed her arm and pulled her back. That broke her hold on Daniel, and he went flying in the opposite direction. The boy landed on the ground and burst out crying like someone was beating him.

Mr. Hoffman jerked her closer, his eyes bulging and his face red and glistening with sweat. "If I ever see you touch my son again, I'll teach you a lesson you won't forget." He shook her hard. "Do you hear me?"

"Yes sir, but I was just trying to stop him from—"

"Don't sass me! I won't stand for it!" He shoved her away, and she fell back, tipping over the basket of wet sheets and falling to the ground. The clean laundry spilled out around her, landing in the dirt.

Katie's breath came in short gasps, and her heart thundered. Why was he so angry with her? She was just trying to stop Daniel from beating Charger. His unruly son was the one who needed a scolding, not Katie!

Mr. Hoffman glared down at her, pointing his shaking finger. "Get up and get back to work! I swear you are the orneriest home child I ever met! You aren't worth the three dollars I paid for you."

Katie gulped in a breath, her eyes stinging. She had tried so hard to do everything he and his wife asked, even though their house was disgusting and dirty and they never lifted a finger to help. She hadn't complained about sleeping in the barn loft with the bats and mice or working all day and never hearing a kind word from them. She glanced at the porch, hoping Mrs. Hoffman would speak up for her, but the woman just stared at them in stony silence, her face like a hard mask.

Daniel's crying slowed to whimpering and sniveling, and he wiped his runny nose on his shirtsleeve.

"You're all right, boy." Mr. Hoffman reached out his hand and pulled Daniel up. He swatted him lightly on the backside, then strode off toward the barn.

Daniel watched his father for a moment, then turned toward Katie. "Pa's right. You're just an ornery home child, and I don't have to listen to you." He stuck out his tongue and wagged his head back and forth.

Katie's face blazed. What an awful boy! It wouldn't do any good to reprimand him. He'd just find a way to blame her and make sure Mr. Hoffman punished her instead of him. She turned away and gathered the damp, dirty sheets.

Tears burned her eyes as she walked back to the fire and dumped the soiled laundry into the simmering pot. At least she hadn't poured out the rinse water, and she could use it to rewash the sheets. She scooped out some soap powder and added it to the water. Then she grabbed the wooden paddle and swished it back and forth. The sheets swirled in the water, and the dirt slowly washed away. The water turned gray-brown, but when she lifted out the sheets, the dirt was gone.

If only she had some way to wash away the

painful stains that had darkened her life. But she was marked as an orphan, a home child, and not worth the pittance people paid to bring her to their homes to do their work.

Please, Lord, help me find my way home.

15

Andrew looked up from the letter he was writing to his mother and stared out the port window. What would she be doing at this time in the afternoon—visiting her friend Charlotte Larkin or walking in the rose garden? Perhaps she was speaking to Mrs. Ellis, the housekeeper, or Mr. Harding, the gardener. Had she found a new lady's maid to replace Laura? He considered asking, but he decided to honor his promise to Laura and not bring up the topic in his letter.

Whatever his mother was doing today, he hoped she was well and finding comfort in her friends and her faith, for she certainly would not find it with his father.

Henry crossed the cabin and stood before the mahogany dressing table with the marble washbasin. He focused on his reflection in the mirror and combed his hair with careful attention. When he finished, he adjusted his tie.

Andrew's curiosity grew as he watched his friend. Henry was always careful about his appearance when he dressed in the morning, but this midday grooming seemed a bit unusual. "Are you going out?"

"Yes. How do I look?" Henry turned toward him.

"You look fine, as you always do."

"Good. I thought I'd take a stroll on deck." A slight smile creased his face. "Miss Carson and her girls are usually there about this time."

Andrew's eyebrows rose. "You're hoping to see Miss Carson?"

"I am." He turned back to the mirror, checking his appearance once more. "I've been impressed by her each time we've met. She is a woman of faith, substance, and compassion, as well as being charming and quite lovely."

Andrew hadn't really taken too much notice of Miss Carson, but he supposed what Henry said was true.

"As I was praying about it this morning, I realized there are only a few more days until our arrival in Canada, and I ought to make the most of that time." He straightened his vest. "So . . . I've decided to invite Miss Carson to dinner."

"Doesn't she dine with the third-class passengers?"

"Yes, but there are two empty places at our table. I spoke to the maître d'. He told me they are reserved for a Mr. and Mrs. Norton, but the man is not well, and he and his wife prefer to take their meals in their cabin. So I asked if I might invite a guest."

"And the maître d' agreed?"

"Yes. He said he'd be glad to seat Miss Carson at our table."

Andrew grinned and nodded. "Why don't I invite Miss Hopkins to dine with us as well?"

"You're interested in pursuing Miss Hopkins?"

Andrew blinked, surprised by the suggestion, and he decided not to answer directly. "I thought Miss Carson might be more willing to accept your invitation if both she and Miss Hopkins were invited." It would also give Laura the opportunity to get to know Henry and see that he would be a trustworthy advocate in their search for her siblings.

"I believe you're right. That's an excellent idea."

Then another thought struck, and Andrew frowned. "But I doubt they'd both be able to get away at the same time. Who would keep an eye on the girls?"

Henry thought for a moment, then smiled. "I think we can find someone suitable to watch over the girls." He glanced toward the door. "Shall we take a stroll on deck and see if we can find them?"

Andrew nodded. "Just give me a moment." He set aside his pen and letter and rose from his chair. While Henry waited for him by the door, he slipped on his suit jacket.

Henry's comment about pursuing *Miss Hopkins* cycled through his mind. Laura was intelligent and attractive, with many fine qualities, but they had very different backgrounds. If he brought home his mother's former lady's maid as his intended, his father would certainly object.

He might push against his father's will when it came to pursuing his partnership with Henry and practicing law in London, but he could only push him so far.

He gave his head a slight shake. Henry could choose to court Rose Carson, but Andrew did not have that same freedom to pursue Laura McAlister, even if the idea was an inviting one.

"Ready?"

"I'm right behind you." Within two minutes, they stepped out on the promenade deck and into the sunshine.

"What a fine day." Henry set off at an easy pace.

"We have had exceptional weather." They passed people lounging in deck chairs and standing by the railing, gazing out to sea. The ship slowly dipped and rose, and he realized he'd grown so used to the movements that they barely registered with him now. He had definitely gained his sea legs.

They strolled on, and he soon heard girls' chatter and laughter. He scanned the view ahead and spotted Laura, Rose, and several of the girls gathered around a shuffleboard court. He glanced at Henry. "There they are."

"Yes, I see." Henry picked up his pace, and Rose looked up as he approached. "Good afternoon, ladies." Even though he said *ladies,* his focus was on Rose. "It looks like you're enjoying the day."

Rose returned a warm smile. "We are, and the girls are becoming quite skilled at shuffleboard."

Laura's gaze darted to Andrew, but then she quickly looked away. Her cheeks glowed pink, and she stepped closer to the girls gathered at the other end of the shuffleboard court.

She was probably remembering their last conversation and hoping to avoid another private encounter. That bothered him, but he wasn't about to push in where he wasn't wanted. She was the one who had run away and left him standing alone on the deck.

Henry joined Rose and engaged her in conversation about the game.

Andrew stood on the side, watching the girls as they used their cues to push the black and red discs to the opposite end of the court. They took turns and cheered each other on no matter how many or few points were scored. That brought a smile to his face. Obviously, someone had been teaching them how to encourage their friends, and he suspected Laura played a big part in that.

She leaned down and whispered in the ear of the girl who was up next. The little girl smiled and nodded, then stepped into place. With a careful shove she sent her disc sliding and knocked her opponent's disc off the court. Her team cheered, and a smile burst across her face.

Andrew clapped. "Good shot."

Laura looked up and returned a tentative smile before she focused on the girls again.

That was enough for him. He crossed and joined her. "You're doing a fine job with these girls."

She kept her gaze focused on the girls rather than Andrew. "They enjoy learning new games."

"You're teaching them much more than how to play shuffleboard."

That sparked her interest, and she looked up at him. "What do you mean?"

"They're learning important life skills."

"From playing shuffleboard?"

"Yes. Learning how to play by the rules and encourage others, whether they're winning or losing, are important skills that will help them in their new lives in Canada."

"I suppose so." She looked down again.

"Miss Hopkins, your girls are truly blessed to have your guidance and care."

She slowly lifted her head. "You mean that?"

"Yes, of course."

She lowered her voice. "You're not angry with me?"

"Angry? Why would I be angry?"

"Because of the way I left our conversation the other night."

"I understand that you're under a great deal of pressure to find the best path forward to help your family. That can't be easy."

"No, it's not."

"Well then, let's see what we can do to help you get your bearings and find that path."

She sent him a questioning look.

He leaned closer. "Henry is going to invite Miss Carson to join us for dinner tonight."

Her eyes widened before she quickly schooled her expression. "He is?"

He nodded. "And I was thinking she might be more comfortable if you'd agree to join us as well."

She stared at him. "You want me to join you in the first-class dining room?"

"Yes. I believe it will help Miss Carson enjoy the evening to have you by her side, and it will also give you the opportunity to become acquainted with Henry and judge his character for yourself. Then you can decide when you're ready to confide in him."

She peered out to sea for a few seconds, obviously contemplating his offer. Finally, she looked back at him. "Thank you for your invitation, but I don't think we can both leave the girls on their own."

"Henry has already thought of that, and he plans to make arrangements for someone to watch over them."

Surprise flickered in her eyes. "Well, if Miss Carson agrees to the plan, then I'd be happy to join you for dinner."

His chest expanded, and he sent her a smile. "Excellent."

She hesitated and looked up at him. "Have you told Mr. Dowd any more about my situation?"

"No. I gave you my word, and I intend to keep it."

"Thank you. I'm relieved to hear it."

He lowered his voice and smiled. "Your secret is safe with me."

Laura made her way down the long corridor toward the first-class dining room with Rose by her side. They entered the lobby where several passengers waited to be seated for dinner. Her stomach tightened, and she ran her hand down the skirt of her light blue day dress. It was the best dress she had, one that would be appropriate to wear on Sunday for church, but it couldn't compare to the lace and beaded evening gowns the other women were wearing.

She turned to Rose and lowered her voice. "All these women look so elegant."

Rose studied the nearest group of women. "Don't worry. Just hold your head up high and smile. That's what my mum always used to say."

"Good evening, Miss Carson, Miss Hopkins." Henry approached, dressed for dinner in white tie and offering them a confident smile. "We're so glad you could join us."

Rose nodded. "Thank you. It was kind of you to invite us."

Henry offered his arm to Rose, and she accepted it with a pleased smile.

Andrew turned to Laura. "Shall we go in?" He offered her his arm.

"Yes." A thrill raced through Laura as she slipped her hand through Andrew's arm and they walked into the first-class dining room together.

Laura could barely contain her delight as she looked around the large, beautiful room and waited to be seated. The walls were covered with wooden paneling, painted white and topped with scrollwork. The tables were set with crisp white tablecloths and napkins, elegant white china, and sparkling silverware. Dark green velvet chairs were arranged around the tables, and blue patterned tiles covered the floors. The most surprising feature was the leaded-glass windows that were lit from behind, giving the impression they were dining at a restaurant on shore rather than at sea.

One of the waiters showed them to their table and seated Rose. Andrew pulled out the chair for Laura, and she sat across from Rose. Henry took the seat next to Rose, and Andrew sat on Laura's left. The waiter placed their napkins on their laps as he welcomed them and told them the menu for the evening.

Rose looked across the table at Laura and sent her a secretive smile. She was obviously as delighted as Laura with their surroundings and company.

Laura glanced at the two empty places at their table. "Will someone else be joining us?"

"Usually Dr. and Mrs. Charles dine with us, but they have other plans this evening." Henry exchanged a look with Andrew that seemed to convey some hidden message. Had the men arranged for just the four of them to dine together tonight?

Laura sent Rose a questioning glance. Her friend smiled and looked down at her plate.

The waiter approached with their first course and set a small plate in front of Laura. "Canapés a l'Amiral."

She looked down at the open half shell with a small mound of something in the center. She had no idea what it might be, but she was relieved to see a small silver spoon beside the shell. At least she knew which piece of glittering silverware to use.

Henry looked around the group. "Will you join me in a blessing?"

They all bowed their heads.

"Father, we thank You for this evening and the opportunity to dine with friends. We're grateful for this food and receive it with thanksgiving, knowing all good things come from You. We ask You to guide our conversation and give us a meaningful time together. We pray these things in the name of Jesus Christ, our Lord. Amen."

Rose looked up and beamed a smile at Henry. "That was lovely. Thank you."

Henry lifted his spoon and grinned. "Bon appétit!"

Laura tried a small bite of her canapé and discovered it was a creamy shrimp mixture with other ingredients she couldn't name. Soon the waiter returned and offered them a choice of a clear consommé or a cream of barley soup as their next course. She chose the consommé and found it was delicious.

Henry turned to Rose. "Miss Carson, I'd be interested to hear how you became an emigration escort."

"All right, I'd be happy to tell you." Rose set her soupspoon aside. "I was raised by very loving parents in London, but when I was eleven, our home caught fire. My father carried me out and returned for my mother, but . . . they both perished in the fire."

"I'm so sorry." Henry appeared genuinely grieved by Rose's words.

"Thank you. I still miss them, but I'm grateful for those eleven years we had together. They gave me a firm foundation of faith and love, and that has made all the difference in my life."

Henry's smile returned, encouraging Rose to continue.

"After that, I went to live with my grandfather, but he was quite elderly and passed away a year later. I had no other relatives nearby, so I was taken into the Moorefield Home for Children." Her expression dimmed, and her eyes clouded. "Life was very different there."

"In what ways?" Henry asked.

"There were more than two hundred girls at Moorefield between the ages of six and eighteen. They have very strict rules and a small staff to carry out all the duties at the home. That did not leave much time for personal interaction."

Andrew was so engaged, listening to Rose's story, he seemed to have forgotten about his soup. Laura's heart grew heavy as she listened to Rose. Why hadn't she asked her friend about her family or childhood before? The answer was obvious. She'd been focused on her own troubles and was more concerned about protecting her secret than showing her friend the kindness and consideration she deserved. She must do better, and she would.

"When I was eighteen," Rose continued, "the matron gave me the option of leaving Moorefield or staying on as a teacher. It was a difficult decision, but after praying and waiting on the Lord, I felt I should stay and try to make a difference for the girls. So I worked at Moorefield for seven years.

"Two years ago, I decided it was time for a change. I learned about the opening at Hughes

Children's Home and applied for the position. And I've been there ever since, helping the girls prepare for their new lives in Canada and sometimes escorting them on the voyage."

Andrew asked, "How many times have you been to Canada?"

"This will be my fourth trip." She smiled. "And I must say, it has been the most adventurous."

Henry smiled. "It sounds as though you've found your calling, working with the girls."

"I believe I have. Many of them come from a situation similar to mine. And I know how frightening it is to be on your own and wish someone would treat you kindly and care what happens to you."

Laura's throat tightened. That must be how her sisters and brother felt as they were taken into the children's homes and then sent off to Canada. They probably had no idea she'd been searching for them in London and Liverpool and was following them to Canada.

Henry's steady gaze rested on Rose. "I admire the way you've taken those lessons from the past and are using them to help others."

Rose's cheeks flushed. "That's my hope and consolation . . . that I can be used to give my girls courage and strength to flourish with their new families."

The waiter returned and removed their soup bowls.

Henry thanked him and turned to Rose again. "Have you had the opportunity to visit any of the girls who were placed from your previous trips?"

"Yes, I was able to see three of the girls who were living close to Belleville."

"And were you pleased with their situations?"

She hesitated. "Two of the girls were doing well. They seemed happy and settled. But the third girl was ill, and the family didn't seem to be offering her good care. I spoke to her and realized it was not a good placement, so I removed her from that family and took her back to the receiving home in Belleville."

Laura clutched her napkin under the table, wishing she could ask more about the situation. She was surprised but thankful that Rose had the authority to remove the girl.

The waiter arrived and placed another plate in front of Laura. "Your salad, madam." Then he served the others.

"My, this looks delicious." Rose lifted her salad fork.

Laura carefully located her own salad fork and took a bite of the tender asparagus and greens. There was a small serving of sliced meat on the side. It looked like beef, but when she took a bite, it tasted like dark chicken. "What kind of meat is this?"

Andrew grinned. "I believe it's squab."

Laura blinked. "Squab?"

Henry leaned forward and whispered, "That's pigeon."

Rose's eyes widened. She lifted her napkin to her mouth to stifle a laugh. "I'm sorry. I've fed many pigeons in the park, but I've never eaten one."

Although Laura pressed her lips together, soon her laughter escaped as well, and the men joined in. "It's actually very tasty," she said when she caught her breath.

Henry finished his salad and looked across at Laura. "How did you become an escort, Miss Hopkins?"

Laura's breath caught, and she almost dropped her fork. "My story is not nearly as interesting as Miss Carson's."

"That's all right. You're among friends."

Andrew turned toward her. "Yes, tell us your story, Miss Hopkins." His mouth tugged up on one side, and a challenge lit his eyes. "We'd love to hear it."

Her face flushed, and she could hardly resist squirming in her chair. He obviously wanted her to tell Henry and Rose the truth about her family, but she wasn't ready to do that—not yet.

"All right." She shifted her gaze to Henry. "I was born and raised in London by very caring parents. I am the oldest of four. I have two sisters and one brother. When I was nineteen, my father passed away from injuries he suffered in a rail accident."

Henry's eyes clouded. "I'm sorry to hear that."

Laura nodded, accepting his kind words. "After that, I went into service to help support my family. First, I worked as a housemaid in London, and then I became a lady's maid for a wealthy family . . . north of London."

Andrew cleared his throat, but she ignored him.

"My mum became ill and I had to return to London. I'm grateful to say she has recovered and is staying with friends. I needed a new position, so when I heard about the opening at Hughes, I applied and was accepted. I only began working there a few weeks ago. This is my first trip as an escort."

Henry gave a thoughtful nod. "I'm impressed with your determination to help support your family."

"I love them very much. I would do anything in my power to assure their health and happiness."

The challenging light in Andrew's eyes softened. "Devotion to family is an admirable quality."

"I quite agree," Henry said.

Rose's gaze traveled around the table. "I've been so pleased to get to know Miss Hopkins on this voyage. Her kindness toward the girls has made her a favorite in their eyes as well as mine."

Laura ducked her head. Hearing Rose's words of praise pricked her conscience and tugged at her heart.

The waiter arrived and set the next course in front of her. A large helping of salmon swimming in a creamy dill sauce filled her plate. She released a shaky breath, thankful she'd been able to explain her background without telling another lie. But wasn't leaving out the whole truth and letting someone believe that was the full story as dishonest as stating a bold lie?

Suddenly, her appetite fled, and she didn't think she could eat one more bite of her meal.

Rose looked her way. "Mary, is everything all right?"

The use of her false name felt like sandpaper rubbing across her heart, deepening her discomfort. She pushed those convicting feelings away and forced a slight smile. "Yes, everything is fine." But when she glanced at Andrew and read the disappointment in his eyes, she knew that was far from the truth.

Katie knelt on the path between the rows of peas and poured a bucket of cool well water at the base of the plants. The dry ground soaked up the water in seconds, leaving a dark stain in the reddish-brown dirt. She hoped watering the peas would loosen the soil and make it easier for her to weed that row, but so far, it hadn't helped very much.

The sun heated her head and shoulders, and she leaned closer to the plants, trying to stay in the shade where the green vines and small white flowers curled up around the strings. She swiped her forehead, grabbed hold of the next big weed, and tugged hard. The stem broke off. She gasped and fell backward, landing in the dirt.

"Oh, you wicked weed!" She huffed and threw the broken stem down the path.

The sound of a horse coming up the road caught her attention. She rose to her knees and peeked through the vines. A man in a black suit and hat drove a two-wheeled open buggy past the kitchen garden. He slowed the horse to a stop in front of the house. Before he could climb down, Mr. Hoffman walked out the door and down the steps to meet him.

The man in the carriage lifted his hat. "Good afternoon, Mr. Hoffman."

"Afternoon, Reverend." Mr. Hoffman's tone sounded cool, even a little suspicious.

"I'm just returning from the Wilsons', and I thought I'd stop by and pay you and your wife a visit."

Mr. Hoffman glanced over his shoulder at the house, then looked back at the reverend. "My wife's still feeling poorly. I can't ask you in."

"I'm sorry to hear that. I was hoping the girl from the home would ease your wife's burden and help her recover."

Mr. Hoffman rubbed his jaw. "Well, the girl is

awful young, and she doesn't know much about farm chores."

"Still, she must be a help to your wife in the house and with the children."

"I suppose." Mr. Hoffman shook his head. "Ella's not herself. It's hard to know what she wants or how to please her."

The reverend sent him an understanding look. "Well, you must be patient with your wife and with the girl."

Mr. Hoffman crossed his arms and frowned toward the barn.

"I'm sorry. I've forgotten the girl's name."

Mr. Hoffman thought for a moment. "Katie. Her name's Katie McAlister."

"Ah, yes. That's right." He glanced around. "May I see Katie?"

Mr. Hoffman shook his head. "She's helping my wife."

"I see." The reverend glanced toward the house again. "We've placed four other home children in and around Roslin recently, three boys and one other girl. They've each settled in and are a good help to the family who has taken them."

Mr. Hoffman's scowl deepened. "There's always one bad apple in the bunch."

Katie pulled in a sharp breath and sat back. How could he say that about her? She'd worked so hard—caring for the children, cooking and cleaning, doing the laundry, and tending the garden, all while Mrs. Hoffman stayed in her room or sat on the porch doing next to nothing.

"I'm sure she'll learn what's needed soon. Patience, training, and time to adjust—that's what most home children need."

Mr. Hoffman grimaced as though the prospect was distasteful.

The reverend shifted in his seat. "So . . . I hope we'll see you and your family in church on Sunday." He lowered his voice. "It might help your wife to get out of the house and see some other women."

Katie's hopes rose. If they went to church on Sunday, she'd be free from her chores, and she might be able to meet those other home children the reverend had mentioned. She leaned forward and strained to hear Mr. Hoffman's answer.

"I don't think Ella is up to going to church. Just tending to the baby seems to tire her out something awful."

The reverend tapped his chin. "Here's a thought. Why not start the preparations on Saturday evening? Let Katie give the children baths and set out their clothes. Then she can prepare a simple breakfast on Sunday morning, and you'll all be ready in time for church."

Mr. Hoffman sent the reverend a doubtful glance.

"I think you'll find worshipping the Lord and

gathering with friends will improve your wife's outlook and encourage everyone." When Mr. Hoffman didn't reply, the reverend's optimistic expression faded. "But if your wife is not up to going, you could come with the children. That would give your wife a quiet morning's rest."

"I'll think about it." Mr. Hoffman stepped back, making it clear he wanted to end the conversation.

"All right, then." The reverend took hold of the reins. "Please give my regards to your wife."

Mr. Hoffman nodded, but he didn't say anything else.

"Good day." The reverend clicked to the horse and set off down the road.

Katie watched him go and determined she'd work extra hard and do all she could on Saturday so she could attend church on Sunday. Just the thought of singing hymns and meeting new friends filled her with longing.

Mr. Hoffman trudged back toward the house, muttering under his breath.

Mrs. Hoffman pushed open the screen door and stepped out on the porch. "What did he want?"

"He was just snooping around, trying to get us to come to church."

"What did you tell him?"

"Nothing."

"I saw you talking to him. You must have said something."

"I told him you were feeling poorly and weren't up to going anywhere."

Her mouth puckered into an angry line. "Don't blame me for us not going to church. That's all your doing."

"What do you mean by that?"

"You're the one who said the reverend is just a loud-mouthed Bible thumper and you don't want to waste your time driving into town on Sundays."

Mr. Hoffman cursed and stomped up the steps. "Hush up, woman!" He strode past his wife.

She turned away as the screen door slammed after him.

Katie sank down on the ground and lifted her hand to cover her stinging eyes. So much for the hope of leaving the farm for a few hours and meeting new friends at church. Would she have to stay here forever with no hope of seeing her brother or sister and no way to make any friends?

16

Laura leaned over Anna May and searched her flushed face. She slept now, but fitfully. Laura placed her hand on the girl's forehead, and heat radiated into her fingers. She bit her lip as worry wove around her heart.

Anna May had suffered with a fever and sore throat for the last two days. The little girl felt so miserable she didn't want to rise from her bunk or go to meals with the other girls. Laura had stayed with her, taking only a few short breaks to eat a quick meal or sleep for a few hours while someone else watched over Anna May.

The ship's doctor had visited each day. He suggested they keep Anna May cool with sponge baths and give her plenty of liquids. He arranged for the other four girls in their cabin to move to new accommodations to prevent the illness from spreading. Other than that, he said they just needed to let Anna May rest and wait for her to get well.

Laura smoothed the sheet across Anna May's chest. She closed her eyes, knowing she wasn't worthy to pray, but where else could she turn?

Please, Lord, comfort Anna May and heal her. She has had such a rough start in life and has already suffered so much.

The cabin door opened, and Rose walked in carrying a bucket. "Here's some more water and another washcloth." She placed the bucket on the floor beside the bunk and handed the cloth to Laura.

"Thank you." Laura reached up and rubbed her tired shoulder. She could feel a slight headache building at the base of her neck.

Rose leaned closer and peered down at Anna May. "I'm glad she's sleeping. That should help. Why don't you go and have some dinner? I'll stay with her."

"I'm not hungry."

"Mary, you have to keep up your strength. Tomorrow is going to be a very long day."

"What will we do if she's not well when it's time to leave the ship?"

Rose's eyes clouded, and she shook her head. "They won't allow her past immigration if she has a fever."

Laura sat on the floor, closed her eyes, and leaned back against the side of Anna May's bunk. Would she have to split off from the group and stay behind with Anna May? Would the immigration authorities end up sending them both back to England? She had no way of knowing what would happen tomorrow, but worrying wouldn't change anything. Perhaps Rose was right. She should go and have dinner with the other girls.

A knock sounded at the door.

Laura looked up. "Come in."

The door opened, and a steward held up an envelope. "I have a message for Miss Mary Hopkins."

Laura rose and crossed to the door. She accepted the envelope and glanced at her name written across the front. Who had sent her a message? She thanked the steward. He nodded and set off down the corridor.

Laura tore open the envelope and unfolded the stationery. She glanced at the bottom first and read Andrew's signature there. Her heartbeat sped up, and she lifted her gaze to read from the beginning.

Dear Miss Hopkins, I was very sorry to hear Anna May is unwell. I will keep her in my prayers and trust the Lord will give her a speedy recovery.

Since we will be landing in Quebec City tomorrow morning, and it seems unlikely we will have time to speak to each other before then, I wanted to inform you of our plans and assure you that I am willing to help you as I promised.

Relief washed over Laura. After she'd failed to tell Henry and Rose her real reason for traveling to Canada, she thought Andrew might not speak to her again. But it seemed he intended to keep his end of the bargain even though she had not fulfilled hers—at least not yet.

Henry and I will take the train to Montreal and stay there for a few days to meet with immigration authorities and visit two children's homes. Then we plan to continue on to Kingston and Belleville. I'm not sure how long that will take, ten days or possibly a bit longer.

I understand from speaking to Miss Carson that you and your party will be taking the train directly to the receiving home in Belleville. I'm sure you are eager to see your girls settled in their new homes as well as continuing with the project we discussed.

How thoughtful Andrew was to write as he did and keep her plans a secret in case Rose or someone else read his note.

I want to urge you to wait until I arrive in Belleville before you discuss that project with those in charge there. I think it would be wise to have legal counsel present when you explain your situation and make your request. I will contact you at the home as soon as we arrive in town.

We can then make arrangements for that meeting.

I want you to know that I take this matter very seriously and will do all I can to help you. Until then I will keep you and your family in my prayers.

Yours sincerely,
Andrew Frasier

Rose watched as Laura folded the note and slipped it back in the envelope. "Is everything all right?"

"Yes, everything's fine." Laura bit her lip and tucked the letter in her skirt pocket. What was the point of keeping the note private? Rose was obviously curious to know who had written, but she was too kind to pry. Laura met Rose's gaze. "The message is from Andrew Frasier."

Rose's eyebrows arched. "Really?"

Laura nodded. "He wanted me to know he'll be coming to Belleville in about ten days."

She smiled. "He hopes to see you then?"

"Yes." For just a moment she savored Rose's assumption that a romance was blossoming between her and Andrew, but reality came rushing back and she silently scolded herself for her foolishness. At least she could tell Rose the truth about Andrew. "I'm sure he doesn't have romantic intentions. He simply offered to help me with a legal matter . . . for my family."

Rose's brow creased, and she sent Laura a questioning look.

That was all she could say for the moment. Andrew didn't want her to reveal her identity to those in charge in Belleville until he was present, so she couldn't very well tell Rose.

She turned back to Anna May and rested her hand lightly on the girl's forehead. Her skin felt cooler now, and her face seemed much more peaceful. "I think her fever has broken."

Rose came closer and laid her hand gently against the little girl's cheek. "I believe you're right." Her expression brightened. "What a wonderful answer to prayer."

Laura gently brushed Anna May's damp hair back from her forehead, thankful the little girl was improving. "If you're still willing to stay with Anna May, I think I will take you up on your offer."

"Please do." Rose settled on the bunk across from Anna May's. "And when you're finished with dinner, why don't you take a walk?" Rose's smile returned, and her eyes twinkled. "Perhaps you'll see Mr. Frasier on the promenade deck."

Laura reached for the comb and small mirror in her travel bag. "I'm sure he'll be at dinner for quite some time, and I need to finish packing tonight."

Confusion filled Rose's eyes. "You don't want to see him?"

Laura released a deep breath. Of course she wanted to see him, but that wouldn't change anything. "I admire Andrew Frasier. He is a fine, honorable man, but there's no point in hoping for something that can never be."

Rose's lips parted, and confusion filled her eyes. "You mean there is no possibility of romance because he's from an upper-class family and you're not?"

Laura nodded. At that moment it dawned on her that Rose was thinking of her own feelings for Henry and the differences that separated them. Laura reached for her hand. "But it's different for you and Henry."

"Do you really think so?"

She didn't want to raise Rose's hopes too high when neither of them knew for certain what the future held, but she didn't want to discourage her either. "I can tell he's very fond of you. Has he said anything about writing to you or seeing you after the voyage?"

Rose's dreamy expression dimmed. "Not yet. I was so hopeful after our dinner the other night that he might say something, but he didn't."

"Then perhaps you're the one who needs to take a stroll later and see if he's on deck."

Rose smiled. "Do you really think I should?"

"Of course. Being in the right place at the right time can't hurt."

"But what about you and Mr. Frasier? He

certainly seems to enjoy your company. Are you sure he doesn't think of you in a romantic way?"

She hesitated, weighing her words. She might not be able to tell Rose the full story, but she could at least reveal part of it. "I'm quite sure all we'll share is friendship. You see . . . I used to work for his family."

"What?" Rose stared at her.

"I was his mother's lady's maid for a few months, but when my mum became ill, I had to leave Bolton and go to London to care for her."

"Why didn't you tell me before?"

Laura lifted her hand and rubbed her eyes. The headache she'd been fighting now pounded behind her eyes. "It's complicated. And when he didn't say anything about it when we were introduced, I decided not to mention it as well."

"You're not ashamed of working in that position, are you?"

"No. It was quite a step up for me, and I'm grateful for my time at Bolton. The Frasiers are a fine family. I wouldn't have left unless my family needed me."

Rose nodded and clasped Laura's hand. "Well, don't worry. You have many fine qualities, and I'm sure, in time, the right man will pursue you."

"You're very kind, Rose." Laura had to force out those words. She might have some good qualities, but at the present she was caught in a web of deceit, leaving her feeling confused and guilty. There was no way she could consider a romance with Andrew or anyone else until these matters with her family were resolved.

Her friend leaned toward her and wrapped her in a gentle hug. "Why don't you go and have some dinner with the girls? And when you're finished, I think I will take that stroll on deck and see if Mr. Dowd is there."

Laura nodded and turned away, surprised by the tears that stung her eyes. Rose might dream of romance and a future with Henry Dowd, but there was no hope for her to ever be more than friends with Andrew, if she could even hold on to that.

A misty fog hung over the harbor the next morning as the ship pulled in next to the dock at Quebec City. Andrew stood at the railing on the promenade deck, waiting with Henry and the other first-class passengers while the crew tied up the ship and prepared to lower the gangplank. The hum of cheerful conversation rose around him. It seemed everyone was eager to step ashore in Canada and be off on business or pleasure.

Henry shifted his briefcase to his other hand and looked down at the dock. "It shouldn't be too much longer now."

Andrew followed his friend's gaze and watched as the first few passengers at the head of the line descended the gangplank and entered the immigration sheds. He glanced to the left where the other line of second- and third-class passengers waited. Rising up on the balls of his feet, he scanned the crowd, searching for Laura.

She hadn't replied to the message he'd sent to her cabin last night, though the steward had confirmed she'd received it. Did she assume he didn't expect a reply, or was she upset that he wanted her to wait until he arrived at Belleville to ask those in charge about her siblings? Either way, there was nothing more he could do now. Still, he searched the crowd, wishing he could speak to her once more before they left the ship.

"Who are you looking for?"

Andrew's neck warmed. He considered ignoring the question, but there was no point in hiding the truth from his friend. "I was hoping to speak to Miss Hopkins once more. I haven't seen her since we dined together the other evening. I believe she's stayed below since then to take care of one of her girls who was unwell."

"Yes, Miss Carson mentioned that last night."

Surprise rippled through Andrew. "You saw Miss Carson last night?"

Henry nodded, looking pleased. "I went out on deck after dinner, and I happened to find her there." He glanced away, but that didn't hide his smile. "We had a very pleasant conversation and walk in the moonlight."

"Are you planning to see her again?"

"Yes. We've agreed to meet in Belleville."

That was good news. Henry's plans to meet Miss Carson would make it easier for him to arrange a meeting between Laura and Henry, then with those in charge of the receiving home at Belleville. But would she wait for him as he'd asked? Her friendship with Miss Carson might be the key. "How long does Miss Carson plan to stay in Belleville?"

"At least three weeks. She wants to see that her girls are properly settled, and she'd like to visit some of the girls from her previous trips. I suggested she might accompany us on some of our visits if the timing is right."

Andrew's thoughts shifted like puzzle pieces sliding into place. Perhaps Laura would join them, and they could all search for her siblings.

Henry's expression clouded. "After that, she'll return to Liverpool."

"And we'll return to London." What would happen after their time in Canada? Would Laura return to Liverpool or London? Would she find her siblings right away, or would she have to stay in Canada for an extended search?

"We may have to write to each other for a time," Henry continued. "But if things progress as I hope, she'll be coming to London in the not-too-distant future."

Andrew placed his hand on his friend's shoulder. "That's very good news. Congratulations."

"It's a bit early for that, but I am hopeful."

The line moved forward a few more steps, and they were almost to the top of the gangplank. He turned and searched the passengers on the left once more. The crowd shifted as some people moved toward the railing, and that made it a challenge for him to see past those in front.

As he stepped down on the gangplank, children's voices rose above the others. He stopped, looked back at the crowded deck, and a jolt of joy shot through him.

Laura stood at the railing in the middle of a cluster of girls about three-quarters of the way down the ship. She wore a dark green traveling suit with a lace collar and small straw hat. The little girls were all dressed alike in their light blue dresses, navy blue jackets, and straw skimmers with dark blue ribbons around the crown.

Henry slowed and looked over his shoulder as the other passengers hurried past them. "Andrew, are you coming?"

"Yes." Andrew's gaze finally connected with Laura, and he lifted his hand.

A smile broke across her face, and she waved back.

If only they weren't so far apart and separated by the crowd. He might not be able to go to her, but at least he could say something. He lifted his hands and cupped them around his mouth. "See you in Belleville!"

Her smile widened, she nodded, and then she waved again. She touched Anna May's shoulder and pointed to him. The little girl's eyes rounded, she rose up on her toes, and she sent him a vigorous wave. Soon the other girls saw him and waved too.

Henry chuckled. "It seems you've made quite an impression on those girls and a certain young lady."

His chest expanded. He hoped the girls would remember him, but even more than that, he hoped he had gained Laura's trust and perhaps even a place in her heart.

"Go on! Get out of this house!" Mr. Hoffman's angry voice vibrated through the hot evening air as Katie dashed out to the porch and let the screen door slam behind her in silent protest. Brushing a tear from her cheek, she marched down the steps.

How dare he yell at her like that!

It was true she had broken a dinner plate. But it had slipped out of her hands when she'd tried to stop Daniel from hitting Daisy. She wasn't being careless. She was simply trying to protect the little girl from her beastly brother.

Mr. Hoffman let loose another string of curses. Katie cringed and hurried around the side of the house. Mrs. Hoffman shouted back at her husband, and the children all began crying.

Please don't let him hurt them, Lord.

Katie sniffed back her tears and strode down the path, past the outhouse, and on toward the barn. Red and gold clouds streaked across the sky where the sun dipped below the recently planted fields in the west.

She stepped through the open barn doorway and pulled in a deep breath of hay-scented air. The Hoffmans' two horses nickered and looked up from their stalls. The milk cow munched on her feed, and doves cooed high up in the rafters. A little mouse skittered around the corner into the farthest stall, but that didn't frighten Katie. She liked the quiet company of the barn animals, even the mice.

She wiped the last of her tears from her cheeks and climbed the ladder to the loft. The temperature rose with each step she took. It felt like all the heat of the day had soaked into the old wooden barn. She usually took a break from her work each afternoon and opened the big loft door to let some of the hot air escape, but she had forgotten to do it today. Now the loft felt like an overheated oven.

She followed the path between the piles of hay and pushed open the loft door, but the air outside felt almost as hot. And though the sun had set, not even a slight breeze stirred the air to cool the temperature in the barn.

She brushed the back of her hand against her sweaty forehead. No way would she be able to sleep up here tonight. She'd have to find a spot down below where it would be at least a little cooler.

She grabbed the raggedy old quilt Mr. Hoffman had given her and was about to throw it down, but she noticed bits of hay stuck to the fabric. She gripped the edge, lifted it higher, and snapped it hard, hoping a good shaking would make the bits of hay fall off.

High-pitched clicking and squeaking sounded overhead. Katie looked up as two bats swooped down toward her. She screamed and dropped the quilt over the side of the open loft floor.

"Get away!" She ducked and tried to dodge the circling bats, stepping closer to the edge. One more step back and her foot met air. She teetered on the edge, gasped, and dove toward the floor.

Facedown in the hay, she felt her heart race and body tremble. *Dear Lord, please let those bats leave me alone!*

Down below, Charger barked. Katie crawled to the edge of the loft floor and looked over.

The collie pranced up and down the aisle of the barn and looked up at her with his tongue hanging out. Poor thing. He was probably thirsty.

Katie looked up, searching for the bats, but in the fading light she couldn't see them anymore. Mr. Hoffman never allowed her to take a lantern or candle to the barn, so she'd grown used to going to bed in the dark. Crouching low, she crept over to the ladder and climbed down as quickly as she could.

Charger met her at the bottom, pressing his warm, wet nose to her hand. She knelt and stroked his back, and he leaned against her leg. She ran her fingers through his warm, silky hair. Her eyes filled, and her nose tingled.

"You're a good boy, such a good boy." She bent down and pressed a kiss to Charger's head. "Come on, let's get you a drink. She grabbed a bucket from the hook on the wall and walked out to the pump at the side of the barn. With a few swift pumps of the handle, water gushed out into the bucket.

Charger didn't even wait until she finished but dipped his head in and lapped up a long drink.

Katie ran her hand along his back again as he continued drinking. Finally, he pulled back and looked up at her with a drippy wet smile.

Katie's heart melted, and she knelt down and laid her head on Charger's neck. The dog nestled closer, his tail wagging at a steady pace. She sighed and looked into Charger's face. "What would I do without you? No one else here cares a fig about me."

Charger nosed her hand as she stood, then he circled around her legs. It almost seemed as if he understood her words and felt the same.

"Come on, boy. Let's find somewhere to sleep tonight." She walked back into the barn, picked up the quilt, and shook it out again. No bats circled around this time, and she released a grateful sigh. Charger waited patiently, then followed her to the fourth stall.

The hay smelled sweet and looked clean. She spread out her quilt and lay down. She should change into her nightgown, but the light was almost gone, and she was so tired she just closed her eyes.

Charger lay down beside her. She scooted closer and rested her arm across his neck. The weariness of the day faded away as the comfort of her companion lulled her into a dreamy sleep.

17

L aura pushed open the window and welcomed the fresh breeze blowing in from the west. It carried the scent of field grasses and forests on the outskirts of town. She hoped it would blow away the stale air, heavy with the unpleasant smell of illness.

More than two weeks had passed since she'd arrived at Pleasantview, the children's receiving home located on the edge of Belleville, Ontario.

She'd spent the first week helping oversee her girls' placements. She knew that was the reason they'd come to Canada, but it had been difficult to say goodbye and see each girl leave with a different family.

Jenny was placed with the Jacksons, a farm family who lived two miles outside of Belleville. They had four children, and one of the girls was near Jenny's age. Laura hoped they would become friends and that would be a comfort to Jenny. She'd given Jenny a hug before she left and encouraged her to write to the home and let them know how she was doing.

Anna May was placed with Mr. and Mrs. Crawford, a middle-aged couple who lived in town and had no children. Mr. Crawford was a quiet man who oversaw the Belleville telegraph office. Mrs. Crawford seemed like a kind woman who was eager to care for Anna May, but Laura couldn't be sure of their intentions, and that had made it hard for her to sleep the last few nights.

Would her girls be well treated, or would they suffer from the stigma of being home children, outsiders with shadowed pasts? With all her heart she hoped for the best, but she couldn't seem to quiet her anxious thoughts.

While she'd helped with the placements, she discreetly tried to learn if her siblings had passed through Belleville or been dropped off at Kingston or some other town. So far she hadn't learned anything, and her worries deepened with each passing day.

She sighed and leaned back from the window. She'd had no word from Andrew, and if she didn't hear from him very soon, she would have no choice but to speak to the matron by herself. When Mrs. Woodward learned her real name and reason for coming to Canada, she would probably sack her, but she had to learn where her siblings had been sent and find a way to contact them.

One of the girls coughed, and her thoughts shifted back to the children in her care. Now that all her girls had been placed, she'd offered to stay on and help out in the third-floor infirmary. A sheet hung down the middle of the long room, separating the boys from the girls. Children who had returned to the home to recover from a serious illness or injury filled eighteen of the twenty beds.

She scanned the room, her stomach tensing as she remembered the sorrowful stories she'd been told about these children.

Thomas, the twelve-year-old boy in the first bed at the far end of the room, had been badly burned in a house fire—one he was blamed for starting, though he adamantly denied he was responsible. White cloth bandages covered his head, hands, arms, and torso, and he'd spent most of the day moaning in pain. Laura had badly burned her hand on the stove when she was younger, and she remembered how much it hurt. Thomas's burns were more extensive, and she couldn't imagine how he could endure that much suffering.

The next boy, ten-year-old Leon, had fallen down an old well on the farm where he'd been working. He'd broken both of his legs and his wrist, and now plaster casts encased his legs and right arm. The doctor said he was lucky to have survived, but he was miserable and begged anyone who would listen to send him home to England.

Six-year-old Holden lay in the next bed with a pale face and blue-tinged lips. He had an illness affecting his lungs, and watching his panicked expression as he struggled to breathe sent tremors through Laura. The doctor had come yesterday afternoon and given him medicine to help him rest, but it lasted only a few hours before he was back to struggling for every breath.

Randal and Oscar, blond-haired brothers who were seven and nine, lay in the next two beds. They both looked so thin and frail, Laura thought they were much younger when she met them. Tears had burned her eyes when she heard the boys had been starved and beaten by the farmer who had taken them in because they couldn't do as much work as he expected.

She shook her head, overwhelmed by the sorrowful stories and harsh treatment some of these children had received. All they had suffered had taken a great toll on their bodies, minds, and spirits, and some of them might never totally recover.

On the girls' side, the stories were no better. Fourteen-year-old Louise lay in the bed closest to the door. She had nearly drowned in a farm pond just outside Belleville. Louise was still alive, but she was unresponsive. The man who brought her in said it was an accident, but one of the other girls who knew her said Louise had been lonely and heartsick and she had probably tried to end her life by drowning. Yesterday Mrs. Woodward had whispered that they didn't expect Louise to last more than another day or two. All they could do was make her comfortable and pray for a peaceful passing.

The ache in Laura's heart deepened as she studied the dark-haired girl. What a tragedy! And soon she would leave this earth surrounded by strangers in an infirmary rather than in a loving home with family gathered around to grieve her passing.

Frieda, a thirteen-year-old with flaming red hair, had a broken arm, multiple bruises, and lash scars across her back and legs. She'd run away from the farm where she'd been working as a domestic. When she'd been found and returned, the farmer had beaten her again. Finally, a neighbor reported her treatment to the local minister and he contacted the home. They removed Frieda and brought her back to Pleasantview to recover. Her scars might fade with time and rest, but would she ever feel safe and loved after all she had endured?

Vivian, the girl in the bed beside Frieda, was weak and sick with a high fever and painful rash. She coughed so long and hard she could barely catch her breath, and that gave her little chance of getting any peaceful sleep. The doctor expected her to recover, but it could take several weeks of nursing care before she would be well enough to return to the family who took her in as a domestic.

Laura shifted her gaze away from the children's

faces and straightened Vivian's blanket. Her throat ached, and tears threatened to overflow her eyes. She pulled in a calming breath through her nose, trying to gain control of her emotions.

Not all of the children who came from England to Canada suffered like those in the infirmary. Rose had reassured her of that fact last night, but Laura couldn't help worrying about her girls and Katie, Grace, and Garth. What if they were ill or had been placed with families who were harsh and uncaring? That thought kept returning, and it made her so anxious she had a difficult time focusing on her tasks.

Rose walked into the infirmary carrying a pile of clean folded sheets. A thin, sloped-shouldered girl walked in behind her. She wore a loose, shabby brown dress and was barefoot. Laura guessed she was fifteen or sixteen, but it was hard to tell for sure.

"Come with me, Jane." Rose set the sheets on a chair and crossed toward Laura.

Jane's wavy brown hair fell forward, covering half of her face.

Rose glanced at Laura, sending her a silent plea, then looked back at the girl. "Jane, this is Miss Hopkins. She'll help you get a bath and give you a clean nightgown."

Jane looked up with wide blue eyes and quickly folded her arms tight across her chest. "I don't want a bath."

"It's all right," Rose said in a gentle tone. "You're quite safe here, and you'll have privacy to bathe and dress."

Jane darted an anxious glance at Laura, then turned to Rose. "Do I have to?"

"Yes, everyone who comes to stay has to bathe and change."

Laura watched their interaction with growing unease. What brought Jane to the infirmary? She didn't look ill or injured. Why was she so wary of them?

Rose nodded to Laura. "Will you please show Jane to the bathroom and be sure she has everything she needs?"

"Of course." Laura sent Jane a tentative smile. "You can come with me."

Jane stared at Laura, her lips quivering, but she didn't move.

"It's all right, Jane." Laura copied Rose's gentle tone. "It's just down the hall this way."

Jane glanced past Laura toward the hall, then finally gave a slight nod.

Questions tumbled through Laura's mind as they walked toward the bathroom and stopped to pick up a nightgown from the wardrobe. Perhaps if she could engage Jane in conversation, that would help her feel more at ease.

Laura glanced over her shoulder at Jane. "Pleasantview is a beautiful old house, isn't it?" The girl nodded but didn't speak. "It was built for the Simpson family back in the 1860s. Mr. Simpson was a railway tycoon, and he wanted his family to have the best of everything. When he passed away, his wife moved to a smaller residence and donated Pleasantview as a receiving home." She pushed open the door to the spacious bathroom. "We even have hot and cold running water."

Jane stopped in the doorway and stared at the claw-foot bathtub.

"Come and see." Laura motioned her closer, then turned on the tap in the tub. She held her hand under the stream of water and turned the two handles to adjust the temperature.

Jane slowly crossed the room and stood next to Laura.

"Is that hot enough for you?"

Jane reached down and tested the water. "Yes. It's fine." Her voice sounded so soft Laura could barely hear her.

"All right." Laura rose and took a bath towel and washcloth from the shelf. She draped them over the side of the tub and smiled at Jane. "I'll leave you to it . . . unless you'd like me to help you undress."

The girl's eyes flashed wide. "No, no . . . I don't need any help."

"All right, then." Laura crossed the room. "You can lock the door after I leave."

Jane nodded but stood frozen to the spot.

Laura stepped out and closed the door behind her. She waited in the hall, and a few seconds later she heard the lock turn.

Rose approached from the far end of the hall. "Did you convince Jane to take a bath?" she whispered.

Laura nodded. "I think so. What brings her to the infirmary?"

Rose's eyes clouded, and she shook her head. "I can hardly speak of it."

A tremor raced down Laura's back. "If you don't think you should tell me, it's—"

"Come with me," Rose whispered. She took Laura's arm and guided her a safe distance away from the bathroom. She glanced down the hall, then turned to Laura. "Jane is with child."

Laura raised her hand to her mouth. "Oh dear."

"But you mustn't think poorly of her. She's not to blame."

Laura cringed, but she had to ask. "What happened?"

"She has been working as a domestic for a farm family up near Roslin." Rose clasped her hands in front of her heart. "And I'm afraid the farmer forced himself on her . . . more than once."

Dread churned Laura's stomach.

"The wife finally realized her . . . condition, and she demanded to know who the father was. Jane told her what her husband had done, and the wife went into a rage. She said it was Jane's fault, and she demanded Jane be sent back here."

"How dreadful! That man ought to go to jail."

"Of course he should, but I doubt it will happen. The wife insists Jane tempted her husband and she is the one to blame."

"That's ridiculous! She's just a girl, and a shy one at that."

Rose glanced toward the bathroom door. "I feel terrible for her."

"What will happen to her . . . and her baby?"

"Mrs. Woodward is going to look for someone to take her in, at least until the baby is born."

"What about after that?"

"I'm not sure. I doubt Jane could find a respectable family willing to take them both under the circumstances." Worry lines creased Rose's forehead. "If she'll give up the child, she might be able to find work with another family."

"But to separate them . . . Is that the only answer?"

Rose lifted her hand to her forehead. "I don't know. It's such a difficult situation. We must be very kind and patient as we care for her."

Laura nodded. "Perhaps she could stay with us rather than in the infirmary. We could bring in another bed."

Rose pondered that for a moment. "Yes, that way she'd have a bit more privacy and wouldn't have to answer so many questions." Rose reached for Laura's hand. "We must treat her like a dear sister."

Those words pierced Laura's heart, and a wave of dizziness washed over her. Katie was almost the same age as Jane. What if some man tried to hurt her as Jane had been hurt?

Conviction filled her soul. She could not wait any longer. She had to move forward with her search for her siblings . . . with or without Andrew Frasier!

The clock struck eleven as Laura crept down the stairs and slipped across the entrance hall. The matron kept all the children's files in cabinets in her office. If Laura was going to discover where her siblings had been sent, she would have to sneak in and search through those files.

All the lights on the main floor had been turned down expect one small gas lamp near the front entry. It provided just enough light for Laura to find her way down the hall without bumping into the side table and chairs.

A door opened somewhere nearby.

Laura pulled in a sharp breath and stepped back against the wall. She closed her eyes and tried to calm her breathing and melt into the shadows.

Footsteps retreated, and she let out a slow, shallow breath.

When all was quiet for several seconds, she continued toward the matron's office. With chilled fingers, she quietly turned the doorknob, slipped inside, and pulled the door closed behind her.

She turned and scanned the dark office. Pale moonlight shone through the windows, highlighting the shape of a desk, bookshelves, and the two tall filing cabinets against the side wall. If she was going to read anything in those files, she would have to light her candle and pray no one passing by would see the glow beneath the door and decide to investigate.

She reached in her skirt pocket and pulled out the short candle stub and box of matches she'd found in the kitchen pantry. Hovering behind the desk, she struck the match and touched it to the wick. The candle flickered, then sent wavering light around the room.

Laura straightened and crossed to the filing cabinets. She placed the candle in a shallow metal bowl on top and pulled open the first drawer. She scanned the tabs and found the files contained bills, receipts, and correspondence with various local merchants. She quietly closed that drawer and opened the next.

This one had records of maintenance and improvements made on the house, taxes, and legal matters. Laura gave an impatient sigh and closed that drawer.

When she pulled open the third drawer, her breath caught. Names were written on each file tab: *Abbot, Charlotte; Adams, Lucile; Addison, Maryann.*

She pulled out the first file, flipped it open, and tilted the papers toward the light. At the top the page read *Admission Sheet* and below that *Child's name: Charlotte Abbot. Date of birth: 27, September 1892. Place of birth: Manchester, England. Mother's name: Mary Jane Abbot. Father's name: Ronald Guy Abbot. Date of entry into Waifs and Strays Home: 14, April 1899.*

She'd found the right cabinet! Now all she needed to do was make her way through the alphabet to McAlister. She quickly scanned the names in that drawer. The last one read, *Campbell, Irene.* She slid open the next drawer and found those names stopped with *Grosvenor, Arlene.* The bottom drawer ended with *Lewis, Elizabeth.*

Laura's pulse sped up as she stepped over to the next cabinet and rolled open the top drawer. After pulling the bowl with the candle closer, she searched the names, and her heart leaped. There they were: *McAlister, Grace,* and *McAlister, Katherine.*

Footsteps approached in the hall.

Laura grabbed Katie's file and blew out the candle. The scent of smoke swirled beneath her nose. The doorknob turned. Laura froze. The door swung open.

A woman stepped in and flipped the switch, flooding the office with light.

Rose gasped. "Mary, what are you doing?"

Relief rushed through Laura, quickly followed by another round of panic. Even though it was her friend who had discovered her, she still had to explain herself. "I was just . . . looking for a file."

Confusion filled Rose's face. "What file?"

Laura swallowed and lifted Katie's file. "My sister's."

Rose's eyes rounded. "Your sister?"

Laura nodded. "I'm sorry. I wanted to tell you, but I was afraid you might not approve of my plan."

"What plan? Mary, you're not making sense."

Another set of footsteps sounded in the hall, and Mrs. Woodward stepped into the open doorway. Her astonished gaze darted from Rose to Laura. "What's going on here?"

Laura slipped the file into the folds of her skirt, her heart pounding in her throat.

Rose turned toward Mrs. Woodward. "I . . . I wanted to drop off this list of supplies we need in the infirmary and return these two books I borrowed."

Mrs. Woodward studied Rose. "At this time of night?"

Rose gave a little chuckle. "I've always been a late-night reader. And I thought I ought to return them as soon as I was finished."

The matron glanced at Laura with an expectant lift of her brows. "And you, Miss Hopkins, are you returning something as well?"

"No ma'am." She couldn't add one more lie to the others she'd already told, so she said nothing more.

Mrs. Woodward stepped over to her desk. "You know I always have an open door for my staff, but I'd feel more comfortable if you'd come in when I'm here."

"Yes ma'am." Laura nodded and backed toward the door.

"I'll be sure to do that next time." Rose placed the list and the books on the corner of the woman's desk and then walked out after Laura.

"Thank you." Laura whispered when they were a few steps down the hall.

Rose sent her a serious look. "I'm not sure what's going on, but I want you to come upstairs now and tell me everything."

Laura swallowed. "Yes. It's past time I do."

Andrew followed Henry and Mrs. Woodward up the stairs toward the top floor of the Pleasantview receiving home. For the last twenty minutes, the matron had shown them around the lower two floors of the facility. She seemed to be an intelligent woman and had answered their questions in a thoughtful, open manner.

Andrew looked for Laura as they entered each

room, but so far he hadn't seen her or Rose Carson. Were they still here, or had they left the home in search of Laura's siblings? He clenched his jaw, hoping that was not the case.

The matron reached the upper landing. "The girls who arrived in the last group have all been placed as domestics with families in and around Belleville."

Andrew thought of Anna May and frowned. She definitely wasn't old enough to work as a domestic. Where had they sent her?

"The girls you met downstairs have returned from one placement and are waiting for the next. We try to keep them happy and occupied while they're with us." Mrs. Woodward nodded toward the landing window.

Andrew stepped over and looked down at the sloping lawn behind the house. Two girls sat reading in the shade of a large maple tree while half a dozen others chased one another across the grass in a lively game of tag. They seemed to be enjoying the time outside on this sunny morning.

Henry turned to Mrs. Woodward. "How many girls can you accommodate?"

"We have beds for one hundred twenty-five. This is one of our dormitories." She opened a door on the left, and he and Henry looked in. "We also have a twenty-bed infirmary on this floor for our girls and the boys from the Masterson Home."

Henry clasped his hands behind his back. "The boys' home doesn't have its own infirmary?"

"No. Masterson is a smaller facility. They don't have enough room there, so we care for both boys and girls here."

Henry gave a thoughtful nod. "We'd like to see the infirmary."

A ripple of unease crossed the matron's face. "I'm not sure that would be wise. Some of the children's illnesses are contagious, and I wouldn't want to put you and Mr. Frasier in danger of catching a disease."

"That's not a problem. Mr. Frasier and I have strong constitutions. I'm sure we can take a quick tour with no danger of contracting an illness."

The matron compressed her lips and shifted her gaze away.

Why didn't she want to show them the infirmary? Was she trying to hide something?

Henry glanced at Andrew, the same question reflected in his eyes. "It's important that we see all areas of the home so we have accurate information for our report." Henry's tone was kind but firm.

The matron looked their way again. "Very well." She stepped past them and opened the door on the right.

Henry led them into the long rectangular room. A fabric curtain hung down the middle, separating the two sides. They set off down the right side.

Henry stopped by the third bed. A young boy with pale blond hair and sky-blue eyes lay propped up with several pillows. The lad looked their way, his breathing raspy.

Henry turned to the matron. "Please tell me about this boy."

Mrs. Woodward turned away from the bed and lowered her voice. "This is Holden Jamison. He is six years old and suffering from asthma. He was placed with a family two months ago, but his health declined and they brought him back to the home last week."

Henry nodded, then stepped up to the bed and laid a hand on the boy's shoulder. "Hello, Holden. I'm sorry you're not feeling well."

"Thank you, sir," the boy said softly.

"I hope you'll soon be back on your feet and playing with your friends."

Holden tipped his head and studied Henry's face. "You talk like my father."

Henry pondered that a moment. "I suppose I sound like him because I'm from England."

"So am I."

Henry smiled. "Yes, we share a common heritage."

The boy nodded, looking pleased.

Henry patted the boy's shoulder. "God bless you, Holden. Rest well and take care."

The boy smiled before pulling in another ragged breath.

Troubled thoughts filled Andrew as he watched the exchange. It would be difficult for a young lad to be so far from home and family while he dealt with such a serious condition. The infirmary seemed to provide adequate care, but it couldn't compare to being cared for at home by family members who cherished him. He sent off a silent prayer for Holden, then walked on down the row to see the other patients.

The lad in the last bed was fast asleep when they approached. His face was barely visible past all the bandages wrapped around his head, and more covered his arms and hands.

Henry stopped by the end of his bed. "What happened to this boy?" He kept his voice low so he wouldn't disturb him.

Lines creased Mrs. Woodward's face. "He was badly burned in a house fire."

"How tragic." Henry laid his hand on the metal bedstead and closed his eyes for a few moments. Andrew bowed his head as well, certain Henry was praying for the boy.

When Henry looked up, the matron motioned for them to follow her around the end of the curtain. "On this side we have seven girls."

Andrew stepped past the curtain and looked down the row. A woman stood next to the first bed, brushing a young girl's hair. Recognition flashed through him, and his steps stalled.

Laura looked up. Her eyes widened, and her hand stilled.

"This is Miss Hopkins." The matron motioned toward Laura. "She recently accompanied a group of girls from England, and she is staying on to help us for a few weeks."

Relief rushed through Andrew. Laura was still here! And even though it had taken him more than two weeks to reach Belleville, she had waited for him and not revealed her identity to the matron.

Mrs. Woodward sent Laura a pointed look. "These gentlemen are here as representatives of the British government. They're gathering information for a report about child emigration."

"Hello, Miss Hopkins." Andrew nodded to her. "It's a pleasure to see you again."

Laura's blue eyes glowed. "Good day, Mr. Frasier, Mr. Dowd."

Mrs. Woodward's eyebrows arched. "You know these gentlemen?"

"Yes ma'am. We sailed to Canada on the same ship."

Henry turned to Mrs. Woodward. "It was very encouraging to see how well the girls were cared for on the voyage across the Atlantic. I have a great deal of respect for Miss Hopkins and Miss Carson. Their devotion to the girls is admirable."

"That's good to hear." Mrs. Woodward looked at Laura with new appreciation.

Rose walked down the aisle toward them, her gaze focused on Henry and her smile spreading wider. She held out her hand. "Mr. Dowd, Mr. Frasier, welcome to Pleasantview."

Henry took her hand with a slight bow. "Miss Carson, I'm happy to see you looking so well."

Rose's cheeks flushed. "Thank you."

"Shall we continue our tour, gentlemen?" Mrs. Woodward walked down the row of beds.

Andrew reached in his pocket and took out the note he'd written to Laura. As he walked past, he pressed the folded paper into her hand.

He heard her quick intake of breath and felt her fingers grasp the note.

He followed the matron, but when he looked over his shoulder, he saw Laura slide the note into her skirt pocket and send him a fleeting smile.

His heart soared as he walked on, rejoicing that she'd waited for him and confident he'd won a bit more of her trust.

Laura stepped into the upper hall and crossed the landing to the empty third-floor dormitory. She slipped inside and quietly closed the door. Her hand trembled as she took the note from her skirt pocket. *Thank You, Lord!* What a blessed relief to see Andrew again. She lowered her gaze and began reading.

> Dear Laura, Henry and I arrived in Belleville yesterday evening and are staying at the Fairmont Hotel on Front Street. I'm sorry it took longer than I expected for us to arrive. We had to extend our time in Montreal to finish our meetings and visit the two homes there. But you have never been far from my thoughts, and I look forward to seeing you soon.

She blinked and reread the last sentence. Did he mean that in a friendly, concerned way, or was he hinting at more? Of course she'd thought of him every day, hoping he'd soon arrive and contact her, but she had tamped down her hopes each time they'd risen. She shook her head. How confusing!

> I know you must be eager to move forward with your search for your brother and sisters, and I am ready to help you in any way I can. As I said in our conversations aboard the Parisian, I believe Henry's legal experience and wisdom will be a great asset. I hope you are ready to confide in him and allow

us both to assist you. I believe that will give you the best chance for a positive outcome.

Can you meet with us tonight at seven? The hotel has a spacious lobby that would give us the opportunity for a private conversation in a public place. If that's not convenient, please send a message and suggest an alternate time.

We expect to be in Belleville a few days, then we begin visiting several children outside of town to see how they are faring in their placements. What we've seen so far has been enlightening, and I look forward to telling you more about it when we meet.

I hope to see you tonight. Until then I remain your trusted friend,

Andrew Frasier

Laura lifted her cool fingers to her lips. Andrew's final words rang true. He had become her trusted friend. Was she ready to meet with Henry Dowd and tell him the full story? What would he say when he learned she'd not only used a false identity to come to Canada but she'd also stolen her sister's file from the matron's office?

She closed her eyes. *Lord, I know I panicked and rushed ahead—again! But hearing Jane's story frightened me so, and I felt I had to do something to try to protect Katie and Grace. I couldn't bear the thought of anyone hurting them the way Jane was hurt. I know I've not been honest and that stealing is wrong, but that was my only choice.*

She stopped, convicted by her thoughts. The truth was, she'd been upset and taken matters into her own hands. She could've taken time to pray and waited for the Lord to direct her instead of stealing that file. If she had waited, would she have found an honest path forward with better results? She'd never know now.

She held the note to her heart and closed her eyes. *I'm sorry, Lord. Forgive me for rushing ahead and not waiting for Your guidance and direction. Please show me Your mercy and provide a way out of these troubles.*

She lowered the note and gazed at Andrew's words again. The letters blurred on the page, and the events of last night filled her mind once more.

After Rose discovered her in the matron's office, they'd gone to a quiet nook on the third floor, and Laura told her everything. Her friend had been surprised and perhaps even a little disappointed, but she hadn't rejected Laura. Instead she'd encouraged her to tell the truth and promised to help in any way she could.

Now Andrew was asking her to take the next

step and confess everything to Henry. Would he understand? Was he a trusted ally, or would he turn her over to the authorities?

What do You want me to do, Lord?

18

Katie trudged down the path toward the pump by the barn, the empty buckets pulling down on her arms like they were filled with rocks. This was her seventh trip to the pump to retrieve bathwater, and it would take several more to bring in enough for the whole family to bathe.

A sudden wave of dizziness swept over her. She stopped and closed her eyes. Maybe if she rested for a moment, it would pass. But painful cramps seized her middle, and fearful panic spread through her. She dropped the buckets and clutched her arms tight across her waist.

What was wrong with her?

She lowered her head, trying to think straight. The last few days she'd been more tired than usual, and today she'd barely had enough energy to complete her chores. But this powerful wave of sickness was something new.

"What are you doing?" Daniel stalked toward her. He dangled a dead frog in one hand and carried a long stick in the other.

Katie blew out a breath and straightened. "I'm just getting some more bathwater."

Daniel glared at the buckets. "I don't want to take a bath, and I don't want to go to church."

Katie slowly continued her walk toward the

pump. "Your father says we're going, so I don't think you have a choice."

Daniel huffed. "All that singin' and sittin' and listenin' to the preacher wears me out."

Katie released a strangled laugh. It sounded wonderful to her. She'd been thrilled when Mrs. Hoffman told her to fetch the water, heat it on the stove, and give Daisy a bath. The reverend had come by again, and now they were going to church on Sunday morning. But what if she felt unwell tomorrow? She couldn't bear the thought of missing her chance to attend church. The way Mr. Hoffman talked, he was going only this one time to satisfy the reverend and keep him from continually visiting.

"Hurry up with that water!" Mrs. Hoffman shouted from the front doorway. "Daniel, get in here. It's your turn for a bath."

"I don't want no bath!" the boy shouted back.

"Don't sass me! Get in this house right now!"

Daniel stood his ground, scowling at his mother.

"You better do as she says." Katie pushed down on the pump handle three times before the water finally started to flow, and still the boy didn't move.

She wasn't overly fond of Daniel, but she knew Mr. Hoffman used his belt to punish the boy when he was angry, and she didn't think any child should be beaten like that, not even ornery Daniel Hoffman.

Mrs. Hoffman stomped across the porch. "Don't make me go get your father!"

Daniel gave a disgusted snort, tossed his frog aside, and set off toward the house.

Katie sighed and continued pumping until both buckets were filled to the top. The woozy feeling was still with her. She swiped her sleeve across her forehead and looked out across the fields. Mum and Laura always took such good care of her when she wasn't feeling well. The strong bond of love they shared had carried them through so many difficult times. But now she was alone. No one here cared if she was unwell or in pain.

Mr. Hoffman strode out of the barn. "What's wrong with you, girl? Stop standing there staring and get that water up to the house!"

Katie gripped the handles and lifted the heavy buckets. With slow, wobbly steps she carried them back up the path. Water sloshed out and soaked her stockings and shoes.

Should she tell Mrs. Hoffman she wasn't feeling well? If she did, would the woman even care? She never spoke to Katie except to issue terse orders, and even those were few and far between. They expected her to do all the work in the house, watch the children, prepare the food, clean up, work in the garden, feed the chickens, and milk the cow. She'd known how to do some of those chores, but others were brand new. She'd made many mistakes while she was learning and suffered for them.

She shook her head and slowly climbed the porch steps. She wouldn't say anything to Mrs. Hoffman. If she did, she might make her stay home tomorrow and miss church. It would be better to keep working and hope whatever was wrong would pass.

Laura pushed open the front door of the Fairmont Hotel and stepped inside with Rose. Her gaze darted around the elegant lobby, and her stomach quivered. Two large, glittering chandeliers hung from the high ceiling, spreading soft light across the smooth, white marble floor. Dark wood paneling covered the walls, and tall potted palms and overstuffed chairs were grouped on the far side of the room.

A tall, somber man in a black uniform stood behind the reception desk, watching Laura and Rose as they started across the lobby.

Rose squeezed her hand. "Don't worry. Everything is going to be all right."

"I hope so." Laura pulled in a deep breath, trying to calm her anxious thoughts.

Before they were halfway to the reception desk, Andrew and Henry rose from chairs by the window and crossed to meet them. Andrew smiled at Laura, looking relieved.

She returned a slight smile, hoping she didn't appear as nervous as she felt.

Henry grinned at Rose. "Good evening, Miss Carson, Miss Hopkins."

A surge of gratefulness rose from Laura's heart. Andrew had kept his promise and not revealed her identity to Henry.

"Good evening." Rose tilted her chin to gaze up at Henry. "Thank you for meeting with us."

Henry sent her a quizzical look, then turned to Andrew. "You knew they were coming?"

"Yes . . . I arranged the meeting." He shifted his gaze to Laura.

Her face warmed, and she quickly glanced away.

"It's always a pleasure to see you," Henry continued, "but is there some particular reason you wanted to see us this evening?"

Rose nodded to Laura, encouraging her to answer.

The time had come, and she summoned her courage. "Yes, I'd like to tell you about my family and ask for your help."

Henry studied her a moment, then motioned toward the four chairs by the window. "All right. Let's sit down, and you can tell me what's on your mind."

Laura followed the two men across the lobby and took a seat. When they were all settled, she looked across and met Henry's gaze. "First, I must tell you my name is Laura McAlister. I've been using my middle name, Mary, and my mum's maiden name, Hopkins, to keep my identity a secret. The real reason I came to Canada is to search for my three siblings."

Henry's eyebrows rose. "Please tell me more."

Laura poured out her story, summarizing what had happened in England, but giving him enough details so he would understand how her family had been separated and why it was urgent that she find her brother and sisters.

Henry listened attentively without interrupting.

"When I arrived at the receiving home in Belleville, my sisters weren't there. And I had no idea what happened to them or where they'd been placed. I wanted to speak to the matron the first day, but when we were on the *Parisian*, Andrew advised me to wait until you both arrived in Belleville."

Henry glanced at Andrew. "You knew about this? Why didn't you tell me?"

"That's my fault," Laura answered before Andrew could speak. "I asked Andrew not to say anything to you until we reached Canada."

Henry's frown made it clear he was not pleased with the arrangement.

Laura hurried on. She had to make him understand. "Rose and I spent our first few days here helping our girls find placements." She clasped her hands in her lap. "I hope they'll do well, but I'm very concerned about them."

"And why is that?"

"I don't know if the people who've taken them in will care for them as they should. I can't believe how little is required. All they have to do is fill out a brief application and pay a small fee, and then they can choose any child they want and take the child home. Shouldn't they at least have to provide character references and prove they're qualified to care for children?"

Henry's expression relaxed as he listened. "Those are good questions, Miss . . . McAlister."

"I feel even more strongly about it now that I've spent a few days working in the infirmary. The stories I've heard there about children who have been mistreated or suffered from illness and injury during their placements have nearly crushed my heart."

Lines creased Henry's forehead.

"And that makes me even more concerned for my brother and sisters. I can't help but wonder if Garth has been beaten or burned like the boys I cared for." Thoughts of Jane's dreadful situation filled her mind, and she tightened the grip on the arms of her chair. "The girls are in a much more vulnerable position. I could barely sleep the last few nights, worrying about Katie and Grace."

Henry listened with growing unease. "It sounds as though your time at Pleasantview has been anything but pleasant."

"I'm afraid you're right, and I decided I had to take action."

Andrew's brow creased. "What do you mean?"

Laura straightened. "Last night I slipped into the matron's office and looked through the files."

415

Andrew tensed, and a muscle in his jaw twitched.

"I know you asked me to wait, but when so many days had passed and you didn't come, I felt desperate to learn what I could."

Henry sent her a serious look. "Did you find your sisters' files?"

Laura nodded. "I took out Katie's. All I intended to do was read it and find out where she'd been placed, but Rose walked into the office and found me there. And before I could explain myself, Mrs. Woodward arrived."

"Oh no." Andrew's expression grew more intense, and he leaned toward her. "What did she say?"

"She asked why we were there, and I was so stunned, I didn't know how to respond."

Rose shifted in her chair. "I told Mrs. Woodward I was returning books and leaving her a note, which was true. She was satisfied, and we left."

Henry focused on Laura again. "What happened to your sister's file?"

"I couldn't put it back, not while Mrs. Woodward was standing there. So I hid it in the folds of my skirt as I walked out of the office with Rose." She glanced at Andrew, then quickly looked away. It was clear he was disappointed in her.

Henry sat back and rubbed his chin for a few

moments. Then he turned to Laura. "We'll have to speak to the matron as soon as possible and try to straighten this out. I doubt she'll be pleased to learn you're using a false name. And you may lose your position for taking that file. Are you prepared for that?"

Laura's stomach clenched. What would she do if the matron sacked her? Why hadn't she considered the consequences when she'd taken that file? But Henry was right. She must admit what she'd done and hope the matron would show mercy. She met Henry's gaze and nodded. "I understand."

"I don't approve of your tactics, though I do sympathize with your situation. Over the past several weeks, we have witnessed some of the challenges of emigration." Henry turned to Andrew. "Miss McAlister will need our legal help."

"I agree. I suggest we inform the matron the children were taken from England without proper consent, request their locations, and retrieve them."

Henry lifted his hand. "I'm afraid that may not be the best course."

Laura's gaze darted from Andrew to Henry. "What do you mean?"

"Even though the children were sent to Canada without your mother's consent, that doesn't mean you have the legal right to retrieve them."

"But my mum was never given time to make other arrangements. That can't be right."

"I understand it sounds unfair, but the law allows agencies to remove children from their parents' care if the situation is unsafe or morally objectionable. They're also allowed to emigrate any child in their care. All that's required is that they notify the parents, but that can be done after the child sails."

A tremor passed through Laura. "But my mum was ill, and she's a widow. It was not her fault the children were left on their own."

"I understand. It's a tragic situation, and it seems unjust, but I'm afraid the law is on the side of the sending agency."

Laura could barely voice her thoughts. "So we have no recourse . . . no legal way to reclaim them?"

A slight smile lifted Henry's lips. "We're not giving up. In fact, I'd say we've only just begun the fight."

On Sunday morning, Katie rode in the back of the wagon with Daisy and Daniel as Mr. Hoffman drove through Roslin with Mrs. Hoffman and the baby seated up front. When they came closer to the white clapboard church with the tall steeple, the sound of people singing a hymn drifted out the open double doors.

The wagon rolled to a stop next to several

other wagons and horses. Daniel jumped down from the back, and Katie took Daisy's hand and helped her climb down. That lightheaded feeling shot through her again, and she swayed slightly. Closing her eyes, she pulled in a deep breath, praying it would pass quickly.

She hadn't eaten breakfast, thinking that might make her feel worse. Now she realized that might not have been the best decision.

Mrs. Hoffman climbed down from her seat and gave Daniel a push toward the church. "Let's go." She took a few steps, then glanced back at the wagon. "Howard, aren't you comin'?"

Mr. Hoffman spit on the ground and adjusted his hat. "Naw, you go ahead. I'll wait out here for you."

Mrs. Hoffman's nostrils flared, and she glared at her husband. "I can't keep Daniel and Daisy quiet in church and care for the baby!"

"You got the girl!" Mr. Hoffman turned his scowl on Katie. "You make the children mind."

"Yes sir." She wasn't sure how she'd manage that since the boy never listened to a word she said and Daisy could cry at the drop of a hat, but she'd try. She followed Mrs. Hoffman up the steps and into the church, hoping all would go well, but she had a feeling it wouldn't.

Light poured through the stained-glass windows, painting soft colors across the shoulders of the congregation. People's voices rose and blended together in harmony, filling the church with energy and life.

Katie's heart lifted with the music, and healing warmth flowed through her. She hadn't been in a real church service since they'd left the flat in London. When she'd stayed at Grangeford and Hughes, the children gathered on Sunday to sing hymns and listen to a message from the matron, but that wasn't the same.

Mrs. Hoffman slipped into the second row from the back, and the people standing there moved down to make room for them. Katie slid in between Daniel and Daisy and prayed they would behave themselves so she could enjoy the service.

The hymn ended, and the song leader told everyone to be seated. Katie settled on the pew and glanced around. It looked like about sixty or seventy people were attending the service—families with children, older couples, young women, and a few young men and older boys. Most were dressed simply in neat, clean clothing. Many of the women wore small, sensible hats, and most of the girls had ribbons in their hair.

Katie glanced down at her two plain braids. She didn't own any ribbons, and she didn't think Mrs. Hoffman would give her any.

The small choir up on the platform stood and opened their hymnals.

Katie sat back and listened to the song, letting the lyrics fill her mind and heart.

Daniel began to fidget, swing his legs back and forth, and kick the pew in front of them.

Mrs. Hoffman glared at him. "Stop that and settle down!" She kept her voice low, but several people turned and looked their way.

Daniel pulled away from her and stuck out his lower lip, but he stopped kicking the pew for the moment.

The choir sang the second verse, and baby Darla began to whimper and fuss. Mrs. Hoffman gave an impatient huff and jiggled the baby up and down.

Katie sighed. Poor dear. There was no way those jerky movements were going to soothe her.

A few more people looked back at them, some with frowns and others with compassionate expressions. Katie slid down a little lower in the pew, wishing she didn't have to sit with the Hoffmans.

Two rows ahead on the other side of the aisle, a young man turned and glanced at Mrs. Hoffman and her squirming baby. He looked like Garth.

Katie blinked and gasped. It was Garth!

Her heart soared, and she gripped the edge of the pew to keep herself from jumping up right then and there. She didn't want to cause a disturbance, but she had to get his attention and make sure he saw her. She reached past Daisy, lowered her hand, and waved it back and forth, praying he'd notice.

His gaze slid her way, and recognition shot through his dark eyes. A smile broke across his face, and he nodded to her. Then he leaned toward the young man sitting next to him and whispered something in his ear. The young man glanced back at Katie.

She stifled another gasp. It was Rob Lewis, Garth's friend she'd met on the voyage to Canada. He smiled, his blue eyes reflecting the light from the window on his left.

Gratefulness welled up in her heart, and she sent him a warm smile. Garth and Rob must live nearby. How wonderful that they were able to see each other and come to church together.

Mrs. Hoffman reached across and pinched Katie's leg. "Stop your flirting!"

"I'm not flirting," Katie whispered back.

"Don't argue with me!" Mrs. Hoffman's harsh whisper made several people turn their way again.

Katie's face blazed, and she forced down the hot reply in her throat. There was no telling what the Hoffmans would do to her when they got back to the farm if she didn't settle down and pretend to ignore the boys.

Katie pressed her lips tightly together and looked straight ahead, but every few seconds Garth glanced at her and she met his gaze. She was so excited to speak to her brother she could barely focus on the sermon or the closing hymn. At last the minister offered the final prayer and dismissed the congregation.

Katie stood, her eyes fixed on Garth. She was not going to let him out of her sight no matter what Mrs. Hoffman or anyone else said. She had to talk to him.

Daniel stepped on Katie's toes, squeezed past, and headed for the door.

"Let's go." Mrs. Hoffman elbowed Katie.

Rob and Garth moved into the aisle, and Katie stepped out of her pew.

Mrs. Hoffman gripped Daisy's shoulder and steered her toward Katie. "Take charge of her." She sent Katie a stern glance, then started down the aisle after Daniel.

Garth walked toward her, his wide smile lighting up his face. "Katie, I can't believe you're here."

"It's so good to see you, Garth." She studied him. "You look . . . older."

He nodded and seemed pleased by her comment. "It must be all the work I'm doing for Mr. Gilchrest. Where are you staying?"

"I'm at the Hoffmans' farm, a few miles north of town." She glanced over her shoulder, looking for Mrs. Hoffman. She had stopped to talk to an older woman who was eager to see the baby. Relief rushed through Katie, and she turned back to the boys.

Rob nodded to her, his gaze warm and friendly. "Hello, Katie. It's nice to see you."

"Hello, Rob." He looked taller and had filled out since she'd seen him on the ship. "Do you and Garth work for the same family?"

"No, I'm staying with the Chapmans, but our farm is next to the one where Garth works."

Katie turned to Garth. "Is it near Roslin?"

He nodded, his smile fading a bit. "I'm working for Mr. Eli Gilchrest. He has a sawmill and large farm about three miles west of town. But I spend Sundays with Rob at the Chapmans'. They're fine folks, and they treat us both like family."

"That's good to hear."

Daisy tugged on Katie's skirt and looked up at her. "I'm hungry."

Garth grinned. "Who's this?"

"This is Daisy Hoffman. She's three." Katie glanced toward the door. Mrs. Hoffman was smiling and speaking to the reverend. Katie blinked and looked again. She didn't think she'd ever seen the woman smile before.

"Let's go outside." Garth motioned toward the door.

Katie nodded, and the four of them walked up the aisle. Garth introduced Katie to Reverend Paxton at the door. She'd seen him when he'd visited the Hoffmans', but they'd never allowed her to come out and meet him.

"Welcome to Roslin, Katie. I hope we'll see you in church often."

"Thank you. I hope so too." She walked outside with Garth and Rob and stepped into the sunshine.

Garth stopped at the bottom of the steps and turned to Katie. "Why haven't I seen you at church before now?"

"I've only been with the Hoffmans a few weeks, and they don't come to church often. Before that I was in Belleville with Dr. and Mrs. Richardson. But they . . . Well, it just didn't work out. They sent me back to the home."

Lines creased Garth's forehead. "What happened?"

Katie shook her head. "I did the best I could, but they had their minds set against me because I was a home child."

Garth and Rob exchanged a serious glance.

Katie searched the line of wagons. Mrs. Hoffman handed the baby up to her husband as she prepared to climb aboard. "I don't have much time. I'm sure the Hoffmans want to get back to the farm." A wave of dizziness swept over her. She swayed and lifted her hand to her forehead.

Garth gripped her arm. "Katie, are you all right?"

"I'm just a little woozy, that's all." She blew out a breath and looked up at him, forcing a smile. She didn't want Garth to worry about her.

Concern filled his eyes as he searched her face. "You look like you've lost weight, and you're pale as a sheet. Are they feeding you?"

She brushed her hand down her loose dress. The Hoffmans didn't have a mirror in their house, but she'd seen herself reflected in the pond and was surprised by how thin her face looked. "The Hoffmans eat what they grow and raise. There's not always enough for everyone."

He slipped his arm around her shoulders. "I'll come and bring you something. I work hard, but I always have more than enough to eat."

"What do you think you're doing?" Mr. Hoffman's voice rang out as he stomped across the grass toward them. "Step back and leave the girl alone."

Katie started to pull away, but Garth held her next to him. "This is my sister. You've no call to shout at us."

Mr. Hoffman narrowed his eyes and scanned Garth. "You don't look like her brother."

Garth straightened and met Mr. Hoffman's hostile glare. "Well, I am, and we're not only brother and sister—we're twins."

"Ha! I don't believe that!"

Rob stepped forward. "It's true, sir. I've known Garth since we lived in England. And this is his twin sister, Katie McAlister."

Mr. Hoffman spit on the ground. "You're a home child too."

Garth scowled, obviously disliking the label. "I'm from England and proud of it. I work for Mr. Eli Gilchrest at his mill and farm west of Roslin."

"I know Gilchrest. How old are you, boy?"

"Fifteen, and I do a full day's work."

Surprise rippled through Katie. Garth was fifteen now, and so was she. Her birthday had come and gone, and she hadn't even realized it. Love and pride filled her as she watched Garth face off with Mr. Hoffman. He was a young man now, tall and strong and able to speak his mind.

Mr. Hoffman huffed. "It's time to go. Get in the wagon, girl." When she didn't move, he grabbed her arm.

Fire flashed in Garth's eyes. "Let go of my sister!"

All over the churchyard, people turned and watched them.

Mr. Hoffman tightened his hold. "Don't try to order me around, boy!"

"You've no call to be harsh with her."

"She works for me, and you've got nothin' to say about it." Mr. Hoffman tugged her toward the wagon. "Get on up there." He gave her a shove, then stood guard, watching while she climbed into the back of the wagon.

Tears burned Katie's eyes as she sat down next to Daisy. Why did Mr. Hoffman have to treat her like that? What had happened to darken his soul and make him lash out at everyone?

Mr. Hoffman climbed into the driver's seat and clicked to the horses. The wagon jerked and rolled forward. Katie sniffed back her tears and turned to look over the side.

Garth lifted his hand, his face somber. Rob stood by his side and raised his hand as well.

Katie waved to them, her throat clogging and a headache pounding behind her eyes.

As the wagon bumped down the road through town, a light misty rain began to fall. Katie wrapped her arms around herself and closed her eyes, wishing she could shut out the painful world around her. A powerful shiver raced through her, making her teeth chatter. What was wrong with her? *Help me, Lord. I need You!*

Whatever it was, she was certain she'd never felt this sick and miserable in her entire life.

19

Birds sang in the nearby trees as Andrew climbed Pleasantview's front steps with Henry at his side. Energy pulsed through him as he considered what lay ahead. This morning Laura planned to meet with the matron and tell her the truth, and he and Henry would be with her to lend their support.

His thoughts returned to the previous evening and their time with Laura and Rose at the hotel. He was grateful she'd found the courage to be honest with Henry. His friend had been surprised by her confession, but he'd listened with an open mind and in the end he'd been sympathetic and offered his help.

Laura's admission that she'd stolen her sister's file had been a twist he hadn't expected. It allowed her to learn where her sister had been placed, but it could end up causing her more problems with the matron. Still, he had to admire her determination. She deeply loved her family, and she would not let anything stop her from finding her siblings and reuniting her family.

Henry lifted his hand to knock on the front door, but then he glanced at Andrew. "You understand we walk a very thin line here. The law is on the matron's side, and there is no guarantee she will understand Miss McAlister's position or tell us how to find Grace."

Andrew's stomach tensed, and he nodded. "I understand."

"Still, I'm optimistic. It seems the Lord has His hand on Miss McAlister and her family, in spite of her questionable methods of conducting her search."

"Her cause is just."

"I believe it is. And if we listen to the Lord and follow His direction, I think we'll see a positive outcome."

Relief flowed through Andrew. "Thank you, Henry. That's what I needed to hear."

Henry knocked and stood back.

A few seconds later, the door opened, and Rose smiled out at them. "Good morning, gentlemen." She opened the door wider and invited them in.

Laura stepped out from behind Rose, her cheeks pink and her golden hair caught up in a pleasing style.

He stared at her until Henry cleared his throat. Andrew blinked and looked away. "Good morning, Miss McAlister."

"Good morning." Laura brushed a strand of hair behind her ear.

He noticed her fingers trembled, and his chest tightened. So much depended on this meeting, and he could tell she was worried. "Everything is going to be all right. We're here to support you. Just remember what we discussed last night."

"Thank you. I will." Her voice sounded soft and strained.

"Miss McAlister, do you have your sister's file?" Henry asked.

She nodded and pulled the slim file from behind her skirt.

"Good. It's important that you return it to Mrs. Woodward, but please wait until I mention it to her."

"All right."

Rose motioned down the hall toward the matron's office. "Shall we?" Henry stepped up beside her, and they all started down the hall.

Laura hesitated and shot an apprehensive glance at the office doorway. Andrew stepped toward her, but he resisted the urge to put his arm around her shoulder and pull her close to his side. That would not be an appropriate way to treat a client. Still . . .

Like a shift in the direction of the wind, the truth blew through his mind. His feelings for Laura ran much deeper than those of a solicitor for his client.

When they'd first met at Bolton, he'd thought of her as a member of the staff who needed his help during a family crisis. But on board the *Parisian* he'd discovered she was a unique young woman with admirable inner qualities and striking outer beauty.

Her commitment to the girls in her care and to her family had struck a chord with him and made him realize how much he admired her. Now he felt a strong desire to protect and defend her against anything that would cause her harm.

He frowned and tried to dismiss those thoughts. This was not the time to contemplate his feelings for Laura. They had an important goal that morning, and he needed to focus his thoughts on how to navigate this meeting.

But as he glanced at her lovely face and read the mixture of courage and anticipation, he knew the time was coming when he would have to make a decision about his feelings for Laura.

They stopped at the matron's door. Laura straightened her shoulders and knocked twice. There was no response, so she knocked again.

Rose glanced down the hall. "I just saw her at breakfast not more than an hour ago. I wonder where she could be." She reached for the doorknob and tried to open the door, but it was locked.

A stout, middle-aged woman in a gray dress and small straw hat walked in the front door and strode down the hall toward them. Andrew recalled meeting her on the day of the tour, but he didn't remember her name or position.

Laura turned toward the woman. "Miss

Hanson, we're looking for Mrs. Woodward. Have you seen her?"

"Yes, I've just taken her to the train station."

Laura's eyes widened. "The train station?"

"That's right."

Rose addressed Miss Hanson. "I didn't know she was planning a trip."

"She wasn't, but she received a telegram right after breakfast." The woman leaned toward Laura and Rose and lowered her voice. "Her sister suffered a terrible fall, and she broke several bones. I'm afraid it's quite serious. Mrs. Woodward has gone to Oshawa to see what needs to be done."

"I'm sorry to hear that." Rose thought for a moment. "Did she say when she planned to return?"

"She has no idea how long she'll need to stay with her sister." The woman puffed up like a peacock. "She put me in charge while she's away."

"Oh, well then perhaps you can help us." Rose motioned toward Henry. "Did you meet Mr. Dowd and Mr. Frasier when Mrs. Woodward gave them a tour of the home the other day? They've been commissioned by the British government to visit some of the receiving homes and offer their recommendations about child emigration."

Miss Hanson pursed her lips and looked them over. "Yes. I met them. Good day, gentlemen."

Henry sent her a winsome smile. "Miss Hanson, it's good to see you again. We had hoped to meet with Mrs. Woodward about an important matter, but since you're now in charge, perhaps we can discuss it with you?"

She relaxed a bit, apparently charmed by Henry's words. "Well, I'll help you if I can."

"Mrs. Woodward gave us a list of children who have been placed in and around Belleville. I'd like to add one more child to the list, but I need to know where she has been placed."

"If you already have your list, why do you want to add another child?"

"We had an inquiry from one of her relatives, and we'd like to see how she's doing in her new situation."

Miss Hanson's expression cooled. "I'm sorry, but I can't give you that information without Mrs. Woodward's permission."

"The girl is only seven years old, and she just arrived a short time ago," Henry added.

Miss Hanson frowned. "As I said, I cannot give you any more information. You'll have to wait until Mrs. Woodward returns."

"I understand, but we're only going to be in Belleville a short time. After that, we have to visit the children who have been placed on farms outside of town." He took a folded paper from his suit coat pocket. "Here's the list Mrs. Woodward gave us. I'm not sure if we'll have time to visit all these children, but I did want to follow up and visit that particular little girl."

"What's her name?"

"Grace McAlister."

Miss Hanson pursed her lips. "I don't recall her. I doubt she came through Pleasantview."

Laura's face flushed, and her fingers coiled around the side of her skirt.

Henry gave a firm nod. "I'm quite sure she did."

Miss Hanson glanced around the group, then focused on Henry again. "Well, we'll just have to wait and see. You can leave a note for Mrs. Woodward, and I'll give it to her when she returns."

"But that might be too late for us to pay the little girl a visit."

Miss Hanson drew herself up. "As I've already said, I can't give you that information. Now you'll have to excuse me. I have important matters to tend to." She turned with a flounce of her skirt and strode away.

Rose blew out a breath. "What are we going to do now?"

"We'll leave Mrs. Woodward a note requesting a meeting. You and Miss McAlister can accompany us on our visits to the children in Belleville."

Laura's gaze riveted Henry. "You mean Katie?"

"You said she's staying with Dr. and Mrs. Richardson on Maple Street."

Laura flipped open her file and scanned down the page. "That's right. The address is 232 Maple Street, Belleville."

Henry pulled another piece of paper from his pocket. "I spoke to the manager at the hotel this morning, and he gave me this map. We have two children to visit who live near Pleasantview. Then we'll hire a small carriage at the livery and drive to Dr. Richardson's home across town."

A smile broke across Laura's face. "Oh, thank you! I'm so grateful!"

Rose looked at Henry. "I'm sure we can ask Mildred and Ethel to cover our duties in the infirmary. That should free us to accompany you."

"Very good." Henry nodded, looking pleased.

"We'll just go up and speak to them, then collect our things. We should be ready in just a few minutes." Rose hooked arms with Laura, and they headed down the hall.

Andrew watched Laura climb the stairs, her face bright with hope.

But unsettling questions stirred his spirit. Would they find Katie today? If they did, would they be able to convince her caretakers to release her into Laura's care? And what would Mrs. Woodward say when she returned, especially if they went over her head and took charge of Laura's sister?

● ● ●

Later that morning, Laura stepped into Nelson's General Store with Andrew, Rose, and Henry. The bell overhead jingled, and the spicy scent of cinnamon, cloves, and nutmeg greeted her. A neat stack of firewood sat beside the door, and rows of canned goods lined the shelves. Piles of potatoes, onions, carrots, and turnips filled the bins by the wall on the right.

A bald man with ruddy cheeks and a wide smile stepped out from behind the counter where several jars of brightly colored penny candy were on display. "Good morning. Welcome to Nelson's General Store."

Henry reached out and shook the proprietor's hand. "Thank you. We're looking for Mr. Walter Nelson."

"You found him. What can I do for you?"

Henry introduced himself and the others. "We understand you've taken in a young girl named Sarah Buxton from the Pleasantview Children's Home."

"That's right. Sarah has been with us about six months." He nodded to the left. "She's in the back, helping my wife cut some fabric." He chuckled. "She follows my Mabel around like a baby duck follows her mother. It's the cutest thing you've ever seen."

Mr. Nelson certainly seemed to be a friendly, talkative man, but how did he treat the little girl?

That was the most important question. From what she had observed in the infirmary, people could say all was well but then treat the children with harshness and cruelty.

Mr. Nelson's forehead creased, and he brushed his hand down the front of his white apron. "Why are you asking about Sarah?"

"My friends and I are visiting some of the children who've been placed to see how they're settling in and to ask if there are any issues or concerns." Henry's tone was warm and friendly, and that seemed to put Mr. Nelson at ease again.

The man rubbed his chin before answering. "Sarah was a little sad and confused when she first came to us, but that's to be expected after all that happened to her back in England. It took some time for her to become accustomed to us and her new home, but now she's doing fine. In fact, I'd say she's as happy as a honeybee in a field of wildflowers."

Henry nodded thoughtfully as he listened to Mr. Nelson.

Laura tensed. Was he just going to take the man's word without question? He might not be telling the truth.

"This address is given as your home as well as your business." Henry glanced at the list he'd taken from his pocket.

"That's right. We live upstairs above the store."

Henry glanced toward the ceiling. "Do you have other children?"

His expression dimmed. "No sir. We do not."

"And you have adequate room there for Sarah as well as yourself and your wife?"

"Oh yes, plenty of space. We had no trouble welcoming Sarah into our home."

"Does she attend school?"

Mr. Nelson nodded. "We enrolled her about a week after she came to us. It was difficult for her at first. She had very little schooling in England, and she had to work hard to catch up. But Mrs. Nelson helped her with her lessons in the evenings, and she's reading well now. Of course, school is out of session for the summer now, but she's learning arithmetic, measurements, and making change while she works with us in the store."

Henry cocked his eyebrow. "So, you'd say she is doing well and you're satisfied with her progress?"

"Oh yes. We're very pleased. She seems quite settled and content now."

Laura bristled. Henry shouldn't make a judgment about the situation without seeing the girl. She shot a pointed glance at Andrew.

He gave a slight nod and turned to Mr. Nelson. "We'd like to speak to Sarah and ask her a few questions."

Mr. Nelson's gaze darted from Andrew to

Henry. "Well, I suppose that would be all right." He walked over to the aisle. "Mabel, would you please come up front and bring Sarah?"

"Yes dear, we'll be right there." The woman's gentle voice floated out from the back of the store.

A few seconds later, an adorable girl with long dark curls walked up the aisle toward them. She wore a ruffled green dress with lace around the collar and sleeves, white stockings, and shiny black shoes. A large white bow was tied in her hair. Her age was listed as eleven, but she looked much younger. Was that due to her circumstances before she came to live with the Nelsons, or were they not giving her enough to eat?

A short, plump woman with bright blue eyes and light brown hair approached with Sarah. She wore a navy blue dress and carried several pieces of fabric draped over her arm. She smiled at them, questions in her eyes.

"This is my wife, Mabel Nelson, and this is our Sarah." Mr. Nelson glanced at his wife, and she moved closer to him. From her uncertain expression Laura could see she was curious about their visit.

Henry leaned down so that he was on eye level with the little girl. "Hello, Sarah. My name is Mr. Dowd."

"Hello, sir." Sarah's serious brown-eyed gaze

stayed on Henry only for a moment, and then she looked down.

"My friends and I are visiting some of the children who've come from England and settled in Belleville. Do you remember living in England?"

She gave a slight nod. "Yes sir."

"Do you have family there?"

She hesitated. "Not anymore."

"Can you tell us about your family and your life in England?"

The little girl looked up at Mrs. Nelson.

The woman laid her hand gently on Sarah's shoulder. "It's all right, dear. You can tell them."

Sarah released a slow, deep breath. "My mum and dad died in the workhouse, so my brother, Ted, and me ran away. We had no one to take us in, so we lived on the streets, looking for food and sleeping wherever we could stay warm."

A pang pierced Laura's heart as she listened. What a heartbreaking story, and Sarah was only one of many facing such terrible hardships.

"One day a kind woman found us sleeping in front of her shop, and she took us to a children's home. I had to stay with the girls, and Ted went with the boys, so I didn't see him much. He left for Canada first, and then I came over a little later."

Henry gave a thoughtful nod. "Do you have contact with your brother?"

"He sends me letters, and we're going to visit him soon."

Mr. Nelson straightened. "That's right. We're planning a trip to Kingston next month to visit Ted. He's staying with a family there and learning how to run a printing press."

"That's kind of you to help Sarah and her brother stay in touch," Rose said. "Not every home child has that opportunity."

"We both come from large families," Mrs. Nelson added. "We know how important it is to stay connected with family members. Sarah has many new friends and cousins to enjoy, but only one brother."

Henry glanced at Andrew, then at Rose and Laura. "Do you have any other questions?"

Rose nodded. "You mentioned Sarah attends school. Does she also attend church?"

"Oh yes," Mrs. Nelson said. "We're members at the First Congregational Church, and Sarah attends with us each Sunday. She enjoys Sunday school, and I've been helping her memorize the Lord's Prayer and Psalm 100."

Their answers seemed appropriate, but the girl's timid spirit made Laura wonder if everything the Nelsons said was true.

Andrew turned to Mr. Nelson. "We'd like to see where Sarah sleeps and spends her free time. Would you show us your rooms upstairs?"

Mrs. Nelson lifted her hand to her chest. "I'm

afraid I was in a bit of a rush this morning and left some of the breakfast dishes in the sink."

"Not to worry, my dear. You're an excellent housekeeper, and we've nothing to hide." He nodded to them. "Please, come with me."

They followed Mr. and Mrs. Nelson and Sarah to the back of the store and climbed the steps to their private rooms above. Laura was the last to enter the Nelsons' flat.

"This is our sitting room." Mr. Nelson motioned toward the couch and two overstuffed chairs grouped near the fireplace. Two sets of shelves filled with books and photographs stood on either side of the fireplace, and an upright piano sat in one corner.

Mrs. Nelson looked to the right. "And through here is our dining room and kitchen."

Laura and the others followed her past an oval table with six chairs and into the sunny kitchen. A worktable stood in the middle, and ruffled blue curtains hung at the windows. A few unwashed dishes and mugs sat in the sink, but the counters were clear, the floor was swept clean, and the glass in the windows sparkled.

"You have a lovely home," Rose said as her gaze swept the kitchen.

"Thank you." Mrs. Nelson returned Rose's smile, looking relieved.

Sarah sent them a tentative glance. "Would you like to see my room?"

"Yes, we would." Henry smiled at Sarah. "Can you show us the way?"

"It's through here." The girl led them back into the sitting room and down a short hall. "This is Mabel and Walter's room." She pointed to a door on the left. "And this is my room." She pushed open the door and they followed her inside.

Laura scanned the room, taking in the details. A pink, yellow, and lavender hand-stitched quilt covered the bed, and a plump white pillow rested by the headboard. White lace curtains hung at the two windows, and a vase of pink roses sat on the dressing table next to a brush and comb. A small bookshelf nearby held a basket of hair ribbons, a doll, and a few books.

Laura crossed the room to the padded window seat and looked out. "I imagine this is the perfect place to curl up and read a book."

Sarah nodded and sent them a shy smile. "I like to sit there and look out the window."

"It's a very pretty room." Rose touched the lace curtain. "Perfect for a girl your age."

The room's decorations and special touches did seem to indicate the Nelsons wanted Sarah to feel comfortable, but still Laura was not sure all was well.

Henry turned to Mr. Nelson. "May I speak to you and your wife in private for a moment?"

"Of course." He turned to Sarah. "Go on downstairs, and we'll be down in a few minutes."

The little girl nodded and walked out of the room.

"Laura and I will go with her." Rose motioned to Laura, and they walked out and descended the stairs.

Sarah met them in the store and showed them around. She said she was learning how to help customers, ring up sales, and give the correct change. Rose asked her if she'd made friends at school, and Sarah listed several girls' names. Then she took them to the back of the store and pointed through the window to her pet bunny, Felix, and said she enjoyed bringing him inside for a visit most evenings. By the time Henry, Andrew, and Mr. and Mrs. Nelson came downstairs, Sarah was smiling and talking freely.

Henry thanked the Nelsons. They all said goodbye to Sarah and walked out of the store.

Andrew paused at the bottom of the steps. "They seem like a nice couple."

Rose nodded. "Sarah seems quite happy with them."

"Yes. It was an encouraging visit." Henry glanced back at the store. "If all the children are treated as well as Sarah, I'd say child emigration is quite a success."

Laura frowned at Henry. "I hope you're not going to draw that conclusion after visiting only one child."

"No, I was simply saying—"

445

"Sarah may have a good situation, but that doesn't mean all the children are treated in a similar fashion."

"Of course." Henry kept his voice calm. "But I'm pleased to see some guardians show genuine kindness toward the children."

"I agree," Andrew added. "And that gives us reason to hope your siblings are treated just as well."

Laura pulled in a deep breath. She could not let their optimism go unchecked, but she also couldn't afford to offend them. "That's also my hope, but I can't help thinking of those children in the infirmary. Most of them were there because those who should've protected and cared for them failed in the worst ways. I'm afraid recalling their suffering compounds my fears."

Their second visit took them to Wolfram's Bakery where fifteen-year-old Lydia Greenfield was working with the older couple who owned the small shop. Mr. and Mrs. Wolfram gave a glowing report about Lydia, saying she didn't mind rising early to help with the daily baking and she enjoyed serving the customers. Her cheerful attitude brightened their days and had improved their business. They considered her a true blessing from heaven.

The Wolframs didn't want to leave the shop to give them a tour of their home, but when Henry and the rest of the group spoke to Lydia privately, she told them she had her own room, had plenty of food and clothing, and was glad to stay with the Wolframs.

Laura checked her watch a few times during their visit. The girl and her guardians seemed happy, and there was no hint of trouble. That made Laura eager to finish the interview and move on to see her sister.

Finally, around three o'clock, after a quick lunch at a nearby café, Henry rented a buggy, and they drove across town toward Dr. and Mrs. Richardson's home.

Laura held tightly to the side of the buggy, scanning the numbers on the houses they passed. She could hardly believe she was about to see Katie after months apart.

"There it is. Number 232." Henry pulled the buggy to a stop. He and Andrew climbed down, and Henry helped Rose.

Andrew reached up and offered Laura his hand. Her heartbeat picked up speed as she took hold and stepped down. He gave her fingers a slight squeeze and sent her a reassuring smile.

She turned toward the large white house and scanned the property. A white picket fence enclosed the wide green lawn, and several large shrubs and bright summer flowers encircled the wraparound porch. It looked like a lovely home, and her hopes rose. Perhaps her sister had been well cared for by the family who lived there.

As they climbed the steps, Henry glanced at Laura. "I think it would be best if I spoke to Dr. and Mrs. Richardson first."

Laura paused. Shouldn't she be the one to speak up for Katie?

As if he'd understood her thoughts, he added, "We have to handle this very carefully if we hope to convince them to release your sister into our care."

Her heart resisted, but finally she nodded, bowing to Henry's legal expertise.

Henry knocked on the door. Laura held her breath and sent up a silent prayer. Andrew stepped closer to her, kindness in his eyes.

The door opened and a stout older woman with gray frizzy hair looked out. She wore a long white apron over her plain gray dress, suggesting she was a servant. "Yes?"

"Good afternoon." Henry nodded to her. "We'd like to speak to Dr. and Mrs. Richardson."

The woman's brow creased. "What's your name, sir?"

"Henry Dowd, and this is my associate, Mr. Frasier. These ladies are from the Pleasantview Home."

She sniffed and looked all four of them over suspiciously. "The doctor isn't in."

"Then we'd like to speak to Mrs. Richardson."

She studied them a moment more. "Wait here. I'll see if she's receiving visitors." She closed the door with a thump and left them standing on the porch.

Andrew shook his head. "Not terribly friendly, is she?"

"That's certainly not your typical Canadian welcome," Rose added.

A few moments later the door opened again, and a tall woman looked out. "I'm Mrs. Richardson. What can I do for you?" Her words were polite, but her cool tone and tight expression made it clear she did not plan to invite them in.

"We understand you've taken in a girl named Katherine McAlister from the Pleasantview Home."

Before Henry finished, Mrs. Richardson shook her head. "She's not here."

Laura shot a glance at Andrew, but his gaze was fixed on Mrs. Richardson.

"Can you tell us where she is?" Henry asked.

"I don't know. She only stayed with us for a few days."

Alarm raced through Laura. "Why? What happened?"

Mrs. Richardson's expression firmed. "Surely since you're from Pleasantview, you know the answer to that question."

A heartsick wave washed over Laura.

"You and your husband are listed as her present

449

guardians," Henry continued, his firm tone matching Mrs. Richardson's.

"I told you she's not here."

"Was there a problem?"

"The girl was too young. She couldn't do the work. Our housekeeper tried to train her, but she was stubborn and disrespectful."

Laura gasped. Her sister was not stubborn, and she'd never been disrespectful!

"She became jealous and lashed out at our children." Mrs. Richardson's lips puckered. "That was the final straw. We sent her back."

Laura shook her head. "That doesn't sound like Katie. She's a sweet girl, and she never gave her family a moment's trouble."

Mrs. Richardson's nostrils flared. "Are you saying I'm not telling the truth?"

"No, I just don't understand how you could describe her in those terms."

Henry reached for Laura's arm. "Please let me handle this." He kept his voice low, but his meaning was clear.

Laura forced down her anger and gave a small nod.

Henry faced Mrs. Richardson again. "Can you tell us when you took Katherine back to Pleasantview?"

"I don't remember. It was weeks ago."

Henry gave a brief nod. "Very well. Thank you for your time. Good day."

Mrs. Richardson stepped back and shut the door without another word.

Laura lifted her hand to her heart. "I can't believe Katie's not here."

Rose stepped closer. "The matron must have sent her to another family."

Laura nodded, remembering a whispered story she'd heard at Pleasantview about one girl who was moved twenty times before she finally finished her indentured contract.

A chill traveled through Laura. "I must have missed a notation about a second placement. Thank goodness I still have her file at Pleasantview."

"Let's head back there now." Andrew motioned toward the buggy.

They drove across town and arrived at Pleasantview within twenty minutes. Laura hopped down and hurried up to the room she shared with Rose and Jane. She quickly retrieved Katie's file from under her mattress and headed back downstairs. Andrew, Henry, and Rose waited for her on the porch.

"Here's the file." Laura opened it and thumbed through the pages. Her gaze caught on the final sheet. She pointed to the top paragraph and read it aloud. "On 20 May, Katherine McAlister was placed with Mr. Howard Hoffman and his wife, Ella. Their farm is located at number 33 Fern Ridge Road, north of Roslin. The family has two young children and an infant. Reverend Paxton from the Roslin Community Church wrote and requested a girl to work as a domestic for the family."

Andrew glanced at Henry. "Where's Roslin?"

"Let's see." Henry took a map from his folder, spread it out across the porch railing, and scanned the center section. "Here it is." He pointed to a small dot miles away from Belleville.

Laura's shoulders sank. They could never reach Roslin today.

"It's quite a distance," Henry continued. "I'll have to inquire about the train schedule." He studied the map a moment more. "I'll let you know what I learn."

Laura's hopes rose. "Can we go there tomorrow?"

Henry nodded. "Of course."

"What about the other children you planned to visit?"

"We'll see them after," Andrew said. "This takes priority."

Laura's throat tightened, and she regretted the way she'd questioned him and Henry earlier. "Thank you."

"Can you be ready to travel tomorrow morning?" Andrew looked at Laura, then shifted his gaze to Rose. "Depending on the train schedule, it may involve staying overnight in Roslin. It would be best if you could both travel with us."

Andrew was right. It wouldn't be appropriate for her to travel alone with two unmarried men.

Rose sent her a reassuring smile, then turned to the men. "We'll make arrangements for others to cover our duties and be ready to travel in the morning."

"Very good." Henry folded his map. "Miss Carson, may I speak to you for a moment?"

Rose's eyes widened, but she quickly masked her surprise. "Of course."

Henry motioned toward the steps, and they walked away from Andrew and Laura.

"I hope you're not too discouraged by this delay." Andrew watched her closely.

"I confess I was at first. I could hardly stand hearing Mrs. Richardson say such dreadful things about Katie. I promise you, she is a caring and thoughtful girl, nothing like Mrs. Richardson's description."

His mouth tugged up on one side. "If she is anything like her sister, then I'm sure that's true."

Laura blinked. Was he serious? Did he really think of her that way?

"Forgive me. I know your thoughts are focused on finding your sister. This is not the time for me to be offering compliments."

Her heartbeat picked up speed. "It's all right. That's very kind of you to say."

"I should go." He glanced at Henry and Rose.

The two stood together in the shade of a tall fir tree near where the buggy was tied, deep in conversation.

"Perhaps you should give them a little more time."

He nodded, light glimmering in his eyes. "Perhaps you're right."

"I'm glad I was able to go with you today," Laura said.

"Yes, I was glad too. I think that made the girls we visited more comfortable."

"It did seem to help."

"It was good to see they were both doing so well."

Laura pondered that for a moment. "How did you choose the girls we visited?"

"Mrs. Woodward prepared the list. Why do you ask?"

"It's possible she might have chosen Lydia and Sarah because she knew they had good situations, and that would give you and Henry a positive impression."

"I doubt that was her motive."

"You don't think she wants to paint the best picture possible for her own benefit?"

"Laura, that doesn't seem quite fair."

"Fair or not, I suspect it's true."

He looked away with a frown. "I know what happened to your family gives you a negative impression of child emigration. That makes sense. But after our visits today, you have to admit some children are happy in their new situations. They've left lives of poverty and hardship behind, and they've been given an opportunity for stable, productive lives in a new land full of promise."

She stared at him, stunned that their opinions could be so different. "What we saw today was one side of the story. There is another side, and our time with Mrs. Richardson brought that to light."

He studied her with a sad, almost pitying look. "I'm afraid your experiences may have clouded your view."

Heat rushed up her neck and into her face. "I've spent the last two months observing firsthand the painful trials these children face when they're forced to leave England and sent to Canada as home children. My experiences have given me insight you may never have, so don't discount them." She turned away and strode toward Pleasantview's front door.

"Laura, please, I didn't mean to upset you."

She spun around. "I don't take offense for myself, but I am offended for all the children who are suffering because of this broken system. If you cannot understand that, then I have nothing more to say. Good night."

He called her name as she walked away, but this time she did not stop or look back.

• • •

Andrew's heart sank as he watched Laura stride away and vanish through the doorway. He huffed out a breath and shook his head. She was just overwrought by the strain of the day and the delay in finding her sister. Surely tomorrow she'd see things more clearly.

Rose walked up the porch steps. "Did Laura go inside?"

"Yes, and I'm afraid she's rather upset."

"She carries a great burden for her family, and she had such high hopes of finding her sister today."

"I understand." But did he really? The weight of conviction pressed down on his heart. "I'm afraid I was careless with my words, and I offended her."

Tenderness lit Rose's expression. "Don't worry, Mr. Frasier. Laura is not one to hold a grudge. I'm sure you can speak to her and make things right tomorrow."

He nodded, but he was not content to wait. "Will you give her a message?"

"Of course."

"Tell her . . . I'm sorry. And I look forward to seeing her in the morning."

Rose sent him a reassuring smile. "I will."

He started toward the steps, but when she called his name, he turned back.

"Laura is on a difficult journey, Mr. Frasier.

456

Her faith is being severely tested. I hope you'll do everything you can to reflect the love of Christ to her through your patience and consideration."

He stilled, struck to the heart by Rose's words. More was at stake than his pride and opinions, even more than finding the McAlister siblings. He was called to help strengthen Laura's faith through offering his support and showing her kindness and grace. But if he wasn't careful, he could squelch it through his prideful words and actions. He must not let that happen.

He met Rose's gaze. "Thank you. I needed to hear that."

She smiled. "If you find my words meaningful, I hope you'll take them to heart and ask the Lord to show you how to live them out."

Warmth and energy flowed through him, and he nodded to her. "I will."

20

K atie stirred and tried to roll onto her side, but a heavy weight pressed her down, making it impossible. Why couldn't she move? What was wrong with her?

In the distance she heard a sweet voice calling her name, and she strained to listen.

"Katie, wake up. I've brought you a slice of apple tart. I know it's your favorite."

Her heart leaped. That was Mum's voice! A moment later Mum appeared, smiling and holding out a plate toward her. The sweet scent of apples, cinnamon, and raisins filled her nose and made her mouth water. But when she tried to lift her hand and reach for the plate, the vision melted away.

Confusion washed over her. Where was Mum? Why had she vanished?

"Katie," another voice called. Before she saw his face, she knew it was Garth, and joy filled her heart.

"Come on, get up!" he called. "Let's run over to the park and see if we can find some of our friends. We'll skip rocks on the pond and then maybe we'll play a game of tag." His face floated above her, his smile broad and his eyes twinkling with light and laughter.

She wanted to answer, but her throat felt terribly dry. She couldn't seem to make her mouth move to form the words.

When she didn't respond, Garth's image turned wavy and drifted off.

Sadness welled up in her heart, and she longed to call him back, but no matter how hard she tried, she couldn't make a sound.

"Katie, come and draw with me." Grace appeared then, a playful smile lighting up her sweet face. "Let's make some pictures for Mum. You know how happy that makes her." Her little sister held out a piece of paper and a pencil.

Katie tried to lift her hand to take them, but her arms felt weighted to her sides. What was wrong with her? Had she injured her arms? Why couldn't she speak or reach out to the ones she loved so much?

Grace shook her head, sadness replacing her happy, carefree expression. "Goodbye, Katie. I'll miss you. Don't forget me . . . Goodbye." Grace's voice and image faded into the darkness.

A scream lodged in Katie's throat, and agony tore at her heart. *Come back, Grace! Don't leave me!*

Another voice came to her through the mist. This one sounded closer and was anxious and fearful. "She's been like this too long. We have to do something."

"Stop your fretting, woman. She'll be all right."

"But she's got a fever, and she's too weak to eat."

Katie fought to recognize the woman's voice. She knew her, but she couldn't recall her name.

"Give her some water." The man's voice sounded rough and angry.

Someone lifted her head, and cool water splashed into her mouth and ran down her parched throat. She gasped and coughed, and another drink slipped past her lips.

"Maybe we should bring her into the house."

"What? You want Daniel and Daisy to catch this?"

"No, of course not. Then maybe we should send for the doctor."

"We ain't got the money to pay for no doctor."

"What are we going to do, then? We can't just let her die!"

"Hush, woman. She's not gonna die!"

"If she don't start eating and drinking soon, she will."

"I don't have time for your foolishness. Do what you want with her. I got work to do."

"Katie, can you hear me?" The woman's voice trembled.

Katie tried to force open her eyes, but they seemed glued shut. She wanted to answer, truly she did, but her dry lips and painful mouth wouldn't move.

The woman raised Katie's head again, and cool water dribbled across her lips and ran down the side of her face. Soft fabric brushed across her cheek, wiping the moisture away.

"I'm sorry." The woman's voice sounded choked and tearful now. "You been a real good help to me, and I surely don't like to see you suffering like this."

More water filled Katie's mouth and washed down her throat. She sighed as she lay back on the hay once more. "Thank you," she whispered.

Someone sniffled, then footsteps faded away.

A dog whimpered, and soft fur brushed her arm. Charger pushed his cool, wet nose against her still fingers and then licked her hand. He lay down beside her and rested his head on her arm with a sigh.

Comforting warmth flowed through her. She was not alone. Her family might be gone, but the Lord was near and had sent Charger. Her thoughts blurred and faded, and soon she drifted away into the silent mist.

The noonday sun warmed Laura's shoulders as the buggy rounded the bend and approached the Hoffmans' farm. Past the trees, the barn and house came into view. Stunned, Laura gripped

461

the side of the rented buggy. The house and outbuildings looked so broken down and choked with weeds she didn't think anyone lived here. But when they came closer, she saw a few pieces of clothing hanging on the line at the side of the house. Bile rose in her throat. This was where her sister lived?

Laura leaned forward. "Are you sure this is the right place?"

Henry glanced over his shoulder. "I believe so." He clicked to the horses and directed them up the road toward the house.

Andrew looked back at her, serious concern reflected in his eyes.

Rose took hold of her hand. "This might not be the Hoffmans' place."

"I hope not." But a dreadful foreboding filled Laura's heart. She needed to prepare herself for whatever they might find.

Henry pulled the buggy to a stop by the broken-down fence not far from the house, and they all climbed down. Chickens squawked and scattered.

A young boy wearing dirty overalls got up from the porch steps and stared at them. As they came closer, he turned and ran into the house. "Someone's here," he called.

A moment later, a thin woman with pale gray eyes walked out the open door. Her brown dress was wrinkled and stained, and lines creased her haggard face. She carried a baby wrapped in a blanket in one arm and held the hand of a young child with the other. The little girl's face was smeared with dirt, and she sucked her thumb as she peered around her mother's skirt.

Henry stepped forward. "Good day. Are you Mrs. Ella Hoffman?"

"I am." Her voice sounded weak and raspy, and her eyes darted across their group. "Who are you?"

Henry apologized and introduced the four of them. "We're here to visit Katherine McAlister."

The woman's eyes widened, and she turned to her son. "Daniel, go get your father. He's in the toolshed."

The boy hustled down the steps and ran around the side of the house.

"May we ask you a few questions while we're waiting for Mr. Hoffman?" Henry's tone was calm and friendly, but he didn't wait for her reply. "How long has Katherine been with you?"

Of course Henry knew the answer, but he chose an easy question to start the interview.

The woman shook her head. "It's best to wait for Mr. Hoffman."

"Come now, that's not a difficult question. We know Katherine came to work for you as a domestic to help you with the children and household chores."

Mrs. Hoffman's chin wobbled. She clutched the baby tighter, and tears filled her eyes. "She was a real good help."

Laura's breath caught. Why was Mrs. Hoffman using the past tense? More questions raced through her mind as Andrew and Henry exchanged a serious glance.

A rough-looking man with blond curly hair strode around the side of the house, followed by the boy.

"What do you want?" Mr. Hoffman's tone sounded threatening.

Henry calmly repeated the introductions. "We'd like to speak to Katherine McAlister."

Mr. Hoffman's face turned ruddy. "You got no right to show up here without warning and poke your nose into my personal affairs."

Henry's eyebrows rose. "We're visiting several children who've been placed through the Pleasantview Home, and we'd like to see Katherine."

"Not today." Mr. Hoffman glared at them. "It's time you get in that buggy and head on back to town."

Henry stepped forward, took a paper from his suit coat pocket, and held it out for the man to see. "We've been commissioned by the British government to check on the welfare of children who've emigrated from England to Canada. This gives us a legal right to see Katherine.

464

If you choose not to cooperate, there will be consequences."

Mr. Hoffman's gaze darted from Henry to Andrew. "I don't want no trouble."

"Then bring Katherine out so we can speak to her."

He licked his lips and glanced at his wife. Then he focused on Henry again. "I can't do that."

"Why not?"

"She ain't here. She ran away."

Laura gasped. "What!" Pain sliced through her heart, and she clutched the sides of her skirt. "Why would she run away? What did you do to my sister?"

Voices stirred Katie from her sleep. Was someone coming to bring her a drink of water? She sighed and tried to understand what was being said, but the voices were too far away. She forced her eyes to open a slit. Sunlight shone into the stall where she lay. It must be morning or midday. She couldn't tell for sure.

Reality came rushing back, and a wave of painful sorrow with it. She was ill, so very ill she could barely move. Her head pounded, and her throat burned.

A woman's voice rose above the others. She sounded tearful and angry. The voice was familiar, and it stirred her heart. She summoned her strength and slowly turned her head toward the outside wall. Bright sunlight streamed through the cracks, making her blink.

She peered out between the boards, trying to make sense of the scene. A horse-drawn buggy sat parked by the house. Three, no four people stood at the bottom of the porch steps, speaking to Mr. and Mrs. Hoffman.

Charger stirred beside her. She touched his warm, furry side, comforted again by his gentle presence. Every time she woke, she found him there beside her like a silent guardian, giving her assurance and peace.

The voices reached her again, and an idea floated through her mind, slowly taking shape. If she could let them know she was here, maybe they would bring her some more water or maybe some soup. Her mouth watered, and her painful stomach contracted at that thought.

She slowly rolled to her side and used one arm to push herself into a sitting position. Her head swam, and her view of the barn stall rippled and swayed.

She winced. The pounding in her head felt like someone was hitting her with a heavy board every second. Closing her eyes, she swallowed against her painful dry throat.

The voices outside grew more intense, rising and clashing, and a few words floated toward her.

"Why would she run away? What did you do to my sister?"

Katie blinked. That sounded like Laura. She squinted, trying to make sense of her thoughts. It couldn't be Laura. Her sister was in England, not Canada. She lifted a trembling hand and rubbed her gritty eyes.

Was she losing her senses now as well as her strength?

"Laura, please, let me question him." The strong male voice rose above the others.

Katie gasped. It was her sister! Laura was really here. She hadn't ignored her letters and pleas for help. She'd come to Canada to find her. Tears flooded her eyes, and she pushed herself to her feet. Somehow she had to find the strength to walk outside and see Laura.

She took one faltering step, then another. Dizziness washed over her, stealing her strength. She reached for the barn wall and opened her mouth to cry out, but her voice failed her. One more step and her knees buckled. She fell to the floor, and the darkness closed over her again.

Andrew slipped his hand behind Laura's back and touched her lightly. He knew this had to be very difficult for her. He could barely resist the urge to grab Mr. Hoffman by the shirtfront and shake him until his eyes rolled back and he was forced to explain himself.

Laura's intense gaze met Andrew's, her blue eyes flickering with painful questions. He

467

hoped his gentle touch would reassure her that they could trust Henry to lead the way in this situation.

She released a long, slow breath, gave a slight nod, and focused on Henry again.

"How long has Katherine been gone?" Henry continued in a serious tone.

Mr. Hoffman rubbed his chin and looked away. "About a week or two."

Henry frowned. "Mr. Hoffman, there is a great deal of difference between seven days and fourteen days. Exactly when did you discover Katherine was missing?"

The man thought for a moment. "I'd say about ten days."

"Mrs. Hoffman, would you agree?"

She shifted the baby to the other arm and gave a reluctant nod.

Andrew studied her anxious expression. She was either afraid of her husband or not telling the whole story . . . or perhaps both.

"Did you inform the authorities and conduct a search for Katherine?"

"We looked for her." Mr. Hoffman glanced toward the fields rather than meeting Henry's gaze. "But she was long gone."

"Did you write or telegraph the staff at Pleasantview, letting them know Katherine was missing?"

Mr. Hoffman rubbed his chin. "Not yet."

Irritation flashed across Henry's face. "And why is that?"

Mr. Hoffman shrugged. "We thought she might come back."

"Ten days is a long time to wait before informing them a child is missing."

Mr. Hoffman set his jaw and remained silent.

"Did she say anything ahead of time to suggest she was thinking about running away, or did she give you any hint about where she might go?"

"Not that I recall."

"Has she made any friends who might offer her shelter?"

"I don't believe so."

"Did she take extra clothing with her?"

"I couldn't say."

Henry turned to Mrs. Hoffman. "You're probably more familiar with Katherine's clothing. Did you look in her trunk? Was anything missing?"

Mrs. Hoffman shook her head. "I . . . I don't know."

"Where is her trunk?"

"In the barn," Mrs. Hoffman answered before her husband could speak.

He shot his wife a heated glance, then started toward the barn. "I'll bring it out," he called over his shoulder. "You can take a look."

Andrew stepped toward Henry and lowered

his voice. "I don't like this. Something is not right."

Rose stepped closer and whispered, "I agree."

Laura's fearful gaze darted from Andrew to the barn. "I don't believe he's telling the truth."

As Mr. Hoffman disappeared through the open barn door, a dog growled and barked.

"Oh dear." Mrs. Hoffman's anxious gaze followed her husband to the barn.

Henry turned toward the woman. "If you know something you haven't told us, I suggest you tell us now."

The baby in her arms whimpered and squirmed. She pressed her lips together and jiggled the wrapped bundle up and down, tears glittering in her eyes.

"Mrs. Hoffman." Henry's voice steeled. "If your husband has harmed Katherine in any way and you choose not to speak up, you will also be held responsible." He glanced at the little girl clinging to her skirt. "I would hate to see you separated from your children because of something your husband has done."

She shook her head. "It's not like that."

"What happened?" Henry stepped toward Mrs. Hoffman. "Tell us the truth."

Before she could answer, Mr. Hoffman appeared in the doorway of the barn. "I've got it!" He tugged a large wooden trunk out and started dragging it toward the house. A large black-and-white border collie followed him, snapping at his heels and snarling.

"Get away!" Mr. Hoffman cursed and waved his free hand at the dog.

The collie continued barking and charging at the man.

Mr. Hoffman dropped the end of the trunk and kicked the dog.

"No!" Mrs. Hoffman's frightened voice rang out.

Henry strode toward the barn. Andrew, Laura, and Rose hurried after him.

The dog circled Mr. Hoffman, barking and cutting off his way of escape.

"You cursed dog! Leave me alone!" Mr. Hoffman lunged toward the collie, trying to grab his collar, but the dog jumped back out of reach. Lowering his head, the collie gave a threatening growl.

"What's going on?" Henry demanded.

"The dog's gone mad!" Mr. Hoffman shouted.

Andrew put out his arm, blocking Laura and Rose. "Stay back. He looks dangerous."

The collie circled around them, ran back to the barn door, then raced out and circled around them again.

Andrew frowned. The behavior reminded him of the dogs who helped herd sheep on his family's estate. But that didn't make sense. He and his friends were not animals that needed to be moved to a new pasture.

Mr. Hoffman lifted the lid of the trunk. "Here, you can look inside. I'll get the dog."

Laura and Rose kept their eyes on the collie as they walked toward the trunk.

Mr. Hoffman held out his hand and slowly approached the dog. "Come here, Charger." He gentled his voice, but his expression remained agitated.

The dog growled and backed away. He definitely did not like his master.

Andrew followed Laura and Rose and stationed himself between them and the collie. The women reached into the trunk and started sorting through Katie's clothing.

Mr. Hoffman crouched low and slowly moved toward the dog, but when he tried to catch him, the dog dashed away and entered the barn once more.

"Crazy dog!" Mr. Hoffman grabbed the hoe leaning against the corral and hurried inside the shadowed barn.

Andrew shook his head and shifted his gaze to Laura and Rose as they bent over the open trunk.

Suddenly, the collie charged out the barn door again. Before Andrew could react, the dog ran directly to Laura and nosed her hand. She gasped and jerked her hand away.

Mr. Hoffman hustled after the collie with the hoe raised in the air. The dog dashed off and into the barn once more. A second later, Charger reappeared in the doorway and gave two sharp barks.

Laura dropped the dress she held into the trunk and started toward the barn.

Andrew started after her. "Laura, stop!"

Laura heard Andrew call her name, but she continued toward the barn. The collie's frenzied actions and Mr. and Mrs. Hoffman's odd behavior raised her suspicions. She had to find out what was going on in that barn.

"You can't go in there!" Mr. Hoffman's hurried footsteps sounded behind her.

Charger dashed past Laura and ran toward Mr. Hoffman, barking and cutting him off.

She strode through the open doorway, blinking as her eyes adjusted to the dimmer light inside. The smell of hay, leather, and animals filled the air. She quickly scanned the interior. Stalls lined both sides, and a long aisle ran down the middle. Most of the stalls looked empty, but a brown and white cow munched on feed in the first stall on her right. A ladder leaned against the open hayloft above.

Outside, the collie continued barking while the men's voices rose.

She started down the aisle, glancing over the half door into each stall. Dirty hay littered the floor, and flies buzzed around, but nothing seemed unusual.

As she approached the last two stalls, Andrew strode through the barn doorway behind her. "Laura? What are you doing?" Urgency and confusion mingled in his voice.

She looked back, uncertain what to say. Then, off to her left she heard a soft rustling. A shiver raced down her back, and she turned toward the sound. "Katie?" She held her breath, straining in the sudden silence.

"Laura." The whispered voice floated toward her from the last stall.

Laura gasped and jerked open the half door. Her sister lay sprawled on the floor just behind the door. "Katie!" Laura dropped to her knees, reached for her sister, and pulled her close.

Katie's eyes fluttered open, and she looked up at Laura. Her cracked lips parted, and she released a pained sigh.

"Oh, Katie." A sob rose in Laura's throat. She clung to her sister, and her tears overflowed. "It's all right, Katie. I'm here now."

Katie's dress was damp and dirty, and heat radiated from her body.

Andrew stepped into the stall and pulled in a sharp breath. "Is this your sister?"

"Yes, and she's burning with fever!" She held Katie against her chest and rocked back and forth.

More footsteps sounded, and Rose and Henry entered the stall. Rose gasped, and her hand flew up to cover her mouth. She quickly knelt next to Laura. "I'm so sorry. What can I do?"

Henry's shocked expression hardened. "We've got to move her out of here."

"She needs to see a doctor." Laura looked up and searched her friends' faces.

"I'll carry her." Andrew bent and gently scooped Katie into his arms.

Laura rose, and a wave of weakness nearly pulled her down again. She took a deep breath and straightened her back. She could not let fear steal her courage. Her sister needed her to be strong. Lifting her chin, she walked out of the barn with Andrew.

Mr. and Mrs. Hoffman stood outside. The woman stared at Andrew with wide, anxious eyes as he carried Katie past. Mr. Hoffman crossed his arms, his face set like stone.

Anger flashed through Laura. "You lied to us!"

Mrs. Hoffman winced and looked away, clutching her baby to her chest.

"You can't blame us," Mr. Hoffman called after them.

Laura clamped her jaw, swallowing back her angry reply. There was no point in arguing with the hard-hearted man. She climbed into the buggy next to Rose. Andrew carefully lifted Katie and laid her across Laura's lap. Blinking back her tears, Laura thanked Andrew. He accepted her thanks with a compassionate nod before walking around and climbing into the front seat.

Henry turned and faced Mr. Hoffman. "I'm appalled by what happened here. This kind of neglect and cruelty is a crime. Trying to cover it up with your lies has only doubled your guilt. You can expect a visit from the local authorities."

"It's not our fault," Mr. Hoffman growled. "She was sickly when she came here."

"Howard, stop!" Mrs. Hoffman pulled on her husband's arm. "You're just diggin' a deeper hole for yourself."

"Let go of me, woman!" He jerked his arm free and spewed another curse.

Henry climbed into the driver's seat. "Your wife is correct. I intend to report everything you said, and it will all be used against you."

Mr. Hoffman's jaw dropped, and a flicker of fear finally shone in his eyes. "I never meant to harm the girl."

"If that were true, then you would've summoned a doctor as soon as she became ill."

"We've got no money for doctors."

"And what is your excuse for lying to us and leaving her in the barn to care for herself when she is so ill?"

Mr. Hoffman shook his head and looked away.

"Stand back and move out of our way. The next time you see me will be in court when I stand as a witness against you." Henry lifted the reins and clicked to the horses. The buggy jerked, and the horses set off at a trot.

Laura cradled her sister in her arms and swallowed back her tears. "Everything is going to be all right, Katie. I'll take care of you. And you'll never have to go back there again, I promise."

21

Laura bit her lip and tried to calm her racing thoughts as she watched the doctor examine Katie. He'd already listened to her heart and lungs and checked her eyes, ears, mouth, and throat—all without a word to Laura and Rose, who stood on the other side of the bed. He pulled his watch from his pocket, lifted Katie's limp wrist, and quietly counted her pulse.

Katie would get better. She had to. Laura couldn't bear the thought of returning to England and telling Mum she'd found Katie, but she was too late to save her life.

She squeezed her eyes shut and forced that terrible thought away. She had to focus on what was true, what was happening right now. She couldn't allow her fearful thoughts to rush ahead to frightening conclusions about the future.

Katie was ill, and she had suffered greatly at the Hoffmans'. But she was alive, and Laura and her friends had rescued her and brought her to a comfortable boardinghouse in Roslin. She and Rose had given her a sponge bath while Henry and Andrew had gone in search of a doctor. They'd returned less than thirty minutes later, and now a kind doctor was giving her sister the medical attention she needed. Still, as she watched her sister's pale face, fear tugged at her heart.

Dr. Taylor returned his watch to his pocket and motioned for Laura and Rose to follow him to the far side of the room.

Laura studied his face, her questions stuck in her throat.

"I believe your sister is suffering from a severe case of influenza that has turned into pneumonia. She has been dealing with this for several days, and she's seriously dehydrated." He glanced at Katie with a concerned frown. "Her weakened condition and the bruises on her arms and back lead me to believe she has been mistreated for some time." Sorrow lined his craggy face. "You were right to remove her from that situation."

Laura's stomach fisted. She had suspected as much, but it was still shocking to hear the doctor state it as fact.

"I don't understand how anyone could treat a child like that," Rose said softly.

The doctor sighed. "Neither do I, Miss Carson. Neither do I."

"What can we do?" Laura asked.

"She'll need constant nursing care until she is past this crisis. Can you handle that, or would you like me to send up a nurse?"

Rose nodded. "We can take care of her. We've both worked in the infirmary at the children's home in Belleville. We'll take turns and stay with her around the clock."

Laura's eyes stung, and gratefulness filled her heart. Rose was a true friend. "Yes, we'll handle the nursing."

Rose asked the doctor, "How long do you think it will take for her to recover?"

"That depends." He studied Katie for a moment. "I'll check on her progress tomorrow morning. Until then, give her plenty of water and clear broth. If she tolerates that, you can add some thinned cooked cereal. Keep her cool and only covered with a sheet or light blanket. We want her body to fight off the infection, but we don't want the fever to get out of control."

Laura nodded. "I understand."

The doctor tucked his stethoscope back into his bag. "If there's any change for the worse—trouble breathing or vomiting—send word and I'll come."

"Thank you, Dr. Taylor."

"You're welcome. I'll keep her in my prayers and trust the Great Physician to do His healing work for that poor child."

Laura's throat grew tight, and she nodded. She would pray, longer and harder than she had ever prayed before. Perhaps the Lord would look past her sins and have mercy on her sister.

The doctor bid them good day and stepped out of the room.

"May I come in?" Andrew looked in from the open doorway.

Relief flowed through Laura. "Yes please."

Rose glanced into the hall. "Where is Henry?"

"He went to send a telegram to Pleasantview. Then he is going to speak to the authorities."

Rose nodded. "I'll go down and ask Mrs. Hadley to prepare some broth for Katie."

"Thank you, Rose." Laura watched her friend disappear down the hallway, once again grateful for her faithful friendship and practical help.

Andrew crossed the room and stood beside Laura. "What did the doctor say?"

Laura repeated the doctor's diagnosis and directions, her eyes stinging as she finished. "He'll be back tomorrow morning to check on her. Rose and I will watch over her until then."

"I'm so sorry, Laura. I know this has to be terribly difficult for you." His tender words nearly undid her.

"I'm trying to keep a clear head and hold on to hope, but I'm so afraid for Katie. My mum will be devastated if . . ."

Andrew slipped his arm around her shoulders, and she rested her head against his upper arm, letting his strength flow in and around her.

"Try not to worry," he said softly. "Dr. Taylor seems like a capable man, and we'll do all we can to help her recover."

"Thank you," she whispered, savoring his

481

caring touch and wishing she could always stay this close to him.

He lowered his arm, then turned toward her. A serious look filled his eyes. Her breath caught, and she knew he had something important to say.

"Before I came to Canada, my opinion about child emigration was based on what I'd seen at Dr. Barnardo's presentations. The children he put on display were all scrubbed clean and dressed alike, singing songs and reciting Scripture. They looked happy and healthy and eager to sail to Canada. And I believed every word the doctor said about giving those children the opportunity to build new lives here.

"I read Doyle's report on child emigration when we prepared for this trip, but I felt certain the problems he wrote about in 1875 must have been addressed by now. I couldn't fathom that conditions might have stayed the same or even gotten worse since then.

"Then I met the girls on the ship." A smile lifted one side of his mouth. "They were delightful, and I was sure they'd have bright futures with their new families. Our visits yesterday seemed to confirm my opinion. All that made me believe Katie would be fine and you were concerned without reason."

He reached for her hand. "I had no idea how wrong I was. You tried to tell me, but I didn't listen, and I regret that deeply."

Laura released a trembling breath and held tight to his hand.

"Will you forgive me, Laura, and give me a chance to make things right?"

Her heart swelled. "Yes."

"I promise you, Katie's suffering will not be in vain. Her story will be included in our report, and I'm confident it will have a great impact on those who have the power to change how child emigration is handled."

She studied his face. Was that all he meant to do? "I have to find my brother and other sister. I can't bear the thought of them suffering as Katie has."

He gave a firm nod. "We'll find them. You can count on that."

Katie shifted her head on the pillow, and her eyes fluttered open. "I've seen Garth," she whispered.

Laura gasped and crossed to the bed. "Katie?"

"Garth . . . I've seen him." Her voice was so soft Laura could barely hear her.

Was she dreaming, or had she really seen their brother? Laura knelt and leaned closer. "Where did you see him?"

"At church."

Laura shot a glance at Andrew, then focused on Katie again. "Here in Roslin?"

Katie pulled in a shallow breath. "Yes. He works for a farmer . . . Eli Gilchrest."

Andrew pulled a small notebook from his pocket and jotted down the name.

"Have you seen Grace?"

Katie's cracked lips trembled. "No . . . not Grace."

Andrew tucked his notebook in his pocket. "I'll go now and make inquiries."

Laura rose, a surge of hope filling her heart. "Thank you, Andrew."

He reached for her hand once more, confidence shining in his eyes. "We'll find them, Laura. I promise."

The next morning Andrew sat beside Henry in their rented buggy and surveyed the rolling fields as they rode toward the Gilchrest farm. Two young men working with hoes made their way down the rows of potatoes, digging up weeds and pitching them into the path behind them.

Andrew scanned their forms and what he could see of their faces beneath their hats. One was a brawny redhead, and the other was a tall, wiry fellow with light brown hair. Both looked like they were in their early twenties, and neither resembled Laura or Katie.

Henry pulled the buggy to a stop in front of the simple farmhouse. They climbed down and started up the path toward the front door.

"Hello," someone called behind them.

Andrew and Henry turned.

A young man in the corral next to the barn lifted his hand. "Can I help you?"

"Yes please," Henry called.

The young man climbed over the fence and strode toward them. At first glance he didn't look like Laura or Katie. But as he came closer, Andrew saw the resemblance in his intelligent eyes, high forehead, and slim, straight nose.

Energy surged through Andrew. "Garth McAlister?"

The young man's eyebrows rose. "Yes?"

"My name is Andrew Frasier, and this is Mr. Henry Dowd."

Garth shook hands with them. "You sound like you're from England."

Andrew nodded. "We are, and we have a message for you from your sisters."

His eyes widened. "My sisters?"

"Yes. We've become acquainted with Laura, and she has come from England to search for you and your sisters and bring you home."

Garth's mouth fell open. "Laura is here in Canada?"

"Yes, she's in Roslin now, caring for your sister Katie."

His joyful expression faltered. "What's wrong with Katie?"

"I'm afraid she was poorly treated by the family who took her in, and she's quite ill."

Garth's expression darkened. "I knew there was trouble when I saw her at church." His Adam's apple bobbed in his throat. "Is she going to be all right?"

"We hope so. She's under a doctor's care, and Laura and her friend Rose Carson are with her."

He clenched his jaw. "I should've done something the last time I saw Katie. I could tell they weren't treating her right."

"What's going on?" A male voice rang out behind them, and a screen door slammed.

Andrew and Henry turned toward the house.

A tall, bearded man in faded overalls hustled down the porch steps and strode toward them. He narrowed his dark eyes as he looked them over. "Who are you?"

Henry gave his name and Andrew's. "We're representatives of the British government's Commission on Child Emigration. We've come to speak to you about Garth McAlister."

Suspicion lit the man's eyes. "What about him?"

"There's been a mistake made concerning Garth. He never should've been sent to Canada."

"That makes no sense."

"I assure you, sir, when you hear the full story, you'll understand and agree he should be returned into the care of his mother."

Garth's head jerked toward Henry. "My mother?"

"Yes, she has recovered, and she deeply regrets that you were sent away without her knowledge or permission."

Garth stared at him. "But . . . I thought she died."

Andrew placed his hand on Garth's shoulder. "I promise you she is alive and well in London."

Garth's gaze darted from Andrew to Mr. Gilchrest. "I have to go back to London. My mum needs me."

Gilchrest lowered his bushy eyebrows. "I have a contract that says you'll work for me until you're eighteen."

"But I thought she'd passed away. That's the only reason I agreed to come to Canada."

"That's not my concern." Gilchrest crossed his brawny arms. "I paid the fee for this boy. I've given him a place to live, food, and a good deal of training. He's obliged to stay and finish his term. After that he can do whatever he likes."

Andrew studied the burly farmer, trying to think of a way to persuade him to change his mind. He softened his tone. "Mr. Gilchrest, do you have a wife and children?"

The man's face turned ruddy, and his expression hardened. "Not anymore."

Andrew eased in a breath, regretting his question. "I'm sorry. But you must know the ties that bind families together are not meant to be broken simply because of a misunderstanding."

Gilchrest glared at them. "Family ties are for sentimental fools. They mean nothing to me. The boy works for me until the contract ends, and that's all there is to say about it."

"Please, sir, don't make a hasty decision—"

"Are you hard of hearing?" Gilchrest's voice rose. "I told you the boy stays. Now get off my land, and don't come back!"

Henry lifted his hand in a calming gesture. "We understand your position, but Garth is here because of a series of misunderstandings. We simply want to straighten those out and return the boy to his family." He turned to Garth. "We'll contact a local judge and present the situation to him. That should help clear up the matter."

Andrew nodded. "When the judge hears the facts, I'm sure you'll be released from the contract."

Mr. Gilchrest huffed. "Go right ahead. That'll be Judge Horace Zebulon. We go way back. He'll never side with two fancy-pants British lawyers against me."

Andrew's mouth went dry. If Gilchrest and the judge were friends, they might never receive a fair hearing.

"It's time to go." Henry nodded toward the buggy.

Andrew glanced at Garth and was grieved to

see the sorrow and confusion lining the boy's face. "Don't worry, Garth. We'll do everything we can for you."

"Tell Laura I want to see her, and that I'm praying for Katie."

"I will." Andrew climbed into the buggy next to Henry.

Henry shook his head as they pulled away from the farmhouse. "That certainly didn't go as we'd hoped."

"No, it didn't." Andrew rubbed his forehead. They'd tried to present a confident appeal, but they hadn't anticipated Gilchrest's stubborn response.

Henry adjusted the reins, urging the horses to pick up the pace. "We're on shaky ground. That signed contract will be the sticking point."

"That and Gilchrest's friendship with the judge."

"I'm afraid you're right. It's going to be more difficult to free the boy than we'd anticipated."

The weight of Henry's words struck Andrew, and he felt as if a heavy pack had been dropped on his shoulders. He'd promised Laura he would find her brother and bring him back. What would he tell her now?

Laura hurried down the stairs of the boarding-house, the note from Andrew in her hand. He was waiting for her outside in the front garden. Was

Garth with him? Her heartbeat picked up speed as she rounded the landing. After her long search, was this finally the day she'd be reunited with her brother?

She stepped outside and started down the front steps. Andrew stood in the shade of a tall fir tree, his hat in his hands. As soon as she saw his serious expression, her steps faltered. "Where's Garth?"

"He's at the Gilchrest farm. We spoke to him and his employer."

"Is he all right?" She stepped into the shade and looked up at Andrew.

"He seems to be in good health and good spirits." But Andrew's concerned expression did not match that encouraging news.

"What is it, Andrew? What's wrong?"

"We explained the situation, but Mr. Gilchrest has a signed contract that states your brother must work for him until he's eighteen."

Laura gasped. "He can't hold him to that, can he?"

"Henry is going to try to arrange a hearing with a judge."

Laura lifted her hand to her heart. "They have to release him! It's not fair to keep him here when his family needs him!"

"I agree, but the contract may be binding. We'll have to work with the local authorities to see what can be done."

Laura folded her arms across her midsection and turned away. How could this happen? She'd always hoped that once she found her siblings and the situation was explained, they would be turned over to her care and she'd be able to take them home.

Andrew laid his hand on her shoulder. "This is just a delay, not a final decision." But something in his voice made her doubt his words.

She shrugged his hand away. "My brother is not a slave. That man has no right to keep him there against his will."

"Your brother is not of age, and those overseeing him have placed him in the man's care. He's within his rights to require Garth to fulfill the terms of the agreement."

She spun around. "You're siding with this . . . Mr. Gilchrest?"

"No, I'm just trying to explain the situation so you can come to terms with it."

She squinted at him. "You want me to just accept it?"

"That's not what I said." He closed his eyes as if searching for the right words. "Please, Laura. We're not giving up. Henry is making inquiries as we speak. As soon as we know more, we can make a plan."

She rubbed her eyes. She must not let anxiety and weariness steal her patience and common sense. None of this was Andrew's fault. He did not have to help her, but he'd done so time and again. She released a sigh and looked up at him. "I'm sorry. I know you're doing all you can. I'm just so . . . tired and worried."

He reached for her hand and wove his fingers through hers. "I understand. This has been a long, difficult trial, and you've borne it all with grace and strength."

His gentle words and the sincere look in his eyes slowed the whirl of her stormy thoughts.

"I believe the Lord is with us," Andrew continued, "guiding us each step of the way. We've done our part, but ultimately, He was the one who helped us find Katie and Garth. That is quite a miracle when you think of the thousands of children who've come from England and been scattered across Canada. And since He's done that, I think we can trust Him to lead us on this next part of the journey."

She soaked in those words and tightened her hold on his hand. "Yes, we must trust Him."

He searched her face. "How is Katie?"

"Her fever comes and goes, but she's staying awake longer and is able to take more broth. The doctor says she's making progress. He'll check on her again tomorrow morning."

Andrew nodded. "Good. We'll keep praying and hold on to hope for them both."

"And for Grace too."

"Yes. I've not forgotten about her, and I'm sure

the Lord hasn't either. As soon as we return to Belleville, we'll speak to the matron and find out where she's been sent. Then Henry and I can go for her even if you have to stay and care for Katie."

Laura's heart warmed. "You'll do that?"

"Of course. I made you a promise, and I'll make every effort to keep it."

"But what about finishing your investigation and writing your report?"

"There will be time for that. Finding your siblings and reuniting your family is important, and it's going to have a powerful impact on countless others when we include your family's story in our report."

She stepped back in surprise. "I'm not sure I want everyone to know the details about what happened to our family."

"No one has to know who you are. We can use different names."

Laura considered it, still feeling uncertain.

"Your family's experiences expose the dangers of the present system in a very personal way. I believe it will motivate those in charge to see the truth and make changes."

She looked up and met his confident gaze. He was certainly persuasive, and matching that with the kindness he'd shown her, she couldn't refuse his request. "I want to help other families, so yes, you may use our story and even our names if you think that would have more impact."

He smiled, lifted her hand to his lips, and kissed her fingers.

Her breath caught, and a delightful shiver traveled up her arm.

He met her gaze, still holding her hand. "Thank you, Laura. You're a very brave woman, and I admire you deeply."

Her lips parted, and her mind spun. She should reply, but she couldn't seem to find the words. She admired him as well, and knowing he felt the same melted away another protective layer from around her heart. She might not know what to say, but one thing was certain—Andrew Frasier had proven he was trustworthy, and that gave her hope for the future.

The next afternoon Laura walked with Andrew and Henry across town to the Roslin courthouse. Henry had arranged a one o'clock meeting with Judge Zebulon. They stopped at the corner across from the courthouse and waited for a wagon to roll past. She ran a hand over her jittery stomach and blew out a slow breath. So much depended on the outcome of this meeting.

She glanced at Henry. "Will Garth be here?"

"I hope so. That might make the judge more sympathetic toward our cause."

She sighed and sent off another silent plea for God's favor and mercy.

Two men on horseback rode past them toward

the courthouse. Laura glanced at the shorter man and pulled in a quick breath. "There's Garth!"

Andrew studied the men on horseback, then started across the street. "The other man is his employer, Mr. Gilchrest."

Garth climbed down and tied his horse to the hitching post in front of the courthouse. He glanced over his shoulder as they approached, and a smile broke across his face. "Laura!"

She hurried toward him and wrapped him in a tight hug. "Oh, Garth." Happy tears filled her eyes as she stepped back and looked him over. "My goodness, you're so much taller."

He grinned. "Yes, I just keep growing."

She motioned to Andrew and Henry. "You remember Mr. Frasier and Mr. Dowd?"

Garth nodded. "Hello, sir." He shook Henry's hand, then greeted Andrew and shook his as well. "This is Mr. Gilchrest. I work on his farm." He nodded to the rough-looking man with the thick, unkempt beard who stood a few feet away.

Laura nodded to the man, but she did not offer a smile. She took Garth's arm and turned away from Mr. Gilchrest. "Is he treating you well?" She kept her voice low so that only Garth would hear.

Garth gave a brief nod. "I'm doing all right."

"Please, Garth, if you're in any danger you must tell me."

"Mr. Gilchrest is strict, and I work hard, but I'm used to it now." He leaned closer. "How's Katie?"

"She's a bit better today."

Garth nodded, looking relieved. "That's good to hear."

"Shall we go inside?" Henry stepped forward and opened the door, and they entered the courthouse. The judge's assistant led them down the hall and knocked on a dark-paneled door. A voice called for them to come in.

Laura sent Garth a hopeful glance, then preceded the men into the judge's office. Introductions were made, and the judge motioned for them to take the chairs facing his large desk.

When they were all settled, Henry began. "Thank you for agreeing to see us so quickly."

The judge scanned the group with a serious expression. His snow-white hair was neatly cut and combed, and his drooping mustache covered his upper lip. "I hope we can solve this issue without the necessity of a formal hearing."

"Yes sir," Henry added. "That is our hope as well."

"I've read your letter, Mr. Dowd. And I've reviewed the information you attached. Now I'd like to hear from Mr. Gilchrest."

The burly man faced the judge. "This is my view of the matter. I applied to the Masterson

Home for a boy to work on my farm. I paid the required fee and chose him." He nodded to Garth. "I agreed to take responsibility for the boy, provide a home, and give him the opportunity to work and learn the farm skills he'll need when he's older. His part of the agreement is to do as he's told and work for me until he turns eighteen."

Laura bit her tongue, wishing she could say that every young man needed more than a roof over his head and *opportunity* to work. He needed love, guidance, and time with his family!

"How old are you, young man?"

"I'm fifteen, sir."

"So that means you made a commitment to work for Mr. Gilchrest for three more years."

Andrew frowned. "Excuse me, Your Honor. But I think it's important to point out Garth was not given a choice in the matter. The agreement was made between the Masterson Home and Mr. Gilchrest. In fact, Garth was wrongly transported to Canada, and that's why we're appealing to you today."

Laura wanted to cheer but held herself back.

The judge's expression soured. "Mr. Frasier, you'll have a turn to speak. Right now I'd like to hear from Mr. Gilchrest and the boy."

Andrew sat back, obviously not happy with the judge's reprimand.

Mr. Gilchrest took a folded paper from his coat

pocket and offered it to the judge. "This is the contract."

Judge Zebulon adjusted his glasses and scanned the paper. "The boy has been with you since this date?"

"Yes sir, he has."

"How is he doing, as far as the work is concerned?"

Laura bristled. Why was he asking that question?

"He's a good worker, better than the other two boys I got from Masterson, that's for sure. They're prone to laziness and bickering, but if I give this boy a job, he gets it done. I don't have to hound him or worry he'll shirk it off."

Laura glanced from Garth to the judge. She was glad to hear her brother was responsible and hardworking, but it seemed those very qualities were what made Mr. Gilchrest reluctant to let him go.

The judge looked down at the open file on his desk and rubbed his mustache. After a few seconds he lifted his chin. "It seems to me the boy has a good situation with Mr. Gilchrest. I don't see any reason to—"

"Your Honor," Henry interrupted. "Garth McAlister never should've been sent to Canada. His mother is a widow, and he is her only son. She needs him to return to London and help support the family."

The judge glared at Henry, then shifted his gaze to Garth. "If your mother is living and needs your help, how did you come into the care of a children's home?"

Garth paused for a moment, as though trying to think of the best way to explain the situation. "My mum became ill, and she had to go into the hospital. I worked as a delivery boy for a butcher, but I was only paid once a month, and we ran low on food and money. I know it was wrong, but I stole some bread from a bakery. A policeman caught me in the act."

The judge's expression darkened. "Stealing is a crime, young man. Certainly there was another way to solve your problem."

"Yes sir, I'm sure there was, but at the time I didn't know what else to do."

Frowning, the judge turned to Mr. Gilchrest. "Did you know you had a thief working for you?"

Anger flared in Laura's chest, and she gripped the arm of the chair. How dare the judge call her brother a thief!

Garth's face colored. "I'm not a thief. I made a mistake, and I learned my lesson. I've never stolen anything since then, and I never will."

The judge studied Garth for a few seconds, then turned to Mr. Gilchrest. "If you're willing to keep the boy, then I don't see any reason to void this contract." He slid the paper back across his desk.

Panic flashed through Laura, and she shot an anxious glance at Andrew.

He leaned forward. "Your Honor, the boy was sent to Canada without his mother's knowledge or consent. She was not given time to reclaim him before he was sent away."

The judge shook his head. "That's a legal matter you'll have to take up with the sending organization and the courts in England."

"But his sister is here now. She's of age, and she wants to take responsibility for him."

The judge turned to Laura. "How old are you, young lady?"

She sat up as tall as she could. "Twenty-one, sir."

"Are you married?"

Her face heated. "No sir, but I can take care of my brother."

"If you're not married, how would you provide for him?"

"I worked as a lady's maid before I came to Canada." She couldn't very well say she was employed by the Hughes or Pleasantview Homes. Once they learned she'd used a false name and had stolen Katie's file, they would sack her for sure.

The judge huffed. "Working as a maid won't give you enough income to support your brother and mother."

"Your Honor, I'd like to call us back to the

main point of our meeting." Henry kept his tone calm, but Laura could sense his rising concern. "This young man was wrongly separated from his family and transported here without proper consent. His widowed mother waits and prays for his safe return. Mr. Frasier and I will cover the cost of his passage home, and we'll make sure his family members have employment and sufficient income to meet their needs. I'm sure you'll agree there is no valid reason to keep him here any longer."

"Well . . . isn't that nice of you?" The judge's mocking expression hardened. "I don't take kindly to highbrow English solicitors coming into my office and telling me what decision I ought to make." He pointed his finger at Henry. "The legal agreement is binding. The boy stays with Mr. Gilchrest and fulfills the contract."

"But Your Honor—"

The judge banged his hand on the desk. "That's my final decision!"

Laura's heart sank to her toes, and another wave of grief washed over her heart.

Laura released a tired sigh, leaned against the train window, and closed her eyes. Every muscle in her body ached with weariness. Caring for Katie around the clock and grieving over Garth's situation had taken their toll on her. Memories of all that had happened floated through her mind

501

as the train rocked and swayed on its way to Belleville.

While Rose watched over Katie at the boardinghouse, Laura, Andrew, and Henry had discussed ways they might be able to overturn Judge Zebulon's decision and secure Garth's freedom. They decided they would speak to the staff at the Masterson Home as soon as they returned to Belleville. If that didn't provide a solution, they would have to take the matter to court when they returned to London.

Laura fought to hold on to hope that her brother would be released and be able to sail back to England with them, but every day it seemed less likely. She tried to take her worries and fears to the Lord in prayer, but it was a struggle to have faith and trust Him when hope was fading.

Katie shifted on the seat beside her and rested her head against Laura's shoulder. Laura looked down and studied her sister's thick eyelashes and the freckles sprinkled across her pale cheeks. These last few days of caring for Katie had drawn them close again, and Laura was grateful for that renewed connection with her sister. It helped ease the pain of not knowing where Grace might be or what would happen with Garth.

Katie still needed more time to recover before she would be ready for a sea voyage, but the doctor said she was well enough to be moved to the infirmary at Pleasantview.

Laura glanced across the aisle at Andrew, and sorrow pierced her heart. He stared out the opposite window, lost in his own thoughts. Since the disastrous meeting with Judge Zebulon, he hadn't sent her any notes asking her to meet him in the boardinghouse garden. When they discussed Garth's case and ate a meal together, he rarely looked her in the eyes, and he never summoned her out of Katie's room for a private talk in the upstairs hall.

Andrew had stepped back from their friendship, and she could guess why.

Listening to Garth tell the story of their family's poverty and hearing the judge call her brother a thief had made all that separated them crystal clear. She swallowed hard and looked away. His choice to maintain his distance hurt, but it made sense and she could not fault him for it. They were not equals, and they would never be considered a good match. It was foolish to think he might truly care for her.

Once and for all, she must put away silly romantic dreams about Andrew Frasier. Nothing good could come of holding on to her feelings for him.

Rose glanced at her from the opposite seat, tender concern in her eyes. "Laura, are you all right?"

Laura blinked away the moisture in her eyes.

"Yes, I'm just tired." That was true, but it certainly wasn't the whole story. Yet this was not the time to confide in Rose, especially with Henry sitting next to her.

Henry studied Laura's face, then glanced at Katie. "I'm sure she'll continue to improve. You mustn't worry."

Laura nodded, her throat too thick to speak.

"As soon as we get her settled at Pleasantview, we'll speak to the matron about the issue of your name, then find out where Grace has been sent. We can visit the Masterson Home and ask for their help with Garth's case. And we'll also make inquiries about Grace's situation."

Laura nodded, grateful for Henry's determination to help her family, but there were still so many unknowns.

She turned her face toward the window again and pulled in a deep breath. She'd never known how difficult this journey would be or how much courage and strength it would take, not just to search for her siblings but also to keep going in spite of setbacks and heartache.

Lord, help me. I don't even know what to pray. But I know I need You and Your grace. Forgive me for doubting You and help me trust You for all that still lies ahead.

Andrew reached out his hand to help Katie descend from the train. Her pale face and unsteady steps prompted him to move closer and slip his arm around the girl's waist. "Hold on to me, Katie."

"Thank you." Her voice sounded as weak as she appeared.

They started across the platform, following Henry and Rose. He glanced over his shoulder as Laura stepped down on her own, toting her bag in one hand and trying to manage her skirt with the other.

She glanced at him and quickly looked away, but he could read the disappointment in her expression. At least that seemed to be the emotion in her eyes, but he couldn't be certain.

He clenched his jaw, regret burning his throat. Ever since he'd failed to find a way to free her brother, he could barely look her in the eyes. He knew what she must think of him—that his prideful words amounted to nothing and he was incapable of fulfilling his promises.

They had located her sister, but Laura was the one who realized the Hoffmans were lying. He'd stood back, missing the clues and thinking she was crazy for running into that barn. But she'd been right. Katie had been there all along, desperate for their help.

Then, when he'd had a chance to prove himself and convince the judge to release her brother, he'd missed the mark and let her down in the worst way. He still planned to speak to those in charge at the Masterson Home, but there seemed little hope that Garth would be reunited with his family any time soon.

Henry turned to him. "Will you see to the trunk while I hail a cab?"

Andrew nodded and handed Katie off to Rose and Laura. They guided her toward a nearby bench. He found a porter and retrieved Katie's trunk from the baggage car.

A few minutes later, the women stood by the hired carriage while Henry and Andrew helped the driver load the heavy wooden trunk on the back.

The driver tightened the rope and tied off the final knot. He stepped forward and opened the passenger door. Rose climbed in first, followed by Katie and Laura. The driver turned to the men. "Where shall I take you?"

"The Pleasantview Home on Chestnut Street," Henry said as he passed one of the smaller pieces of luggage inside to Rose.

The driver's brows dipped. "Is that the children's home?"

"That's right." Andrew handed the last bag to Laura.

The driver rubbed his bristled chin. "I don't think you want to go there today."

Andrew frowned. "What do you mean?"

"There was a big fire there last night."

Laura gasped and leaned out the carriage doorway. "A fire?"

Rose looked out with Laura. "Was anyone hurt?"

"I'm afraid so." Sadness lined the driver's face. "I heard two children on the top floor lost their lives. They were too sick to flee, and by the time the fire company arrived, it was too late to rescue them."

Rose gripped the side of the open carriage door. "Please, we have to go there now and see if we can help."

The driver shook his head. "I'm sorry. I'm afraid it's too late for that."

Henry's expression firmed. "Take us to Pleasantview." He climbed into the carriage. Andrew stepped inside and sat next to Henry, across from the women.

A heavy silence filled the carriage as they rolled through the streets of Belleville.

Andrew glanced at Laura. She held Katie's hand and stared out the window, her mouth set in a grim line.

His chest grew tight as he watched her. How much pain and disappointment could one woman carry?

The carriage rounded the corner of Chestnut Street, then slowed to a stop. They all leaned toward the window on the right.

Andrew steeled himself, but the shocking sight hit him like a physical blow. Three brick chimneys, scorched and blackened by the fire, were all that was left standing of the Pleasantview Children's Home. The rest was a smoking pile of charred rubble.

"Oh my stars," Rose whispered.

"I can't believe it," Laura said, staring at the startling scene.

They stepped down from the carriage, and Henry directed the driver to wait for them.

The acrid smell of smoke hung in the air as they walked past the open gateway. All the branches of the trees near where the house had stood were singed and bare. The bark on their trunks was burned away on the side facing the fire.

A policeman stood off to the left, talking to two men. When he saw them crossing the lawn, he ended his conversation and started toward them. "You have to stay back," he called. "No one is allowed on the property."

Henry stepped forward. "These ladies are members of the staff. We've just returned to town, and we heard about the fire. Can you tell us what happened to the children and staff?"

"There were twenty-three children and six staff members in residence. Those who survived were taken to First Congregational Church last night. I believe they're staying with various church members."

Henry lowered his voice. "Is it true two children lost their lives?"

The policeman gave a solemn nod. "Yes sir. I'm afraid that's true."

Katie lifted her hand to cover her mouth and stifle a cry. She turned into Laura's arms and sobbed. Laura cried as she clung to Katie, and Rose quickly enfolded them both in a hug.

Andrew's gut clenched as he watched them. Then a frightening thought hit him. If Laura, Rose, and Katie had returned to Pleasantview sooner, they could've died in that fire. He shuddered and turned to Henry. "Thank the Lord they were not here last night."

Henry's mouth firmed, and he nodded.

Laura broke away from Rose and Katie, her eyes wide. "Grace's file!" She spun toward the remains and ran across the lawn.

"Laura, no!" Andrew dashed after her and grabbed her arm.

"I have to find her file!" She tried to pull away, but he held her tight.

"It's too late! It must have burned with everything else."

Her tears overflowed again, and he wrapped her in his arms and held her close. "I'm so sorry," he said gently. But her broken sobs continued as though his words had no power to soothe her.

Rose hurried toward them and placed her hand on Laura's back. "I'm here, Laura. It will be all right."

"No," Laura cried. "Grace's file is gone. How will I ever find her?"

"We'll speak to Mrs. Woodward. She might remember where Grace was sent."

Laura shook her head and stepped away from Andrew. "How could she? Grace is only one of hundreds of girls she placed."

Rose slipped her arm around Laura's shoulder. "I know this is difficult, but we have to think of Katie now and do what's best for her."

Laura brushed her fingers across her cheeks. She gave a reluctant nod, and Rose guided her back across the lawn to where Henry and Katie waited with the policeman.

Andrew trudged after them, his spirits sagging.

"I don't think there is anything else we can do here." Henry looked from the women to Andrew. "I suggest we go to the hotel. We could all use a rest, and I'm sure we can find rooms there for you ladies."

Laura glanced at Rose, reluctance in her eyes.

"Please don't worry about the expense," Henry quickly added. "We'll take care of that."

Rose and Laura discussed it quietly for a moment, then agreed and thanked Henry. They returned to the carriage and set off across town for the hotel.

Disappointment burned Andrew's throat, and he focused his gaze out the window. He couldn't bear to look at Laura and see the pain in her eyes. The fire had destroyed the only source of information that would lead them to her sister.

How would he ever fulfill his promise to Laura now?

22

Laura's head throbbed as they climbed down from the carriage and walked into the lobby of the Fairmont Hotel. It seemed to take all her strength to remain upright and support her sister. The image of Pleasantview's burnt wreckage filled her mind and sent sickening waves through her stomach.

How frightening it must have been for the women and children who were trapped there last night. Had Mrs. Woodward returned and taken charge, or had some other staff member overseen them?

She pictured the children in the infirmary, and tremors traveled down her arms. Most of them were too sick to walk more than a few steps. How had they escaped in time? She hadn't even thought to ask the policeman how many had suffered burns or damage to their lungs from the smoke.

She lifted her hand and rubbed her stinging eyes. It was too much. She couldn't think about it right now. After they had time to rest, she would be better able to deal with this news and see what she could do to help.

Henry touched Rose's arm. "It will be just a moment, and we'll take you up to your rooms."

Rose met his gaze. "One room would be fine."

"Yes, we'd like to stay together." Laura slipped her arm around Katie, knowing she would rest more securely if the three of them shared a room.

Henry nodded, and he and Andrew stepped up to the front desk.

The clerk, a bald man in his sixties, smiled and greeted them. "Mr. Dowd, Mr. Frasier, welcome back to the Fairmont."

Henry asked for rooms for himself and Andrew, then a third for Laura, Rose, and Katie.

The clerk took three keys from the hooks on the wall behind him and passed them across the desk. "Oh, I almost forgot. Mr. Frasier, you received a telegram yesterday." He opened a desk drawer and pulled out an envelope. "I held on to it, knowing you planned to return."

"Thank you." Andrew accepted the envelope and tore it open. He quickly scanned the message. His eyebrows dipped, and he turned to Henry. "It's from my mother." His voice faltered. "My father is gravely ill. She needs me to return home as soon as possible."

Laura stared at Andrew, too stunned to speak. Memories of their conversations aboard ship rose in her mind. He was not on good terms with his father. The journey home would take at least nine or ten days. What if he didn't arrive in time to speak to his father and restore their relationship? She well remembered the pain of losing her father and how it had devastated their family. If the worst happened, how would Andrew deal with that kind of loss?

Andrew stuffed the telegram in his pocket and turned to the desk clerk. "Is there a train to Quebec City tonight?"

"I believe the next train east would be tomorrow morning."

Andrew passed his suitcase to Henry. "Can you take this to my room? I want to go to the telegraph office and send a reply to my mother."

"Of course." Henry took the suitcase. "What else can I do to help?"

Andrew shook his head. "I can't think of anything else right now."

Henry placed his hand on Andrew's shoulder. "I'm sorry. This is sobering news. I'll pray for you and your family."

"Thank you." Andrew glanced at Laura, pain etched across his features. Then he walked past her and out the door.

Laura brushed aside the lace curtain and pushed open her hotel window. Lamplight glowed on the quiet city street below, illuminating the businesses and park beyond. Above the rooftops, the fading light of sunset turned the sky dusty blue, and the first star in the west winked at her. That glimmering light seemed to send out a message of hope. Was it truly a sign of better things to come, or was that only wishful thinking after such a difficult series of painful events?

She stepped back from the window and settled in the chair nearby. Across the room, Rose sat at the desk, writing a letter to the matron at Hughes, and Katie slept in one of the two beds. She studied her sister's peaceful expression, thankful she was finally able to rest after their long, trying day.

A light breeze from the open window ruffled Laura's hair and cooled her warm cheeks. Her uneasy thoughts returned to the events earlier that evening.

Andrew hadn't joined them for dinner, and when Laura asked Henry why, he said Andrew had some business to finish before he started his journey home tomorrow. She wasn't sure what kind of business it might be, and Henry didn't seem inclined to explain. She would have to wait to see him until breakfast tomorrow morning. It would be difficult to say goodbye, but she had to thank him for all he'd done for her and her family.

Rose looked up from her letter. "Laura, are you all right?"

She forced a slight smile. "Yes, I'm fine."

Rose watched her a few more seconds. "I'm sorry Andrew has to leave," she said softly. "I know that must be hard for you."

Laura quickly glanced away. It was hard, so very hard. If only Katie were well enough for a sea voyage, he could escort them home. But even if she were, Laura couldn't leave Canada until she had made every effort to find Grace and see what else could be done for Garth.

What would happen to her search efforts now? With Andrew leaving, would Henry still be willing to help her? His workload would double, and he had to finish his investigation and prepare his report.

Rose set her pen aside. "I'm sure you'll miss Andrew. I've noticed the way your friendship has grown. Has he spoken to you about his feelings or intentions?"

Laura's face warmed. "No, he hasn't."

Rose's hopeful expression faded. "I'm sorry. I shouldn't have asked, but I thought he might have."

Laura sighed. "It's all right. I shouldn't be disappointed. He has been a kind friend, but I'm afraid I let my heart hope for more."

"I can see why you did. He was very attentive, and I thought . . ." Her words faded, and she shook her head. "I've said enough."

Laura leaned back in the chair and closed her eyes. She had to let go of wishing for more than friendship with Andrew. If she didn't, it would only cause her more heartache. He had done what he could to help her. Now his family needed him, and she couldn't begrudge his decision to return to England at once.

Still, releasing him from his promise felt like she was tearing away a piece of her heart. But it was time to let him go and stop expecting anything from Andrew. That was the only way she'd ever get past her pain and disappointment.

After tossing and turning half the night, Laura steeled her emotions and approached the hotel dining room the next morning. She'd prepared herself to thank Andrew, wish him well, and say goodbye, but Henry was the only one seated at the table.

"Good morning, Henry." Laura glanced at the other four empty chairs. "Katie is still asleep, so Rose is staying with her. Will Andrew be joining us?"

Henry hesitated. "No, I'm afraid he already left for the station."

Laura's heart clenched. How could Andrew leave without saying goodbye? She glanced away, hoping Henry would not read the hurt in her eyes.

He took an envelope from his pocket and held it out to her. "He left this for you."

Hope flickered in her heart, and she reached for the envelope. She glanced at her name written on the front in bold handwriting. Should she open it now or wait for a private moment?

Henry sent her a sympathetic look. "I think you'll want to read it right away. There are a few things we need to discuss."

Laura took a seat and slid her finger under the flap of the envelope. She pulled out the single piece of stationery.

Dear Laura, I'm sorry I must leave before we were able to find Grace and secure Garth's release from Mr. Gilchrest. I've asked Henry to continue our efforts and do what he can for you and your family. I regret I was not able to fulfill my promise to you. I hope you will understand my need to return home and forgive me.

Please keep my family in your prayers. There is much I need to say to my father, and I am asking the Lord to extend his life and give me that opportunity. I will pray for you and your family as well and trust the Lord to see that justice is accomplished and you are all reunited soon.

Sincerely,
Andrew Frasier

Laura released a breath and refolded the note. Andrew's formal words brought little comfort to her aching heart, but she would do as he asked and pray for him and his family. She understood he needed to go, and that helped her take the first step toward forgiveness, but moving past the hurt would take some time.

Henry took a sip of his coffee and set the cup aside. "Andrew wanted me to assure you I'll speak to the authorities here about holding Mr. and Mrs. Hoffman accountable for the way they treated Katie. And I plan to visit the Masterson Home on Monday to ask if they'll help us with Garth's case. Would you like to accompany me?"

"Yes, I would. I'll ask Rose if she'll stay with Katie."

He smiled at the mention of Rose's name. "I'm sure she will." His growing affection touched Laura's heart. Henry and Rose seemed a perfect match in so many ways. She hoped Henry would soon speak to Rose and make his feelings clear, if he hadn't already.

"The fire at Pleasantview will make it more challenging to find out where Grace was sent," Henry continued. "But I think our first step should be to try to contact the matron and take care of matters with her."

Laura gave a reluctant nod. She wasn't looking forward to confessing her use of the false name and admitting she'd taken Katie's file, but knowing it had helped them rescue her sister from such dreadful circumstances boosted her confidence. "Yes. We need to speak to her about Katie, and I also want to ask about the children and staff who survived the fire."

He took a folded newspaper from the table and passed it to her. "There's an article on the front page. It will give you a few more details."

Laura accepted the newspaper and scanned the headline, "Fire Destroys Pleasantview Children's Home." She quickly read on, stunned again by the description of the destruction. The building was a complete loss. Two staff members and four children were treated for burns and smoke inhalation. Her breath caught as she read the names of the two children who had perished, ten-year-old Leon Rafferty and fourteen-year-old Louise Childs. With two broken legs it was no wonder Leon hadn't been able to flee the fire. And Louise had been unresponsive since she'd returned to Pleasantview.

She closed her stinging eyes. *I'm thankful they're safely home in Your arms, Father, where they will no longer suffer the painful trials of this life.*

"Did you know the children who died?" Henry's voice was gentle.

"Yes, I knew them both from my time working in the infirmary."

"I'm very sorry. It's truly a tragedy of great proportion."

"If only they hadn't been sent here, they never would've faced such a terrible end."

He nodded. "It brings to mind again the importance of our investigation and the recommendations we'll make."

It pleased Laura to hear him say *our,* including Andrew even though he was returning to England before they'd finished their work here.

"It's kind of you to take time to help me when you have such important work to finish."

"What I've learned about child emigration has made a deep impression on me. I can't sit back now and make impersonal recommendations, then wait years to see changes made. The child emigration system is faulty and unjust, and your family has suffered greatly because of it. I may not be able to force change as quickly as I'd like, but I can help your family find justice."

Her spirits rose as she listened to Henry state his convictions.

"I'll keep working on this until all your siblings are returned to England and safely back in your mother's care. You may even be due some compensation."

That thought surprised her. "I just want my family reunited."

"I understand, and I'll do my best to see that happens." He clasped his hands on the table, his gaze steady. "You can count on me, Laura. I'll see this through."

Andrew stood at the railing of the steamship *Adonis* and looked out across Quebec City's busy harbor. Although sunshine warmed his face and a light breeze ruffled his hair, they didn't ease the tightness in his chest or quiet his troubled thoughts.

The urgent words of his mother's telegram flashed through his mind again. Would he arrive home in time to see his father? If he did, what could he say to bridge the great divide that had separated them for so long? The thought of his father passing from this life without knowing how much Andrew loved and respected him pressed down on his shoulders like a crushing weight.

He thought he had followed the Lord's leading when he'd made the commitment to Henry and continued his legal training in London. But had he misheard? Was it a mistake? Would it have been wiser to heed his father's warnings and stay at Bolton? If he had, he would be there now to comfort his mother and help his father through this difficult time.

Now he might never have that chance.

He bowed his head. *Please, Lord, don't let it be too late. Give me another opportunity to see my father and assure him of my love and commitment to our family.*

His thoughts shifted to Laura, and his regrets

resurfaced. He hated leaving her behind with so much that still needed to be resolved. Henry would do his best. Andrew was confident of that, but it was not the same as being there to see it through himself.

He'd made her a promise, and he had not fulfilled it . . . at least not yet. Was there still a chance he might somehow finish what he had begun?

Please help us, Lord. Watch over Garth and see that he is released at the right time. Take care of Grace, wherever she is, and help us find her. Restore Katie's health and spirit and give her a bright future when she returns home to England. Most of all, comfort Laura, take care of her every need, and give her all her heart desires.

He wanted to ask that this not be the end of their friendship, but he held back, not wanting to be selfish.

Whatever is best for Laura, Lord, whatever Your will is, guide us toward it and confirm it in our hearts.

As he finished his prayer, a new sense of peace filled him. The future was in the Lord's hands, and that was where it needed to stay.

Laura held her breath and gripped the sides of her chair in Reverend Archer's parlor as she waited for Mrs. Woodward's response to her confession.

The matron glanced at Reverend Archer and

Henry, then studied Laura with a curious look. "You used a false name to secure your position as an escort?"

Laura shifted on the chair. "Yes ma'am. I did."

Mrs. Woodward's brow creased. "And you did that so you could follow your brother and sisters to Canada?"

"Yes. My mum was frantic with worry. I had to come."

"I don't understand. Why didn't you speak to those in charge in England? Surely they would've listened to you and returned the children to your mother's care."

"I tried, but they wouldn't release them until I could prove guardianship and pay their exorbitant fees. Before I had a chance to do that, they moved them to Liverpool and assigned them to emigration parties."

"So, you brought that group of girls to Pleasantview with the intention of looking for your sisters, and when they weren't here, you took your sister's file without my permission."

Laura glanced at Henry. He gave a slight nod, urging her to admit the truth once more. She focused on the matron again. "Yes ma'am."

Mrs. Woodward sighed. "I wish you would've been honest with me and come forward as soon as you arrived. I would've given you a fair hearing and done what I could for you at that time." She looked away for a few seconds, then refocused on Laura. "I understand you felt the situation was urgent, and I was absent for several days, caring for my sister."

The tightness in Laura's shoulders eased a bit. Perhaps Mrs. Woodward had a caring heart beneath her starched and pressed appearance.

"I can't condone dishonesty," Mrs. Woodward continued. "However, considering your sister's situation, I'm thankful you learned her location and removed her from the Hoffmans' home."

Henry leaned forward. "If we hadn't arrived that day, Katie might not have survived."

The reverend shook his head. "Such a dreadful situation. I'm appalled she was so poorly treated."

"I'm sorry as well." Mrs. Woodward seemed sincere, but her voice was also wary. "I hope you understand it was never our intention that any child should suffer as she has."

Henry met the woman's gaze. "Good intentions must be backed by concerned and thoughtful actions."

The matron straightened. "Are you suggesting we haven't done our best to oversee the children?"

"What I'm saying is, Katie McAlister nearly lost her life because those who were responsible for her failed to care for her as they should."

The reverend lifted his hand. "Now, Mr. Dowd, I don't think it's fair to blame Mrs. Woodward for what happened to Katie. She has placed hundreds of girls, and most of them are doing very well."

"That may be true, but if even one child is treated as Katie was, then there are serious issues that must be addressed."

The matron shifted in her chair, obviously unsettled by Henry's conclusions.

Henry's gaze remained intense. "How often does someone from Pleasantview check on the children who have been placed to make sure they're being well treated?"

"We have several volunteers who visit the children at least once a year."

Henry frowned. "A lot can happen in a year."

"Well, some of the other organizations don't even believe visits are necessary or helpful. But we've gone out of our way to follow up on our children, and that is no easy task when we've placed more than five hundred girls. Some live a great distance from Belleville, and the winters in Ontario are much more severe than those in England. Our visitors can only make those trips to the outlying farms during the warmer months when the weather allows."

"How will you check on your most recent placements now that the fire has destroyed their records?"

"That will be a challenge, but we can post a notice in the newspaper and ask families who have taken in a child in the last few months to write to us and give us their information."

Henry frowned. "I doubt that will help you find every child."

"Then what would you suggest, Mr. Dowd?" The matron's tone sharpened.

Laura's stomach tensed. If Henry continued to press her, she might not be willing to pass on any information she received about Grace.

Henry seemed to sense he'd gone as far as he could on that point and lifted his hand. "I understand you're facing a difficult challenge."

"I am, and I take my responsibilities very seriously," Mrs. Woodward continued. "I hope your report will be fair and reflect the positive outcome for our girls who are doing well in their placements."

"I'll report what I've observed in an honest and objective manner. But I'm thankful we visited some children who were not on the list you provided so that we could have a balanced view."

Mrs. Woodward's brow creased. "Mr. Dowd, do you think I only gave you the names of children who had the best placements?"

"Was that your intention?"

"No, it most certainly was not!"

"Please." Laura reached out her hand toward Mrs. Woodward. "We don't mean to criticize you or question your devotion to the children. During my time at Pleasantview, I saw your kindness and sincerity toward the girls and the staff."

Mrs. Woodward's expression eased. "I've always tried to do what's best for the children."

Laura nodded, hoping to calm the conversation. "We wanted to say how very sorry we are about the fire."

"Yes, such a dreadful situation." The reverend bobbed his head in agreement.

"We realize this is a difficult time for you," Henry said, "and we don't want to add to your burden."

"Thank you." Mrs. Woodward's voice still sounded cool and guarded.

Laura pulled in a deep breath and focused on Mrs. Woodward. "Do you remember my sister Grace? We'd like to know where she was placed."

"How old is she?"

"Seven. She turns eight in November."

"Do you have a photograph?"

Laura took the family photo from her skirt pocket and passed it to the matron, thankful Rose had encouraged her to bring it to the meeting.

Mrs. Woodward studied the photo with a slight frown.

"That was taken about three years ago, but Grace looks much the same." At least she did when Laura had seen her last Christmas.

The matron shook her head and passed the photo back. "I'm sorry. I don't remember her.

If you had asked me before the fire, I could've checked her file, but that information was destroyed along with everything else."

Laura sighed and slipped the photo back in her skirt pocket.

Henry focused on Mrs. Woodward. "Is there someone else who might remember Grace or know where she was placed?"

"The escorts who oversaw her group might remember, but they are back in England. I usually send a quarterly report to Liverpool listing all the new placements. Her information would have been included in the applicable report, but all that information is gone now."

Laura swallowed hard, fighting her disappointment.

Mrs. Woodward shifted her gaze to Laura. "The children from the infirmary who escaped the fire have been placed in the Belleville hospital. Families from the church have taken the girls who were waiting for new placements. I'm hopeful those situations will become permanent. I've released the other staff members. Miss Lewis and Miss Porter are returning to England. You and Miss Carson are released as well."

Laura swallowed and nodded. "I understand."

"I believe it's time for us to go." Henry rose. "Thank you for your time." He nodded to Mrs. Woodward and the reverend.

Laura stood, her legs feeling slightly shaky.

The path to finding Grace had become much more difficult, but she was not giving up. Her sister was out there somewhere, and Laura would find her no matter how long it took.

Katie took Laura's arm as they stepped down from the carriage and started across the Belleville train station platform. A child cried out off to the left. Katie startled and held tighter to her sister's arm.

"It's all right." Laura's voice was soft and soothing.

Katie nodded and released a sigh. How long would it take for her painful memories to fade? Laura had told her the best way to banish those troublesome thoughts was to replace them with new, better thoughts, but it wasn't easy.

Katie lifted her chin and purposed again to put the past behind her and think instead about the present and the future. She was grateful for Laura's loving care, Rose's kindness, and the doctor's assurance that she was finally ready to begin the long journey home. Those were worthy thoughts.

After stopping to read the schedule posted on the station wall, Henry checked his pocket watch. "The train for Quebec City is due in twenty minutes. I'll speak to the porter about tagging our bags." He strode off and flagged down a porter.

"Let's wait over there." Rose nodded toward a bench by the ticket window.

They crossed the platform and took a seat. Katie glanced around the busy station where several people waited with suitcases in hand, ready to board the next train. A few feet away, a young man called out the headlines from newspapers and a young girl sold small bunches of flowers.

Henry tipped the porter and walked back toward their bench. He'd made all the arrangements for their train trip east and the sea voyage to England, and he'd paid for their passage. How grateful they all were for his kindness and protection.

Then a thought struck Katie's heart, reminding her of a painful truth—they were headed home, but Garth would not be going with them.

Henry and Laura had met with those in charge at the Masterson Home and appealed to a second judge in Belleville, but none of them were willing to release Garth from the agreement the home had made with Mr. Gilchrest.

Laura, Rose, and Henry had spent hours talking through the issues, and it seemed the only option now was to return to London and take it before a judge there to try to prove the children had been sent away before their mum had been given the opportunity to reclaim them.

Knowing they had to leave Garth behind had been a bitter blow for Katie. It slowed her recovery, and it still burdened her heart.

Why, Lord? You rescued me, and You're healing me. Why must Garth stay in Canada? It doesn't seem fair or right. And what about Grace? How will we ever find her?

Laura had assured Katie they were not giving up. They would keep fighting for Garth's freedom and continue the search for Grace, even from England. Still, it was hard, so very hard, to leave without them.

"Katie!"

She gasped and turned, scanning across the platform.

Garth lifted his hand and wove his way through the crowd toward her, a smile lighting up his face. He wore his work clothes and heavy boots, and Mr. Gilchrest followed a few feet behind. He carried nothing in his hands. Katie's heart sank, and hot tears filled her eyes. He'd not come to join them on the journey. He'd come to say goodbye.

She rose and stepped into his embrace. "Oh, Garth."

He held her for a moment, and when he stepped back, his eyes glistened with unshed tears. He'd visited her twice while she was recovering at the hotel, but today's visit was an unexpected gift.

Katie swallowed. "I'm glad you came."

He nodded. "I told Mr. Gilchrest I wanted to see you off, so he said we could come to town and pick up supplies."

Katie glanced past Garth to the bearded farmer. The man looked away, as though he was unwilling to meet her gaze.

Laura joined them and hugged Garth. "It was good of you to come."

He patted Laura on the back, and Katie was surprised to see he was taller than their older sister.

Laura brushed her hand down his shirtsleeve. "Write to us often and let us know how you're doing. That will ease Mum's mind."

Garth nodded. "I will. Tell her not to worry. I'm all right. And give her my love."

Laura touched his cheek. "We'll keep you in prayer and trust the Lord will bring you home soon."

He nodded again and smiled, but when he looked at Katie, she read his true thoughts and they pierced her heart. He was not counting on coming home, at least not any time soon.

She reached for him again and hugged him tight. "We'll do everything we can. I promise."

"I know you will, Katie. Let's put it in God's hands. He'll make a way when the time is right." He kissed her cheek and stepped back.

The whistle blew, and the train rolled into the station with a screech of brakes and a hissing cloud of steam.

Mr. Gilchrest approached, his face a stern mask. "It's time to go."

Garth nodded to the man, then turned back toward Katie and Laura. "God bless you both and give you a safe journey home."

Katie swallowed down her tears. She must be brave for Garth's sake. Crying now would only make their parting harder. She forced a smile, lifted her hand, and waved, matching Garth's farewell gesture.

He nodded to her once more, then faded into the crowd and vanished from sight.

23

Laura held Katie's hand and looked out the side window of the motorcar as Henry drove through London's busy streets. The day was warm and sunny, with only a few clouds in the summer sky.

Rose sat up front next to Henry, holding on to the light scarf tying down her hat. She looked over her shoulder and smiled at Laura and Katie. "It won't be long now. You're almost home."

Katie's eyes sparkled. "I can't wait to see Mum and tell her everything that happened."

Laura squeezed her sister's hand. "You might not want to tell her everything at once."

Katie nodded. "I understand what you mean. I'll be careful."

Laura smiled, reminded again how much Katie had matured through her experiences in the last few months. Yet, in spite of those trials, she'd held on to her hopeful outlook, and for that Laura was amazed and grateful.

It had taken almost a month for the doctor to agree Katie was well enough for an ocean voyage. Laura thought he was being overly cautious, but Henry also needed time to visit several more children and gather all the information he needed for his report.

Laura had exchanged two letters with Mum while they stayed at the hotel in Belleville. She'd been surprised to learn Mum had gone back to work for Mrs. Palmer and moved into the flat above the shop. After Laura's harsh encounter with the owner of the dress shop, she thought their furniture and clothing had been sold or given away. But Mum reported it was all still there when she returned.

Mrs. Palmer was not an easy woman to work for, but Mum was thankful for the position. Her income would help meet their needs until Laura could secure a new position nearby. Never again would she work so far away from her family. Her experiences in the last few months had sealed this truth in her heart: family bonds were not meant to be broken. Whatever the future held, she would always want to be close to her family.

"There it is!" Katie leaned forward to better see out the window and pointed to Palmer's Dress Shop.

Henry pulled the car to a stop in front and glanced over his shoulder at Laura. "Why don't we leave your luggage here until you have a chance to greet your mother?"

Laura agreed. She and Katie hurried around the building and into the alley that led to the entrance to their flat.

Katie raced ahead, pulled open the door, and

charged up the stairs. "Mum? Mum, we're home!"

The door to their flat flew open, and Mum appeared on the upper landing. Joy lit up her face as she stretched out her arms. "Oh, Katie, Laura!"

Katie launched into Mum's arms and Laura followed, wrapping them both in a hug. Happy tears overflowed Laura's eyes, and their laughter mingled with kisses.

"Oh, my girls, my girls," Mum kept saying. "I've missed you so much."

"And we've missed you," Katie cried, kissing Mum's cheeks.

Mum stepped back with a teary smile. She looked down the steps and spotted Rose and Henry below. "Please, come upstairs."

"Yes, I'm sorry." Laura turned, grinning and breathless. "These are our dear friends, Miss Rose Carson and Mr. Henry Dowd."

Rose and Henry climbed the stairs and greeted Mum. She nodded to them and welcomed them into their flat.

Soon the four of them were seated as Mum scurried around, offering tea and lemon biscuits and helping everyone feel welcome. A rush of happiness swept through Laura as Mum hovered around Katie and urged her to take another biscuit. They were safely home, and experiencing the joy of their reunion felt like a cherished dream had finally come true.

"Please tell me, is there any more news about Garth?" Mum sat down next to Laura and balanced her teacup on her lap.

Henry turned to Mum. "Garth is still working on the farm for Mr. Gilchrest. We saw him the day we left Belleville, only a few days before we sailed from Quebec City."

Katie popped the last bite of her lemon biscuit into her mouth. "Mum, you won't believe how much he has grown. He's taller than Laura and ever so strong."

Laura smiled at Mum. "You'd be so proud of him. He's keeping his spirits up and working hard, and he attends church every Sunday."

"That's right," Katie continued, "and he has a good friend named Rob Lewis who works on a neighboring farm. I met him when we traveled to Canada on the same ship."

Mum lifted her hand to her heart. "I can hardly believe you sailed across the sea and now you've come back to me." Tears glistened in Mum's eyes again. She took a handkerchief from her pocket and dabbed her eyes. "I'm sorry, I'm not usually so tearful."

"It's all right." Rose smiled at Mum. "We understand. This is a happy reunion worthy of tears."

Mum tucked her handkerchief away. "What can we do to bring Garth home?"

"I believe the next step is to take the information

we've gathered and present it to the courts here in London," Henry continued. "We have to prove you were not given a fair opportunity to reclaim the children before they were sent away."

Mum nodded. "That's certainly true."

"Now that you've recovered and are able to provide for your family, I think a judge might be persuaded to nullify the contract and return Garth to England."

"And what about Grace?"

Henry's brow creased. "Her situation is more challenging, but not without hope. We've sent her photograph and information to the authorities in several cities and towns in Ontario. We're praying that will give us a lead."

Mum gave a slight nod, her tense expression easing. "It's been very hard to be separated from my children and trust they'll all come home, but seeing Katie and Laura today helps me believe. God answered my prayers for them, and I trust He'll bring Garth and Grace back as well."

A lump lodged in Laura's throat as she listened to Mum express her faith and trust in such a tender, personal way. *Lord, I know I've not always followed You as closely as I should, but You've been so faithful to me. Help me trust You and have a stronger faith like Mum.*

Henry glanced at Rose, then turned to Mum. "I'm glad we were able to bring Grace and Laura home and have a chance to meet you."

"I'm so grateful for all you've done for them." Mum's eyes glistened.

"It was my pleasure." Henry glanced around at each person present. "I think it's time for us to be going. Miss Carson and I are driving down to Kingston to meet my family this afternoon." He smiled at Rose, and her cheeks flushed.

Laura studied them with growing excitement. Did that mean what she thought it meant?

"I'll be in touch with you in a few days." Henry stood. "We'll arrange a time to meet and discuss Garth's case."

Mum rose. "Thank you so much, Mr. Dowd. I don't know how I can ever repay you for the kindness you've shown my family."

"I'm happy to be of service. Meeting Laura, Katie, and Garth has been a privilege. It's given me important insight about child emigration, and that will be a tremendous help when I present my findings."

Mum and Katie followed them to the door, and Laura continued down the steps with Rose and Henry.

When they reached the motorcar, Henry untied Katie's trunk and recruited a young man passing by to help him carry it upstairs.

While they waited for Henry to return, Rose took Laura's hand. "I'm so glad we could see you and Katie safely home and meet your mother. She's a delightful person."

"Thank you." Laura searched her friend's face as memories of all they'd experienced together filled her mind.

Rose pulled Laura close. "I'll miss you."

Laura closed her eyes and held on to Rose. "I'll miss you too. You've become the dearest friend."

Henry walked back toward the motorcar but waited a few feet away to give them time to say goodbye.

Rose sniffed and stepped back. "We can write, and I'll visit as often as I can." She glanced at Henry, a soft smile gracing her lips. "I'm hopeful I'll have some happy news to share very soon," she whispered.

Laura clasped her friend's hands. "Oh, Rose, I can't wait to hear. Write to me as soon as things are settled."

"I will." Rose hesitated and glanced toward Henry once more. "He hasn't heard from Andrew yet, but I expect he will soon."

Laura's throat tightened. Why hadn't Andrew written to her or at least to Henry? Had he been able to spend time with his father, or was he too late and now dealing with all the legal and family obligations that would fall on his shoulders? She pushed those questions aside. It was best not to let her thoughts stay on Andrew.

She focused on Rose again. "When you see Andrew, please tell him I wish him all the best."

Rose searched Laura's face. "Is there anything else you'd like us to say?"

Laura's heart clenched. If only she could send a message through Rose, but it would only extend the pain of their parting. She shook her head. "There's no other message. I understand his decision. He has responsibilities to his family, as I do to mine."

"If you're sure . . ."

Laura nodded. She needed to accept the finality of the situation if she was ever going to have peace. "Even though we're both back in England, there is still so much that separates us."

Rose nodded, sympathy reflected in her eyes. "I understand."

"I'll find a new position, help Mum and Katie, and do everything I can for Garth and Grace."

Rose squeezed her hand. "I admire your courage to move forward with your life. I'll keep you in my prayers."

"Thank you." Laura kissed Rose's cheek. "Take care and write soon."

"I will." Rose climbed in the motorcar, and Henry closed the door for her.

"Goodbye, Laura. We'll be in touch," Henry called before climbing into the driver's seat.

She lifted her hand and waved to them as the motorcar drove down the street and turned the corner.

The soft afternoon light filtered through the

clouds that had appeared, and the sounds of the city filled the air—horses' hooves clattered on the cobblestones, and the bells of St. Anthony's rang out their song.

She was home at last, and her future lay before her like a blank journal. What kind of story would she write? Looking back, she saw a series of difficult trials but also joyful moments when she'd experienced the love of family and friends and the kindness and mercy of God. So much more was yet to be written.

She looked up at the open windows of her flat and caught the sound of Katie's laughter and Mum's happy voice. Her heart lifted. Mum and Katie needed her, she needed them, and that was enough for now.

Katie tilted the light green dress toward the sunlight pouring in through the kitchen window and took the next few stitches around the hem. She settled back in the chair, glad for the sense of peace that filled her now that she was home with Mum and Laura.

After all the work she'd been expected to do for the Richardsons and the Hoffmans, helping Mum with sewing and household chores was such a comfort and relief.

But sometimes she'd hear a boy's voice in the street below and look out the window expecting to see Garth. Or she'd see a little girl with blond wavy hair in the park, and for a split second she'd think it was Grace. Then reality would come rushing back, filling her with a fresh wave of sadness and reminding her Garth and Grace were still in Canada.

She sighed and let those melancholy thoughts fade away. *Watch over them, Lord. Keep them safe.* She picked up her needle once more and focused on the next few stitches.

Across the kitchen at the worktable, Laura kneaded a huge mound of dough. Flour smeared the front of her blue apron and dusted her cheeks.

Katie grinned. "How many loaves of bread are you making?"

"Enough so we can share some with the Grahams."

"That's a kind thought."

Laura looked up. "We would've been out on the street if they hadn't opened their home to us when Mum was recovering."

"I'm sure they'll appreciate the bread."

"I wish we could do more for them, but this will be a start." Laura plunged her hands into the dough, grabbed hold, and rolled it over with a sturdy thump.

Katie chuckled. "You look like you're wrestling a wild animal."

"I feel like it!" Laura brushed her arm across her forehead and continued her vigorous kneading. "Remind me not to double the recipe next time."

Footsteps sounded on the stairs, and the door opened. Mum smiled at them and held up two envelopes. "The post arrived."

Laura stilled and stared at the letters, hope glimmering in her eyes. It was the same reaction she had every time Mum brought up the post, and Katie knew why. Her sister longed to hear from Andrew Frasier, though she would never admit it.

Katie had met Andrew the day Laura had found her in the Hoffmans' barn. He had carried her out like she weighed nothing. She vaguely remembered him lifting her into the buggy, then seeing him standing at the door of her hotel room. He'd helped them on the return train trip to Belleville, but then he was gone. While she was recovering, she'd heard Rose and Laura talking about him a few times, and she'd seen the longing on her sister's face—that same longing she couldn't hide now.

"Who are they from?" Laura asked, a slight tremor in her voice.

"One is from Garth, and the other is from Rose."

The hope in Laura's expression faded. She thanked Mum and offered a smile, but it didn't reach her eyes.

"Let's see what Garth has to say." Mum tore

open his letter and scanned the first few lines, reading aloud:

"Dear Mum, Laura, and Katie, I hope this letter finds you well and happy to be together in London. I'm doing fine, although I miss you all very much."

Mum lifted her hand to her heart and blinked her moist eyes.

"We are busy with the harvest. The days are long, and I'm tired by the time the sun goes down. After dinner I usually fall right into bed. When the weather cools, I expect our workload will be lighter and I'll have more time to write to you and to visit Rob and Mr. and Mrs. Chapman."

Mum smiled at that and kept reading.

"The Chapmans own the neighboring farm, and they have been very kind to me. Rob works for them, but they treat him like a son, and they usually invite me to their home on Sunday after church to enjoy a good dinner. Sometimes Rob and I go fishing. After that we all play games, sing around the piano, and sit out on their porch and talk until the sun goes down.

They are good people, and spending time with them almost feels like being home."

Katie leaned forward. "Remember I told you about Rob?"

"Yes, dear, I remember." Mum continued reading.

"I spoke to Mr. Gilchrest about going to school when harvest is finished, and he is considering it. Please pray he will agree. Rob will be going, and I don't want to fall behind."

"Garth should be allowed to attend school," Laura insisted and punched the dough again. "That's in the agreement Mr. Gilchrest made with the Masterson Home."

Mum nodded. "I'll speak to Mr. Dowd. Perhaps he can write to Mr. Gilchrest and remind him to abide by the agreement."

"If I were still there, I'd do more than that," Laura muttered and smacked the dough down on the table.

Katie pursed her lips. "That old Mr. Gilchrest is a stubborn, selfish man. I don't like him at all."

Mum sent them both an understanding look. "Loving our enemies and praying for them is much more effective than grumbling against them."

Katie sighed and sat back in the chair. Mum was right, but that didn't make it easy.

Laura's tense expression smoothed, and she continued kneading.

"There's a little more to Garth's letter." Mum held up the page.

"I think of you often and pray for you every night before I go to sleep. I hope Mr. Dowd and Mr. Frasier will find a way for me to come home, but until then, I am doing my work the best I can and trusting God for the days ahead. Write to me soon. I send you all my love.

"Your son and brother, Garth."

Mum lowered the letter. "He sounds like he's doing well, but I wonder if he's only telling us part of the story."

Katie laid her sewing in her lap. "Don't worry, Mum. Mr. Gilchrest might be strict, but he doesn't beat Garth or make him stay out in the barn."

Mum shook her head and sighed. "I hope you're right."

Laura dried her hands on a towel and crossed the kitchen to stand beside Mum. "He'll be all right." She placed her hand on Mum's shoulder. "We have to believe that."

Mum's throat worked, and she finally nodded.

"Yes, I'm sure the Lord hears our prayers and is working everything out even though we can't see it right now."

Katie swallowed and blinked away hot tears. They would hold on to hope and trust the Lord to watch over Garth and Grace, and one day they would be together again.

Mum pressed her hand over Laura's. "Thank you, my dear. I have to go back to the shop, but I hope you'll enjoy your letter from Rose and . . ." Her eyes widened as she noticed the expanding pile of dough on the table. "My goodness, Laura, what are you making?"

"Bread, lots and lots of bread." She grinned and returned to the worktable. "Don't worry. I have a plan."

Mum chuckled and kissed Laura's cheek. "I'm sure you do, my girl. I'm sure you do."

Laura stood by the ironing board in the kitchen and lifted the hot iron off the stovetop. She ran it over the damp skirt of the coral dress Mum had left for her earlier that morning. Pressing the finished dresses and helping with hand sewing provided a little extra income, but it was not enough.

Yesterday she'd finally gone to an employment office and filled out paperwork to seek a position as a lady's maid. She'd listed Mrs. Frasier as her previous employer, and she hoped Andrew's mother would give her a recommendation in spite of the way she'd left Bolton and never returned.

She sighed and placed the iron back on the stove to reheat. Mrs. Palmer was quite particular about this final step. If she found one tiny wrinkle, she would send Laura back upstairs to press it out.

As she waited for the iron to reheat, her thoughts drifted to Rose and the happy news she'd included in her last letter. Henry had proposed during a moonlight walk the second night of her visit with his family. Rose had happily accepted, and his family had welcomed the news with warm hugs and hearty congratulations.

Laura smiled picturing that scene—Henry wearing a proud smile as Rose showed his parents the engagement ring he'd placed on her finger. After losing her parents and being on her own for so many years, Rose deserved to be loved and cherished, and Henry was just the man to do it—her perfect match. Rose would always have a special place in his heart, and her long-cherished dreams of a home and family would finally be fulfilled.

Laura lifted the hot iron and pressed the next section of the dress as thoughts of her own hopes and dreams rose in her mind. Would she spend her days working long hours as a maid for a meager wage and be able to see her family only on Sunday afternoons? Was that what the future held for her?

She turned the dress and scolded herself for her gloomy thoughts. It would be wiser to focus on all the reasons she had to be grateful rather than pining over what could never be. The Lord had done so much for her and her family. He had proven His faithfulness in so many ways, healing Laura's heart and strengthening her faith.

Mum had recovered from the illness they feared would take her life. She was able to return to work and enjoyed her evenings with Katie and Laura. Katie had been restored to them, and she'd grown stronger through all she had endured. She was home where she belonged, healthy and happy again.

Mr. Gilchrest had agreed Garth could attend school, even before Mr. Dowd had written to him. And Garth was thankful he could keep up his studies and see his friends on school days. The date for the court hearing had not yet been set, but Henry's commitment to help them bring Garth home had never wavered.

They had received two leads in their search for Grace, and Henry had hired a man in Montreal to check into those. They might hear good news about Grace any day.

Laura closed her eyes. *Please, Lord, watch over Grace. Send Your angels to guard and protect her. Lead us to her and help us find her soon.*

Quick steps sounded on the stairs, and Laura opened her eyes.

Katie burst through the door, breathless and grinning. "Come downstairs. There's someone here to see you."

"Who is it?"

Katie's eyes twinkled. "Come and see."

"All right." Laura set aside the iron and started toward the door.

"Take off your apron!"

Laura shook her head, but she reached around and untied the strings. "Is it someone from the employment office?"

"No, but you'd better hurry up! You don't want to keep him waiting." Her sister turned and flew down the stairs before Laura could ask any more questions.

She glanced in the mirror by the door and smoothed down her hair. Maybe it was Mr. Graham or his son, Jacob, stopping by to thank her for the loaves of bread she'd dropped off last week. But she doubted it would be them. They were both at work this time of the day.

Her curiosity rose as she walked through the back storage area and into the main room of the shop. Mum, Katie, Mrs. Palmer, and her two daughters all stood behind the counter. Each one wore an expectant smile, even Mrs. Palmer.

Laura stopped by the end of the counter. "Where is this mysterious man?"

"He's waiting for you by the front window." Mum nodded toward that area of the shop.

Laura pressed down her questions and started up the aisle past bolts of fabric and spools of ribbons. When she reached the end, she saw the man standing by the front window with his back to her and his hat in his hand.

Recognition rippled through her. "Andrew?"

He turned, and a smile broke across his handsome face. "Laura." His gaze traveled over her, drinking her in like a thirsty man savors a glass of cool water. "I've missed you."

Her cheeks warmed, and her smile bloomed. She wanted to say she'd missed him too, but that seemed too forward. "How are you?" *My goodness, I sound almost breathless.*

"I'm fine." His steady gaze remained focused on her as she came closer.

"How is your family?" She didn't want to ask about his father, but she hoped this would open the door for him to tell her more.

"They're all well. Thank you for asking."

Laura blinked. "Your father . . ."

"He gave us quite a scare, but he's doing much better now. The doctor says he can expect a full recovery as long as he limits his activity for a few more weeks."

"Oh, Andrew, that's wonderful. I'm so glad."

"Yes, it's quite a relief. I can see the Lord had a purpose in it all."

"What do you mean?"

"My father's illness caused us both to slow down and think about what's most important in life. It softened him considerably toward my mother and me. She rarely left his side during his illness, and they've grown much closer now."

"That's such good news."

"Father and I had some important conversations while he was recovering. I think we understand each other more now. I've agreed to spend more time at Bolton, learning how to manage the estate, and he has given me his blessing to work part of the time in London." He looked away for a moment, and when he met her gaze again, some undefined emotion filled his eyes. "The events of the last few months have also helped me think about the future, and as soon as the doctor confirmed my father was out of danger, I decided to come to London and look for you."

Her heartbeat quickened, and she searched his face. Did she dare hope he was thinking about a future with her?

He looked down and turned his hat in his hands. "First, I want to apologize for the way I left you in Belleville."

"Oh no, I understand. Your father was ill, and your family needed you."

"Yes, but I made a promise to you, and with your permission I'd like another opportunity to keep that commitment."

Confusion swirled her thoughts. "You want to help with Garth's case? That's why you came to London?"

"Yes, and I want to double our efforts to find Grace."

Her heart tripped. That was all he wanted, nothing else? She swallowed hard. "I'm sure Henry would appreciate your help. He has some new leads in the search for Grace."

"Yes, I've just spent the last two hours with him, and he gave me an update."

She nodded, looking away to hide her disappointment.

"Laura?" He reached for her hand. "Look at me."

She slowly lifted her head, trying to blink away the moisture in her eyes.

"You're not crying, are you?"

"No, of course not." She pulled in a deep breath, willing herself to hold back her foolish flood of emotion.

"The last thing I want to do is upset you."

"You haven't," she insisted. "I'm fine."

Tenderness filled his expression, and she knew he'd seen through her attempt to hide her true feelings.

"I have something else I want to ask." He tightened his hold on her hand.

She didn't know how she could stand any more dashed hopes, but she met his gaze once more.

"While we were apart, you were never far from my thoughts. When I was worried about my father, I would remember our conversations and the courage you showed as you searched for your brother and sisters. You inspired me to hold on to my faith and not give up."

She shook her head. "But I've made so many mistakes. I can't imagine inspiring you or anyone else."

His gentle smile returned. "We all make mistakes, Laura. It's what we do about them that matters. You've chosen to learn from yours, and you've taken those lessons into your heart and become an even more honest and loving person because of them."

His words soothed the ache she'd carried for too long. She'd asked for God's forgiveness and had set her feet on a better path, but she'd had a hard time believing that was enough. Knowing Andrew understood her journey and was proud of her made all the difference. Finally, the burden eased from her heart and she felt free to truly receive the comforting wave of God's forgiveness.

"Thank you," she whispered, wishing she could explain how much his words meant to her.

He knelt on one knee before her and took a small black velvet box from his jacket pocket.

She gasped and lifted her hand to cover her mouth. She shook her head, and her gaze darted from the box to his face.

"Laura, I love you with all my heart. You are the one I want to cherish and protect for the rest of my life. Would you do me the honor of becoming my wife?"

Joy burst from her heart, stealing away her words.

He watched her, expectation and a flash of uncertainty crossing his face. "I know this may be unexpected. I planned to tell you my intentions when we sailed back to England together. But then I received that summons home, and I had to put my own hopes aside until I knew what would happen to my father."

"Oh, Andrew." Tears filled her eyes. "I do love you, but what about your family? I have nothing to bring into marriage. How could they ever approve?"

He offered her a confident smile. "I've already told them I planned to propose to you, and they've given their consent."

She gasped again, and a new wave of hope washed over her.

"I admit they were surprised at first, but what you may not know is that my mother came to England as a companion of a wealthy young heiress. She was her cousin and had a background very similar to yours. But that never stopped my father from pursuing her."

Laura stared at him. "Your mother was a companion?"

"Yes, I understand that's something similar to a lady's maid. She had nothing more than a trunk of clothes and a hope of finding a husband when she came to London."

Laura could hardly believe it was true, but if Andrew's father had looked past his wife's lack of money and social standing, then perhaps they might accept her into the family as well.

Andrew opened the velvet box and looked up at her once more. "Laura, my love for you could never be greater, even if you were a wealthy heiress or Princess Mary herself."

Laura's laughter mingled with her tears. "Oh, Andrew."

"Will you marry me, take me into your heart, and build a future with me?"

Confidence and joy flooded her. "Yes, yes, I will!" She lifted her trembling hand to him, and he slipped the sparkling ring on her finger.

He stood, gently brushed her tears from her cheeks, and leaned closer. "My darling, you've made me very happy."

She was so overcome she couldn't speak. Instead, she rose up on her toes and lifted her face to welcome his kiss. He wrapped his arms around her, pulled her close, and deepened the kiss, offering her a blissful glimpse of the love they would share in their marriage.

When they finally parted, she sighed and rested her head against his chest, savoring his nearness and listening to the strong, steady beat of his heart. She had dreamed of a moment like this, but in the last few years, she'd given up believing her dream would ever come true. And then Andrew had walked into her life and proven he was a man worthy of her respect and lifelong love.

Voices and soft laughter floated toward them from the back of the shop.

Laura stepped away from Andrew and glanced down the aisle. Mum, Katie, Mrs. Palmer, and her two daughters hovered behind a mannequin a few yards away, watching them with guilty smiles.

"Mrs. McAlister." Andrew slipped his arm around Laura's waist, holding her close as he called to her mother.

"Yes?" Mum replied.

"Would you and Katie and your friends come and join us? We have something to tell you."

Mum hurried toward them, her face aglow, Katie right behind her. The others followed, and they all circled around Laura and Andrew.

He grinned at the women, then focused on Mum. "I've asked Laura to marry me, and she has accepted. We want you to be the first to know and ask for your blessing."

Mum lifted both her hands to her mouth, happy delight shining in her eyes.

Katie grinned up at Mum and tugged on her sleeve. "Say yes!"

The other women laughed, and Mrs. Palmer patted Mum on the back.

"Of course you have my blessing." Mum's smile faltered. "Though I must admit it will be hard to part with Laura again so soon."

Andrew gave an understanding nod. "I know how close you are to Laura and Katie, so I was thinking all three of you might like to come and stay at Bolton. You could be guests in our home, or there's a lovely cottage just a short walk from the house where you could set up housekeeping and live nearby, permanently if you'd like. Either way, you and Katie, and in the future Garth and Grace, will always be welcome at Bolton as a treasured part of our family."

Laura's heart melted as she listened to Andrew's thoughtful plan. How kind he was to offer his support and care for her family. It was more than she could've hoped for.

Mum lifted her hand to her heart. "My goodness. I don't know what to say. That's such a generous offer."

"Tell the man you agree," Mrs. Palmer said in a firm voice. "You don't get an invitation like that every day of the week."

Laura looked up at Andrew. "That sounds like a wonderful plan." She shifted her gaze to Mum, waiting for her to reply.

"Well, if you're sure it wouldn't be an

imposition, we'd love to move to the cottage and stay nearby, especially after Laura marries."

"Excellent!" Andrew sent her mum a triumphant grin. "My parents are looking forward to meeting you and Katie and welcoming Laura home to Bolton."

His words sent a thrill through Laura as memories of the beautiful estate filled her mind. Bolton would be her country home, and Andrew would be her loving husband. It was almost too much to comprehend. They would inherit his family's estate one day, and perhaps in the not-too-distant future, they would have children and raise a family of their own at Bolton. That wonderful vision of the future filled her with joy and anticipation.

"Thank you, Mr. Frasier." Mum extended her hand. "We're most grateful."

Andrew took hold of her fingers and smiled at her. "Now that we're going to be related, you must call me Andrew."

Mum's face shone as she looked up at him. "Laura told us how kind and helpful you were when she was in Canada. I can see that's very true."

Andrew turned to Laura. "You told your mother I was kind and helpful?"

She laughed. "Yes, I did. And you were . . . or, I should say, you are."

"If I am, it's because you bring out those qualities in me."

She looked up into his handsome face, mentally tracing the lines and planes that had become so dear to her. Gratitude washed over her heart for the love they shared and the hope and future that would surely be theirs.

Author's Note

Dear Reader,

I hope you enjoyed getting to know Laura, Katie, Grace, and Garth and learning what it was like for British families caught up in the child emigration system more than one hundred years ago.

Are you wondering what happens to Garth and Grace? I'm writing their stories now, weaving together the experiences of the McAlister and Frasier families in my next novel, so I hope you'll be watching for it in 2020. I'm eager to share the rest of the story with you and give Grace and Garth the pages they deserve!

Between the 1860s and the 1930s, more than one hundred eighteen thousand poor and orphaned children were sent to Canada as British Home Children. Most became indentured workers on farms or domestics in homes. Some were welcomed and treated well, but many others suffered greatly from prejudice, neglect, and abuse. Their stories need to be told, their lives need to be remembered, and their trials must never be forgotten. I hope this novel will spark your interest, and you'll want to learn more.

The British Home Children Advocacy &

Research Association was a wonderful resource for my research. Lori Oschefski and those who work with her answered many of my questions and provided outstanding information through their website, Facebook group, newsletters, and articles, as well as books they recommended. I hope *No Ocean Too Wide* gives more people a chance to learn about British Home Children and honor their memory.

If you'd like to learn more, these are some of the resources I used in my research:

- The British Home Children Advocacy & Research Association: www.britishhome children.com
- The British Home Children Advocacy & Research Association Facebook group: www.facebook.com/groups/Britishhome children
- *The Golden Bridge: Young Immigrants to Canada, 1833–1939* by Marjorie Kohli
- *Promises of Home: Stories of Canada's British Home Children* by Rose McCormick Brandon
- *Nation Builders: Barnardo Children in Canada* by Gail H. Corbett
- *Labouring Children: British Immigrant Apprentices to Canada, 1869–1924* by Joy Parr
- *The Camera and Dr. Barnardo* compiled

by Valerie Lloyd. Based on an exhibition staged by the National Portrait Gallery, London, July–November 1974

Blessings and happy reading,
Carrie

READERS GUIDE

1. Had you heard about British Home Children before you read *No Ocean Too Wide*? What is one thing you learned that made an impression on you about child emigration and British Home Children in particular?

2. People have compared the British Home Children to those children who were taken from New York City and sent west on the orphan trains. Are you familiar with the orphan trains, and what similarities do you see between these two groups? What differences?

3. What motivated those in Britain to want to send poor and orphaned children to Canada? What do you think of their reasons? What about the families or businesses who received them in Canada?

4. Why were people prejudiced against British Home Children? How did this impact the McAlister children in this story?

5. Laura went to great lengths to search for her siblings, even using a false name. What do you think of her decision? What were the results of that choice?

6. Andrew Frasier had a privileged background, but he wanted to study law and make his life count. What are some of the qualities Andrew demonstrated in this story?

7. Friendships play a key role in the story, as Henry and Andrew shared a special friendship and Rose became a caring friend for Laura. How did Henry's influence help Andrew mature through the story? How does that differ from the ways that Rose helped Laura?

8. Katie endured some very difficult treatment from the two families that took her in. How did she cope? What qualities do you admire in Katie?

9. How do you feel about the judge's decision for Garth to stay in Canada and fulfill his indentured contract?

10. James 1:27 says, "Religion that God our Father accepts as pure and faultless is

this: to look after orphans and widows in their distress and to keep oneself from being polluted by the world" (NIV). What is one way you could extend love and care to widows or orphans?

ACKNOWLEDGMENTS

I am very grateful for all those who have given me their support and encouragement and who have provided information in the process of writing this book. Without your help, it would never have been possible! I'd like to say thank you to the following people:

- My husband, Scott, who always provides great feedback and constant encouragement when I talk about my characters, plot, and what's happening next. Your love and support have allowed me to follow my dreams and write the books of my heart. I will be forever grateful for you!
- Steve Laube, my literary agent, for his patience, guidance, and wise counsel. You have been a great advocate who has represented me well. I feel very blessed to be your client, and I appreciate you!
- Shannon Marchese, Charlene Patterson, Laura Wright, and Tracey Moore, my gifted editors, who help me shape the story and then polish it so readers are able to truly enjoy it.
- Lori Oschefski, Norma Cook, and all the members of the British Home Children

Advocacy & Research Association Facebook group. Many told me their stories and shared photographs of their family members who were British Home Children.

- Kristopher Orr, the multitalented designer at Multnomah, for the lovely cover design. He went above and beyond to bring all the elements together and satisfy all those involved. I appreciated the opportunity to give input and enjoyed our partnership!
- Jamie Lapeyrolerie, Chelsea Woodward, Lori Addicott, Laura Barker, and the entire Multnomah team for their great work with marketing, publicity, production, and sales. This book would stay hidden on my computer if not for your creative ideas and hard work. You all are the best!
- Cathy Gohlke, fellow author and friend, who constantly encourages me to trust the Lord for grace to write stories that will transform hearts and draw people closer to the Lord. You have blessed my life in so many ways! I love our times together at Sea Isle. Let's both keep pressing on to serve the Lord with the gift of writing.
- My children, Josh, Melinda, Melissa, Peter, Ben, Galan, Megan, Walter, and Lizzy, and my mother-in-law, Shirley, for all the ways you cheer me on. It's a blessing to have a family that is so supportive!

- My readers, especially those in the Carrie's Reading Friends Facebook group who encourage me with their kind reviews and help me spread the word about my books. Your thoughtful posts and emails keep me going!
- Most of all, I thank my Lord and Savior, Jesus Christ, for His love, wonderful grace, and faithful provision. I am grateful for the gifts and talents You have given me, and I hope to always use them in ways that bless You and bring You glory.

ABOUT THE AUTHOR

Carrie Turansky has loved reading since she first visited the library as a young child and checked out a tall stack of picture books. Her love for writing began when she penned her first novel at age twelve. She is now the award-winning author of twenty inspirational romance novels and novellas.

Carrie and her husband, Scott, who is a pastor, author, and speaker, have been married for forty years and make their home in New Jersey. They often travel together on ministry trips and to visit their five adult children and six grandchildren. Carrie also leads the women's ministry at her church, and when she's not writing, she enjoys spending time working in her flower gardens and cooking healthy meals for friends and family.

She loves to connect with reading friends through her website, http://carrieturansky.com, and via Facebook, Pinterest, and Twitter.

Books are produced in the United States using U.S.-based materials

Books are printed using a revolutionary new process called THINKtech™ that lowers energy usage by 70% and increases overall quality

Books are durable and flexible because of Smyth-sewing

Paper is sourced using environmentally responsible foresting methods and the paper is acid-free

Center Point Large Print
600 Brooks Road / PO Box 1
Thorndike, ME 04986-0001 USA

(207) 568-3717

US & Canada:
1 800 929-9108
www.centerpointlargeprint.com